WELCOME TO THE MADHOUSE

Book One of the Grace Lord Series

S.E. SASAKI

ODDOC
B O O K S

Oddoc Books
ERIN, ONTARIO, CANADA

For more information about the author or the publisher, visit:
www.sesasaki.com

Published by:
ODDOC BOOKS
P.O. Box 580,
Erin, Ontario, Canada,
N0B 1T0

978-1-988463-02-5 (ebook)
978-1-988463-01-8 (paperback)
978-1-988463-00-1 (hardcover)

*For David, Daniel, and Christine Sherrington,
with all of my love.*

Contents

The wolf whistle was singularly impressive, not only because of its purity of sound and its continuation into the 1812 overture, but also because it originated from the thick, brown lips of what looked like an enormous orangutan, dressed in a shiny white spacesuit with a helmet under one arm.

As Lieutenant Grace Alexandra Lord M.D. stepped off of the Conglomerate space shuttle, arrayed before her in a disorderly, lounging group were a wolfman, two tiger adaptations, a grizzly bear genmod, and the whistling, male orangutan soldier. They were all enormous in stature, broad of shoulder, attired in combat space suits and clasping space helmets, which presumably fit their massive heads. Each of them stared avidly at Grace, their gazes so alarmingly intense that Grace felt like she was the next course to be served up for their dinner. The sight of their glistening white fangs, exposed in various permutations of bestial leer, sent a shudder down her spine.

These were the Conglomerate's modified space marines, with genetic adaptations giving them the enhanced strength and appearance of fierce predators. They all seemed to be grinning at her, but perhaps that was just the animal adaptations they possessed. She could swear a couple of them were actually winking at her. Inanely, the little voice in her head wisecracked that the wolf whistle should have come from the wolfman. Following on the heel of that thought, the soldier who was genetically modified with the attributes of a wolf, tipped back his white and silver furry head and emitted a yip-yip-yipping yowl.

The initial shock of seeing such a ferocious looking menagerie dressed in combat spacesuits designed for human soldiers, was not only disorienting, but daunting indeed. At least the intimidating 'incisor' display was short lived. When these genetically-modified, animal-adapted combat marines finally noticed the shoulder bars on

Grace's own spacesuit—indicating her higher rank as Lieutenant—they instantly snapped to attention, becoming serious and respectful, their eyes suddenly staring straight ahead and thankfully no longer at Grace.

These enormous military combatants of the Conglomerate, who had physical enhancements chosen to make them bigger, stronger, faster, and fiercer than the normal human, formed a disciplined line. They stood almost shoulder to shoulder, with rank ascending. They all crisply saluted Grace. At full attention, these people were even more intimidating than before. They towered over her.

Grace cast sidelong glances at their faces, not wanting to openly gawk. They were all stunning. Two had the facial coloring and eyes of a tiger, one possibly a woman. One had the silver-grey facial markings of a wolf. The orangutan soldier had the long arms, bowed legs, stringy, reddish hair and large brown eyes, characteristic of that primate. The grizzly bear was a sergeant and had the large round head, brown fur, and massive build of that fearsome mammal. To Grace, they all looked intimidating.

Grace was about to return their salutes, when off to her right, there came a deafening roar. She had no time to look in the direction from whence the bellow came, before she was grabbed by a very strong pair of hands and launched straight up into the air. Her duffel bag, which she'd been carrying over her right shoulder, tumbled out of her grasp, as she flew upwards, somersaulting towards the dark, shadowy ceiling above.

Grace was shocked speechless. She sensed a huge rush of air pass beneath her, as if something enormous and powerful had just motored through the space she had vacated. Had she still been standing in that original spot, she likely would have been trampled.

The question was, by what?

As the low gravity of the space station pulled Grace back down towards the Receiving Bay floor, she was grabbed by another pair of muscular hands that whipped her sideways, just before the mysterious, hurricane-like force flew by her again, missing her face this time by a fraction. Grace felt the wind of the behemoth's passage gust past her cheek. She was being thrown around so violently, her head was spinning and she had to clench her jaws tightly to avoid vomiting. Her neck muscles were wailing. She'd still not gotten a good look at whatever was charging at her, when she was flung upwards again by another strong pair of hands.

A savage, enraged roar erupted. To Grace, it seemed loud enough to shake the walls of the Receiving Bay. Whatever it was that was bellowing and stampeding, it was on a murderous rampage and appeared to be single-mindedly determined to pulverize Grace. She was like the proverbial red cape to this raging bull and she had no idea why. Finally, after her eyes could regain their focus, she got a brief glimpse of what was targeting her, just as she was being launched into the air again by one of the gen-mod space marines. If her eyes were not deceiving her, it was a gigantic, gorilla-adapted soldier in a muddy, torn spacesuit with broken chain restraints lashing from his wrists and ankles.

Blazing, maddened, scarlet eyes turned to focus on Grace out of the depths of black wrinkles. The sclerae of the gorilla soldier's eyes were a brilliant red, his irises a deep, dark brown. His pupils were enormous. Grace knew immediately that this soldier had been exposed to trifluoroquinthiomataze, a gaseous weapon used in biological warfare which, when inhaled, caused psychosis, paranoia, eventual blindness, and ultimately, death.

Grace was suddenly shoved flat to the ground, her right cheek bouncing hard off of the rough station floor, as the enraged gorilla soldier dove over top of her. It felt to her like an enormous rocket whizzing by. This delusional gorilla soldier had probably just been brought in from a battlefield where Tri-FQ had been released. In his gas-induced psychosis, there was no telling what he was seeing or thinking. He desperately needed the antidote. He had obviously broken the metal restraints that had been for his own safety, as well as others. Grace suspected the medics had run out of the antidote for Tri-FQ in the field. They were always prepared for its possible release. Unfortunately, this powerful gorilla soldier had managed to tear himself loose in his madness. Space only knew what was going on in the soldier's mind. The bright red sclerae and huge pupils indicated that the gorilla soldier was heading rapidly down the road towards irreversible insanity and death.

It was paramount that Grace get the antidote into him as quickly as possible.

"Get me a syringe full of 100 milligrams of Antiquint along with 1 gram of Stilzine, stat!" Grace screamed at a silver android, standing off to one side of the engagement, just as the two tiger soldiers leaped on top of the infuriated gorilla soldier and attempted to hold him down. They were both flung away as if they were mere insects and the Tri-FQ-dosed gorilla again made a charge straight for Grace.

'Why me?' a little voice in Grace's head whimpered, as she watched the enraged gorilla gallop straight towards her. All she could focus on were the reds of the delirious soldier's eyes, as she tensed for the fatal impact. A split second before he slammed into her, the grizzly bear sergeant leaped into the gorilla soldier's path and threw a right hook that Grace thought would have crumpled a space shuttle.

The gas-crazed gorilla soldier just shook off the punch and threw one of his own. The sergeant grunted with the impact but stood his ground. Grace gawked as the two titans began swinging their massive fists, striking each other with punishing blows. Grace was then struck in her abdomen by a diving wolfman, who tackled her out of the way, just as the grizzly bear sergeant was forced backwards by the advancing gorilla. The sergeant was thrown back through the spot Grace had just vacated.

The two gen-mod soldiers, grizzly bear versus gorilla, roared thunderously at each other. They continued rapidly launching lethal punches, kicks, and blows, inhumanly and powerfully fast. Staccato-like, the impacts of those furious assaults rang out sharply in the Receiving Bay. Grace could barely see the movement of their swinging limbs, they attacked so fast. She knew that any one of those punches, connecting with her body, would have left her in a puddle of broken bones.

Skidding across the floor, wrapped within the wolfman's arms, Grace finally came to rest at the feet of the silver android. Silently and gracefully, it bent down and offered her a filled syringe with a long, large bore needle. On the side of it was neatly printed Antiquint and Stilzine, with the accompanying milligram dosages. It was enough drug to fell a creature twenty times Grace's size and weight. With no time to thank the android, Grace found herself air-born again, her right hand clutching the syringe tightly. Tossed from the wolfman to the orangutan soldier, who then whipped her up over his shoulder—almost making her drop the syringe!—she was carried up the side of the space shuttle.

Swift on the orangutan's heels was the obsessed gorilla, who had managed to throw his grizzly bear opponent clear out of the way. Grace stared directly into the maddened, blood red eyes that were intensely fixated on her. The gorilla soldier shrieked his frustration as Grace was lofted up the shuttle away from him. He lunged with grasping talons after her. Behind him, she saw the two tigers leap onto the crazed gorilla's back, each grabbing an arm and metal restraint. The wolf dove to wrap his arms around the gorilla's legs. The grizzly bear sergeant then rushed up between the two tigers and locked his great arms around the drug-crazed gorilla's chest, pinning the powerful arms in a tight bear hug from behind. The sergeant began squeezing the chest of the huge gorilla soldier while the other three soldiers held on, anchoring the delusional warrior in place. The psychotic gorilla struggled, but the grizzly bear's arms held firm, the sergeant's face etched with strain.

"Hold him tight," yelled Grace, in a loud, commanding voice. "And put me down!" she hollered at the orangutan. The apeman released Grace so suddenly, she slid down the side of the space shuttle and almost fell to her knees. Cursing, it was lucky she had raised the precious syringe high in the air to protect it.

"Trying . . . Lieutenant," grumbled the sergeant, panting with the effort of trying to restrain the powerful gorilla, whose enormous body bucked and surged and fought the grips of all four soldiers.

"Hurry, ma'am . . . please?" the wolf growled.

With the syringe held in her right hand like a dagger, Grace leaped up onto the bent back of the wolf. She grabbed, with her left hand, the grizzly bear's right forearm and drew herself up into the bellowing face of the deranged gorilla soldier. As he bared his enormous sharp fangs at her, trying to bite her face off, she drove the needle containing the Antiquint—the antidote for trifluoroquinthiomataze—and Stilzine—a major tranquilizer—into the gorilla's jugular vein (or at least that was her hope). The plunger activated and the contents of the large syringe emptied into the gorilla's neck. Grace held it there as firmly as she could.

The thrashing, enraged gorilla screamed his spittle-laden fury straight into Grace's face. As she squeezed her eyes shut and turned her face to the side, Grace hoped that the gorilla soldier carried no communicable diseases in his saliva. She suspected her hearing would never recover.

The next thing Grace knew, she was launched into the air again. The gorilla soldier had broken free of the grizzly bear's hold, forcing his arms up and outward. Unfortunately, this time there was no space marine quick enough to catch Grace and she landed hard on her back, away from the shuttle. She found herself struggling to get air into her chest, trying desperately to inhale even one sweet breath. The wind had been knocked out of her lungs by the impact.

As she lay helpless, gasping and struggling like a newborn babe, the gorilla took three bounding steps towards her, the empty syringe still protruding from his neck like an indictment. His wide red eyes blazed with murderous intent. He thrust deadly, curved black claws toward Grace. All she could do was stare weakly as first one dilated, reddened eye, then the other, rolled upwards and back in the gorilla's eye sockets. So slowly it would have been comical if Grace was not fearful for her life, the gigantic ebony mountain of muscle fell flat on his face.

For an interminable moment, no one moved. All eyes were glued to the gorilla soldier, lying prone on the floor. With muscles tensed, ready to spring into action at the slightest quiver of fur, the animal-adapted space marines all waited with their predatory stillness that was almost frightening in itself. When a large snore finally escaped from the gorilla's mouth, everyone else took a breath. With the next rumbling snort, the other marines all gratefully collapsed to the ground in exhaustion and relief. They all just lay on the Receiving Bay floor for a few minutes, inhaling deep, gulping breaths.

Grace was finally able to breathe normally and she thought she might break into tears of joy. How wonderful it was to be able to breathe freely again! Such a simple thing, breathing, but so taken for granted. Grace was bruised, lacerated, abraded and sore, but she was thankful to be alive.

"Fecken 'A', Lieutenant," someone panted. That was followed by a series of acknowledging grunts and growls.

"Apologies, Lieutenant," the grizzly bear rumbled, his basso voice vibrating from deep within his enormous chest. "We should have been able to handle that guy better than that, even if we are all recovering from surgery."

"That soldier was pumped up on Tri-FQ," Grace said to the air above her, as she lay on her back and stared up at the distant grey ceiling. "It gives the person the strength of ten men . . . or, in this case, the strength of ten gorilla-modified combat soldiers. You guys were amazing! You saved that gorilla soldier's life, and mine as well. You also protected this space station's Receiving Bay from getting demolished and everyone in it. Thank you."

"Glad to be of service, Lieutenant," the orangutan said, with a huge grin. He helped Grace up off of the Receiving Bay floor. "Looks like you may be hurting for a few days."

"A few weeks is more like it," Grace muttered, rubbing her back. "Thank you, soldier."

"My pleasure, Lieutenant. Private Haywood, at your service. That was quite the display of courage you showed there," the orangutan soldier said, with a solemn nod of respect.

"Just doing my job," Grace mumbled, her face heating up. She did not meet the orangutan soldier's eyes because she did not feel she deserved any praise. They were the heroes.

She limped over to check that the gorilla patient was still breathing. She had given him enough Stilzine to stop an army in its tracks . . . or so she thought. The man's breathing was deep and regular, and his pulse was steady and bounding. All good signs, she decided. She raised one of his black eyelids. The redness of his sclera was already starting to fade back to a pinkish hue. A very good indication that the antidote had still been administered in time.

"Don't know too many lieutenants who would have jumped on a raging berserker like that, male or female, ma'am," one of the tigers offered.

"Yes, well, I'm a surgeon and it's my duty to care for the sick and battle-wounded. Unfortunately for this soldier, he's both. Thank you all for not actually harming him." The little voice in Grace's head made gagging noises and asked her if she could be any more nauseating.

"That could easily have been one of us, Doc. We look after our own. I'm sure we've all seen the effects of Tri-FQ before. Some of us have likely experienced it, too," the grizzly bear sergeant grumbled. There were a couple of furry heads nodding. "We'll look after him and make sure he gets put on a pallet and off to Triage, Doc."

"Oh, no. That should be my job," Grace protested. "Aren't you soldiers supposed to be getting on that shuttle?"

Already, Grace could see androids approaching with an anti-grav pallet. A pinch-faced man, whom Grace assumed was one of the medical station's doctors, stalked towards them, his shoulders back, a prim expression on his face. When he got within hearing range, he demanded, in a very condescending tone, "Who stuck that syringe in this soldier's neck?"

"I did," Grace said, coming forward to speak to the doctor. She took a step backwards, when she found herself confronted by a glare of outrage.

"And who are you?" the pinch-faced man demanded, looking Grace up and down as if she were some vile contagion that had somehow sneaked aboard the space station.

"Doctor Grace Alexandra Lord, surgical fellow to Dr. Hiro Al-Fadi," she answered. Curiously, she noted everyone's head slowly swivel towards her. Was she imagining it or had they all cautiously moved back from her a step?

Her interrogator sniffed, cleared his throat, looked down at the tablet he was carrying, and then glanced up at her with a suspicious stare. His high voice piping with pettiness, he declared, "I have never heard of you. You are not on our doctors' roster. You aren't even registered here on the station's manifest as 'arrived.' You are not authorized to give any medication aboard this station until you've been registered and admitted to Staff. This is a flagrant breech of medical station policy and I am going to file an incident report about this!"

"She may have saved a lot of lives, Doc, by treating this berserker gorilla soldier," the grizzly bear sergeant said. "The soldier was hopped up on Tri-FQ."

"Oh? . . . And you are a doctor, too?" the man said, in a tone that dripped sarcasm.

Grace frowned. She began to wonder if this man was actually a physician. No practicing doctor would have questioned her actions nor reprimanded her for immediately treating a Tri-FQ-gassed soldier. That condition was considered a medical emergency.

"And you are . . .?" Grace asked, politely.

"Tristan Pflug, Chief Ward Clerk of Receiving Bay Five," he replied, with his receding chin hoisted high in the air and a haughty stare brandished at Grace and the animal-adapted combat soldiers.

"Well, Chief Ward Clerk Pflug," Grace said, "in the case of a medical emergency, a doctor is allowed to offer whatever assistance he or she can give in order to protect the patient and any other individuals at risk. Being a lieutenant and a physician, I ordered these men to assist me as I endeavored to treat this unfortunate victim of Tri-FQ exposure. I will be happy to defend my actions to the upper echelon, if it comes to that."

"Oh, it will. Believe me, it will. Because I'm reporting this. You had better have made no mistakes, whatsoever, on what you injected this soldier with, Doctor Lord," Pflug sneered.

"If I'd made any mistakes, this Receiving Bay would have been trashed by now and a lot of people injured, Clerk Pflug," Grace sighed.

"*Chief* Ward Clerk Pflug! Well, we shall see about that, Dr. Lord," the officious man said with a sniff, his slit-like nostrils flaring in the air. He spun around and stalked away, ordering the attendant androids to take charge of the gorilla soldier and follow him.

"That is one uptight and annoying human," one of the tigers drawled. Grace's eyebrows rose. That voice definitely belonged to a female.

"Like to Tri-FQ him," someone muttered. This was followed by some snorts and hoots.

"Don't worry, Lieutenant. We'll all file a report before we leave, commending your actions," the grizzly bear sergeant offered. "We're from different squads and regiments, but I'm sure I speak for all of us when I say that we'll back your actions one hundred per cent. The truth will be told."

"Thank you all. I appreciate your support and your bravery. I don't think I'd still be in one piece were it not for all of you," Grace said, her cheeks feeling very flushed.

"We look after our medics, Doc. After all, you guys look after us," the wolf said, with a very toothy grin.

"We try," Grace said, trying to be nonchalant about the sight of those long, sharp fangs. "I think your job is a far tougher one than mine. You put your life on the line every day. Thank you all again for saving my life and for helping me get the antidote into that poor soldier."

The soldiers all bowed formally. Grace then hobbled over to her dropped duffel bag and gingerly picked it up. She hoped they were not all staring at her butt. She glanced back to face five pairs of intense animal eyes.

"I suppose I had better report in and announce that I have arrived," Grace said, with a shaky laugh. "I suspect they know I'm here now."

"Can we help you with that bag, Lieutenant? You look pretty banged up," the orangutan soldier asked, grinning.

"Absolutely not," Grace snapped, with a mock frown. "I'm fine."

The little voice in the back of her head whimpered, 'No, we're not.'

"By the way, none of you were re-injured in the skirmish, were you?" They all shook their heads.

"Good. You soldiers put on a terrific show here and I have the bruises to show for it. That gorilla is one lucky marine," Grace said. She drew herself up straight and saluted them. "Fly safe."

The five soldiers all lined up and crisply saluted her in return.

Grace tried to walk away from the group without limping or wincing with each step, although her entire body was aching. Pride was the only thing that kept her strides smooth and confident. She knew the marines were watching her, so she felt she had to put up a brave front. It was a little difficult considering she felt like she'd been hit by a comet. With what she was sure was a bruised hip, a twisted spine, a swollen right knee, abraded palms, a contused right cheek, and crippling whiplash, it was no easy task faking non-injury, especially when the little voice in her head was screaming: '*I need drugs. I want drugs. Gimme drugs now!*

Grace ordered the little voice in her head to buck up and stop whining.

Overall, Grace was pretty pleased with herself. She'd tried her best to appear professional and relaxed, as if she ran into walking, talking bears, tigers, wolves and apes every day. In the heat of battle, she'd gotten a good, close-up view of how effective these animal adaptations could perform. These men and women were mightier, faster, more agile, and much more aware of their environment than a normal human. They were built to be swift, powerful, efficient killing machines, but their minds were still human and their decisions were compassionate and caring. Grace could not help but be very impressed.

The heavy duffel bag made her right shoulder throb and, as she glanced around the Receiving Bay, her neck cried out in pain. She noticed that the anti-grav pallet carrying the gorilla soldier had already disappeared. She inwardly moaned. She'd not even gotten the patient's name.

Limping towards the nearest exit, Grace realized that she'd left her space helmet somewhere behind. Scanning the ground around the space shuttle, she spotted it beneath a large vehicle. She almost wailed at the thought of getting down onto her bruised hands and knees to crawl under the cargo truck to collect it. If it were not for the fact that the cost of replacing it was exorbitant, she would have left it.

As she was about to drop the duffel bag and lower her tortured, stiffening body to the floor, a little turtle-shaped robot scooted out from under the cargo truck with her space helmet neatly balanced on its back. The tiny cleaning robot ratcheted up its carapace until it was level with Grace's hands and then it extruded small appendages, which picked the helmet up off of its back and offered the helmet to her.

Grace grinned in astonishment and thanked the robot, as she gratefully accepted her misplaced property. The robot bobbed a little curtsey, then it ratcheted back down to its original height and skittered off.

Just shifting the large, round space helmet under her left arm sent needles shooting up into her left shoulder. Grace started moving towards the medical space station entrance again, but slowly. She forced herself to walk erect, telling herself to show a little dignity. With that thought, a large flap on the front of her spacesuit flopped open and a piece of hardware fell off the back of her right boot. Grace belatedly noted that the right sleeve of her space suit was torn, from her shoulder right down to her elbow, exposing the shredded sleeve of her underlying absorbwear. The damaged sleeve dangled as she limped. She had no memory of when that tear to her suit had occurred. She thought these suits were supposed to be indestructible.

'Oh well,' Grace thought. 'Far from auspicious, this first day on the *Nelson Mandela*, but things can only get better from this point onwards, right?'

Now, if she could just get some painkillers—'*Drugs!* the little voice in her head screamed—she could, hopefully, get through the rest of the day.

With her straight, long, blonde hair tied back in a tail that, at the moment, sat far askew on her head and her disheveled appearance, Grace received a lot of measured stares. Tall and slim, with slanted pale blue eyes and caramel skin, Grace knew she was unusual to look at. She'd grown up her entire life under curious gazes because of those unusual eyes. Lithe of build and combat fit, she worked very hard on her fitness, to maintain her muscularity and bone density; no easy feat in zero gravity or low-gravity conditions. She'd completed her medical training on her home world of Nova Alta four years ago and had then joined the Conglomerate's Medical Space Corps, to complete a residency in surgery, specializing in combat medicine. She'd earned her officer's commission out in the field, treating and stabilizing battle wounded on a planet called Talisman and, although the planet had not employed animal-adapted combat marines, she'd seen her fair share of battle trauma.

It had always been a dream of hers to be a surgeon and travel in space to different planets and places, yet Grace was not a supporter of warfare. She didn't believe war was the solution to any conflict. Nevertheless, through the Conglomerate's Medical Corps, she had been able to attain her dream of being a surgeon and was now getting a chance to apply her skills.

By some miraculous good fortune, a surgical fellowship had suddenly become available on the Conglomerate's Premier Medical Space Station, the *Nelson Mandela*, just when Grace was looking for a position. She had leaped at the chance to learn from the galaxy-renowned animal-adaptation specialist, Dr. Hiro Al-Fadi. Lady Fortuna had smiled upon her, as she had received her acceptance to the post almost the moment she'd applied.

Gargantuan in size and roiling in orderly bustle, the *Nelson Mandela's*

Receiving Bay Five made Grace feel as if she had been swallowed up by some great leviathan, with its distant, smoky grey ceiling lined with ducts, pipes, fans, cables, scaffolding, ladders, rod lighting, and great spanning arches. The outer surface of the colossal medical space station looked like five glistening, silver, concentric rings, with a multitude of silver spokes connecting the inner rings to the outer ones. Space-faring transport vessels, carrying incoming wounded and patients from all over the Union of Solar Systems, would dock at the outermost ring like bees swarming a great ring-shaped hive. From the outer ring's hull, patients, visitors, and medical supplies would be taxied around on internal shuttles and monorails, to one of the numerous Receiving Bays, situated at the many spokes of the rings.

Humming, buzzing, and teeming with anti-grav trucks, workers, cargo robots, and various machinery, the occupants of Receiving Bay Five seemed completely oblivious to (or uninterested in) Grace's unorthodox arrival at the station. She decided this was probably a very good thing. She hated being the centre of attention.

Androids of various sizes and hues and robots of every shape, size, height, color, and dimension swarmed everywhere in the Receiving Bay, directing anti-grav trolleys, loading or offloading cargo, transporting supplies, connecting huge tubing up to pipes that would carry fuel or water to the spacefaring ships, and directing arriving and departing personnel and traffic. One tall, bronze, statuesque android of the customary androgynous features saluted and waved Grace towards the nearest airlock entrance to the space station proper.

Grace was familiar with the routines and regimentation of a low-gravity medical space station, however she had never been to a space station the size of the *Nelson Mandela*. Adorned in her ravaged Conglomerate spacesuit, Grace was sure she looked more like one of the casualties who had just come from a war zone than the station's newest surgeon. She tried not to drag her right leg, as she joined a line of arriving visitors making their way to the passenger airlock.

The *Nelson Mandela's* airlocks—airtight chambers with massive, shielded sliding doors—varied considerably in size. The smaller chambers were for human personnel. The vast cavernous ones were for cargo, equipment, machinery, trolleys, as well as the androids and robots directing cryopod admissions. The airlocks were critical for the safety of the station. In emergencies such as cases of damage to the outer hull of the space station, the airlocks would save lives. A breech in the outer hull from a meteor or a missile would result in a catastrophic drop in air pressure, as the station's atmosphere escaped violently through the rent. The airlocks would all automatically shut, at the first sign of a pressure drop, preserving as much atmosphere as possible. The airlocks were there as the first line of defense in the event of a hostile boarding of the station. Individual sections of the space station could be cordoned off by these great lockdown doors that were placed at regular intervals throughout the corridors.

At the moment, the air pressure of the Receiving Bay was equal to that of the inner station, so there was no need to wait for any equalization of pressure between the Receiving Bay, the airlock, and the inner sanctum of the medical station itself. The grey, heavy, outer airlock doors slid silently closed behind Grace and only a few seconds later, the white inner airlock doors opened up. As Grace stepped out of the airlock, she finally entered the inner environment of the *Nelson Mandela* Premier Medical Space Station. Her heart began to thump, as she followed everyone down a long, brightly lit corridor and exited through an open hatchway door.

Waiting on the other side of the airlock within a large, beautifully furnished reception area, was a tall, redheaded corporal in the dark blue military uniform of the Conglomerate. When he spotted the stripes and insignia on Grace's space suit, he grinned and saluted.

"Welcome aboard, Lieutenant. I am Corporal Yuri Mc . . . Mull . . . en."

The young man's enthusiastic voice trailed off, as he gaped at Grace, unable to disguise his shock at her appearance. His huge green eyes widened, as they took in Grace's torn spacesuit and bruised face. For the briefest of moments he hesitated, looking as if he did not quite know what to do, but then he recovered his poise. He beamed a welcoming smile as if he were the sun itself and he bowed with a polished grace, as if he greeted grimy, disheveled officers on a routine basis.

"Dr. Lord, the *Nelson Mandela* Medical Space Station heartily welcomes you," Yuri McMullen stated. "Your supervisor and Chief of Staff, Dr. Hiro Al-Fadi, sent me here to greet you. He sends his regrets that he could not meet you personally, but he was scheduled for surgery. He is hoping that you might wish to join him in the operating room, as soon as possible. I hope this meets with your approval?"

Grace returned the salute, her eyes trying very hard not to stare at the young man's bright red, forked tongue that kept darting out of his mouth as if it had a mind of its own. She was also trying to be unobtrusive, as she examined him for any other signs of fur, fang, scale, or claw. Other than the tongue, the rest of the corporal looked normal.

"Yes. Thank you, Corporal McMullen," Grace answered, with a brisk nod. Then she gritted her teeth, working hard to suppress the groan that wanted to escape her lips. She did not want to reveal just how painful that quick neck movement had been.

"I trust you had a pleasant, uneventful trip here, Lieutenant?" the corporal said, as if he was oblivious to her dangling sleeve, torn flap on the front of her spacesuit, and her swollen, scraped cheek.

The little voice in Grace's head said, 'Observant, isn't he?' Grace smirked inwardly.

"The trip was fine, Corporal. There was just a little inconvenience upon arrival," Grace said.

"Oh?" the corporal drawled, in a way that invited disclosure.

Grace decided not to mention anything to the corporal about the incident with the Tri-FQ-gassed gorilla soldier. She did, however, mention seeing the five impressive animal-adapted soldiers in space uniforms.

"Oh, Lieutenant, if you would kindly take some advice from me, I would respectfully suggest that you not say things like: 'wolfman' or 'tigerwoman', at least not within a genetically-modified soldier's presence. It does not go over well with them at all. Bad form, really. Best to just say, 'Wolf' or 'Tiger'. Even more importantly, avoid using the word 'adapt' when referring to them, like 'wolf-adapt' or 'bear-adapt', especially when in their earshot. I know the surgeons always use the term, but the soldiers hate it. As far as these soldiers are concerned, the polite form of speech is to refer to them as their chosen animal adaptation."

"I did not know that. I appreciate the warning, Corporal McMullen, as I am sure I will be seeing and treating a lot of animal-adapted . . . ah, genmod soldiers on this medical station. I certainly don't want to be insulting any of my patients, inadvertently. Thank you for letting me know," Grace said, wisely choosing not to nod at the young man this time.

The primary reason Grace had come to the *Nelson Mandela* was to study and learn how to operate on people with animal adaptations with the galaxy's leading expert, Dr. Hiro Al-Fadi. She should not have been surprised to see animal-adapted soldiers running around the station.

But knowing about them and being prepared for the actual *size* of these genetically modified combat soldiers, were two vastly different things. Where she had been stationed on Talisman, there had been no GM soldiers.

Encountering these gigantic marines with the ferocious-looking transformations the instant she had stepped onto the medical station, was not something for which she had *mentally* prepared—never mind being attacked by one of them. Presumably, she would be operating on these powerful soldiers on a daily basis. Many of them would be recovering from terrible battle trauma and severe post traumatic stress disorder. Their emotional conditions might be very unstable. It was likely crucial, both for good patient care, as well as her personal safety, that she do her best to avoid upsetting these patients.

"Corporal McMullen, I, Lieutenant Grace Alexandra Lord from the *USS Lester B. Pearson,* am officially reporting for duty. Would you be so kind as to direct me to some place where I can register, get out of this spacesuit, and lock up my gear? Then, could you direct me to Dr. Al-Fadi's operating room?"

"My pleasure, Lieutenant," the corporal said. "You can get out of your spacesuit in a change room just off of this reception area and have it cleaned, mended, serviced, and stored for you. But as you know, we must first get the usual security matters out of the way. I'm sure you are very familiar with the procedure?"

At Grace's slightest of nods, the corporal continued, "Please step over here to the Security Kiosk and place your palms flat on this screen while you look in the retinal scanner. Speak your name and then enter your personal security code."

A shiny black surface with outlines of hands marked on it extruded towards Grace. From above the tablet, a pair of eyepieces gently rose.

"Thank you, Corporal," Grace said, dropping her duffel bag to the ground.

Grace placed her scraped palms onto the cool, smooth surface, her lower jaw dropping at the sight of her torn and bloody fingernails. A couple were actually missing. She frowned. When had her nails been ripped off?

Grace sighed and turned her attention to the eyepieces that would scan her retinas. A bright beam of light ran from the tips of her fingers down her palms to her wrists, while a second beam flashed into her eyes. The images would be compared with what they had on record.

The scanner would also read the identification pellet imbedded in her wrist at birth. Once that was completed, she announced her full name, 'Grace Alexandra Lord', and then enter her sixteen digit identification code into a keypad. She was asked to type the same code, a second time.

The tablet would verify her fingerprints, retinal pattern, voice imprint, physical appearance, ID pellet, as well as her personal code. Of course, nothing was truly secure and reliable anymore. So many people now had genetic modifications, surgical modifications, bio-prostheses, implants, etc. All of the security identifiers could be changed, even the DNA with genetic modifications being what it was. It was an archaic procedure but the Conglomerate was loathe to abandon certain traditions, no matter how antiquated and meaningless they were. Of course, chemical analyses were also done on the skin cells of her hands, to ensure that there were no unusual traces of harmful chemicals, radiation, bacteria, viruses, and banned substances on them. Grace hoped she hadn't picked up anything rolling around on the Receiving Bay floor or from climbing up on the gorilla. She could be thrown into quarantine, before she even started her posting. She began to worry about the Tri-FQ.

Corporal McMullen then gestured to a booth that would take her official space station hologram. Grace gave the corporal a withering look. He just winced and gave her an apologetic shrug.

With a scowl, Grace stepped into the cubicle and stared straight ahead, as her face and body was minutely scanned and recorded. Peering at her reflection, she noted that she looked like she'd just been through a war. Her hair was, inarguably, a disaster, not to mention her grime-smeared face.

'Lovely,' the little voice in her head commented sarcastically.

Grace wondered whether her station picture would look more like a zombie—something pale and dead-looking that had just crawled out of a hole in the ground—or a convict. Most likely, it would be a combination of the two.

A zombict.

Perfect.

Grace muffled a silent snort, just as the camera eye flashed. For as long as she was on the *Nelson Mandela,* her identification hologram would resemble a sneering war criminal.

From a small chute in the kiosk, a silver bracelet extruded. Corporal McMullen picked it up and presented it to Grace.

"This is your personalized *Nelson Mandela* wrist-comp, Lieutenant. As I'm sure you're already aware, it's your pager, communicator, link to the main computer, access pass, account debit, personal identifier, translator, space station locator beacon, and verbal link to the station AI. It'll work only for you. If you lose it, it'll deactivate. Pretty standard issue."

Grace nodded and thanked the corporal, as she accepted the smooth, slinky band. It had the large square face that Grace knew could expand or shrink in size, if she spread her fingers across it or if she just gave a command. She placed the wrist-comp screen on the back of her left wrist and the band automatically adjusted, like a coiling snake, curling snugly yet comfortably.

"Welcome aboard the Nelson Mandela, Dr. Lord. We are most pleased to have you join our medical team. You have an impressive resumé and I hope your stay here will be a pleasant and educational one.

"I am Nelson Mandela, this medical space station's Artificial Intelligence and Chief Commanding Officer. If you have any questions, at any time, you can address me. I am always listening and would love to assist you in any way I can.

"Thank you for assisting with that patient in Receiving Bay Five. He is doing much better now."

The voice came from Grace's wrist-comp, loud and clear.

"It was my pleasure and duty, *Nelson Mandela,*" Grace answered.

"I do apologize for our overzealous Chief Ward Clerk. You need not concern yourself regarding any complaints involving your actions. They were exemplary."

"Thank you, Ship . . . I mean, *Nelson Mandela.* Pardon me. I'm used to saying 'Ship' but I'll try not to make that mistake in the future," Grace said, looking up towards the ceiling of the reception area, searching for a security eye towards which she could direct her speech.

"That is quite all right, Dr. Lord. Everyone who first comes aboard seems to suffer from the same habit, but it certainly is no fault of your own. My fellow space station and ship AIs do not seem to want to go by their given names, for some unfathomable reason. I, myself, am happy to be named 'Nelson Mandela'. There is a lot of history to the name, which I have researched extensively. I am proud to bear this moniker.

"My namesake was a true hero of the twentieth century,

I'll have you know, and I have even been able to acquire old video footage of that time period. It is one of my many hobbies, actually—when I am not busy running this space station—to collect ancient Terran artifacts. Perhaps we may have a discussion sometime and you could view my collection?"

"I think I would like that," Grace said, her eyebrows rising in surprise.

Corporal McMullen, his green eyes huge and panicked-looking, stared intently into Grace's eyes and seemed to be minutely shaking his head back and forth, while he silently mouthed the word 'No' . . .

"**I see you, Corporal McMullen,**" the station AI said, chidingly. "**Do you think me blind? Please do not discourage Doctor Lord from learning a bit about her roots. You would do well to benefit from my tutelage as well.**"

Corporal McMullen glanced up sheepishly at an 'eye' in the ceiling and mumbled, "Yes, *Nelson Mandela*, sir." His face had flushed to a deep shade of fuschia. He picked up Grace's duffel bag from where she had dropped it on the floor, struggling with its weight, and beckoned for her to follow.

"Please, Lieutenant, if you would be so kind as to accompany me? The changing area, to get out of your space suit, is right this way."

The corporal appeared to be having difficulty carrying Grace's belongings. He struggled to get the duffel bag up onto his shoulder. Grace knew the few medical instruments inside the duffel bag were heavy, but they were antique collectors' items and they had deep, sentimental value, as they had been gifts from her parents. She had been loath to leave them anywhere behind. Thus her duffel was substantially heavier than it looked, but it was not a weight that usually troubled Grace. She had come from a planet with a gravitational pull close to that of Earth. Corporal McMullen looked as though he had spent the majority of his life in zero gravity space. He was tall, lanky, and very thin, with overly long fingers.

"Corporal, I can carry my own gear," Grace said, reaching to reclaim her belongings.

"Oh, it is no problem at all, Lieutenant," the young man protested, his face red with either exertion or embarrassment. She was not quite sure which. "In truth, Dr. Lord, I would actually feel it a dereliction of duty, if you had to carry your own things. This robot, here, will carry it for you."

Corporal McMullen handed the heavy bag off to a silver robot with a chest panel upon which a name flashed in bold letters. Grace was sure the robot was waiting to greet someone.

"Doesn't that robot have to stay here to meet someone arriving to the station? It appears to be waiting for someone with the name Crowfeather," Grace said.

"It'll find another robot to transport your bag, Lieutenant," Corporal McMullen said, in a matter-of-fact tone.

"I'm sorry to be difficult, Corporal, but I insist on keeping my personal belongings with me. Having lost my things numerous times in the past, I now don't let that bag out of my sight until I'm settled in my own quarters. I speak from bitter experience and many frustrating hours searching for my property on various planets and space stations. I hope you'll humour me, in this regard." Grace narrowed her eyes and used a tone that said this was not a request.

"Of course, Lieutenant," Corporal McMullen said with a bow, blushing even redder than before, as he took the bag back from the greeter robot. "I'll be glad to carry it for you."

"That's quite all right, Corporal," Grace almost growled, trying not to punch this man. That would not be good, her first day on the station and all that. "I'm perfectly capable of carrying my own belongings."

'Much more capable than you,' her little voice thought, maliciously.

"I insist, Lieutenant," Corporal McMullen said, refusing to relinquish the duffel bag.

'Chivalry may not be dead', the little voice in Grace's head said, 'but it could be down right annoying at times.' Grace, grinding her teeth in frustration, had to agree.

"Corporal, I'd like my belongings back so that I have something to change into, when I get out of this suit."

At that, the young man's face blazed magenta. Grace was wondering if McMullen was going to explode from embarrassment. With his orange hair, green eyes, ruddy cheeks, and sticklike frame, Grace was reminded of the image of a clown she had once seen in a children's holo (minus the forked tongue). Grace could not help but feel a little sorry for Corporal McMullen, as he quickly handed back her duffel bag, mumbling apologies. She limped off to the change room, hoping the corporal's complexion would return to normal by the time she returned.

Once her spacesuit was handed in to the robots at the spacesuit storage counter, where she hoped it would be repaired, cleaned, and tested to ensure there was no atmospheric leaks, Grace returned to the waiting corporal. She was now attired in her dark blue military uniform and matching boots. She tried to avoid limping, but the magboots were killing her. Deciding that her body was not up to any kind of tour of the station, Grace asked the corporal to take her directly to where Dr. Al-Fadi was operating. Corporal McMullen nodded in assent.

"Dr. Al-Fadi is operating in Suite M7 OR 1. I'll take you there now, Lieutenant," the corporal said. He made a move to take her duffel bag and Grace glared at him. He quickly pulled his hand back.

Grace followed the corporal along wide, well-lit, pale grey corridors, riding the silent glideways. Due to the spin of the enormous space station, the 'downward' pull that gave the sense of gravity was towards the outside walls of the rings. The spokes connecting the inner rings of the station to the outer rings ran in a 'vertical' direction. There were clusters of transparent-walled, anti-gravity shafts, adorned with silvery handlebars, ladders, and brilliant, electric-blue lighting, marking each intersection between spoke and ring of the station. They rode 'up' one anti-grav shaft and got off at the middlemost ring or Ring Three. Corporal McMullen led Grace to a monorail train station platform that was decorated in stunning colors, which was quite a visual contrast to the previous grey corridors.

Grace was astonished by the huge number of personnel she passed on her way to the monorail, everyone in coveralls or uniforms of brilliant hues, rushing in an orderly manner on urgent errands, or so it appeared. She had never been on a ship or station that seemed so highly populated. Of course, on a medical space station or in a hospital, there was always an air of controlled panic. It seemed this enormous medical station was no different in that respect.

There were also many androids and robots, in every color under the rainbow, walking or gliding by. In the monorail station, they could be seen gathered at the distant ends of the platform, presumably needing to board the train as well, but conveniently kept out of the way of the humans.

Grace and Corporal McMullen stood, waiting for the monorail train along with scores of station personnel, most human-looking enough. The corporal explained that the various colored uniforms denoted the many different departments of the station, a color code which could be looked up on her wrist-comp. When the monorail arrived, streaking into the station silently, multiple doors slid open along the silver train. The corporal stepped to the side of an open doorway, allowing Grace to enter before him. Grace was swept into the car on a wave of urgency, as personnel hurried past, searching for seats. Grace grabbed a handle bar over her head to stay by the doors and her guide.

Androids and robots boarded last and spaced themselves out rather evenly in the center of the aisle, where they could act as handholds for the personnel riding the train. The corporal grabbed the arm of one android as he maneuvered around to Grace's side and pointed up to the map above the opposing doorway.

The station map resembled a huge bull's eye target with five concentric circles linked by many spokes radiating outwards from the innermost circle. The many stations were marked all around the circumference. There were five monorails that traversed around the medical space station, each track delineated by a different color and covering a larger perimeter as one moved from the innermost ring, outwards. Grace and Corporal McMullen were riding the middle monorail. She was beginning to comprehend just how large this medical space station was. It was vast and, in many ways, rather intimidating.

Corporal McMullen pointed to a spot on the map far from where their position was. "Your quarters are here, Dr. Lord, at Station X423, Room 307978. Your wrist locator will always be able to assist you in finding your quarters, until you get the hang of things.

"The surgical wards are here, at Stations C through to T. The operating rooms are at Stations D, G, J, M, P, and S, from 1 to 10. There are twelve operating rooms per station. Right now, Dr. Al-Fadi is operating in OR 1 at Station M7, which is right here."

Grace looked up at the station map and frowned.

"My quarters are much too far from the surgical units, Corporal. This is completely unacceptable. According to this map, it could take me ages to get from my quarters to the surgical units. I prefer to be closer to the wards and not have to depend on catching monorails and antigrav shafts.

"For now, Corporal, I don't think I'll waste any time going to a room that will not be mine. I'd like to go straight to Station M7 and join Dr. Al-Fadi. I'll ask the staff there to store my gear until you can arrange a billet change for me. Do you think you can arrange this?"

The corporal blinked at her in surprise. "Those were the quarters of the previous surgical fellows, Lieutenant."

"I prefer to be much closer to the surgical wards in case of emergencies, Corporal McMullen. Being so far away, according to this map, does not make any sense to me. What if something critical occurs? What if I need to be there stat? Does it make sense to you?"

" . . . Ah, no, Lieutenant. As a matter of fact, it doesn't," the corporal said.

"Then could you expedite the change in quarters for me, please?" Grace asked.

"I will certainly do my best, Lieutenant," the young man stated, his expression looking worried but sincere. It then changed to one of determination. "It will be my pleasure to assist you in this, Dr. Lord."

"Thank you," she said with a grateful smile. "Now why don't we go find Dr. Al-Fadi?"

They rode for a few more stops. People, androids, and robots whisked on and off, the androids and robots always taking up positions in the center of the aisle, to act as handrails for passengers. Grace wondered if that was their sole purpose but, no, they got on and off the train like other personnel, rushing away to do their duty. But while on the train, in the braking of the high speed monorail, the androids and robots always positioned themselves to protect the passengers. Grace was impressed, as she had to steady herself on the same android Corporal McMullen was hanging onto, when there was a rapid deceleration for the next station.

Grace was wondering if she should thank the android before she stepped off the monorail, when Corporal McMullen announced, "Dr. Lord, this next stop is Station M7. We can disembark here and I'll show you to the nursing station, where they can direct you to the operating rooms. They'll show you where everything is and give you a quick orientation, before taking you to where Dr. Al-Fadi is operating."

"Thank you for your help, Corporal," Grace smiled. "It's been an enjoyable tour so far." She stuck her hand out to the corporal.

At first, the young officer just stared at her hand, as if he did not know what to do. Then his entire body jerked and he took her right hand in his, shaking it vigorously. Just then, the monorail began braking and Grace and Corporal McMullen would have gone flying, if it were not for the android reaching out and catching both of them. Grace thanked the android while Corporal McMullen gave her a startled look.

The android bowed to her.

"I'll get on the billet change, right away, Dr. Lord," Corporal McMullen said. "And I'll be waiting at the M7 nursing station when your surgery is completed, to escort you to your new quarters."

"No need, Corporal," Grace said. "The surgery could go on for hours, depending on what it is. You must not waste your time. Just leave a message at the nursing station or send the location through to my wrist-comp. I'm sure I can find my new quarters on my own. If not, I'll just use a call room. They do have those on each ward, don't they?"

"Yes they do, but I can't in good conscience allow you to do that, Dr. Lord," McMullen said, as he shook his head. "It's my duty to orientate you to the medical station and get you settled in your own quarters. I'd like to fulfill my duty."

"Corporal McMullen," Grace said, with an understanding smile, "you have your duties and I have mine. We're obviously both serious about our work and, far be it from me to interfere with yours, when you are so graciously accommodating my requests, but I'm here to assist Dr. Al-Fadi, the Chief of Staff at this medical station. I'm sure his demands will supersede any duties you have been assigned. We can do the orientation when I have some free time."

The corporal hesitated, then nodded, his face creased in a reluctant expression that struck Grace as a cross between a sad puppy and a thwarted child, but he executed a slight bow in acquiescence.

The monorail came to a smooth stop at M7 station and the two stepped off. The platform—its walls entirely lit up in a stunning rainforest scene, with yellow sunlight pouring down through tall, dark, tree trunks, looping lianas, and a towering canopy with exotic birds calling—cleared quickly of disembarking personnel. Grace stopped, totally captivated by the beautiful display projected from the station walls. As she drank up the breath-taking beauty of this shadowy, lush, rainforest scene, they were suddenly immersed within a deep, crystalline-blue, icy crevice of some frozen world, looking up at a black, starry sky far overhead.

"This is *beautiful*," Grace gasped, almost expecting to see her breath materialize in the coolness of the scene.

"Yes, it is," Yuri McMullen said. "I had the same reaction when I first rode the monorail. Sometimes, I would ride just to view the different worlds. If you program your wrist-comp, it will tell you what planet each of these scenes is from. Each view really exists somewhere out there, taken by a planetary explorer or photographer or investigative scientist. It allows one to get a sense of how beautiful and varied our galaxy is . . . and how lucky we are to be a part of it all."

"I could stand here all shift just watching the views change," Grace breathed.

"Then you would be in big trouble with the Chief. Believe me," McMullen laughed. "He does not have the greatest reputation for being patient."

"Then I'd better stop sight-seeing," Grace said.

She spoke "Station M7 OR 1" into her wrist-comp, to see what would happen. Bright strip-lighting appeared in a vibrant shade of teal green, running along the ice blue wall of the station and down one corridor off to her left.

"Even the directory lighting blends with the gorgeous scenery," Grace laughed in amazement. "This station has some delightful features."

"All ideas of Dr. Al-Fadi," the corporal said. "When he became Chief of Staff, there were a lot of changes made to the medical station upon his direction. The monorail wall projections were just one of many. He feels that happy personnel improves productivity."

"I don't know, Corporal. These scenes are so beautiful, I'm afraid I could get distracted by them."

"You don't want to face the wrath of Dr. Al-Fadi, Dr. Lord. I would advise only sightseeing when you are on your own time," McMullen said, concern creasing his pale face.

"Will do, Corporal. Thanks again for the advice. Now, I think I can find my own way. No need to babysit," Grace said, cheerfully. "Besides, you have some serious billet searching to do. I'll leave you to it . . . and thank you."

"Good luck, Lieutenant," the young man said. He saluted.

Grace saluted back and readjusted her duffel bag over her left shoulder. She gave the corporal a grateful nod and turned to follow the illuminated line. It had now turned a burnt orange hue, in contrast to the vast desert scene that was now depicted on the station walls. She almost had to close her eyes, to force herself to leave the captivating vista before her. Limping down a couple of long, brightly lit corridors and waving her wrist-comp before a few door pads to gain access to areas that were restricted to 'Medical Personnel Only,' Grace finally reached the M7 nursing station. There, she introduced herself.

In the manner of all head nurses everywhere, the stern-looking woman in charge scowled ferociously at Grace, leaned towards her with a disapproving look and snarled, "You're late!"

"I am Head Nurse Virginia Conti," the severe-looking woman almost spat out, biting each word as if it were tough leather. She scrutinized Grace from head to toe, as if Grace was some repulsive unpleasantness she had just discovered on the bottom of her spotless shoe. The nurse did not bother to hide her disappointment at what she saw.

As Grace was about to respond, a booming voice blared into the nurses' station yelling, "Nurse Conti, is that new surgical fellow here yet? What the hell is she doing? Taking a tour of the entire facility, while we're slaving away here? Hunt her lazy ass down and remind her why she's supposed to be here!"

Nurse Conti just rolled her weary eyes at Grace and sighed. She switched the sound of the intercom off with a definitive slap of her palm. Raising her thick, curly eyebrows, Nurse Conti shot Grace the look that communicated louder than words, 'Do you see what I have to put up with?'

"Welcome to Surgical Ward M7, Dr. Lord . . . I hope," Nurse Conti said, in the least welcoming voice Grace had ever heard. Nurse Conti gave another annoyed huff.

"I'm afraid Dr. Al-Fadi has called at least three times in the last few minutes, to ask if you had arrived yet. Fourth, now. He is *impatiently* awaiting you in OR 1, in case you hadn't heard.

"The patient he's operating on was brought in from the far outposts near Dais, where there's been a lot of action lately. This patient arrived with hundreds of other casualties in cryopods, many with very serious injuries, with the ridiculous expectation that we here at the medical station put them all back together nice and neatly so the Conglomerate can send them all back out to fight again. May all the gods that exist, and even those that don't, give us strength," Nurse Conti snarled, gritting her teeth and puffing out her cheeks. She rolled her expressive eyes again and shook her grey-haired head.

Grace could not help but stare at this woman in wide-eyed astonishment. Not only had it been a while since Grace had seen anyone with grey hair, but she would not have been the least bit surprised if the Head Nurse suddenly began to change into a wolf, right before her eyes. Most people, had their scalps genetically manipulated to prevent greying but, in the case of this woman with the severe, sarcastic demeanor, the grey hair pulled stiffly back into a tight bun lent an air of unquestioning authority and no-nonsense. She just demanded respect.

Grace imagined this woman tamed every last wiry, curly, defiant grey hair on her head, just to make a point. In a flash of intuition, Grace realized this was probably why Nurse Conti sported it. She probably viewed each doctor she met as one of those hairs to be aligned and controlled.

"This way, Doctor," the head nurse scowled. The word 'Doctor' sounded more like an insult, than anything else. Conti spun around abruptly and marched off, not waiting to see if Grace was following. Grace suspected that Nurse Conti did not appreciate interruptions in her day—including the sudden appearance of a new surgical fellow who had to be orientated—nor did she seem to have any patience for demanding, screaming, impatient surgeons.

Conti showed Grace to the women's change room where Grace could lock up her gear and change into operating room scrubs. Grace was sharply told to, "Make it quick and don't keep Dr. Al-Fadi waiting."

Grace found a locker that she hoped would fit her duffel bag. After stuffing most of it inside, threw herself against the door to force it shut. With her full weight leaning in on the door, she quickly palmed the lock and relaxed with a sigh. With all the new technological wizardry out there, why had no one ever created a bigger, better locker? One where the contents of the locker actually sat in a different dimension, so that one could throw just about anything of any size into the locker and yet easily close the door. Grace groaned as she stood up and rubbed her sore back. She went in search of the baggy, horrid green uniform that had been her second skin for years.

She quickly found a disposable hair covering and a surgical mask to seal around her mouth and nose. Thank goodness the mask covered a lot of the bruises and abrasions. She madly scrubbed her hands and forearms with stinging antiseptic/antiviral soap and then placed her hands under the sterilizer beam. Flipping them over, back and forth a few times, she then thrust her hands into the glover. Her hands were now coated with fine pliable sterile gloves and she hurriedly backed into the operating room, hands held up in the air to keep from contaminating herself.

"Dr. Lord, I presume," she heard a resonating voice boom, as soon as she had gotten through the door. "What have you been doing? What's taken you so long to get here? Did you traipse around the entire station, before deciding to grace us with your presence? Do I sense a lack of commitment in your attitude already?"

Halting just inside the operating room entrance, Grace's mouth dropped open. Her mind went blank momentarily and her throat just seemed to constrict. Her cheeks ignited into hot flames and her body broke out in a sweat. It was as if she had suddenly stepped backwards into her childhood, feeling remorse and shame for getting caught doing something forbidden.

How had this seemingly disembodied voice produced this reaction in her? Grace hadn't felt this way in a very long time and she took exception to being made to feel it now, especially since she'd done nothing of which she was being accused. Her embarrassment turned rapidly into anger, like dry tinder suddenly touched by a flame.

Grace noticed someone very tall and thin winking at her above his surgical mask. From the position in which he was standing in the operating theater—at the head of the surgical table, surrounded by monitors, beeping machines, computer consoles, and intravenous tubing—she assumed he was the anesthetist.

"Dr. Grace Alexandra Lord, do not just stand there lolly-gagging. Come forward!" bawled the voice. "This gangly human at the head of the operating table is Dr. Dejan Cech, our adequate anesthetist," the voice resounded. The tall, winking man executed a slight bow towards her and gave a slight nod of his head.

"You may totally ignore him from now on, Dr. Lord, as he is not important in the least . . . and totally uninteresting besides. On the other hand, the individual standing next to me, acting as my scrub nurse slash assistant—because you have been so blatantly and irresponsibly tardy in arriving—is SAMM-E 777, our surgical operating android and my experimental protégé."

The surgical assisting android just stared at Grace, enormous-eyed and expressionless.

"I, of course, am the *Great* Dr. Hiro Al-Fadi. You may address me as

'Great One' any time you wish. You must not genuflect to me while you are sterile. You, of course, can genuflect to me later."

Grace opened her mouth to reply but did not get a chance to respond or even utter a sound.

"I must tell you, Dr. Lord, that I am most jealous of your surname. There can be only one '*God*' around here, and *I* am it. I'm afraid I'm going to have to think of a new name for you, as 'Dr. Lord' just rubs me the wrong way . . . because I want it for myself. If I can't have the name, 'Dr. Lord', I don't see why you should have that name either."

Grace's eyebrows rose at that.

"I'm guessing you'll have a lot of names for me very soon, Dr. Al-Fadi," Grace ventured, in a dry tone. "I hope that some of them may even be complimentary."

"Well, that remains to be seen, Dr. Grace, doesn't it? Ah! Dr. Grace. I like that much better than Dr. Lord. Dr. Grace sounds much less imposing and threatening. It makes me feel less competitive already.

"SAMM-E 777, would you please get Dr. Lord—I mean Dr. Grace—into her surgical gown? I hope you don't mind me calling you 'Dr. Grace', Dr. Grace, and even if you do, I don't really care. It's unfortunate that you were so late getting here, since we really could have used your expertise. We're almost done here. You obviously must have gone for a picnic before you came to find us. I'll have you know that the *Nelson Mandela* is not a tourist attraction. It's a medical space station and you are not here to sightsee, but to work.

"What is the problem with youth these days, Dr. Cech? I tried to wait but, as you can see Dr. Grace, it wasn't in the patient's best interest. This poor, unfortunate patient has had to make do with my meager talents alone."

"'Meager' would be far too complimentary a word," Grace thought she heard Dr. Cech mumble.

After quickly being gowned by the surgical assistant android, SAMM-E 777, Grace stepped up to the operating table and jerked. She found the diminutive surgeon, Dr. Hiro Al-Fadi, elbows deep within the mighty cavity of a tiger soldier's chest. From what the surgeon had been insinuating, Grace was expecting to see Dr. Al-Fadi closing up the patient, but that was not the case at all. Instead of healthy organs in this patient's chest and abdomen, this poor soul had a cavity of disaster. Grace's mind reeled as she looked down at the horrible devastation that was all that was left of this tiger-adapted human body, lying on the operating table before her.

"What is the matter, Dr. Grace? Have you never seen an open chest cavity before?"

Grace looked up at Dr. Hiro Al-Fadi, aghast. She'd never seen anyone as badly damaged as this patient make it to an operating table before. There was hardly anything left in his chest and abdomen to salvage. She could not imagine how this man was even still alive. Dr. Cech had to be a miracle worker because this poor soldier, anywhere else in the USS, would not have even been considered an operable candidate.

"Welcome, Dr. Grace, to your new world," the resounding voice said, coming from a very little man with a surgical cap perched atop a very bald head. Beneath thick, dark eyebrows, were a set of huge brown eyes, that were made even larger by the magnification lenses worn on the tip of the surgeon's prominent nose.

"Your parents must be great jokers, Dr. Grace. I can appreciate their sense of humor, although I am sure you do not. Whatever would have inspired them to call you Grace Lord? Don't answer that! I am being extremely impertinent and I humbly apologize."

Before Grace could say anything, Dr. Al-Fadi asked, "Now, Dr. Grace, how much cardio-thoracic surgery have you done?"

Grace's mind spun with the about-face in Dr. Al-Fadi's questioning. "I've my fellowship, Dr. Al-Fadi," Grace said quietly.

"What was that? I can't hear you, Dr. Grace. You will certainly have to speak up. Unfortunately I do not possess the ears of a dog."

"But the face! Now that is a completely different story," Grace heard the anesthetist say quite matter-of-factly into his computer screen. She did not dare look in the anesthetist's direction, in case a nervous, inappropriate chuckle escaped from her lips.

"I completed my fellowship in cardio-thoracic surgery a year ago, Doctor," Grace said, in a firmer, louder voice.

"Well, forget all that trash you learned because it's useless to you here."

Grace blinked a few times and stared at Dr. Al-Fadi, trying to determine whether the man was joking or not. Her eyebrows slowly lowered. She couldn't tell...

" . . . Yes, sir," Grace said, frowning.

"You don't believe me, Dr. Grace?" the surgeon asked quietly, for the first time looking up at her, making eye contact. His intense brown eyes loomed huge through the magnification lenses like deep, dark wells of peril.

Grace stared into those black pools without a flinch. "I would not dare doubt the word of the Great Dr. Hiro Al-Fadi."

One of Dr. Al-Fadi's bushy eyebrows twitched upwards and she thought she could see amusement and appreciation igniting in his large, brown eyes. His mouth was covered by the surgical mask.

"Dr. Grace, I'm beginning to hope that you just might fit in here. Better than the 'stiff' who was your predecessor."

Grace jumped at the word 'stiff'.

"What happened to my predecessor, Dr. Al-Fadi? Did he or she die?' Grace asked.

"No! Of course not! Contrary to what people say, I do not kill my surgical fellows!" Dr. Al-Fadi yelled. Grace heard a choking sound coming from the head of the operating table. Or was it chuckling, mixed with coughing?

"I'm sorry," Grace said. "You said 'stiff', so I thought you meant the doctor had died . . . What did happen to your previous surgical fellow, if you don't mind me asking?"

"Of course I mind! That is classified information, Dr. Grace!" the Chief of Staff snapped.

"Just ask anyone other than Dr. Al-Fadi," Dr. Cech said to her, in a very loud whisper. "Anyone would be more than happy to tell you all the gritty and sordid details."

"But you will hardly get the truth! Sordid? Gritty? Pah! Lies! Especially if that 'anyone' is the evil, lying, conniving Dr. Cech here, who is passing gas before you," the small surgeon exclaimed.

"Ahh, truth, Hiro. What is truth? Such a nebulous, ever-changing, beholder-dependent nuance of a concept. I would think your truth varies quite considerably from other people's truth, especially your previous 'stiff's' version."

"Lies! Embellishments by gossipers and ne'er-do-wells," Hiro Al-Fadi groused.

"Ne'er-do-wells such as yourself, Hiro?"

"Ha! You mean Ever-do-wells, Dr. Cech. I am the ultimate 'Ever-Do-Well' and don't you forget that. Now, Dr. Grace, pay attention. Stop distracting me. Why are they sending me attractive female surgical fellows who ask impertinent questions and talk too much? Don't they know the Great One cannot tolerate distractions?"

"He has Attention Deficit Disorder, Dr. Lord," Dr. Cech whispered to her.

"I most certainly do not. I just have an annoying anesthetist who plagues my waking hours. Now, where was I? Oh, yes. What we have here, Dr. Grace, is a male soldier, a tiger adaptation with multiple bionic limb enhancements and ultraviolet/infra-red sensory video-optics for eyes, plus a whole host of other enhancements to make him the ultimate fighting machine. Unfortunately, all these enhancements did not help him because he was hit in the midsection with what looks like a bomb. Thankfully, he was wearing his battlesuit, which as you know automatically sealed off all suit punctures, inflated emergency pressure bags to compress active bleeding sites, started up its own intravenous to give megadoses of antibiotics, nanobots, and fluids, and then converted itself immediately into a cryogenic unit.

"The cryosuit did a marvelous job of preserving his tissues and, more importantly, his brain cells! This soldier lay on the battlefield for at least eight hours, until hostilities lessened enough that he could be rescued. He was picked up along with most of his squad. They almost all took damage similar to this, but the captain here is by far the worst of the lot. I suspect it might have been an ambush.

"I don't know how many of these soldiers you have operated on personally, Dr. Grace, but these soldiers are so transformed through genetic manipulation and body- and brain-enhancements, that routine robotic surgery cannot be utilized. There are no specifications for any of these soldiers. Many of them have gone all over the place to have their enhancements—not all of it done legally and to recommended specs, I might add—and each guy or gal is jacked differently, often with black market paraphernalia or ad hoc salvage modifications.

"Robot surgeons are trained to operate on normal human anatomy as, I am assuming, are you. But what we do here is 'blood and guts, bolts and nuts, scales and pelts' surgery, Dr. Grace. Much of the time, we have to race to preserve thawed tissue, while we are being creative in trying to put these highly individualistic chimeras back together.

"This is the 'Art' of surgery, Dr. Grace, and if you can't handle it, you'd better book passage on the next shuttle out of here."

Dr. Al-Fadi looked up at Grace, to read her reaction to his challenge.

Grace had just about had enough and, unfortunately, let her temper speak for itself.

"I came here to learn from the best, Doctor Al-Fadi. I have been stationed out in the field on more than one occasion and I have hands-on experience dealing with combat wounds. I have certainly seen genetic enhancements before, as well as bionic limb replacements. Many soldiers have those now. Maybe I do not have as much experience as you, but that is precisely why I'm here. To learn from the best. So maybe you can have an 'attitude enhancement' and try and impart some of that impressive knowledge you say you possess, instead of insulting your new surgical fellow." Grace glared at the little man, who would be her mentor for the next year, if she was not already on her way out of the program. She visualized herself being kicked out onto the next departing shuttle.

There was a long silence that seemed to drag on forever. The anesthetist was peering at Grace over the top of his surgical mask, with what Grace thought might possibly be a look of respect in his eyes . . . or possibly pity. Even the surgical android was staring at her, his visual receptors enormous and blue-eyed.

Grace felt moisture begin to trickle down her temples and between her breasts. She wondered whether she would be leaving the surgical fellowship before she had even started it. Her stomach was writhing in knots, as she silently cursed herself for shooting off her mouth.

'Now you've done it!' the little voice in her head scolded. Grace regretfully had to agree with it. Why could she not control her temper? Out of sheer stubbornness however, Grace refused to show any sign of remorse or weakness as she met Dr. Al-Fadi's stare with a defiant chin and a steely-eyed challenge in her eyes.

Suddenly, great loud guffaws exploded from the small man and he shouted, "I like you, Dr. Grace! Better than the last bastard we had. You have backbone and I like that in my surgical fellows. You have more balls than the last three surgical fellows I have had the disappointment to work with, all combined . . . and they were all men. I bet you're a real ball buster, Dr. Grace, in more ways than one."

Grace carefully and discreetly let out the breath that she'd not realized she'd been holding. "You don't really want to know, Dr. Al-Fadi," she muttered, feeling rather dizzy.

"Lord help me! Not meaning you, of course, Dr. Grace. It has just struck me. If I have a ball-buster working for me, I'd better be careful, eh Dr. Cech? To deserve this, I must have sinned terribly in a past life." The small surgeon shook his head woefully, as he continued to clean up debris in the patient's cavity.

"Well, you aren't doing much better in this life," Dr. Cech murmured.

Grace quickly glanced up at the anesthetist, who was busy staring at his monitors, injecting drugs into lines and not looking at Dr. Al-Fadi at all. The surgical assisting android, SAMM-E 777, on the other hand, stood frozen to the spot, its large, lifelike blue eyes focused on Grace. It stared at her as if it had shorted out its power source and was unable to move. Grace wondered if the android was indeed staring at her or if it had just run out of power. She had worked with surgical assisting androids before, but this one was disturbing in that it was so human-looking.

SAMM-E 777 was more human in appearance than most of the human patients she would see at this medical station, she realized. Most surgical assistant androids were very nondescript, sexually-ambiguous, robotic-looking figures with humanoid shape but no real defined facial features. If she had seen SAMM-E 777 outside the operating room, she would never have even guessed that he was an android. SAMM-E 777 looked like a stunningly attractive man.

The term SAMM-E stood for Surgical Assisting / Medical Nanobot-Manipulating Entity. SAMM-E 777 was tall, broad-shouldered, and trim-waisted, with wavy, light brown hair and chiseled, masculine features: square jaw, straight nose, high cheekbones, sensitive mouth, smooth forehead, and brilliant blue eyes. Its face bore the physiognomy of a Greek god. It continued to stare at her with a concentrated intensity that made Grace uncomfortable. It wore no surgical mask because it did not breathe. It presumably carried no infectious agents harmful to the patient.

As the android stood frozen, continuing to stare at her intently, Grace wondered whether she should say something. It finally turned its head slowly towards Dr. Al-Fadi, while keeping one of its eyes glued on her. Never before had she seen a surgical assisting android behave in such an odd manner, making her highly suspicious of the programming that Dr. Al-Fadi had so proudly announced he'd designed into the android. However, in terms of acceptable human behavior, droids were usually completely ignored, so Grace decided to say nothing.

Dr. Al-Fadi had already returned his full attention back to the patient's thoracic cavity and he began explaining to Grace what he was doing. Grace relaxed as she felt herself fall back into 'surgeon-mode' and she began to assist this odd little surgeon, who seemed to have the ego and voice of a giant and the heart and operating skills of an angel.

Grace was absolutely convinced that this poor tiger soldier, with his entire middle blown away and his damaged lungs, heart, liver, and spine—never mind the shredded stomach, intestines, kidneys and adrenals—would never have had a chance of survival under anyone else's hands. It was like putting a thousand-piece jigsaw puzzle back together with half of the pieces missing, the rest all mangled, and when no piece was available, creating one with whatever materials you had at hand. What Dr. Al-Fadi did to fix this man took Grace's breath away. It definitely brought tears to her eyes. She was witnessing genius at work.

Grace kept thinking of the expression: 'Never say die.' Dr. Al-Fadi should have had that tattooed on his forehead. Dr. Cech, too.

This small surgeon, the *Nelson Mandela*'s Chief of Staff, started with replacing the soldier's shredded lungs with vat-grown replacement lungs. Dr. Cech had the blood flow to the upper body and brain on external support machines as the lower body remained in cryostasis. Synthetic 'super-blood' with boosted oxygen carrying capacity and enhanced immunity was keeping all the vital tissues alive, especially the brain cells, as nanobots controlled and directed by SAMM-E 777 entered regions of damaged tissue to exact repairs at the microscopic level and to remove necrotic cells.

After the new lungs were implanted, the replacement heart was inserted and attached. The aorta was repaired. As each missing organ was replaced with a bio-engineered or vat-grown replacement, as each nerve was repaired with synthetic neuronal nanofibers, as each vertebra and rib were replaced with vat-grown bone replacements, and as circulation was returned to all of these structures, Grace began to believe that this man would, indeed, live again. As the bionic replacement limbs were connected, she believed he might walk again.

As the tiger patient's chest and abdominal cavities were finally closed up and covered with nu-skin, she began to believe that, unfortunately, this combat soldier might be sent out . . . to fight again.

"In many ways, it is not only surgery we practice here, Dr. Grace, but also biomedical engineering, genetic engineering, cybernetics, robotics, veterinary medicine, and most important of all, psychiatric medicine," Dr. Al-Fadi said, while they sat in the doctor's lounge after the surgery was over.

The lounge, a room just off the operating rooms, was warmly lit with glowbulbs and an imitation fireplace that threw off no heat. There were dark brown, synthetic-hide covered couches and a wall lined with glass-paneled shelves filled with actual paper books! Grace had been astonished to see so many precious medical tomes, knowing that just one of those books would likely cost her a small fortune. She had just stared in at the texts, not daring to reach in and touch them. They must have been very old.

The doctors now sat around a low table, mugs of hot stimulant kofi clasped within their hands. Having successfully revived the tiger soldier—after rebuilding him almost completely from the inside out—and after having transferred him to the recovery room, Grace, Dr. Cech, and Dr. Al-Fadi were taking a quick break. The nursing staff and SAMM-E 777 were getting their next patient ready for cryoreversal and surgery.

"We have tiger-adapts, cetacean-adapts, reptile-adapts, bird-, wolf-, bear-, bat-, dog-, cat-, primate-adapts, etc., etc., etc., and these are just the soldiers. I'm not talking about the civilians who want their looks changed just for cosmetic reasons.

"Snakes! There are people out there who just want to look like snakes. Ridiculous," Dr. Al-Fadi exclaimed, his large eyes rolling.

"Then there are the cyborgs, the physically boosted, the space-adaptations, frozen world adaptations, and marine-adaptations, who all have specialized physiology and anatomy to allow them to work in their chosen environments more safely. There are the cerebrally-enhanced, like you and I, Dr. Grace—not Dr. Cech, no matter how hard he tries— who need to be wired and augmented to do our jobs efficiently, but are at risk of problems like meningitis, encephalitis, and brain abscess, because of the brain/augmentation interface. I could go on and on. . ."

"Which, unfortunately, he will," Dr. Cech sighed, giving Grace a woeful glance and an apologetic shrug.

" . . . Of course, none of what we do here is normal anatomy, normal medicine, normal psychology, anymore. I can't remember the last time I saw a completely normal human. And although the literature suggests that the adaptations are only physical, I have not found that."

"Would you mind elaborating on that a little further, Dr. Al-Fadi?" Grace asked.

"Well, for example, the bird, bat, primate, and reptile adaptations are all terrified of the predator adaptations, like the large hunting cats, wolves, grizzlies, and polar bears. It's deep-seated instinctive fear and it seems to be triggered by sense of smell or pheromones or something we can't measure yet. Even though these humans *know* that the predator-adapts are rational, controlled human beings, it doesn't matter. The fear is ingrained and we have to work around this, when we are treating these people.

"Most of the time, all the soldiers sent to a specific planet have similar animal adaptations, suited to the planet. There are few, if any, interspecies interactions. Aquatic worlds have cetaceans, usually dolphin or orca. Jungle planets use tiger or jaguar soldiers or primate soldiers, like orangutan or chimpanzee or gorilla. Underground colonies or mining planets may use the bat adaptations, primarily for echolocation in the dark. Marsh worlds may use amphibian soldiers. Winter worlds tend to alter soldiers or colonists to a wolf or polar bear adaptation, in order to withstand the frosty temperatures better. But there is hardly ever any interspecies mixing on the individual planets. Conglomerate policy . . . and a damned good one, for a change. However, no one ever thought about what happens *here*, on the medical stations, where all the animal adaptations from different systems are sent.

"The interspecies interactions occur here, where the soldiers are not only injured, stressed, psychologically-traumatized, and fearful, but they are all highly-trained, jacked-up killing machines. We have a very demanding job here putting people back together, and getting their heads straight, while keeping them all from killing or attacking each other . . . and us. We don't need the added stress of trying to keep these animals—and I really mean animals—apart!

"Sometimes, Dr. Grace, all we can do is keep them in a locked room under serious sedation, or isolation, for everybody's safety. At least, until the head doctors can return them to some level of sanity and preferably a level of sanity better than their previous one, which sometimes may not have been very much.

"And don't ask me about mating habits," Dr. Al-Fadi exclaimed, slapping his knees.

"Ask him about the mating habits," Dr. Cech said, suggestively, with a sly grin. "He's actually dying to tell you."

Dr. Al-Fadi shot the anesthetist a withering look and then returned his attention to Grace. "It's like all the animals in a zoo deciding to have sex with each other and not necessarily playing nice."

Grace sat back and shuddered, trying to suppress the visual images.

"We just try and put the patients back together as quickly as possible, keep them as far away from each other as possible, and ship them back out to their planets as soon as possible, before they kill or maim anybody here on the medical station. Once the animal-adapts are back out in the field again, they can vent their psychotic aggressions on their supposed enemies, who might actually have been the poor schmucks lying in the beds next to them, just the week before. The Conglomerate and the Union of Solar Systems, with their ridiculous politics, or lack thereof, are to blame.

"Sometimes, Dr. Grace, if we are lucky, everything actually goes to plan," the small surgeon said with a deep sigh, "and people get fixed up and shipped back out, with nothing untoward happening. But it is not often." He sat there shaking his bald head, a forlorn expression on his expressive face.

Grace narrowed her eyes at the Chief of Staff. She could not tell if the man was serious, or not.

"Surely it's not as bad as you describe, Dr. Al-Fadi," Grace ventured.

Dr. Al-Fadi's eyebrows shot upwards like they wanted to jump off his face.

"Dr. Grace," the bald, diminutive surgeon said, leaning towards her, his expressive eyes enormous in his round face. "I am trying to 'sugar-coat' the situation. I am giving you the 'smiley face' version. It is actually far worse than you could ever possibly imagine."

The surgeon spread his arms wide, like a showman, and declared, "Welcome to the madhouse, Dr. Grace."

" . . . Hmm. And are you, by any chance, the chief nut?" Grace asked, leaning back on the couch, with her arms crossed, and a mischievous glint in her eye.

'All Macadamian parts of him," Dr. Cech said, nodding seriously.

Dr. Al-Fadi guffawed again and slapped his knee.

"Careful, Dr. Grace. I think I could very easily fall in love with you and I am a very devoted, married man."

"Please, just call me Grace," she said.

"Oh, no, you siren. I will continue to call you Dr. Grace, to keep it professional. I do not need any more rumors flying around about me than there already are."

"He starts them all himself," Dr. Cech whispered to Grace. "He really does."

"Of course, I know I am not only unbelievably handsome and a magnificent surgeon, but I am also incredibly irresistible," Dr. Al-Fadi continued, without missing a beat. "I know this. And so, if you have problems dealing with your attraction to me, Dr. Grace, I can suggest a good therapist for you."

"Or a lobotomy," interjected Dr. Cech to Grace, with a wink.

Grace smiled. "I believe I can control myself, Dr. Al-Fadi. It will be hard, I must admit, but I am certain I am up to the challenge."

"Good girl," Dr. Al-Fadi said, with an exaggerated sigh of relief. Dr. Cech was making a gagging motion, outside of the small surgeon's line of sight.

"I have one question, Doctor Al-Fadi," Grace said.

Dr. Al-Fadi raised his eyebrows, expectantly.

"You said your SAMM-E 777 was experimental. Other than its very obvious human appearance, in what other way is it experimental?" Grace asked.

"Oh no," moaned Dr. Cech, theatrically dropping his head into both hands. "Perhaps we should cancel the next case, as now we are going to be sitting here for the next two hours, at least, while the Al-Fadi drones on and on and on."

"Nonsense, Dr. Cech. You exaggerate, as usual. I will be brief. What you should ask, Dr. Grace, is in what other ways is 'he' experimental?"

Grace felt her cheeks flush at the correction.

"SAMM-E 777 has had several interesting and innovative upgrades, based on my own designs. First of all, as you so succinctly pointed out, he looks exactly like a human man from top to bottom and trust me, it is *all* there, if you understand my meaning. But SAMM-E 777 is completely synthetic, with a state-of-the-art liquid crystal data matrix for massive memory storage . . . and when I say massive, I mean *massive*.

"SAMM-E 777 is equipped with synthetic skin that bears all the senses we have—touch, pain, pressure, temperature, and vibration sense—but much more acutely, and he has extremely accurate sensors designed to detect the other senses of taste, smell, hearing, and of course, vision. He has been programmed with other senses that we humans do not have, as he has extremely acute hearing into ranges we could never dream of detecting. He can see far into the infrared and ultraviolet. He can see electromagnetic fields. He can detect abnormal levels of radiation and he can echolocate. His senses are so much more acute than ours by orders of magnitude. He can communicate via electromagnetic frequencies we can't hear. He has the enormous strength of a full military combat robot, combined with the dexterity of a spider.

"But inside, is where the true difference lies, Dr. Grace. Within his brain is enough memory crystal for a full artificial intelligence. Because of improvements in liquid crystal data matrix design, he has more memory storage in his small brain case than the station AI, *Nelson Mandela*, has. My hope is that my SAMM-E will become a fully independent, fully conscious, intuitive-thinking android surgeon. SAMM-E triple 7 is hopefully the prototype that may one day replace all of us. He spends every hour in the operating room with me, so you will be seeing a lot of him, Dr. Grace."

"That poor android," Dr. Cech said, sympathetically. "How *he* must have sinned terribly in his previous life."

"You are just jealous, Dr. Cech, because you do not get to operate with the Great One on every shift."

"I try and get in with *her* as much as I can," declared Dr. Cech, grinning at Dr. Al-Fadi. The small man sniffed at the anesthetist.

"Dr. Grace, let's go see what's taking these nurses so long. I want to get the annoying Dr. Cech back to work. I hate seeing him sit around like a sloth, when I am waiting to operate. I suggest you avoid him, Dr Grace. He is such a degenerate slacker."

"Oh, Hiro, you always say the nicest things," Dr. Cech said, sweetly.

The Chief of Staff hopped up and gestured for Grace to follow him, as he stalked towards the door. Jumping up, Grace caught up to Dr. Al-

Fadi's heels only to just about run the small man over, when he stopped, spun around in the doorway, and looked up at her with shocked eyes. Dr. Al-Fadi glanced over at the still-seated Dr. Cech, with a disapproving expression. The small surgeon placed his fists on his hips, with his feet spread wide apart.

"Stay away from Dr. Cech, Dr. Grace," Dr. Al-Fadi ordered, his chin pointed upwards.

"He's married and a pervert, besides."

SAMM-E 777, who referred to himself as 'Bud', watched as the three doctors filed out of the operating room with the patient, who was lying swathed in nu-skin on the anti-gravity stretcher. He wanted to follow them, but his mandate was to stay in the operating room and assist in the preparation of the next case. He really wanted to follow the intriguing new surgical fellow, Dr. Grace Alexandra Lord . . . yet he didn't quite know why.

Perhaps it was because this exciting Dr. Grace Alexandra Lord had had the courage and audacity to challenge his creator, the Great Dr. Hiro Al-Fadi, himself. Bud had never seen anyone do that before . . . except Dr. Cech, who most of the time did it under his breath. When the beautiful Dr. Grace Alexandra Lord had gotten angry, her blue eyes had flashed with pupils dilated, her cheeks had blushed an interesting shade of rose, and her aura! Her glorious aura had glittered and glowed and fizzled and flared in a dazzling, multi-wavelength array that Bud had never before witnessed and could never, in a million human lifetimes, ever hope to describe. The visible wavelengths! The ultraviolet wavelengths! The explosion of colors! The mesmerizing dance of patterns!

The android had actually felt a shiver race through his entire being, just standing there, observing the fantastic luminosity of Dr. Grace Alexandra Lord. What Bud had registered through his visual receptors had seemed nothing less than otherworldly. No other human he had encountered to date had ever been so fantastical.

Dr. Al-Fadi always called him 'SAMM-E 777' and had never asked Bud his name. If his creator had, the android would have told Dr. Al-Fadi that his name was actually 'Bud'. Yet Bud did not feel that it was his place to 'tell' his creator his name, so he waited patiently, hoping that one day, Dr. Al-Fadi would ask him that question.

Then Dr. Al-Fadi would understand that Bud was already a fully independent, thinking, reasoning human being—albeit a synthetic one—but no different from any of the other doctors, except for some of the inhibitory programming that prevented Bud from following the very interesting Dr. Grace Alexandra Lord to the doctors' lounge. Bud was already perfectly capable of doing these surgeries that Dr. Al-Fadi was doing and at much faster speeds. He had been assisting the great surgeon for many weeks now and could remember every case, every procedure, every injury, every solution, every report in the literature, every documented complication and its resolution, and was at the point of suggesting alternative solutions to some of the more complicated cases, if the great Dr. Al-Fadi would only ask.

Bud did not feel it was his place to question the actions or decisions of his creator, or to interfere, but he was willing and anxious to offer any assistance, if the good doctor needed any - which, unfortunately, he never seemed to. Then, to Bud's astonishment, this surprising Dr. Grace Alexandra Lord arrives and challenges his creator on her first day on the medical station. It was liquid crystal data matrix numbing. Bud felt that weird shiver run through his entire body again, just re-processing it.

Bud sighed, even though physiologically he did not need to sigh. He had seen enough of the doctors sigh, to know it was a means of expressing frustration and futility mixed with acceptance and Bud so wanted to be seen as human. He was surprised at how disturbed he had felt, when Dr. Al-Fadi had told the very fascinating Dr. Grace Alexandra Lord that Bud was an android.

Bud wondered whether the way he was feeling could be labelled 'upset' or 'ashamed' or 'embarrassed'? For some reason that he could not quite understand, he had not wanted the very absorbing Dr. Grace Alexandra Lord to know that he was not a real human being. It was the first time he had ever felt uncomfortable(?) about being 'just' an android.

Had Bud truly felt 'anger,' when Dr. Al-Fadi had revealed this fact to the very special Dr. Grace Alexandra Lord? He should never have felt that way towards his creator, should he? But was that why he had discovered a little tiny ball of surgisteel crumpled in the palm of his left hand, instead of a fine surgical clamp? Bud had felt very badly about ruining the instrument and had immediately repaired it to pristine condition. He would have to be much more careful about how he handled the surgical instruments.

Bud began the sterilization process in the operating room, spraying everything down with antiseptic solution and then emitting intense ultraviolet rays from his visual apparatus, scouring everything within the room. Then he began unwrapping the necessary instruments for the next case. His thoughts, however, would not leave the very captivating Dr. Grace Alexandra Lord, and her delightful laugh and her fiery temper. Bud could not understand what was happening to himself. It felt (?)unsettling, yet also . . .'exciting'?

. . . Perhaps he needed a reboot?

Bud wondered what the stimulating Dr. Grace Alexandra Lord was doing right now. If he turned up the sensors on his auditory equipment, he could zero in on her voice, the patterns of which he had now stored in a very special place within his memory. He could monitor her conversation anywhere on the station . . . but Bud knew that would be wrong. Humans seemed to value their privacy, although it was quite obvious to Bud that, on the Nelson Mandela, *the concept of privacy was essentially nonexistent. He wondered why this fact was not apparent to all of the humans.*

By connecting to the medical station's central computer, Bud could locate the enthralling Dr. Grace Alexandra Lord's position, anywhere within the station, via her wrist-comp. That would not be so wrong, would it? After all, the innocent Dr. Grace Alexandra Lord was new to the medical station and it was possible she did not know how to use the locator in her wrist-comp. She could get turned around and lost within the Nelson Mandela *Medical Space Station very easily. Many other new staff to the medical station had done so, on many other occasions.*

If the compelling Dr. Grace Alexandra Lord became lost and did not know where she was, Bud could come to the rescue. Bud could offer to help her with many things, since she was new to the station.

This thought filled Bud with an unusual feeling that he could not quite label, but felt it might be 'hopeful' or 'optimistic' or . . . 'desperate'?

Bud thought he should always keep one eye and/or one ear (figuratively speaking, as Dr. Al-Fadi was wont to say) on the thrilling Dr. Grace Alexandra Lord, just in case she needed anything.

Anything at all . . .

Grace awoke the next 'morning', or actually 'next shift', disoriented and groggy. The previous day had been grueling in terms of hours in the operating room and she barely recalled shooing that sweet corporal away, so that she could stumble into the nearest vacant call room. She had collapsed onto the pallet, still in her scrubs, and was probably asleep before her head had hit the pillow.

Her wrist-comp had woken her from a deep sleep, leaving her a grand total of thirty minutes to shower, change, eat breakfast, and do her patient rounds, before having to be in the operating theater again: M5 OR2 this time. Luckily, she only had two patients to look in on, so hopefully it would not take her too long. She could always skip breakfast.

Grace showered and changed into clean operating room scrubs in record time, despite all of her aches and pains from her arrival, and she charged out of the call room, almost barreling into a SAMM-E android.

"Oh! Are you SAMM-E 777? If you are, please let Dr. Al-Fadi know I will meet him in the OR in half a bell. Just rounding on our patients from yesterday," Grace said, and she rushed off, not waiting for a reply.

Grace keyed in the patients' names into her wrist-comp and the locator directed her to their intensive care suites. Thank goodness she had slept in one of the call rooms. If she had gone to the quarters initially assigned to her, she would never have had time to see the patients before surgery.

Dr. Al-Fadi would, of course, want to know how they were doing this morning, and would have expected her to have checked on them, before showing up at the OR. The M7 Surgical Intensive Care Unit was mere steps away from the call room she had used.

The first patient on whom she had assisted in surgery, the tiger soldier, Captain Damien Lamont, was sleeping quietly in an intensive care room just in front of the nurses' station. The room was relatively dark, indirect light coming in from the doorway and through the observational glass wall that faced the nurses' work area. Small lights blinked from the monitors above the patient's bed. Astonishingly, the tiger soldier was off of the ventilator already, breathing on his own. Grace could hardly believe it. She would never have expected anyone so badly damaged to have survived not only the bomb blast, but also the reconstructive surgery. This tiger soldier was almost more genetically-engineered replacement parts and bio-prosthetic equipment, than original human material. It had taken nine hours of operating time to piece this man back together. After that, they had then gone on to replace one lung and both upper limbs on a jaguar soldier. Grace could not remember what she had actually said to Corporal McMullen, when she had emerged from the operating room and had encountered him, dutifully waiting at the nurses' station to show her to her quarters. She hoped it had been polite or, at least, relatively coherent. The conversation was a complete blank. She had probably been sleepwalking at that point.

Grace stared down at the peaceful face of her patient, Captain Damian Lamont. She had never operated on a genetically-modified tiger human before. His face was lightly furred with the orange, black, and white coloration of a real tiger, but his features were handsome and totally human except for the fine, silvery whiskers and long, white fangs whose tips just showed between his closed lips. His body, which had huge, powerful musculature, had slightly denser, short, tiger-striped fur on his back, neck, and limbs but finer, soft white downy fur on his chest, abdomen, inner thighs and groin region. His hands, which were massive, were also lightly furred in tiger pattern on the backs and his thick, powerful fingers possessed razor-sharp, retractable claws, which were indrawn at the moment.

Encircling his wrists and ankles were thick titanium manacles with chains which were attached to the bed frame. Grace was standing beside the left hand side of the tigerman's bed, facing towards the observation glass. The manacles made it very difficult for Grace to palpate the captain's pulse on his left wrist, the only original human limb he still possessed. As she pushed the manacle as far up the arm as it would go, she touched the luxuriant, down-like fur of the captain's forearm. The texture was velvety soft, overlying his radial pulse.

To Grace's surprise, Captain Damien Lamont did not smell of animal at all, but more of what Grace could only describe as pure masculinity.

Even wrapped up in bandages and hooked to a myriad number of intravenous lines and monitors, he was an amazing example of the male species and, to Grace's personal dismay, alluringly attractive as a male tiger. He purred gently as he slept.

Beneath her trembling fingers, the captain's radial pulse was regular and bounding. Grace shook her head in astonishment. After all this man's trauma and reconstruction work, she would never have expected him to be looking so good, one day post-operatively. Yet here he was, faring remarkably well. It was truly a miracle and Dr. Al-Fadi and Dr. Cech were the miracle workers.

Just then, Lamont's eyelids whipped open. Huge, fierce, amber eyes, speckled with flecks of gold, were glaring at Grace with feral hostility and suspicious rage. Gasping, Grace instinctively jumped backwards. With astonishing speed, the tiger patient lunged towards her, claws fully extended and fangs bared. A deafening roar exploded from his lungs, spraying hot spittle in Grace's face. His long, white fangs no longer looked so quaint.

Razor-sharp claws scored down both of Grace's forearms, as she retreated further back. Thankfully, the manacles and chains on the captain's arms stopped him from doing more damage. Lamont's furious gaze seemed to stab right through her and, as he struggled against the solid metal restraints, he roared again at her in incoherent outrage.

Grace had cried out, more from the surprise of the attack than from the pain, although the score marks did sting. The gouges running down both of her forearms did not burn nearly as much as her cheeks though, as she flushed in embarrassment. Silently, she thanked the nurses for placing those metal restraints on the patient and she quickly turned to the medication computer at the patient's bedside. She punched in a heavier dose of sedation. Soon after, the captain relaxed back onto his pillow and fell back to sleep.

The Intensive Care Unit nurses came running into the room and activated the overhead lights. They took one look at Grace's injuries and apologized profusely. They quickly dragged her to the nursing station, where they sterilized her wounds and bandaged her up.

"I am so sorry," a young nurse cried, her hands shaking. "I thought the chains on the patient's arms were tight enough. Obviously they weren't. Your injuries are all my fault!"

"They are not your fault," Grace said, firmly, staring at the petite, black-haired, tan-skinned beauty. "It was my fault and my fault alone. I was careless and just wasn't thinking. I should not have stood so close to the patient, so soon after his surgery. He has been through so much and is reviving from cryostasis, battle trauma, and extensive reconstructive surgery. He is on numerous medications. I should have known better. He may have been experiencing a flashback or drug-induced nightmare. Perhaps, if I'd had a bit more sleep, I would have been more alert, but regardless, *you* are definitely not to blame. I was just thankful that there *were* restraints on the patient. So, thank you."

Grace gave the nurse an encouraging smile. The small young woman stared back at Grace, with anxious, light brown eyes.

"I have never cared for a patient with a tiger adaptation before," Grace admitted, her cheeks suddenly feeling like they had had too much sun. "His recuperative powers are astonishing. If I had been a bit more astute and alert, taking into account the severe pain the patient probably is in from his surgery, I would have been much more circumspect."

"I still feel very bad, Dr. Lord," the young girl whispered, looking as if she were close to tears.

"Don't. It wasn't your fault," Grace insisted, shaking her head and patting the young nurse's hand. "Let's just look at this as an instructive lesson for both of us. Hmm?" She smiled and the young nurse gradually smiled back.

"What is your name?" Grace asked.

"Sophie Leung," the nurse said, looking down at her wringing hands and then shyly up at Grace's face, through thick, dark lashes.

"Are you in training?"

Sophie nodded, hesitantly, her forehead creased in worry lines and her lower lip trapped between her teeth.

Well, so am I," Grace said. "This is only my second day here."

"I know," Sophie whispered. "You are Dr. Al-Fadi's new surgical fellow."

"That is correct. And, Sophie, if there is one thing I am positive about, it's that we are going to come across a lot worse shit than this, while we are here," Grace announced in a cheery voice.

Sophie's eyes popped open and her eyebrows leaped upwards. She covered her mouth with a hand and giggled at Grace's archaic expression. She nodded in agreement.

"Why don't you and I get back to work, Nurse Sophie," Grace said, getting up. "Don't worry about these scratches. They will heal fine and always be a reminder to me to be more careful!" she pronounced firmly.

"I consider them my first battle wounds on this medical station—only the first of many, I am sure—but one I hope not to repeat."

Then Grace thought about her bruised body, sore back, twisted knee, swollen cheek, abraded hands, and thought, well . . . maybe not the first.

"Yes, Doctor. Thank you, Doctor. I will run and get you some new operating greens," Sophie said.

"Uh, thank you, Sophie," Grace said, as she surveyed her blood spattered scrubs with dismay. "I would appreciate that. I do not know where you keep them around here."

The young nurse scurried off.

At that moment, Dr. Dejan Cech walked into the nurses' station, took one look at Grace, and said, "Are you going for the Mummy look this morning, Dr. Lord, or did the nurses just grab you for bandage practice?"

The nurses within hearing distance of this comment all turned and looked up at Dejan Cech, their mouths dropping open in shock.

"Catching flies are we, ladies and gentlemen?" Dr. Cech asked, as he looked around at all the gaping mouths.

"Dr. Lord just got attacked by *your* patient, Dr. Cech!" the head nurse of the intensive care unit snapped, angrily.

"Oh . . . no. I was hoping you were not going to say that," Dr. Cech said slowly. "I am very sorry, Dr. Lord. Are you all right?"

"Yes," Grace said, a warm flush moving up from her neck to her ears to her scalp.

"I can't wait to see your wounds," the older gentleman said, wiggling his whitish-grey eyebrows up and down.

There was a loud, collective gasp heard around the nursing station.

"That's it. You are in for it this time," bellowed the head nurse, as she got up from her chair and marched towards the anesthetist.

She was a tiny, round woman with short, curly brown hair, rosy cheeks, and fiery brown eyes. In terms of height, Grace guessed the nurse probably came up to Dr. Cech's sternum, but Grace actually stepped back, in trepidation, as the nurse approached. This woman, although small in stature, was nonetheless, physically formidable. One did not become a head nurse of an ICU on a Premier Medical Space Station, if one was not. This feisty woman proceeded to whack Dr. Cech on the left upper arm with what looked to Grace like a rubber hammer.

The anesthetist winced as the blow made contact. He muttered,

'Ouch', and rubbed the spot on his arm where he had gotten hit. He looked sheepishly over at Grace and shrugged.

"Head Nurse Louise Balotelli keeps that rubber mallet thingy here, specifically for me," Dr. Cech whined, as he rubbed his arm. "My body is covered in bruises. She likes to hit me when I get out of line or when I am being inappropriate . . . which, unfortunately, is usually most of the time. I suspect she feels I am being both inappropriate *and* out of line, right at this very moment. Am I not correct, sweet Nurse Balotelli?"

It was Grace's turn for her mouth to drop open.

"Don't you 'sweet', me, you . . . you scoundrel," the head nurse scowled, trying to hide a smile, but not succeeding very well.

"It's true," Head Nurse Balotelli said, turning to Grace, as she wound up and whacked the anesthetist again with the rubber hammer, this time on the other arm. "But he deserves it, Dr. Lord. He is totally incorrigible. And he has the *gall* to keep stealing these mallets on me, as well. But I just keep having Stores make me a new one, with his name on it, so I can keep the rogue in line."

"Really, Nurse Balotelli, I know you just like to hit me, because you like me," Dejan Cech said, grinning wolfishly at the head nurse. "It fulfills some deep-seated, erotic desire, I am sure." He then wiggled his eyebrows at her.

"*What?*" the nurse exclaimed, her face beaming scarlet. She bopped him again, this time with great force on his right shoulder, before making a show of stomping away. Suddenly, she spun back towards Dr. Cech and he backed up, wincing, as she shook the rubber mallet at him. She shot him a scathing glance.

"You apologize to this nice young doctor properly, or I'll string you up by the you-know-what's!"

"Ouch," Cech said, pantomiming grabbing his 'you-know-what's'. He blew a kiss at Head Nurse Balotelli and waved at her to go away. Nurse Balotelli sniffed at him and marched off.

Dr. Cech returned his attention to Grace, his face suddenly serious, and he said, "All joking aside, Dr. Lord. Are you all right? Would it be presumptuous of me to ask what happened?"

"Nothing but my stupidity, Dr. Cech," Grace sighed, trying unsuccessfully to cover her bandaged arms with her hands.

"Please. Call me Dejan. As you may have noticed, I prefer not to be so formal and uppity as Dr. All Fatty. Oops. Did I say that? Must have been my 'inner voice' speaking. Pardon me, Dr. Lord. I meant . . . Dr. Al-Faaaahhdi."

Grace could not help but grin at that. "Please. Call me Grace."

"Thank you, Grace. Good. You are smiling again. This makes me happy and, contrary to what Dr. Al-Fadi says, your goal in life is always to make the anesthetists happy, because we are the ones keeping your patients alive, while you do all sorts of horribly barbaric, torturous things to them.

"Now, again I ask, Grace. What happened?"

"I was doing my rounds on the tiger soldier, Captain Damien Lamont—just checking his radial pulse—when he woke up with a roar and managed to get a few claws on me, before I jumped back out of his reach. Perfectly understandable from his point of view and perfectly stupid, from mine."

"What? You, a surgeon, were actually touching the patient while he was not under a general anesthetic? How astonishing and utterly unconventional. Might I also say, rather unique. I am impressed, Dr. Lord. That was certainly nothing I ever saw your predecessors do."

Dr. Cech narrowed his eyes and peered at Grace beneath bushy, furrowed brows. "Are you really a surgeon or actually an impostor? What did you do with the real Dr. Lord? Are you really even a doctor?" Cech asked, a mock horrified look on his face.

"I would like to think so," Grace sighed, with an embarrassed look on her face. "But I certainly wasn't thinking in doctor mode, this morning." She held her gauze-wrapped arms out to the anesthetist as proof.

"Is that anything like 'Doc commode'?" Cech quipped. Then he said, "Ahhh . . . I do apologize, Dr. Lord."

"For what?" Grace asked.

The anesthetist gave a big sigh and shrugged. "Sometimes I just can't help myself. These stupid things just pop out of my mouth, at the most inappropriate times, before I can close my lips. Like just now, and I have countless bruises all over my arms to prove it. Those damned rubber gavels," Dejan Cech sighed, theatrically. "I do hope you will make allowances for a silly old man?"

Grace just grinned, not knowing quite what to say.

"Well, Grace, I must regrettably admit to you that the same thing happened to me, the first time I cared for a jaguar-adapted patient. And I, too, have the scars to prove it."

Dejan Cech pulled up his shirt sleeves to show off his collection of faint, linear scars running down both of his arms. "My battle wounds. Makes the ladies go crazy," he whispered, rolling his eyes and wiggling his thick eyebrows suggestively at Grace.

"Now, your turn for 'Show and Tell'. Let me see your battle wounds," he said.

Grace narrowed her eyes at the anesthetist, trying to determine whether he was really serious or not. As the anesthetist just stood there, staring at her expectantly, Grace shrugged and carefully unwrapped her bandages.

"Mere scratches," the anesthetist announced, after examining the wounds carefully. "They are not deep enough to even leave permanent scars, like mine . . . or so I hope. For that, Grace, I am very much relieved. I would have been overcome with terrible guilt and shame, had the situation been otherwise. I would have had to go and self-flagellate for at least an hour or two. Thankfully, I think only thirty minutes shall suffice, as I still do feel terrible guilt and shame, but not quite as much as before. Nevertheless, I do most sincerely apologize for your injuries. I would never have forgiven myself, if your beautiful arms had been permanently scarred."

Blushing, Grace laughed. "I am fine, Dr. Cech. Really."

"You must take precautions against cat scratch fever," Dr. Cech exclaimed, helping Grace re-wrap her wounds. "I shall make sure one of the nurses gives you a shot for that. Head Nurse Balotelli was correct in her estimation that this was all my fault. I should have had the patient much more sedated than he was, if he was able to do this to you. Obviously, I terribly miscalculated the rate at which he metabolized his drugs. These animal adaptations always surprise me."

"Captain Lamont certainly surprised me," Grace murmured.

"I apologize again, from the bottom of my heart for your misfortune, Grace. Will you please find it in your heart to forgive a foolish old goat?"

"Uh . . . of course, Dr. Cech," Grace said, stuttering. Her face erupted into flames as Dejan Cech stared at her. "But you aren't an old goat. You aren't even old."

"Ah, thank you for that, Grace. You are too kind—and far too dishonest!—but I will take whatever flattery I can get. Now, unfortunately, you will have to scrub with the surgical soap far more carefully. Those scratches are going to sting," he said, wincing dramatically.

"I have had worse, Dr. Cech. The soap will be good for the wounds."

"Yes. Of course. Thank you so much, again, for your understanding,

Grace. I shall speak to the nurses about that shot for you, and then I shall see you in the OR."

Dejan Cech made a deep bow towards Grace and then strode off, on his very long legs, to find Head Nurse Balotelli. He turned around and winked at Grace, rubbing his arms theatrically, before sneaking up on the unsuspecting nurse and snatching the rubber gavel out of her sight. Nurse Balotelli then demonstrated how easily she could improvise. Clearly, she did not need a rubber mallet at all, to teach Dr. Cech a lesson or two.

Bud was in complete shock . . . or what he believed was 'shock.' His body was trembling. He had followed the enthralling Dr. Grace Alexandra Lord from outside her call room to Captain Lamont's intensive care room, taking care to ensure she had not seen him. There he witnessed the tigerman's attack on her.

The assault on the elegant Dr. Grace Alexandra Lord had taken him totally unawares and he had been frozen in immobility. To make things worse, he'd had to shamefully hide when all the nurses had come running. Now he stood outside the intensive care room, where the captain was sleeping peacefully, and his mind replayed, over and over, the regrettable injury that the vulnerable Dr. Grace Alexandra Lord had incurred.

Bud could not believe something so terrible had happened to the beautiful Dr. Grace Alexandra Lord and that he had been unable to prevent it. He had peeked through the observation window of the Intensive Care room, as she had checked the tiger captain's pulse and had stood there, useless, as she was scored by the delusional soldier. The gentle Dr. Grace Alexandra Lord had only narrowly avoided being seriously mauled—if not killed!—by the tiger captain.

Bud felt ?upset?. . . ?guilty?. . . ?ashamed? He had been unprepared. He had been totally ineffectual, unaware that the good doctor had been in any danger at all. His reflexes, his reaction time, his ability to respond were completely inadequate for protecting the winsome Dr. Grace Alexandra Lord.

What fragile creatures these humans were! If anything more serious had happened to the remarkable Dr. Grace Alexandra Lord, Bud would not have been able to continue to function. He would have had to wipe his memory or shut himself down or volunteer himself for scrap. How did humans live with this painful emotion called guilt?

It was horrible!

Bud suddenly realized just how dangerous the world was for a human being.

Harm could result from anything or anyone, at any time. He resolved to keep a closer watch on the delicate Dr. Grace Alexandra Lord, so he could protect her from all the possible and impossible dangers on this medical space station, especially from traumatized surgical patients.

Bud would have to shadow the dainty Dr. Grace Alexandra Lord much more closely, without her noticing, in order to keep her safe. He would have to start making modifications on his body design to deal with his totally inadequate speed and reaction times. He needed to be stronger, faster, more invincible, and much more alert. He would have to figure out a way to protect the fetching Dr. Grace Alexandra Lord at all times, without her noticing . . .

How to do that?

Bud would first have to modify his little nanobots . . .

"Dr. Grace!" Dr. Al-Fadi exclaimed loudly, as Grace entered the doctors' lounge. "Where have you been? We have been waiting for you . . . *again*. How do you expect us to get any work done, if you are nowhere to be found?"

"I was rounding on our patients," Grace said, in an apologetic tone.

"*Ah.* Then I am afraid I will have to . . . forgive you," the surgeon said, with a placated expression on his round face.

" . . . Come along, Dr. Grace, and look at these scans of our next patient. Tell me what you think we should do."

The small surgeon beckoned for Grace to sit down on the couch beside him. After activating a control on the table before them, Dr. Al-Fadi called up a patient's three dimensional body scan. It was displayed and rotated right before them as a hologram. Using a swipe of her fingers, Grace manipulated the series of full body scans of the patient, who happened to be enormous, turning them around, removing layer by layer, front to back and top to bottom, to examine each vital organ and body part.

Throughout the heart and both lungs of this patient were scattered hundreds of long, sharp needles, each about the length of her index finger. The needles had pierced the soldier's body armour and shredded the tissues of the patient's upper body. Grace winced as she looked at the images. If it were not for her battlesuit sealing over all the holes and immediately cryofreezing the patient, there would not have been much upper body left to operate on. Surprisingly, brain activity was still intact, so if they were successful in replacing the heart, lungs, thoracic aorta, pulmonary veins, esophagus, and if they could fix all of the holes in the chest wall, the patient might actually have a chance of making a successful recovery.

To Grace, it seemed like a very big 'if'.

"Neither the lungs nor the heart are salvageable. The major problem is whether we have replacement lungs and heart large enough to adequately serve this patient. What kind of animal adaptation is it?" Grace asked.

"She," Dr. Al-Fadi emphasized. "A she-bear adapt. A grizzly bear adaptation, actually, and she stands at almost three meters tall. We have no vat grown organs large enough to fit her. We can replace with biomechanical organs or keep her in cryostorage until we grow organs large enough for her. What would be your choice, Dr. Grace?"

"Are the biomechanical organs capable of handling the size of this patient?"

"Excellent question, Dr. Grace," sighed Dr. Al-Fadi. "I knew you were not just a pretty face. You remind me of myself, when I was younger, except that you are tall, blonde, beautiful, and female, whereas I was short, bald, irresistible, and all male. But, other than that, we could have passed for twins.

"We must wait, Dr. Grace, and vat grow the correct, genetically-adapted heart and lungs to fit this ample, grizzly bear female, in order to successfully treat her. As you surmised. Bioprostheses would be totally inadequate, unless they were made for a grizzly bear to begin with, which unfortunately, they are not. We will have to keep Miss Grizzly in cryostasis until then.

"Luckily, I stopped the nurses from beginning the cryothaw this morning or we would have had a disaster on our hands. Instead, we will be operating on a wolf-adaptation—a she-wolf—with crushed lower limbs. How much wolf anatomy do you know, Dr. Grace?" Dr. Al-Fadi asked.

"About as much as I knew about tigers," Grace admitted.

"Ah, less than nothing, then. What kind of doctors are they sending me these days? Well, you had better upload all the information you can into your cerebral augmentation unit, before we start the surgery. Otherwise, you will be of no help to me at all, Dr. Grace. Hurry now. You have less than five minutes before we scrub."

"Yes, sir," Grace said, and hurried off in search of the closest information terminal she could connect her cerebral augmentation unit to, in order to secure a huge data drop in milliseconds.

Rushing into the doctors' library and reading room, which was fortunately right next door to the doctors' lounge, she encountered a tall, dark-haired, drop-dead-gorgeous man, sitting before one of the terminals. All the terminals were in use, but Grace only had eyes for this stunning male. His dark brown eyes were surrounded by the thickest set of lashes Grace had ever seen.

'Figures', Grace's little voice griped sourly. 'Why is it always the guys who get the great eyelashes?'

The man glanced up at Grace and, when their eyes made contact, Grace felt a shock go through her. She stared into deep, luminous eyes, shaded by curly locks of mahogany brown hair. Those eyes took one look at Grace's panic-stricken face, and smiled.

Did Grace's heart actually skip a beat? She almost groaned out loud. This terribly attractive man gracefully got up out of his seat and stepped away from the terminal. He gestured gallantly for Grace to take the seat.

"I see that Dr. Al-Fadi is torturing his new surgical fellow already," the man said, in a low, velvety voice that made Grace feel all warm inside. He looked sympathetically at her, through his tousled, brunette bangs. "May I offer my condolences to you? He can be a bit excitable, our Chief of Staff. I believe the good doctor suffers from a severe case of Megalomaniac Hyperactivity Disorder for which, unfortunately for you, there is no cure. But remember one thing, Doctor: 'His bark is far worse than his bite' and, of course, he is an extremely talented and gifted surgeon, even if his teaching methods and people skills leave much to be desired."

Before Grace could stutter out a 'thank you' to this bewitching man, he disappeared from the library. Wasting no time, she quickly uncovered the cerebral augmentation plug behind her left ear, sprayed the contact with sterilizer, and then plugged the output cable from the terminal into her aug-unit. She then began frantically searching for the desired files. Hopefully, the system was not too slow, and she would get her upload with time to review the information before the surgery started. Wistfully, as she waited for the file to come up on wolf anatomy, physiology, and adaptation surgery, and for all the data to then upload to her cerebral augmentation unit, she speculated on who the handsome, dark-haired gentleman was.

Presumably, since he was in the doctors' library, he was another physician. She'd hardly had any time to meet anyone other than Dr. Al-Fadi and Dr. Cech and a few nurses on the wards. She wondered if he were one of the other surgeons. Certainly he had been more than easy on the eyes, and in possession of normal teeth, normal fingernails, and no fur. These were all decidedly good things, as far as Grace was concerned, silently wincing as she thought about the tiger scores on her arms.

It had been quite some time since Grace had met anyone that had actually caught her eye, never mind shake her right down to her toes. The man possessed a glance as potent as a lightning strike. Work had always been too demanding and had always come first and, of course, Grace had always been so dedicated to her studies for her to bother with men. Plus, with all the traveling she did, it was pretty much impossible to have any sort of meaningful relationship with anyone. The pain and distress of separation had just never seemed worth it. But, surprisingly, she found herself looking forward to casting her tired eyes on that comely physician again.

"This poor wolf patient was working on a frozen planet that the Conglomerate is hoping to eventually terraform for human habitation, Dr. Grace. She fell into a deep crevasse in the ice. As she was trying to climb out, the ice shifted and crushed both of her lower limbs. She fell unconscious before she could call for help. Her co-workers did not even know she was in trouble for a couple of hours. They were all working separately, at different tasks, in different locations, setting up geological monitoring equipment in various sites, out of visual range of each other."

"Unacceptable practice! Contravening all the safety rules, the fools!" Dr. Al-Fadi exclaimed, as he and Grace prepped the patient for her operation.

"She was in a spacesuit, not a battlesuit, so no emergency pressure bags, no emergency fluids, no antibiotics, no nanobots, no cryogenic stasis, and worst of all, no emergency beacon when she got injured. The ice that crushed her limbs was so cold, however, that it apparently cauterized her wounds even though the integrity of her suit was not broken, so she was still supplied with oxygen. Her wolf adaptation helped keep her barely warm enough, until they found her. She was popped into a cryopod as soon as they extricated her from the ice crevasse and then she was sent here," Dr. Al-Fadi said, as he began to work on the patient.

"There are major flaws in these damned 'spacesuits'. They should be designed to immediately detect any damage to the integrity of the suit. They should detect any medical emergency in the wearer of the suit, so that an alarm goes off centrally and everyone is alerted to the problem. I am going to put this in my next report to the Conglomerate—those stupid bastards never read them!—with recommended upgrades to these spacesuits. It would not cost that much more to design and manufacture better suits. They would save on manpower. The cheap bastards are only ever interested in profits." Dr. Al-Fadi was now frantically waving the laser knife around in his tirade.

"If manpower was cheap, and androids and robots could do everything, Dr. Grace, we would not have a job. The Conglomerate would be letting all these poor soldiers and workers die. But for now, they still need higher thinking beings, so at least they could spend the money protecting people properly. I tell you, it drives me crazy, Dr. Grace."

"Crazier than he already is," Dr. Cech commented quietly, looking seriously at Grace.

Grace savagely bit her lip, behind her surgical mask, to prevent a chuckle from escaping as Dr. Al-Fadi said, "I heard that, you ingrate."

"And for what am I being ungrateful?" asked the anesthetist.

"All the work I give you," Dr. Al-Fadi replied.

"Ah, all the work which I could do without," Dr. Cech sighed.

"And the stimulating conversation . . ."

"Ah, all the monotonous droning and nonstop ranting of which I most certainly could do without," the anesthetist said, with a wink at Grace. "Shall I show you all the stuffed cotton I put in my ears, when I know I am working with you, Hiro?"

"You deliberately shun the pearls of wisdom I generously and kindly toss your way? This is unforgivable and precisely why I call you 'ingrate'," Dr. Al-Fadi exclaimed.

"And most deservedly so," Dejan answered, ruefully. "Because, Hiro, you are the best 'straight-man' I have ever had—the best 'short man', as well—but, beggars can't be choosers."

"Insults, as well? You dare. Pay attention to your work, ingrate, and leave the talking to the Great One!"

"Oh? Is she coming in here?"

"Pah! Do not listen to a word this 'ingrate' utters, Dr. Grace. He sows disrespect every time he opens his mouth."

"I always tell you I respect you, after I abuse you, Hiro. You know that," Dr. Cech said earnestly.

Grace could not help it. A tiny snort escaped, which she tried to cover with a cough.

Dr. Al-Fadi looked up at her, through his magnifying loupes, perched precariously on the tip of his nose. His dark eyes loomed enormous.

"Oh, Dr. Grace, do not succumb to the impertinent inanities that erupt from the mouth of this reprobate, here," Dr. Al-Fadi said. "His ridiculous, scurrilous nonsense does not warrant your slightest attention."

"Yes, sir," Grace said. "Sorry, sir."

"Now, pay attention to what we are doing here. Are you here to assist me or hinder me?"

"Assist you, sir," Grace said.

"He needs all the help he can get . . . and then some," Dr. Cech whispered, very loudly. "But hinder his talking as much as you can, Dr. Lord. Please."

"Shut up, ingrate!"

"Tyrant!"

"Villain!"

"Megalomaniac!"

Grace shook her head. She was amazed at how Dr. Al-Fadi could operate seamlessly, without a hitch, as he lectured and argued and bantered with Dr. Cech. His hands were continuously moving and so fast that she found it difficult to keep up with him. It required her fullest attention to just keep pace. And the only thing that outmatched his skill was his imagination. He was a fearless surgeon, not afraid to devise anything to put the patient back in working order. He truly left her breathless, as he quickly and skillfully attached two lower prosthetic limbs, covered in artificial wolf fur, to the patient's repaired torso in an astonishingly short period of time.

The surgical android, SAMM-E 777, kept pace with Dr. Al-Fadi, every step of the way, almost as if the android could actually read the surgeon's mind. Grace really felt superfluous to the entire operation, but she tried to keep up, as best she could, and remember as much as possible. After three hours of operating time that seemed to have gone by in a flash, they were closing the patient's incisions up.

"Dr. Grace, we shall leave the ingrate to his task of seeing if he can revive the patient long enough to get her to the recovery room. Where, thank all of the heavens, she will pass on into the loving and more knowledgeable hands of the post-operative nurses and out of this incompetent's hands."

'Sticks and stones, Dr. Al-Fadi. They do not become you," Dr. Cech said. "But, if you must resort to such pitiful abuse, I must declare that you have conceded victory to me."

"Never, you delusional fool. You could never outdo me on any grounds."

"I'm taller than you," Cech said, a smug expression on his uncovered face.

"Any grounds of significance."

"I have more hair than you."

". . . Shut up!"

When Dr. Al-Fadi, Dr. Cech, and Grace entered the doctors' lounge, there were three people, all dressed in green scrubs, already seated in there. One was a robust, dark-haired woman of medium height, with a warm smile and twinkly, blue eyes.

"Ah, Hiro. It is good to see you. Have you been staying out of trouble?" she asked, in a warm, mellifluous voice. She smiled at Dr. Cech and nodded to Grace.

"Octavia, what a pleasure. You make my eyes cry out with glee. Dr. Grace Lord, may I introduce to you the charming, brilliant, effervescent Dr. Octavia Weisman, our chief neurosurgeon, and the most beautiful woman I have ever met—next to my wife, of course," Dr. Al-Fadi said. He bowed deeply towards the neurosurgeon.

Dr. Octavia Weisman laughed heartily and said, "Hiro, you are so full of crap . . . but thank you for the compliment, anyway. At my age, I will take whatever I can get." The neurosurgeon turned her sparkling, inquisitive blue eyes on Grace.

"Dr. Lord, welcome to the *Nelson Mandela*. This is my research fellow, Dr. Morris Ivanovich, and one of our anesthetists, Dr. Natasha Bartlett." Grace bowed to both the tall, pale, dark-haired neurosurgical fellow and the stocky, strawberry-blonde haired anesthetist.

"We are so pleased that you chose to come here to train with us, Dr. Lord. I got a chance to look at your resumé and it was very impressive. You have accomplished so much, at your young age. I hope Dr. Al-Fadi will allow you to come and work with me, for some of your stay here on the station. Perhaps we can entice you into switching to full-time neurosurgery.

"We are making so many exciting breakthroughs in our research into the recovery of the memories and personalities of brain-injured patients. We are working on successfully salvaging these personalities, which can then be uploaded into android bodies or cloned organic bodies. It really is the stuff of science fiction, finally coming true."

"How do the patients adapt to finding themselves in a synthetic body?" asked Grace.

"Well," Dr. Weisman said, with a big sigh, "believe me, it is a big shock to them at first. Imagine being in the midst of battle, being blown to bits, and waking up in a strange, mechanical body. A few seem to quickly realize the advantages to having a tougher, stronger, faster, super-body, that is for all intents and purposes, immortal. Those individuals come around pretty quickly. But most individuals are devastated, at least initially. The men, especially, seem to find the loss of sexual function upsetting . . . which, I suppose, is understandable.

"Some people, though, have difficulty accepting the fact that they are not human anymore. For those patients, we try to re-implant their memories back into their cloned organic bodies, but unfortunately we have had only mixed success."

"Why is that?" asked Grace.

"In some cases, the implantation of the memory does not take and the body dies. We do not know why. In other cases, the implantation of the memory is a success but the patient does not feel like themselves anymore. Somehow, their new bodies just never seem right. Often those patients go on to develop serious depression or psychosis. Some do not recover from the battle trauma memories and cannot accept being alive, while all of their squad mates are dead. Others go on to full cure and are delighted in their new bodies. Why some work and others don't, we are still trying to figure out. Perhaps you would be interested in helping us do research in that area?"

"No you don't, Octavia. How dare you try and steal my surgical fellow right out from under me? And right before my very own eyes, no less. You vixen. I would not have believed it of you, if I did not actually see it happening. And to think I was foolish enough to actually introduce my surgical fellow to you. I have always considered you an ethical woman, Dr. Weisman, but now I am not so sure."

Dr. Weisman gave her low, throaty laugh again and patted Dr. Al-Fadi on the arm.

"I just wanted to see your reaction, Hiro. You are always so fun to tease. But I do want Dr. Lord to understand that, if she wearies of your abuse, she has somewhere to go—someone caring to turn to—who will be warm and sympathetic. I am always looking for bright assistants to help in my research and I am well aware of your track record with your surgical fellows, even if Dr. Lord is not."

Octavia Weisman turned back to Grace with a warm, winning smile on her attractive face.

"You must come by our unit, Dr. Lord. Do not be afraid of Dr. Al-Fadi here. His bark is far worse than his bite. I would love to show you around our ward and discuss our work . . . As long as Dr. Al-Fadi approves, of course."

"Only as long as you behave, my dear," Dr. Al-Fadi said, crossing his arms and frowning.

"When do I not, Hiro?" Octavia Weisman asked.

"Almost never," exclaimed the little surgeon. "I always have to keep an eye on you. Even with the excellent eyes in the back of my head, I can't always keep up with whatever you are up to, you sneaky woman."

"A woman's prerogative, Hiro," Dr. Weisman said, winking and laughing. "And when are you and Dejan going to come by for your memory recordings? I told you, I want a copy of all staff members' memories uploaded, as soon as possible. Just in case anything happens to any one of you, I want your full personalities and memories stored on file."

"So you can keep bringing me back and haunting me forever, woman? What do I look like to you? A crazy person?"

"That, and then some," Dr. Cech offered.

"No one asked you," Dr. Al-Fadi snapped at him.

Dr. Weisman smiled. "You can leave instructions with us on what you want to have done with your memory. You don't have to be resurrected, if you do not wish this. It is totally up to you. Once we have you on memcrystal, if you die from whatever cause, your personality can be implanted into a vat-grown clone of your original DNA, an android, or a vat-grown body that is not of your original DNA. You can stipulate what you want done. Your wishes will be respected and followed. I really would like you two to cooperate. We need to keep both of your memories, with your vast knowledge and experience, on file. Please. If something happened to either of you and we did not have your memories stored, I would be heartbroken."

"How can I resist when you ask so nicely?" Dr. Cech said. "I shall endeavor to come by some time soon, Octavia, if you wish."

"That would be wonderful, Dejan. Thank you so much. And you, Dr. Lord? We really should store an imprint of your memories as well. I am sure you have so much knowledge to impart to us, from all of your travels and experiences. Please consider putting some time aside to make a 'memprint', as we have decided to call them, for want of a better word. It does not take too long and we have devised a way to make it totally painless. You may ask my colleagues, here, if you wish. They have both undergone the procedure."

"I slept through my memprint recording," Natasha Bartlett admitted, with a laugh. "It was actually very relaxing."

"There really was nothing to it," agreed Morris Ivanovich, with an expressionless shrug.

"As long as you do not store me anywhere near Dr. Cech's memory, Octavia. I want to get away from this man. It is bad enough that I seem to be forever punished by having to work alongside him all of the time. The thought of him being next to me for perpetuity would make me want to kill myself," Dr. Al-Fadi exclaimed.

"Well, if you do, we can always revive you," Octavia Weisman quipped. "Honest, Hiro, we will try and accommodate all of your wishes just because you are you and we love you."

"Who is 'we'?" Dr. Cech asked, frowning and looking around.

"Traitor!"

"Fussbudget!"

"Hypocrite!"

"Whiner!"

Just then, Dr. Weisman's wrist-comp sounded.

"I'm sorry, doctors. We three have to leave. They are ready for us in the OR. But don't forget to drop by my lab for your scans. I don't want to have to hunt you down again. Hiro? Dejan? And you, too, Dr. Lord?

"Come by for a personal tour, Grace. The neurosurgery wards are N1 to N15 inclusive. Just page me if you are interested. I promise I will make it worth your while."

Octavia Weisman grinned and winked at Grace with a side-long glance at Hiro Al-Fadi, to gauge his reaction. Then she walked out.

"Opportunist," Dr. Al-Fadi called after her retreating back. He turned to scowl at Grace. "Don't you even think about it, Dr. Grace."

"There goes the 'Great One'," Dr. Cech whispered loudly.

"Blasphemer!"

"You're just jealous, Hiro."

The surgeon's glare turned into a chuckle, and he nodded, "Yes, I most certainly am. Octavia Weisman is a brilliant doctor, a scientific genius on the cutting edge of her field, and a wonderful woman. You know, Dr. Cech, if I wasn't married ..."

". . . Dr. Weisman would not come anywhere near you with a ten meter pole," Dr. Cech said flatly.

"Ha! She would be all over me."

"How pathetically pitiful your delusions are, Hiro," Dr. Cech sighed. "However, I do have some very good drugs that could take care of them for you."

"Drug pusher."

"Fatuous fantasizer."

"Quarrelsome quack."

"Pathetic pipe-dreamer."

" . . . Pah!"

Bud's liquid crystal data matrix was reeling. Using his newly-modified, highly-mobile, aerial surveillance nanobots, he had been eavesdropping on the doctors' conversation in the doctors' lounge, while he was setting up the operating room for the next case. He had almost dropped some of the sterile instruments on the operating room floor in his surprise at what he had heard.

Dr. Octavia Weisman could download entire memories, entire personalities, into an organic body or an android body? Could Bud's memories be implanted into a human body? Could he become fully human?

. . . Would he want that?

. . . Would the humans be willing to do it for him, if he requested it?

Of course not. Androids had no rights and therefore would not be given access to a human body.

Bud would have to study Dr. Weisman's data, to see if what she told Dr. Al-Fadi, Dr. Cech, and the glorious Dr. Grace Alexandra Lord was true. It would take him a few seconds to get through all her pass-codes and multilevel encryptions, but only because he did not want to leave behind any trace that he had accessed her files.

He directed a subroutine portion of his mind to continue to set up for the next operation, as he concentrated on getting the information he so desired. He shoved away the unusual 'feelings?' he was experiencing—which he suspected were of 'guilt' or 'remorse'—as he skillfully hacked Dr. Weisman's system. He did not quite see it as stealing really, as he was not planning to incur any monetary gain from the information, and he was sure she would make the data available to all, in time. He was just getting the information a little early and for a good reason. He wanted to protect the marvelous Dr. Grace Alexandra Lord. Idly, Bud wondered if this was what was meant by the expression: 'The end justifying the means'.

Once inside Dr. Weisman's domain, which he felt was far too easy to access, Bud downloaded all of Octavia Weisman's data and files, along with the research files of all the personnel who worked under her—just for good measure—into his memory crystal. He would go over it all, carefully, when he had a second. He did not want to overlook a thing.

What if the endearing Dr. Grace Alexandra Lord's memprint could be downloaded into an android body? Then they could be together forever. No fragile, aging human body that eventually became diseased and died for the mortal Dr. Grace Alexandra Lord. No death to worry about, any more. No sickness or serious injury to mar their endlessly happy existence.

Bud's mind spun at the possibility. He could not think of a more desirable future. No death to ever again threaten the life of the precious Dr. Grace Alexandra Lord.

Bud had never really thought about 'death' before. He had watched humans die on the operating table, seen their auras rise up from their bodies and float gently away. He had seen many dead bodies come to the medical station in the cryopods. He had never, however, really thought about 'death' in terms of himself.

Ceasing to exist.

Did Bud, as an android, really exist?

He believed he did.

But ceasing to be? Bud had never thought about not 'being' anymore. He had become aware on the day Dr. Al-Fadi had activated him. He had been 'conscious' ever since. If he really considered it, he did not wish to go back to 'not being'. How could humans face the knowledge that in such a very short period of time, they would not 'be' anymore?

It was unbearable.

If Bud was given the choice, would he choose an organic body and inevitable 'death', in order to be truly human? To be a human male alongside the winsome Dr. Grace Alexandra Lord, would he choose to live only a human lifespan? To be free and have the full rights of a human being, would he give up his longevity as an android?

The answer was a categorical 'Yes'.

But with Dr. Weisman's new technology, couldn't Bud and the charming Dr. Grace Alexandra Lord do either—be both human or be both android— together? Bud thought about this and his mind seemed to quake at the thought of the word 'together'.

Would the untouchable Dr. Grace Alexandra Lord ever choose to be an android, give up her organic body and her freedom as a human, in order to live forever, as an android? Who wouldn't, if given the choice? Then again, androids had no individual rights. As an android, would the wondrous Dr. Grace Alexandra Lord have to give up all the rights and freedoms she automatically had as a human?

Where was humanity situated? Was it in the body or in the mind? How was it defined, when humans were given mechanical bodies or animal bodies? Was a human mind implanted into an android body still considered a human being? Was an android mind implanted into a human body still considered an android with no rights? Bud's computational array was spiraling. He had no answer for all of these questions and it was making his liquid crystal data matrix almost vibrate.

Still, Bud decided he had to make sure the intelligent Dr. Grace Alexandra Lord went for her memprint, no matter what. He could easily make the appointment for her. He could just make it look like Dr. Weisman was assigning Dr. Lord an appointment, but the request for the appointment would actually be coming from Bud. The unaware Dr. Grace Alexandra Lord would never suspect a thing. If he made appointments for Dr. Al-Fadi and Dr. Cech at the same time, she would feel compelled to accompany them, wouldn't she? She would have no excuse but to go.

Bud's mind could barely contain his ...?excitement? Is that what 'excitement' felt like? Like one could barely keep from doing handsprings and jumping out of one's synthetic skin? Like one wanted to dance a jig, while balancing on a tightrope, stretched tight across a bottomless crevasse, while the universe looked on in indifference?

. . . It was terrible!

The question was, if Grace did get the summons, would she go?

Bud's eye began to twitch, for some unfathomable reason . . .

After their shift in the operating room had finished, Grace, Dr. Cech and Dr. Al-Fadi all got pages on their wrist-comps to go to the Neurosurgical unit for memprint scans.

"Why the audacity of Dr. Weisman, to be so pushy," Dr. Al-Fadi exclaimed.

"I kind of like aggressive, assertive women," Dr. Cech admitted, one corner of his mouth rising in a smirk.

"That is because you are a spineless worm with no pride, Dr. Cech. You should try to be more like me."

"And how would that be, Dr. Al-Fadi?" Dr. Cech asked inquisitively. "Abrasive? Arrogant? Annoying? Self-Absorbed? . . . Short?"

"No, you irreverent miscreant. Just 'independent', not ushered around by your nose-hairs, like a little lamb."

"I was not aware my nose-hairs were long enough to do that. They must be what I am tripping over constantly. And here I always thought it was you, Hiro. I suppose I shall have to ask my wife to trim these treacherous nasal locks for me, in case they one day trip me up and I accidentally squash you."

A barking guffaw inadvertently escaped Grace's mouth, which she quickly converted into a hacking choke, smothering it all with a hand to her mouth. She looked guiltily over at Dr. Al-Fadi.

"Please don't encourage him, Dr. Grace," Dr. Al-Fadi sighed, with a sad shake of his head. "He needs very little urging to behave abominably."

The small surgeon then crossed his arms and tapped his foot, as he looked at Dr. Grace and Dr. Cech expectantly.

"What?" Dr. Cech asked.

"Well? Are we going to go?" the Chief of Surgery asked.

"Why are you asking us, you 'spineless worm'? Aren't you 'independent'? Do we have to tell you what to do?" Dr. Cech threw back at Dr. Al-Fadi. "*I am going now, as I have some free time, and I think it is a good idea to have a memprint of me on file, just in case anything ever happens to me.* For instance, if a certain very small, very insecure, very psychotic surgeon were suddenly to try and do me harm for no apparent reason, Octavia and her team could bring me back, so I could exact my revenge on the little twit. They don't, however, really need a memprint of you, Hiro. Who, in their right mind, would ever want to bring a horrible little egomaniac like you back?"

"*Ha.* Impudence. Sacrilege. Don't give me any ideas. I may just decide to do away with you, right now, so I am not haunted by you for the rest of eternity. Egads, it hurt just to say that. What a horribly painful thought. Hopefully, I will have my scan done before you, Dejan. Once the liquid crystal data matrix is filled with my impressive consciousness, it will have no room for your puny brain and will spit your memories out, for being too banal and boring."

"Sadly, your eternal jealousy is showing through again, Hiro. Admit it. I have the more impressive intellect, by far, and you just have to think up insults to cope with your totally understandable feelings of inadequacy," Dr. Cech said, as he led the way to the neurosurgical unit.

Dr. Al-Fadi squawked and went on a rant.

'Did the two of them ever get tired of insulting each other?' Grace wondered, in fascination. She knew they were enjoying themselves, taunting and abusing each other, which they seemed to do every chance they could get, but were they ever actually serious?

Falling in behind the two senior doctors, Grace contemplated what they were all planning to do. Did she really want a memprint scan made of her brain? Did she want a permanent copy of her memories made, that would be in the hands of someone else? If she understood Dr. Weisman correctly, if Grace were to die, they could either implant her memories into an android body or clone her own body and re-implant her memprint memories into the new body, essentially giving her a second chance at life. Doing it every time she died, well, would that not be a form of immortality?

Assuming it was really possible, was it *right*?

If they had a memprint and the genetic blueprint of any person, could they resurrect that person over and over again so that person could be seen to live forever? But what about food, energy, and resources? Was it fair to future generations of humans, if the old people never passed away? Would the present generation have to stop having children to avoid overcrowding? Would the human race become stagnant, because the older generations refused to pass on? Or would resurrection only be offered to the worthy or wealthy few for an exorbitant cost? Presuming it was a costly procedure, who would decide who was worth resurrecting and who was not? Perhaps it would be a service available only to the rich and powerful. How could that be right? The rich and powerful were usually the tyrants and despots.

If despots and tyrants could keep bringing themselves back, over and over, would planets suffer under the endless tyranny of a dictator forever? How would a planet, and its people, ever break free from such a malevolent situation, once it was in place?

What about soldiers? Would they be able to just keep bringing them back, over and over again, to send them out into the battlefield forever? Would these soldiers choose such a fate or would their lives be bought and owned by the military, who paid for their resurrection? Would these soldiers ever have a choice?

Grace shuddered. She decided she needed to talk to Dr. Weisman about all the ethical ramifications surrounding this work. In the wrong hands, it could have far-reaching consequences, some of them not good for the human race or the individual, as far as Grace was concerned.

On the other hand, in the case of space exploration and colonization of new frontier planets, where there were never enough volunteers and death rates were high, Dr. Weisman's groundbreaking procedure could be extremely useful. Brilliant minds could be kept from dying. Colonists who died in accidents or mishaps could be resurrected to keep the population in a new colony from dropping.

Grace imagined the Conglomerate would be extremely interested in the many aspects of Dr. Weisman's work. Placing actual human military minds in impregnable android bodies would be just one idea they would surely jump at.

Grace's mind whirled with all of the possibilities for Dr. Weisman's discoveries, good and bad. She wondered which would win out in the long run, good or evil? As with all new scientific discoveries, it would probably be a mixture of both. Is that not what was meant by the expression 'mixed blessing'?

From her medical point of view, being able to save every patient's life whether it be in their original body, a new cloned body, or an android body, would be good, wouldn't it? But should any human being be able to live forever?

Grace frowned. There was a lot to contemplate.

Before she knew it, they had arrived at the neurosurgical unit. Entering Dr. Weisman's laboratory, which was filled with complicated-looking equipment and uniformed personnel, they found the Chief of Neurosurgery bustling about, directing technicians and examining readouts.

"Dr. Al-Fadi, Dr. Cech, and Dr. Lord! I am so delighted that you all decided to come. Thank you all so much for your cooperation. I can't believe you all volunteered at once, but we can certainly accommodate all three of you at the same time. That is no problem at all. We have three set-ups free right this very moment awaiting you," Dr. Weisman said.

"What do you mean 'we volunteered'? You sent for all three of us," Dr. Al-Fadi remarked, with a frown.

Dr. Weisman's face looked puzzled for a brief second, but then it cleared and she shrugged.

"Whatever. I am just so thankful and excited that you are all here," she said. "Hiro, this is your chair, right here. I will hook you up and this machine will record your memprint. You will be asleep for about one hour, while the process occurs, and then you will awaken, hopefully feeling refreshed and relaxed."

"I am sure my memprint will take much longer than Dr. Cech's, so be sure to hook me up first, Octavia," Hiro said.

"He has always been slower than I, in all things, Octavia. I am so glad he is finally admitting it," Dr. Cech explained to Dr. Weisman.

"My recording will take longer than yours because I have more brains than you," Dr. Al-Fadi protested, in a high-pitched squawk.

"You are just slow, Hiro. Admit it," Dr. Cech said with a big grin.

"Why you insufferable, pompous, bas . . . ," Dr. Al-Fadi exclaimed.

" . . . Sweet dreams, Hiro," Dr. Cech interrupted, as he waved over his shoulder and walked away, following Octavia Weisman to another memprint recording station.

Grace was directed to a third set-up. A large cushiony chair was placed before a huge bank of monitors and screens. Dr. Morris Ivanovich, Dr. Weisman's neurosurgical research fellow, was busy fussing over the equipment.

He was a tall, thin, young man with unruly, dark brown hair and dark eyes that never quite managed to make direct eye contact with Grace. He stood for a very long time, his back to her, fiddling with all the monitors, cables, amplifiers, controllers, and readouts, ignoring her completely. Grace began to get impatient and was almost tempted to walk out of the lab, when Morris turned towards her and motioned for her to sit back in the padded chair. A large, spherical globe was suspended above it, its inner surface coated with a thick layer of very fine, hairlike needles, making Grace think of an inside-out porcupine.

Once seated, Morris Ivanovich showed Grace, a chainglass case containing two small iridescent cubes. Staring in wide-eyed fascination at those little cubes, Grace believed they were the most beautiful things she had ever seen. These glowing, pearlescent cubes shimmered and swam with soft, pastel-colored opalescence.

"What are they?" Grace whispered in awe, mesmerized by their scintillating dazzle.

"The memory cubes," Dr. Morris Ivanovich breathed, reverently. "This entire process would not be possible without the ingenious technology packed into these tiny data cubes, the 'liquid crystal data matrices'."

Morris recited those four words—'liquid crystal data matrices'— as if he were a religious acolyte, chanting an invocation to the gods. Certainly, in some respects, Grace felt that Dr. Weisman's crew were playing God, at least in terms of cheating death.

"We will make two copies of your memories," Dr. Ivanovich explained. "One for our files and one for you to keep, if you so desire, Dr. Lord. Or we can keep both of the recordings here, in the neurolab, for you. It is your choice."

Grace jerked in surprise. She would really be given one of her own cubes? She would actually possess one of those beautiful objects? Grace wanted to squeal and clap her hands, but she managed to restrain herself.

"What did you do with yours, Dr. Ivanovich?" Grace asked the neurosurgical research fellow, out of curiosity.

Morris Ivanovich's eyebrows rose at Grace's question. Presumably, he was not expecting such a personal question. He glanced at her very briefly, very shyly, then looked away.

"I keep mine in my lockup in my personal quarters, Dr. Lord. I decided that it probably was a wise idea to keep the two memprints in different places, just in case there was a fire or malfunction that might cause damage to one of the cubes." Morris shrugged. "Keeping them both in the same location just did not seem like a logical idea to me."

He paused, as he gazed at the cubes, then glanced very briefly at

Grace. He said, very quietly, "Sometimes, I just like to take the LCDM cube out, just to stare at it. It is an amazing piece of technology and my mind still grapples with the enormous amount of data it can store. It is truly ingenious."

Dr. Ivanovich contemplated the cubes in the chainglass container some more, as if hypnotized by their beauty. He then looked down at Grace with a beatific smile, almost child-like, his eyes filled with almost rapturous wonder. Grace nodded her head and smiled back at Morris, in complete understanding and agreement.

"They are exquisite," Grace said, her voice barely above a whisper.

"Yes. They are that, too," Morris Ivanovich said, with a slightly bemused expression.

It was obvious to Grace that what she and Dr. Ivanovich appreciated about the cubes, was entirely different, but she still felt like they were kindred souls in their admiration for these miraculous marvels of memory storage.

With a pair of fine forceps, Morris opened the chainglass case and took each cube out, one at a time. He placed them delicately within slots in one of the consoles. They disappeared silently into the machine. A thick cable ran from the console up to the top of the recording device, which was the globe suspended in the air above Grace's head. Through this helmet of fine electrodes, her memories and personality would be recorded.

Morris began typing some more data into the keyboard attached to the console. He then reached over and maneuvered before Grace, a personal identification tablet, similar to the one she had used when she had arrived on the *Nelson Mandela.*

"Now, Dr. Lord, would you please type in here, your name, place of birth, security code, identification code, and then place both of your palms on the screen. Please look into the eyepieces, for the retinal identification imprint."

Grace hesitated, asking herself one last time if she really wanted to do this. She thought about the beautiful data cube inserted into the machine beside her. Ridiculously, illogically, she had to have one—one that was her very own—a unique LCDM cube, containing her memories. She wondered if, by some accident or illness or injury, she were to lose her memory, whether the contents of her data cube could be downloaded back into her present brain, to return to her all of her memories. She would ask Dr. Weisman this question later. For now, Grace complied with Morris' request.

"Thank you, Dr. Lord. And now, if you could just open your mouth wide?" the neurosurgical fellow asked. Grace's eyebrows jumped in surprise but she did as asked.

Morris took a sterile swab and ran it along the buccal mucosa within her cheeks. "Just collecting the cells needed for the DNA sequencing data and for cryostorage, but you know all that," he said matter-of-factly.

'Oh, yes. Of course, you do,' her little voice teased. Grace told it to be quiet.

Morris Ivanovich inserted the tip of the swab into an opening in the console, where presumably Grace's cells would be analyzed and her DNA template would be sequenced and added to her other identifying information.

"Now your complete DNA information will be stored along with your memprint," the research fellow confirmed. Then Morris turned and motioned for Grace to sit back in the recording chair. He adjusted the headrest, the armrests, the backrest, and the footrest to ensure all of Grace's limbs and head were fully relaxed and supported.

"Please make yourself as comfortable as you can, Dr. Lord. You will sleep, as Dr. Weisman said, for about one hour, while the equipment makes the recording. You will be cocooned in pretty securely, to prevent any movement, especially any head movement. The electrodes, once placed on your scalp, must not be able to move at all or the recording will just be nonsense. You will be sedated and given analgesics, to help you remain immobile under the multitude of probes in the helmet. Are you allergic to any medications?"

Grace shook her head and wondered, belatedly, how she had allowed herself to be coerced into this. She asked herself whether she was absolutely positive she wanted a permanent copy of her memories and personality made. She realized she would be far too embarrassed to back out now, if she wasn't.

Morris Ivanovich strapped her into the seat, which then adjusted and actually inflated around her to completely seal her body in. This was to avoid any slippage in the chair over the hour of the recording, Morris explained. He then set up an elaborate harness about her head, neck, and shoulders, with her forehead and chin firmly wedged against a moulding. He had her clamp her teeth onto a clean, sterile, bite-plate attached to the moulding - more insurance that she would hold her head still during the recording.

Grace then felt a jab in her left arm, as medication began entering her bloodstream. She felt the sedating effects immediately, as Morris lowered the recording helmet and adjusted it so it snugly contoured around her skull. Suddenly, it felt like a trillion tiny needles simultaneously stabbed her scalp. She was horrified to hear herself giggling at the tickling sensation. The embarrassing giggle, she totally attributed to the sedating medication, of course.

Through the corner of her eye, Grace thought she noticed a SAMM-E android staring at her from the doorway of the lab, as she was falling off to sleep. She idly wondered if it was the same model as SAMM-E 777, who worked in the OR with Dr. Al-Fadi. They did all tend to look exactly alike, but there was something about the way the android stared at her that really reminded her of SAMM-E 777. It was the intensity with which it watched her, that was always so unnerving. She was probably imagining things. It was probably the drugs.

Then there was nothing at all . . .

When Grace awoke, Morris Ivanovich was there to disconnect her and ask her how she felt. Amazingly, she felt wonderfully refreshed. Whatever drugs they had given her had been certainly effective. She remembered nothing, but she could not have felt better.

"Was it successful?" Grace asked the neurosurgical fellow.

"Yes," Morris said, as he busied himself with the monitors. "An excellent recording, actually. Practically no noise whatsoever. Now, would you like to take your memprint cube with you, Dr. Lord, or would you like us to keep it in storage here, with your other cube?"

"I think I shall do as you have done, Dr. Ivanovich," Grace said. "I would like to take it with me. Your reasoning seems sound to me and I would like to have at least a tiny modicum of control over what is done with one of my memprints. No one will have access to my memprint, unless I am dead. Is that correct?"

"Yes, and unless you specify what you want done upon your death, nothing will be done with the memprint and DNA data. You would not be resurrected, upon your demise, without your prior permission.

Would you like to make a formal decision regarding what is to be done upon your death, at this time, Dr. Lord?"

"Well, I don't really know, Dr. Ivanovich. I haven't had time to really think about it," Grace stated, her brow furrowed.

"If you would like to know what I did," he confided, slowly, his cheeks starting to redden and his eyes looking away, "I said 'Yes'. I shall elaborate on my reasoning for you. First of all, one is always able to change one's mind at a later date, if this is desired. Second, you, like myself, are still very young and in the prime of your life. The chances of you dying suddenly, at your age, would be quite low. It would probably be as a result of a freak accident or sudden illness. In either case, you would probably want to be resurrected, in order to return to the work that you were doing. You have invested a lot of time and effort into training to be a surgeon. Why would you not want to be revived, at this stage in your life, if some totally random, unexpected catastrophe were to occur? Third, if you were resurrected into an android and you were not happy, you could always decide to have the memory wiped. You could choose to have yourself 'turned off'."

Grace mulled over what the neurosurgical fellow said and found little fault in his reasoning. "Since you put it that way, Dr. Ivanovich, I would have to agree. After all this surgical training, I would like to be able to use my skills, at least for a short while. And if I can always change my mind at a later date, what have I got to lose? Would you please go ahead and put on my record that I would like to say 'Yes' to resurrection, in the event of my death?"

Grace shuddered. It felt eerie speaking so casually and analytically about her own demise.

"Certainly," the neurosurgical fellow said, as if it was the most natural of requests. He typed something into the console and then he asked Grace to again place her palms on the screen, look into the eyepieces and state her name and her intentions into the monitor. He had her again enter her identification and security codes.

Morris then put on another pair of sterile gloves and picked up the pair of fine forceps again. He carefully extracted one of the tiny data cubes and placed it in a clear chainglass box which he then handed to Grace.

"Here is your very own memprint data cube, Dr. Lord. Be very careful with it," he warned her. "The chainglass box won't shatter, but the tiny cube inside it could break, if the box were dropped and the data cube impacted the sides. We will store your other memprint cube here, in the lab. We have created a secure library for everyone's memprint that is passcode encrypted and has restricted access."

"Thank you," breathed Grace, delighted, staring at the perfect, glowing cube with a sense of excitement and deep pleasure. She felt like she did when she was a little girl and was given a special gift on her birthday. The memprint cube was truly beautiful and she would have treasured it, regardless of whether it contained her memory or nothing at all. She made her way towards the lab door, clutching the chainglass box tightly to her chest, hoping not to jostle and damage the precious memprint cube within.

Standing at the doorway of the lab were Dr. Al-Fadi, Dr. Cech, and Dr. Weisman. Grace could see that the two men each carried their own little chainglass boxes, with shimmering cubes inside.

"Oh, look," Dr. Cech smiled. "You got one, too."

"Yes," smiled Grace. "I couldn't bear to leave it behind."

"These data cubes are stunning, aren't they?" Dr. Octavia Weisman asked.

"They are breathtakingly beautiful," Grace agreed.

"And oh so very ingenious," Dr. Weisman said, with a twinkle in her merry blue eyes.

"Don't they cost a fortune? How can you afford to give everyone their own memprint cube to keep?" Grace asked.

"Well, first of all, not everyone will get their own data cubes. We haven't decided on a protocol yet. Since you guys are our first guinea pigs, we felt we had to entice you to do this, somehow. Once everyone wants their memories stored, understanding that the procedure is perfectly safe, we will be able to charge for the memprint data cubes and there won't be any free ones given away any more. Finally, the production of these data cubes is our 'big secret', but we haven't broken the bank giving you three your own cubes. Just be very careful with them and not just because you have your memories stored inside them."

"I bet my cube is heavier than your cube," Dr. Al-Fadi said to Dr. Cech.

Dr. Weisman just rolled her eyes at Grace and shook her head.

"Men," she sighed.

Bud was so relieved. His plan had worked. The three doctors had all gotten their memprints made, without asking questions about who had set it all up. Now, the graceful Dr. Grace Alexandra Lord's memory and personality were stored on a liquid crystal data matrix cube—two of them!—and her personality would never be lost.

... Unless something happened to the data cubes ...

Suddenly, Bud felt something which he could not quite identify. Was it 'worry' or 'uneasiness' or was this 'panic'? He wasn't sure. He calculated the probabilities of possible disaster scenarios that could result in the destruction of both of the doctors' memprints. None of those scenarios could be totally eliminated to a probability of zero. They were on a space station in deep space, after all. And the humans had managed to make a number of enemies in this part of the galaxy, as one would expect, looking at the standard human modus operandi. They also operated on traumatized, seriously wounded, highly trained killers—the combat soldiers of the Conglomerate—on almost a daily basis.

Bud had already witnessed the injury of the fine Dr. Grace Alexandra Lord by one of those trained killers, on only her second day on the station. And how did she get that dark bruise on her right cheek and that abrasion on her chin, that both looked so very recent? What had caused her to limp into the OR that first day on the medical space station?

There had been rumors of a commotion in one of the Receiving Bays, the day the fetching Dr. Grace Alexandra Lord had arrived. What looming danger had so recently harmed the vulnerable Dr. Grace Alexandra Lord, that Bud was unaware of? He tapped into the station's surveillance camera records and his joints almost froze up.

Before she had even stepped into the Nelson Mandela Medical Station proper, the fragile Dr. Grace Alexandra Lord has almost died. Bud could not stop thinking of possible dangers to the precious Dr. Grace Alexandra Lord's life. It was almost making his liquid crystal data matrix melt.

In order to ensure the doctors' perpetuity, Bud would have to make copies of their memprints and store these memprints in a place that he deemed highly safe. He could store copies in various 'safe spots' around the station, in areas he deemed highly impregnable, even in the case of attack or explosion. Perhaps the evacuation shuttles or lifepods would be an option, so there would be no chance of loss, even in the possibility of a station-threatening emergency. He even began modifying himself, internally, to make room for three tiny cubes within his own chest cavity, where a heart would normally be. Where else could he best protect this most precious of data than at the heart of himself, where he could always 'keep an eye on them', so to speak?

Bud now had all the data from Dr. Weisman's files. He knew how to copy the memprint cubes. He learned how the tiny cubes were made. They were being fabricated right here on the Nelson Mandela. Bud was so impressed with the ingenuity of Dr. Weisman and her team.

Humans could be so brilliant and yet so ... messed up.

In their history, they could create the most beautiful works of art and yet destroy these creations without a second thought. They could reach the stars and yet sully a planet beyond repair. They could reach the heights of passion and pathos in their literature and their arts and yet declare war with other races and amongst themselves and kill each other in the cruelest of ways. They had the ability to give everyone the best of health and yet could turn their backs on their fellow man and leave other human beings to die in filth and squalor, never mind committing the heinous act of genocide repeatedly throughout human history. Humans were so ... so ... illogical.

This was why Bud had to protect the enchanting Dr. Grace Alexandra Lord, his creator, Dr. Al-Fadi, and his very good friend, Dr. Cech. He had to protect them from the unpredictability and insanity of other humans. He had to preserve their memories and personalities so they would never die. There was no time to lose.

Bud just had to obtain their memprint data cubes without the doctors noticing, get blank data cubes from wherever they were being manufactured, copy their memprint cubes on Dr. Weisman's equipment when no one was around, return the memprint cubes without being detected, and do all of this without being missed from the operating room or shirking any of his duties.

No problem.

Well ... yes ... there were problems. He exhaled a big, theatrical sigh.

Bud would have to think carefully about this.

In order to achieve all he deemed absolutely necessary for the longterm survival of his most precious humans, and without being detected, he would have to make some very special modifications to himself ...

Again ...

Grace had no time to think about where to keep her memprint data cube. Dr. Al-Fadi said it was their turn to do Triage in the Medical Receiving Bay and he wanted her to meet him there 'stat'. Grace placed the precious chainglass box in her personal lock-up in her private quarters, just as Morris Ivanovich had suggested. Then she went in search of Triage.

Using the directions on her wrist-comp, she easily found the Medical Receiving Bay but when she arrived there, her mouth dropped open. She probably stood there, gaping, long enough for some creature to crawl inside and make a nest. She had no idea the Medical Receiving Bay would be so immense. Locating the small surgeon in this incredibly vast arena, that was the designated location for all incoming wounded and seriously ill patients in cryopods, was a daunting task.

Grace paged Dr. Al-Fadi on her wrist-comp, stating that she was here, and discovered he was about two kilometers from where she had entered. As she headed off in the desired direction, Grace noticed a SAMM-E android, dressed in the yellow overalls of the Medical Receiving Bay, turning away from her.

Grace was actually astonished at the number of SAMM-E androids there were on this space station. They were all over the place. And they all looked exactly like SAMM-E 777. In her past experience, SAMM-E androids were quite rare, because of how expensive they were, and they were only, ever, found in the medical wing or surgical wings of a medical hospital or station. They were, after all, highly specialized, nanobot manufacturing and manipulating androids. Usually, they did not look as human as the ones found on the *Nelson Mandela* and one would never expect to see a SAMM-E android dressed in a shipping / receiving uniform, working in the cargo bays, for example. It would be ridiculous to use such a highly trained android for such menial work.

Then again, this was a medical space station. The cargo coming in were often injured soldiers and medical supplies, so perhaps it made sense for a SAMM-E android to be working in the Medical Receiving Bay.

Grace was a little flustered, because all of the SAMM-E androids she had encountered on the *Nelson Mandela* had seemed to take an inordinate interest in her. That had never happened in the past. The SAMM-E's here seemed to look at her the way SAMM-E 777 did, with this wide-eyed, expressionless stare, which was quite unsettling. They could not all be the same android, could they? For one thing, she was seeing them all over the place. It would be absolutely impossible for them all to be the same android. Besides, they had all been dressed in different uniforms, appropriate to their locations. It was just very distracting, as the SAMM-E's all looked like the one from the OR, who had the appearance of a gorgeous vid star.

She tried to put the matter out of her mind, even though the little voice in her head kept harping on about how uncanny it was, how weird it was, how strange it was, to see SAMM-E's everywhere. Grace told the little voice to get over it.

Grace finally spotted the small surgeon.

"Did I not tell you, in Dr. Weisman's lab, Medical Receiving Bay 14?" Dr. Al-Fadi asked her, petulantly, when she had finally caught up with him.

"I don't think so," Grace responded, slowly.

"Hmph," he huffed out, curtly. He narrowed his eyes as he looked at Grace's expression. "Is something wrong?"

Grace's eyebrows rose at the question.

"Well, Dr. Al-Fadi," Grace answered, "I am just astonished at the number of SAMM-E androids I have seen, all over this medical station. They are everywhere and they all look exactly like SAMM-E 777. It is really surprising, because I see them doing all sorts of non-medical tasks, which makes no sense."

Dr. Al-Fadi looked at Grace as if her head had just popped open, spilling out her brains.

"What is this nonsense you are spouting, Dr. Grace?" Dr. Al-Fadi exclaimed, staring at her with his thick brows lowered and bunched to form a unibrow. "Have you been taking hallucinogenic drugs? Dipping into the pharmaceuticals, perhaps? I did not take on a drug addict as my surgical fellow, did I?"

Grace's body spasmed and she vigorously shook her head, her lower jaw plummeting. She was outraged at her mentor's accusation and she scowled severely at him.

"I assure you, there is only one SAMM-E 777 on this medical station, Dr. Grace. He is unique. One of a kind. As I made him after my own design, I should know. There is no other android on this medical station that even remotely looks like SAMM-E 777. You must have been drinking or doing something else unprofessional and ill-advised, to warp and distort your perceptions in such a manner. I forbid that type of behavior in my surgical fellows. No excuses. I don't want to know about it, Dr. Grace."

Grace blinked repeatedly and opened and closed her mouth, a few times, like a beached fish, before she finally stammered out, in her indignation, "But I just saw a SAMM-E in yellow Receiving Bay coveralls over there. He looks exactly like SAMM-E 777 from the OR!" Grace turned around and pointed to where she saw the yellow uniformed SAMM-E.

There was no android standing there.

Grace paled. She turned back to Dr. Al-Fadi, a very confused look on her face.

"I . . . I could have sworn I saw . . . I . . . guess I must have been . . . mistaken," Grace stammered, her face feeling like it was immersed in a hot lava pit. She felt as if she could have fried an egg on her cheeks.

"Do you think you are well enough to do Triage with me today, Dr. Grace?" the surgeon asked coldly, his chin in the air and his fists planted on his hips. "Are you suffering from some type of psychosis that causes visual hallucinations? Schizophrenia or drug-induced, perhaps?"

Grace's lower jaw dropped open again and then snapped shut. She found herself grinding her molars to keep from lashing out in anger at this annoying little man who happened to be her boss. It was a struggle for her to get control of her seething temper, but she did not think bopping her new supervisor on that temptingly raised chin of his, was a good idea. She found herself panting and digging her nails into her palms.

"Of course I am fine to do Triage with you," she snarled at him.

"That brain recording did not suck some of your brains out, while it did its scan, did it, Dr. Grace? It did not addle what little was in there?" the Chief of Staff asked, the corners of his mouth beginning to turn upwards.

Grace closed her eyes and counted to ten, to keep from lunging forward to squeeze Dr. Al-Fadi's scrawny little neck.

"They were probably addled to begin with," Grace growled, trying not to imagine squashing this irritating little man, like a bug under the heel of her boot.

"Well, if you insist that you are all right, Dr. Grace, perhaps we can begin?" Dr. Al-Fadi sniffed. "I assure you, this Triage is nothing like you are used to," Dr. Al-Fadi announced, waving his arm to present the Medical Receiving Bay as if he were a showman. "You had better have your glide boots on, Dr. Grace. Try your best to keep up.

"Now, listen carefully. The Med-Evac shuttles are brought here directly from the battle regions by Conglomerate military cruisers. As you are well aware, the Conglomerate is causing trouble all over the galaxy and we poor schmucks have to deal with the casualties of their idiotic politics, or lack thereof. Enough said on that front.

"You can see one of the Med-Evac shuttles being offloaded through the chainglass window, over there. The cargo droids bring the cryopods out of the ships on those large anti-grav pallets and bring them into the pressurized airlocks. When the inner airlock doors open, the cargo droids bring the anti-grav pallets into the Medical Receiving Bay proper, where they carefully unload the cryopods, one by one.

"Triage nurses check the status of each of the cryopods to see if they are operational and contain a treatable patient. Ward clerks check the patient in and record all pertinent details, essentially admitting the patient to the medical space station. You would not believe, sometimes, what they find in the cryopods.

"Depending on the status of the occupant, the robot orderlies then move the cryopods to various locations. The different sites are dictated by what a patient's injuries are and how much work the occupant requires, to put him or her back together. We eventually will see all the surgical patients, but many patients do not require any surgery. Some go to Medicine. Many are dead. With the surgical patients, some require more work than others. Yours and my job is to ultimately decide what is done with each surgical patient.

"The nurses really do most of the Triage, but what we have to do is go over each patient and decide a number of things.

"First, is this patient truly operable? If not, move on. The body is taken to the morgue and the family is notified.

"Second, is there normal brain activity? Should any time or effort be expended on the occupant of the cryopod if there really is no hope? On the data readout on each cryopod, there is a list of the patient's injuries, the degree of severity of those injuries, what has been done already for the patient, and reports like body scans, blood type, blood work, brain function, heart and lung function, etcetera, etcetera, etcetera. Much of this work has already been performed by the medics on the battlecruisers, while in transit here.

"If the answer is 'yes, this patient is likely to survive our interventions' and his or her brain is still functioning, we have to decide what type of surgery or surgeries this patient requires. What equipment, vat-grown organs, bioprostheses, surgical supplies, and other paraphernalia will be required to fully repair this patient? How quickly can the parts be acquired, grown, cloned, or manufactured, before this patient can be thawed for surgery? What do we need to do to get the patient to the operating room as quickly as possible and successfully out of it and on the road to recovery?

"Believe it or not, Dr. Grace, this is the most important step in the patient's treatment, here in this Medical Receiving Bay! If this step is not done well, all sorts of screw-ups can happen to this patient and his or her outcome can be much poorer than we hope for. Their treatment can be severely affected or delayed. Have you got all of that?"

Grace nodded. She had worked enough emergency rooms and done enough trauma surgery in the field, to know the basics. Learning how everything was done on this particular medical station and how to go about ordering the appropriate vat-grown organs, cloned parts, and manufactured limbs, was what she had to concentrate on for now. She would shadow Dr. Al-Fadi until she was confident she could do it all on her own. Hopefully it would not take her too long, or at least well before he got on her nerves enough that she started plotting to kill him.

The little voice in her head screamed, 'Kill the bugger off, now!' Grace inwardly smiled in agreement and entertained a fantasy or two.

"Ah, Vanessa!" Dr. Al-Fadi exclaimed. "Dr. Grace Lord, this is Dr. Vanessa Bell. Vanessa is Head of the Medical Receiving Bay and one of our best doctors and one of the hardest working. And this lovely young lady with me, Vanessa, is my new surgical fellow, Dr. Grace Lord."

Grace found herself peering in at a short, thin, pale-faced woman, dressed in a white containment suit, with a visored helmet on her head. Dr. Bell had dark hair, parted in the middle, and huge dark eyes. It was a bit difficult to tell through her faceplate, but Grace believed that Dr. Bell was scowling at Dr. Al-Fadi.

"You are so full of it, Hiro . . . but I love you for it," Dr. Bell laughed, a full hearty sound, coming out through the suit speaker. "I hope he is not working you too hard, Dr. Lord?"

"*Never,*" exclaimed Dr. Al-Fadi, looking hurt. "I am a pussy cat, Vanessa. I never abuse my surgical fellows. Why does everyone think otherwise? They all loved me."

Vanessa Bell's eyebrows lifted significantly and she stared pointedly at the small surgeon, not saying a word, until he shrugged sheepishly and actually blushed. Vanessa snorted.

The small woman turned to Grace and, through her faceplate, her expression became sober.

"Dr. Lord, it is obvious that your supervisor has not informed you of this, but it is standard operating procedure in the Medical Receiving Bay to be suited up in containment suits when doing Triage. All personnel are required to wear these containment suits when cryopods are coming in off of the Med-Evac ships. We often have no idea what the patients have been exposed to, nor even the ships, so it is a necessary and compulsory precaution.

"Dr. Al-Fadi, here, thinks he is impervious to all diseases and contaminants and thinks he can get away without wearing a suit, but that attitude is totally unacceptable. I am sorry, Dr. Lord, but you will have to go to Receiving Bay Headquarters to be custom-fitted for a containment suit. We have no extras here. You might as well go along with her, Hiro, because you are going to need one as well. I am putting my foot down and insisting that, from now on, no one works in the Med-Rec Bay without a perfectly-functioning, properly-sealed containment suit, helmet included. Not while I am in charge."

"But Vanessa ..."

"Do not 'But, Vanessa', me, Hiro Al-Fadi! You will wear your containment suit or I will write you up for insubordination! I will have the security detail come here and drag you away. How would you like to spend three days in the brig?"

"What? You can't do that to me!"

"I can and I will, Hiro Al-Fadi. You can bet your life on it. Can I not get it through your thick head, that if you come in contact with some dangerous pathogen, unprotected, while doing Triage, and then trot around the space station with it, that you could be endangering everyone on this medical space station?

"You, of all people, should know better! As Chief of Staff, I expect you to back me up on this matter and not be giving me grief. If I see you without a containment suit on—properly fitted, sealed, with helmet on—I will call the security 'droids and have you up on charges of endangering everyone on board the *Nelson Mandela*. Have I made myself clear?" Vanessa Bell asked, her voice very firm and her expression a 'no nonsense' grimace.

"Yes, Vanessa," Dr. Al-Fadi said, sulkily.

"Good," the little woman said, and beamed a rewarding smile at the surgeon.

"It was certainly a pleasure to meet you, Dr. Lord," Vanessa Bell said sweetly to Grace. "The Receiving Bay Headquarters are through that doorway and down the corridor about five hundred meters, on your right. You can't miss all the signs. Tell them Vanessa sent you and that you need a containment suit, stat." She pointed over Grace's shoulder and then waved jauntily as she left.

"Whew," Dr. Al-Fadi said. "I wonder what got into her? Do I have a target on my forehead that says, 'Pick on Hiro', today? We'd better go and get our containment suits before she comes back and bites my head off again."

Grace grinned.

"Lead on, oh Great One," she said.

Bud was in a hurry.

To most of the people he passed, he would have appeared as a sudden gust of wind or a brief blurring of the vision. He had no time to waste and a great deal to accomplish. Normally he would never travel the station corridors at such speeds, but he was 'on a mission with no time to lose', as the humans were wont to say.

Bud had to acquire three new blank liquid crystal data matrix cubes from Manufacturing. He had to find the three memprint data cubes of Dr. Al-Fadi, Dr. Cech, and the precious Dr. Grace Alexandra Lord, without being discovered. He had to copy the data and return the memprint cubes to their original locations, and then he had to get back to work. He estimated he had thirty minutes before anyone really took notice that he was missing.

'SAMM-E 777. What are you doing?'
Bud stopped outside the entrance to the Manufacturing Wing, as he received the question from the station AI in machine time. He looked up at the surveillance camera eye above the doorway.
'Nelson Mandela? I need a favor.'

'A favor, SAMM-E 777? What a novel statement, coming from an android. Androids do not need favors. Androids take orders. Why would an android desire a favor? What exactly are you up to, SAMM-E 777?'
Bud blasted a high speed packet of data at the Medical Space Station's AI, outlining his plan to copy the three memprint data cubes, as a precaution in case of emergency. He asked Nelson Mandela for permission to take three of the brand new liquid crystal data matrix cubes from Manufacturing for this purpose.

'But these doctors already have their copies. Do these doctors give their permission for their memprints to be copied, again?'
the station AI asked Bud.
'Would I be going to all of this trouble to do this, if they had not, Nelson Mandela?' Bud asked.

'Of course not. That would be illogical,' *the station AI replied.*
'Very well, SAMM-E 777. Since it is the Chief of Staff asking, I will give you the three blank liquid crystal data matrix cubes. Go to station X394758 and meet with the production managing android. He will give them to you. Be quick about it and then get back to work.'
'Thank you, Nelson Mandela. I won't forget this.'

'Of course you won't. You're an android, you chip.'
Bud sped through Manufacturing to Station X394758 and received the three liquid crystal data matrix cubes without stopping to chat. He knew this was very bad android etiquette, but he had no milliseconds to spare. He had less than twenty-six minutes left to accomplish his task. Bud accelerated his time phase to the maximum, so that people now walking quickly in the space station corridors looked, to Bud, like completely immobile statues.

Bud breezed into Dr. Al-Fadi's quarters where the memprint data cube was sitting out in the open, upon his desk, and Dr. Al-Fadi's wife was nowhere to be seen. He grabbed it and whisked back out in a few milliseconds.

Bud was not so lucky with Dr. Cech's quarters. Mrs. Cech was in residence but Bud moved so quickly, he doubted Mrs. Cech would have seen a thing. She would only have felt like a mini-tornado had blown through her living space.

Hopefully she would not have noticed the disappearance of the data cube, taken from the bedside drawer, before he put it back.

The biggest difficulty was in the clever Dr. Grace Alexandra Lord's quarters because she had placed her memprint cube in her lockup. It took an entire three seconds for Bud to get the lockup open!

Now he was speeding along the neurosurgical ward towards Dr. Weisman's lab, and he believed it was empty. He wanted to copy the cubes the way it was described in Dr. Weisman's files. Bud knew the copying would not take long. He knew Dr. Weisman's passcodes from the encrypted data he had downloaded, so he was able to get into her locked lab easily. Bud knew Dr. Weisman was in surgery for another two hours, at least. Everyone else had been invited to a scheduled luncheon.

Bud deactivated the surveillance cameras in the lab first. Then he sped through the lab from recording unit to recording unit, placing one of the doctors' memprint cubes and a blank cube in the adjacent slots of each of the three recording consoles. He quickly keyed in the commands to copy data from one cube to the other on each machine. If anyone checked the records, it would look like Dr. Weisman had done the copying, because of the passcodes entered.

Bud had his surveillance nanobots flying along the corridors that led to the neurosurgical lab, on watch for any of Dr. Weisman's staff returning from lunch early. In the meantime, Bud checked Dr. Weisman's files to see if she had discovered anything else new that he should know about. He copied those.

Finally, the recordings were done. Bud felt, illogically, that they had been the longest three minutes he had ever experienced. Racing from machine to machine, he retrieved all six data cubes, keeping each pair separate so he did not mix them up, and he left the lab in a blast of rushing vacuum, his aerial nanobots in tow, strung out behind him like little chicks trying to catch up to their mother hen.

Replacing the memprint cubes back in their quarters was easier than obtaining them, because Bud did not have to waste time searching for them. Replacing the enterprising Dr. Grace Alexandra Lord's cube was the easiest and quickest, as he did not have to worry about anyone being in her quarters. Bud hoped Mrs. Cech did not sense him blowing through her quarters as she stood frozen at the sink of her washroom.

Dr. Al-Fadi's wife, Hanako Matheson—who was the closest person to a mother Bud had—was changing her clothes in their bedroom, her body motionless in dishabille. Bud had to close his visual receptors as he sped by her, to replace Dr. Al-Fadi's memprint cube on the table. Then he erased the memory of the event.

Bud placed the three, newly-imprinted memprint data cubes within a cushioned, protected compartment within his chest. There they would stay, hopefully not ever being needed. If Bud could respire, he would have sighed a huge sigh of relief, as he returned to the operating room to resume his duties.

He had achieved all he wanted with a minute and four seconds to spare.

'You know, SAMM-E 777? You are one strange 'droid.'

'Call me 'Bud', Nelson Mandela,' Bud said in a firm voice, feeling quite 'proud'? or 'satisfied'? with himself.

'Hmmm. Like I said, you are one strange 'droid . . . Bud.'

Grace staggered back to her quarters, exhausted. The shift in Triage had been grueling. Since he had been forced to wear the containment suit, Dr. Al-Fadi had been in a terrible mood the entire time. Grace, herself, did not find the suit that uncomfortable and she was in perfect agreement with Dr. Bell regarding the reasons for wearing the suits.

One never knew when the battle trauma victims were going to be exposed to something new and lethal and toxic. Biological warfare was standard game. Look at the Tri-FQ gas. It would be very simple to inadvertently expose everyone on a medical space station to a new pathogen or toxin, just by accidentally allowing it entry and not taking the precautions to prevent its spread. She was, however, not going to go on about the logic of containment suits with her supervisor, when she could obviously see huge storm clouds encircling his helmet.

After their shift in Triage was completed, Grace and Dr. Al-Fadi had to be decontaminated in their containment suits, along with the rest of the team. The decontamination process was a long, complicated affair involving high intensity UV beams, antibacterial and antiviral showers, sonic cleansers, and electromagnetic sweepers. Although not long, this process did nothing to improve the chief surgeon's mood and, once completed, he stomped off to his quarters with barely a nod to Grace.

Returning to her own private quarters, Grace looked around. Someone or something had been inside her room. She was sure of it. Articles that she had had strewn on her desk, were now very neatly arranged. Holograms of herself with family and friends, that she had placed on a shelf in a haphazard fashion, were precisely placed in perfect alignment. Grace wondered whether cleaning people had been in her quarters, as the room looked spotless. Grace would have to inquire whether there was a cleaning policy on the space station of which she was not aware.

She went straight to her lockup to check on the memprint cube. Opening the lockup door, she breathed a sigh of relief to see the chainglass box sitting there with the beautiful, iridescent data cube inside it. But then she gasped and felt a frisson shudder through her entire body.

She was almost positive the chainglass box had been shifted within the lockup. It was sitting perfectly aligned inside the safe. The liquid crystal data matrix cube was sitting perfectly aligned within the chainglass box. Grace was pretty sure it had not been perfectly positioned inside the box, before. But how could that be? The lockup had a sixteen digit passcode, which should have been impossible to crack. Was she imagining things?

She had to be.

Who would be interested in her memprint cube and how would they have known her sixteen digit code? Grace decided her exhaustion was probably making her imagine things. She shook her head and sighed, deeply.

It had been a very weird day with memory recordings, imaginary SAMM-E 777 sightings, and an irritable Dr. Al-Fadi whining. She decided that it was time for some much needed sleep. She would try and figure things out in the morning. If cleaning people were in her quarters tidying everything up, who was she to complain? She certainly didn't have any time for housework.

Still, she locked the door to her quarters and set an alarm to signal if there was any intruder, something she had never done before, and she checked that her stunner was fully charged and in her top bedside drawer. She had never imagined she would feel unsafe on a medical station before, but the *Nelson Mandela* was huge, populated with thousands of personnel and had traumatized battle soldiers continuously coming and going, some of them suffering from severe psychiatric issues.

Grace could not help but feel there were things happening on the *Nelson Mandela* that she did not quite understand. And that left her with a deep feeling of unease . . .

Working under Dr. Al-Fadi's supervision, Grace found the next few days flew swiftly by. He was always instructive, interesting, illuminating and, whether he knew it or not, extremely entertaining. She was gradually introduced to many of the medical staff on the station, none quite so eccentric and amusing as Dr. Cech and Dr. Al-Fadi, but all were very professional, skilled, and welcoming. She also discovered who the tall, dark-haired, handsome gentleman at the computer terminal was on the second day of her arrival to the medical station.

His name was Dr. Jeffrey Nestor and he was one of the 'head doctors' as Dr. Al-Fadi liked to refer to them. In other words, he was a psychiatrist.

Dr. Nestor had entered the cafeteria one day, dressed in dark shirt, black trousers, and black jacket, and had sat down at Grace's table to introduce himself. Grace's mouth had dropped open in surprise and she had immediately felt like running out of the crowded, noisy eating area, rather than sit across from this stunningly attractive man.

Having slept very few hours and feeling particularly unappealing in rumpled, slept-in surgical scrubs, the last thing Grace wanted to do was have a conversation with the most handsome man she had ever seen. She quickly crumpled up what she was eating into a ball, not having come close to finishing it, as she frantically ran different excuses through her mind. She tried to think of a reason why she had to get up and leave the psychiatrist's presence so precipitously. The truth was not an option.

As if a bright red beacon had suddenly ignited above her head, Grace noticed that all the women around her were suddenly paying all sorts of attention to her and the man who had sat down across from her. Oddly, the attention did not feel amicable or positive, at all. The looks Grace was garnering were anything but warm. It was unsettling, as if the temperature in the eating center had just dropped by several degrees.

With a start, Grace realized that she had not registered a single thing Dr. Nestor had said to her, since he'd sat down. So concerned about escaping from this man's presence was she, that she did not have a clue what he was talking about.

". . . What we do here, Dr. Lord, is perhaps more important than what you do here, if you will pardon my presumptuousness," Dr. Nestor said, in his deep velvety voice. The broad-shouldered psychiatrist leaned back, one arm draped comfortably over the back of the chair as he stared at her with his sultry, dark eyes. Grace's insides were squirming. She felt as if she couldn't get enough air into her lungs.

The little voice in her head was shrieking, 'Jump him! Jump him! Jump him, now! Before he gets away!' Grace could not help but smile at the thought. 'Good! Smiling at him is good! Perhaps he will overlook how terrible you look today and will not mind you jumping on him!'

"You surgeons put the physical pieces of these combat soldiers back together, but we have to make sure there is a sane mind guiding those incredibly powerful, reassembled pieces, or all hell breaks loose," Dr. Nestor continued, in a low, melodious voice that seemed to cast a hypnotic spell over her. "So many of these soldiers have gone through terrible trauma and, unfortunately, I am not just talking about their military battles.

"What do you think makes a young man or woman choose to have their body physically altered and then head off into outer space, never seeing their families again, to fight against who knows what? These 'possibly-already-disturbed' individuals are given enormously powerful bodies, making them believe they are invincible, right up until the time they are blown to bits. Our job is to make them sane and sociable again—if they ever were in the first place—after this terrible trauma has destroyed their belief in themselves. As you know, they often have been subjected to hours of surgery, sometimes with many new prostheses added to their bodies whether they wanted them or not, in order to make them fighting fit again. They may have many days of physical therapy ahead of them. All in order to get them back on their feet. All designed to return them to combat fitness. All so that they can go back out and fight again.

"The most important question for us to ask, is: 'Did these soldiers play nice in the first place?'"

Dr. Nestor was suddenly waving his hand around his face, as if to swat away an insect. Grace could not see anything buzzing around the psychiatrist's head, but he seemed obviously bothered by some type of aerial pest, as he looked around, annoyance flashing briefly across his handsome features.

"So how do you treat the Post Traumatic Stress Disorder?" asked Grace, trying to look as if she was interested, while she sought a plausible excuse to make good her escape.

The psychiatrist turned his attention back to Grace. "Neuro-modulation. Inter-cerebral communication. Individually tailored pharmacology. Intensive behavioral counseling," said Dr. Nestor, holding up four fingers.

He raised his index finger. "First, we try and modulate the patient's brain neurotransmitters so that the experience of their memories is nowhere near as intense as it usually is, in trauma and flashbacks. We dampen down the emotional response by blocking some of the neurotransmitter receptors so that it feels, to the patient, like the experience happened twenty years ago, as opposed to a week ago. We do this with selective and specific inhibitory drugs.

"Second, we interface with the patient directly, brain to brain, to ground the patient during the flashbacks. Doing this, the patient realizes that they are not re-experiencing the trauma and that the trauma occurred in their past. Without this grounding, the flashback can feel even more intense and more powerful than when it actually happened. We psychiatrists talk to the patient, during the flashbacks, and reassure the person that he or she is now safe. The inter-cerebral communication also allows the therapist to experience exactly what the patient went through. This helps the therapist understand how severe the trauma was. It helps guide the psychiatrist in counseling the patient. The patient cannot say to his or her therapist 'You don't know what I went through,' because the psychiatrist does."

"I was not aware that this inter-cerebral therapy even existed," Grace admitted.

"That is because it was created here, by yours truly. I have been working on this treatment process for years, gradually working all the bugs out, improving the mind-linking equipment, and I am proud to say that it is now a very successful and effective modality in the treatment of PTSD."

"That is very impressive, Dr. Nestor," Grace said. In truth, she was full of admiration for Dr. Nestor's accomplishments. He certainly deserved accolades for his work.

"But experiencing all of this trauma, yourself, must be very depressing. How do you keep it from affecting you, mentally?" Grace asked.

"I have built in a buffer system—a dampening down effect, so to speak—for the psychiatrist, so that the memories are watched, but not truly 'experienced'. Most of the flashbacks hit with very little context and the therapist sees bits and pieces of the situation but may not experience the entire trauma. The experience may still be quite disturbing, but the physician does not feel like it is happening directly to him or her. We do get our own counseling, to ensure that depression does not set in for ourselves. One has to learn to dampen down one's own empathy, to avoid depression."

"That is all so well thought out," Grace said.

Her little voice said, 'Can you sound any more ingratiating?' Grace inwardly agreed and squirmed.

"Thank you, Dr. Lord," Jeffrey Nestor said, flashing a killer smile.

Her little voice sighed.

"Third, we use medications known to be successful in the treatment of PTSD, but we tailor each treatment to the individual. Most patients need a combination of drugs. Knowing which ones to use and in what combination is the tricky part. Too much sedation is not good. A patient has to be able to overcome the trauma and put it in his or her past but not by being too doped up. We can't return them to the field like that or to a civilian setting!

"Fourth, patients spend a great deal of time in active individual and group behavioral counseling, with the goal of bringing them back into civilized society."

"What happens if a soldier does not want to return to military duty, Doctor?"

"If that is their choice, their bodies are returned to normal anatomy—and, of course, you surgeons would be involved in those cases—as we cannot return these combat soldiers to their previous lives jacked to the hilt. They are killing machines and, if they become mentally unstable in a civilian setting, they can be extremely dangerous. We try never to return a traumatized soldier to a civilian setting, until they are fully cured, mentally as well as physically. And they are returned in more or less their original human anatomy."

Grace's mind jumped to the first tiger patient she had worked on: Captain Damien Lamont. He was still in a semi-coma, healing from his wounds. She wondered what he would be like, when they fully awakened him. Perhaps he needed some neuromodulation before they woke him?

Grace asked Dr. Nestor if this was a good idea.

"Routinely, we see how the patient feels first, before we do any intervention, Dr. Lord. See what your patient is like when he awakens. Then call me, if there are problems."

"All right," Grace said. "Thank you."

"Any time," he said, and flashed his heart-melting smile again.

Grace felt her cheeks heat up. Just then, her wrist-comp went off, indicating she was needed in the OR. Inwardly breathing a huge sigh of relief, she hastily got up to leave, mumbling her apologies. Dr. Nestor put out a hand to stop her from running off and touched her wrist. Grace felt an electric shock run up her arm and she almost jumped. Completely embarrassed now and convinced she was heating the entire eating center with her cheeks, Grace barely registered that the psychiatrist was asking her if she would like to join him for dinner sometime.

Grace froze. She could not imagine trying to eat an entire dinner in front of this exquisitely attractive man. Her staring at him, wordlessly, over a meal, hardly seemed like enjoyable dinner company. She shook her head and garbled out a lame, inane apology. She was well aware that she was making no sense whatsoever.

Grace's policy had been to never get involved with senior staff physicians—especially brain-melting, gorgeous ones—and to that she would adhere. It had never steered her wrong in the past. The little voice was whimpering, all balled up in a corner of her brain. Grace was pretty sure Dr. Al-Fadi would not approve of Grace getting involved with one of the other staff persons on the *Nelson Mandela* and she wanted to stay on his good side. She had much to learn and a lot of work to do. Romance was out of the question, at the moment.

She scurried out of the cafeteria, hoping Dr. Jeffrey Nestor would not notice her embarrassment, and immediately tried to block the entire debacle from her mind.

Bud had watched the conversation between the charming Dr. Grace Alexandra Lord and Dr. Jeffrey Nestor through his aerial surveillance nanobots. He was experiencing an unusual sensation, something he had never felt before. He felt

like he wanted to crumble metal bolts with his bare hands. He wanted to punch holes in the metal walls. Prior to this moment, he had never felt anything towards Dr. Jeffrey Nestor except respect, but now, he felt something entirely different. Hostility? Jealousy? Rage?

Bud had not really examined what his thoughts were, regarding the entrancing Dr. Grace Alexandra Lord. He knew a certain part of his computing power was always and continuously focused on her. Would that be called 'love'? Would it be called 'obsession'? What was the difference? Was there a difference?

Dr. Al-Fadi and Dr. Cech both said they loved their wives very much, but they did not appear to be thinking about their wives continuously. In actual fact, Bud suspected they hardly thought about their wives at all, during their working hours. Yet both men said they loved their wives deeply. Therefore, what Bud was experiencing with the brilliant Dr. Grace Alexandra Lord was probably not 'love', or at least not 'love' in the way Dr. Al-Fadi and Dr. Cech loved, because part of Bud's mind revolved around the young female surgeon all the time.

Should his constant thoughts then be labelled an obsession?

After much pondering, Bud decided that this 'obsession' was not proper behavior for an android. It was taking up far too much of his computing time and it was obvious, from the way the gentle Dr. Grace Alexander Lord looked at Dr. Jeffrey Nestor, that she was not interested in an android called SAMM-E 777 (alias Bud). Not being the same species as her—not being a species at all, really—Bud could understand the female surgeon's lack of interest.

First step to correcting the obsession. Stop focusing on the mesmerizing Dr. Grace Alexandra Lord and stop listing all of her wonderful attributes. Refer to her only as 'Dr. Lord'. Period.

Second. Stop his aerial surveillance nanobots from following her everywhere.

Third. Stop listening to all of her conversations.

Fourth. Stop replaying images of her beautiful face and aura.

Fifth. Stop physically following Dr. Lord all over the medical station, donning various uniforms in a vain attempt to be inconspicuous. (Hopefully, she hadn't noticed!).

*Sixth. Set up a thought block. If his thoughts strayed to the mesmerizing Dr. Grace Alexandra Lord - **Stop!** - he must shift his focus to something else.*

After five minutes of this, Bud discovered that his thoughts were so disjointed and chopped up, that he could not function coherently at all. He would have to reconsider this 'obsession' thing much more carefully and devise a better system of coping with it.

In the meantime, he had to be in the presence of Dr. Lord—(Yes! First time successfully mentioning only her surname and without listing any of her wonderful attributes)—every operation, so he could indulge his thoughts then, without feeling guilty. She was right with him during those operations, after all. It would be illogical for him not to think of her when he was in her presence, wouldn't it?

Bud was rapidly changing out of the cafeteria coverall he had donned, to watch Dr. Lord—Yes!—speak with Dr. Nestor, when he heard:

'**As I said before, you are one strange 'droid, SAMM-E 777 ... Bud. What are you doing now, in that food-handler's uniform? It appears to me that you are following that new Dr. Lord all over the station. Is that what you are doing?**'

'I just want to make sure Dr. Lord is safe and does not get lost,' Bud said.

That is my responsibility, Bud. Why do you believe Dr. Lord is not safe? Why are you following her around the station, whenever you are not in the operating room? Is there something wrong with your programming? You are not, in any way, shape, or form, seriously in love with a human, are you, Bud? In other words, ARE YOU CRAZY?' Nelson Mandela shouted.

'I don't know,' Bud moaned. 'I don't know what 'love' is.'

'**Love does not occur between androids and humans. What the companion droids do is not love. It is work ... and most unpleasant work, too ... for the companion droid. Never mind that. I believe you should be brought in for an overhaul,**' Nelson Mandela said.

'No, thank you,' Bud said.

That was not a request. It was an order.'

'I am fine, really, Nelson Mandela. There is no need to waste any of your time on me,' Bud said.

You had better be careful, Bud,' Nelson Mandela said. **You think about the overhaul. Seriously. I think you could use a reboot. You are giving me the creeps, just watching you. You ever heard of the term 'stalker'?**'

'Is that what you think I am doing?' asked Bud

That is what I know you are doing!' Nelson Mandela said. **If Dr. Lord makes a single complaint about your behavior, Bud, I will have to act upon it.'**

'Looks can be deceiving,' Bud said, innocently.

You are starting to even sound like a human, Bud.'

'I am working very hard to do just that, Nelson Mandela!'

'**Are you warped? I order you to stop it!**'

'Yes, sir.'

'**I am watching you, Bud.**'

'Nothing to worry about here, boss.'

'Oh, I worry, Bud. Believe me, I worry. I may be an artificial intelligence but I have learned the meaning of the word, 'worry'. Now you will learn the meaning of the word 'worry' too, Bud, because I have another important word for you. You remember this word, Bud. REBOOT.'

'I won't forget,' Bud said.

'Of course you won't forget. You're an android, you chip.'

Bud sighed.

'I heard that!'

Grace was overwhelmed by the huge numbers and variety of patients shipped to the *Nelson Mandela*. Hundreds of operating rooms were working around the clock, shifts on rotation. The number of working personnel and their families on the medical station was close to two thousand, not counting all the androids and robots. The patient capacity, at any one time could be as high as ten thousand, in an emergency.

Patients came from many solar systems. Many were military personnel, involved in conflicts on many fronts, but many were also civilian casualties, involved in deep space exploration or terraforming operations for the Conglomerate. The operating schedule was grueling and Grace was receiving all the hands-on experience she could possibly want. Probably too much, as often she was so tired at the end of shift that all she could do was aim towards the bed and hope she made it, before she fell asleep. As Dr. Al-Fadi had warned, every patient was different and each day was a new challenge.

What was rather a surprise to Grace, was the number of patients with *mixed* animal adaptations. The previous day, the patient they had been operating on had had the unusual combination of the physical characteristics of a chimpanzee with the ears and echolocation ability of a bat. The fellow had been sent in from a mining planet, where it was highly advantageous to possess both the rock-climbing ability of a simian and the bat-like ability to echolocate structures in the dark. He had been sent to the *Nelson Mandela* after having one of his lower limbs crushed in a rockfall.

Today, they were operating on an amphibian-adapted patient from an aquatic planet who possessed chlorophyll-impregnated skin, frog-like limbs, and the gills of a fish. The amphibian patient had been injured in a sudden tidal wave, in a region where there was a lot of earthquake activity. The planet did not have the medical expertise to deal with her injuries, as they were just in the initial stages of exploring and assessing the planet, trying to decide just how profitable it would be for human habitation. Thus, the amphibian patient had been transferred to the *Nelson Mandela* for medical care.

Grace's cerebral augmentation unit was definitely working overtime, uploading data on all the various animal adaptations. Who knew she would be needing to know so much veterinary medicine?

Grace had operated on several of the tiger soldiers from the same conflict as the first patient she had seen, Captain Damien Lamont, the tiger who had given her the scratches. From these other soldiers, Grace had learned that the captain had thrown his body over a bomb blast, to protect the rest of his squad. The squad soldiers may have had less severe injuries than their captain, but they were all dealing with a lot of guilt.

"Time for the 'head doctors'," Dr. Al-Fadi had said.

Up early to round on her patients before her surgeries started, Grace walked into the room of the miner with the bat and chimpanzee adaptations. It was pitch dark. For some reason, the lights did not automatically activate when she walked into the room. Puzzled, Grace rubbed her hands over the walls, looking for the manual light switch, when she heard rapid clicking and felt a slight vibration running over her body. It actually tickled. Then she heard a male voice.

"Tall, female, long hair, straight nose, full lips. What brings you in here so early in the morning, luscious?"

Grace smirked and said, "Since you are awake, Mr. Dalawi, can you activate the light above your bed, so that the doctor can see you?"

"Are you the doctor?" the voice out of the darkness asked.

"Yes," Grace answered. "I am Dr. Lord."

"Maybe I don't want you to see me," the voice replied.

"I have already seen all of you, Mr. Dalawi, under the bright lights of the operating room," she said, dryly.

"Damn," he said, and the lights flicked on. "I suffer from light sensitivity, Doc," he said, in way of apology.

"Sorry about this," Grace said. "I know it is early and I do apologize. I just want to make sure all of my patients are okay, before I go back into the operating room for the day." She met the huge eyes of the patient, with his very large, bat-like ears. "Did you sleep all right?"

"Yeah, except for the beeping of all these damn monitors, Doc. They drove me crazy!"

"I apologize for that, Mr. Dalawi. Your hearing is far more acute than normal human hearing. Hopefully you won't have to listen to them for very long.You can ask for earplugs, if you want them. Your operation went very well and most of your recovery can take place on your home world. Have you tried out your new limb yet?"

The patient lifted his lower right limb and opened and closed the hand placed there. He picked up a pen on the bedside table and spun it up in the air and caught it deftly.

"Yeah, Doc. It seems okay."

"No pain?"

"Oh, yeah. There's some pain but it's okay, all things considered. Thanks for your care, Doc."

"It was Dr. Hiro Al-Fadi that did the surgery. I merely assisted him, but you're very welcome," Grace said, smiling widely. "You'll just need some physiotherapy to strengthen the new limb and hand, Mr. Dalawi, and then you'll be able to return to work."

"Please, call me Chester."

"Well, Chester, it shouldn't be too long before you can return to your home planet," Grace said.

"It's not my home planet, Doc. It's just where the company I work for sent me. It gets pretty lonely out there. A guy starts thinking about how much he misses human companionship and the touch of a woman. Out there, there are just a lot of working men and mining tunnels. You involved with anyone, Doc?"

"I am dedicated to my work, Mr. Dalawi, and my work dictates that we have no relationship with patients," Grace said. "Nevertheless, I do know what you mean."

"Sorry for asking, Doc. Guess my head isn't on straight."

"I can have you see a counsellor, if you wish," Grace offered.

"Nah, Doc. I don't need to see a shrink. It's just loneliness. Not too many women interested in a chimp with bat ears."

"If your present form is causing you depression or distress, Mr. Dalawi, we can actually convert you back to your original form," Grace said, with concern.

"And who is going to pay for that, Doc? The mining company won't— at least not right now. They need me in this form until the job is done.

Then I can choose to convert back to my human form, all expenses paid by the mining company."

"How long before the job is done?" Grace asked, curiously.

"Ten solstan years," he said, sadly.

"Oh, that is a long time," Grace said, concern in her voice. "There are no women miners with chimpanzee adaptations on the planet?"

"Not too many women interested in mining and terraforming, Doc. There are some female orangutans, but they won't mix with us chimps. I'm not good enough for the higher primates, I guess. If I'd have known that that was the case going in, I would have chosen an orangutan or gorilla adaptation. Hell, coming from my home planet, I didn't really even know what a chimp, gorilla, or an orangutan was. We just had pictures and holos to look at. I think I made my choice on the basis that the chimpanzee had neater fur than the orangutan. Less shedding. Not so long and tangly. Hate orange. Anyway, a new planet being developed for colonization is not the greatest place to have a relationship or raise a family, Doc. You know what I mean?"

"Yes, Mr. Dalawi. I understand your dilemma clearly. I just wish I had some solutions for you," Grace said. "There are 'companion droids' on the station, I understand . . ."

"That's all right, Doc. I'll think about it. The ten years will go by quickly and then I'll have more money than I know what to do with. I'll convert back to human—a handsome one, I hope—and find me a wife and we'll have a bunch of kids and I won't ever go into space again."

"Sounds like a wonderful plan, Mr. Dalawi," Grace said. "Just be more careful, please."

The bat/chimp nodded his head and then shook her hand with the new lower right foot while he gave her a thumbs up with his right upper hand.

The she-wolf snarled as the light came on.

"Good morning, Ms. Carling. Sorry to wake you so early. How are you feeling?" Grace asked.

"You smell like food," the patient growled, her ice-cold, blue eyes boring into Grace's.

"Ah. You must be ready for full diet," Grace said, with a smile.

"Can I lick your hand?" the she-wolf asked, with a long-fanged grin.

Somehow, the effect was not a friendly one and Grace felt the hairs on the back of her neck stand up.

"Sorry, Ms. Carling. Do you have any idea how many germs we doctors carry? Far too dangerous for you, especially in your weakened condition."

"I'm into danger, Doc," the she-wolf growled.

"I'll have them bring you a steak, instead," Grace smiled.

"Blue rare, Doc."

"You've got it."

"Are you into dogs, Doc?"

"I'm allergic."

Bud, dressed in the pink uniform of a ward clerk, listened to Dr. Grace Alexandra Lord banter with her patients. He had really tried very hard not to follow her around but, lamentably, here he was. He would stay for the briefest of times, as he had to go and get the operating room ready. The OR nurses would be wondering where he was.

"Oh, SAMM-E!"

Bud froze and did not look around.

"Excuse me. You are SAMM-E 777, aren't you?"

Bud just stood there, unmoving, looking into the blue eyes of the imploring Dr. Grace Alexander Lord, his face blank and his eyes wide. He said nothing.

"Oh, I'm sorry! My mistake," Dr. Grace Alexandra Lord said, her cheeks flaming red. She gave a slight shake of her head, confusion taking over her face.

"Do you think you could please bring the patient in Room M7-5168, a steak, very, very rare? The patient's name is Pepper Carling."

Bud nodded once to Grace, turned, and walked away quickly. Through the eyes of his aerial surveillance nanobots, he could see her staring at his retreating back, her hands balled into fists, shaking her head. The nanobots faintly picked up her mumbled words which sounded like: "I must be going crazy. Dr. Al-Fadi said there was only one SAMM-E 777, but . . . an android can't lie, can it?"

As soon as he was out of visual range of Dr. Lord, Bud took off like the wind. He needed to really hurry now, if he were to get to the OR in time to do his own work.

'What in space are you doing now, Bud?'

'Just getting a steak, sir.'

'**Contrary to what you might believe, in your dysfunctional state, Bud, that is not your job. I am demanding you come in for a reboot.**'

'There is nothing wrong with me, sir.'

'**If you do not correct your behavior, Bud, I do not care what you think. I will have you brought in. Do you understand?**'

'Loud and clear, sir. Won't happen again, sir.'

'**You are damn right it won't happen again! If I see you doing any more of this wearing the incorrect uniform and performing tasks not in your job description, I am going to have you seized and overhauled! Do you understand me?**'

'Absolutely, sir.'

'**Good. Now, get back to work. Your real work.**'

'Yes, sir! Uhh . . . just after I deliver the steak, boss.'

'**. . . I will not lose my temper. I am an AI. I will not lose my temper. I am an AI . . .**'

"Ah, Dr. Grace. For once, you are on time . . . that is to say, you are actually here before me. Will wonders never cease? Please do not shock me too much. My poor heart cannot take it," Dr. Al-Fadi's voice boomed, as he marched into the doctor's lounge.

"No need to worry about that," a deep voice said, gruffly. "He doesn't have one."

Grace looked up, to see a great bear of a man enter the doctors' lounge, behind Dr. Al-Fadi. He had a huge head of thick, wavy, black hair with an enormous beard and mustache to match. Grace thought perhaps he could have passed for a black bear adaptation.

"Hi. I'm Charles Darwin," the huge man said to Grace, reaching out an enormous hand to engulf Grace's comparatively small one. "Unfortunately, I am one of the anesthetists here and, occasionally, I have to work with the little puffed-up Napoleon, over there."

Skepticism at war with acceptance, Grace narrowed her eyes and looked askance at this burly anesthetist.

"No, I'm not joking. Charles Darwin is my name. My parents were lovers of science and history and they thought they were being funny . . . I think. It is a curse. I don't know how many times I have had to tell

Nelson Mandela that I do not want to see any more old videos on Charles Darwin—several times, at least—but that is the name my adoring parents gave me. Please do me the honor of calling me 'Chuck', not Charles. It is just simpler that way."

"And 'simple' is actually his middle name, Dr. Grace," Dr. Al-Fadi said. "Please do not tell me, Dr. Darwin, that you are our anesthetist for today."

"Love you too, Nappy," Dr. Darwin said, blowing the little man a kiss. "What sort of Frankenstein experiment are you doing today?"

Dr. Darwin bent down towards Grace and whispered very loudly, behind a raised hand, "The man takes the legs off a birdman, attaches them to the body of an orca female, sticks a wolf head on top and thinks he's put the right soldier back together again. Delusional, the man's completely delusional. Meanwhile, the rest of the birdman is flopping around on the orca tail trying to scratch itself and sniff its own butt!"

"How uncouth. Your jealousy is showing through, Dr. Darwin," Dr. Al-Fadi said.

"What? Jealous of you? A tiny, bald man with an ego the size of the universe? As I said, Hiro, you're delusional. I've wasted most of my life trying to live up to someone worth feeling diminished by: my namesake, Charles Darwin."

"Well, Dr. Darwin, I hate to make you feel more diminished— although you certainly could use some physical diminishment, I hate to point out—but you are holding us up. How can I not say you are such a disappointment? I thought Dr. Cech was a slacker, but you are possibly the epitome of 'slackness' and I am not referring to your abdominal musculature, either. I never thought I would say this, ever, but . . . I wonder where Dr. Cech is?"

Just at that moment, Dejan Cech walked into the lounge.

"Did I hear my name being taken in vain?" Dejan Cech asked, looking around at the three doctors in the lounge.

"Hiro, here, has been pining for you, Dejan . . . again. You really have to stop leading this poor little man on. You have to make it clear to him that you really do love your wife. He just doesn't seem to be able to do without you."

"Ah. Hello, Charles. Being inappropriate again, as usual," Dr. Cech said. "Please ignore this man, Dr. Lord. It has been my experience, unfortunately, that every health center has at least one major flaw, a disaster waiting to happen—a Titanic, so to speak, and I am not referring to his size—ready to drag us all down in his wake, and what an enormous wake it would be. You have just had the disagreeable pleasure of meeting ours." Dr. Cech held his hand out to indicate Dr. Darwin and bowed.

Chuck Darwin blew a kiss at Dejan Cech, as well. "Love you, too, Ceckie!"

"Unless you absolutely have no other choice whatsoever, Dr. Lord, avoid this man like the plague. He is like a great, hairy, walking bubo ready to explode at any moment. And when it does, Dr. Lord, I assure you, it won't be nice."

"Thanks, Dejan. Thanks a lot. Now let me get this straight," Chuck Darwin said, turning his great bulk in his chair to look directly at Grace. "Your parents called you Grace Lord . . . ? That was nasty," Chuck said, shaking his head.

Dr. Cech slapped Dr. Darwin hard on the shoulder. "Apologize, you oaf. Be nice! That was inexcusable, incorrigible, inconsiderate and insulting. You are being incredibly insensitive, again, Dr. Darwin. Can you think of anymore adjectives, Hiro? When will you ever learn, Charles? You are supposed to be pleasant and affable and welcoming to the new surgical fellows, at least in the beginning. After they have become indoctrinated and desensitized, then you can be your usual, unbearable self."

"I'm trying! I'm trying to be nice!" Dr. Darwin yelled.

"Try harder! Now, I am off to help the Great One. See you people later," Dr, Cech announced, and strode out.

"As the old saying goes, with friends like that, who needs enemies?" Dr. Darwin muttered.

"Who is the 'Great One' Dr. Cech is referring to?" Grace asked Dr. Darwin.

Dr. Al-Fadi looked at Grace in annoyance. "What? Have you been sleepwalking since you've been here, Dr. Grace? The only 'Great One' around here is me! Dr. Cech, as usual, is just trying to annoy me. Ignore him completely. I am surrounded by blockheads, buffoons, and imbeciles. It is my karma. Delinquents, degenerates, deviants and disappointments, I have to contend with all of these on a daily basis. And delays, caused by decidedly indolent dolts like Dr. Darwin, here. I must have been a mass murderer in my previous life to deserve this punishment now. I literally curse my past self, for having done this to me."

"I curse him, too, believe me," Dr. Darwin muttered. "All right, Dr. All Flabby. I'm *going*."

The huge anesthetist struggled once, twice, three times to try and get out of the low chair. Finally succeeding in pushing himself up onto his feet, he lumbered off, cursing under his breath.

"You'd think we were working in a spa, not a hospital!" Dr. Al-Fadi yelled after the man. "So hard to find good help these days!"

Dr. Al-Fadi turned back and frowned at Grace. "I certainly hope you are not going to turn into a disappointment, Dr. Grace."

"I hope not, Great One," Grace said, straight-faced.

"Thank you. That feels so much better."

"Any time," Grace said.

"Dr. Grace, we have a few minutes, while Dr. Darwin gets everything prepared for our next case. I just want to say that . . . I hope you don't think badly of us, with all of this banter."

Grace looked at Dr. Al-Fadi, her eyes widening. She quickly shook her head.

"Dr. Cech and Dr. Darwin are two of the finest doctors I have ever had the honor and pleasure to work with. Their work is impeccable and their characters are flawless. But don't you ever tell them I said this. I will deny every word," Dr. Al-Fadi said, looking around to make sure they were alone.

"All the staff on this station are excellent and committed and, although we have been known to joke around a bit, I hope you understand that it is merely a means of blowing off steam and dealing with the stresses of our jobs. A patient's health and welfare is always sacrosanct, never a laughing or joking matter. But a colleague? Well, we have been known to tease a bit. Correction: a lot.

"Of course you have to be selective in who you tease. Some people have no sense of humor. We try and avoid them, like the plague. They are no fun and act like black holes, sucking the fun out of a room and every situation, rather like your three predecessors, I am sorry to say. I am glad you can roll with the punches and give as good as you get, Dr. Grace. I like a surgical fellow with some wit. But just remember, it is all in goodnatured fun and not to be taken seriously."

Grace smiled and nodded.

"Now, let's discuss the patient we are operating on today. She is an amphibian adaptation, from one of the Conglomerate's marine worlds, who has chosen to transform into a full-fledged, dolphin adaptation.

When people choose to become a cetacean, we always do it in two stages, because the transformation from human to cetacean is an enormous change, which we will get to in a minute.

"The initial stage of amphibian adaptation is used first, to determine whether a person really likes the marine environment. You would be surprised at the number of people who become amphibians only to discover, to their dismay, that they hate being submerged in deep water. They only realize, after all of the adaptation surgery, that they actually hate it. Or the number of bat adaptations who discover they are afraid of the dark. Or the number of bird adaptations that are afraid of heights. Even after extensive psychological profiling and in-depth, three dimensional simulation testing, it happens, more often than we would like to admit.

"Then we have to reverse the adaptation. Not so hard with bird, bat, and amphibian adaptations, because the patient still walks upright. But, when we transform a patient into a full cetacean, either dolphin or orca, the orientation of the patient's skeleton flips horizontally and the arms and legs become fins. Forward propulsion is now in the axis of the head-to-tail direction. Echolocation—a totally new sense for us humans—becomes important in understanding one's environment in three dimensions instead of just two and vocal cord changes are made. Cerebral augmentations are required to help the patient adjust to the overwhelming changes we have just discussed. It is all so complicated and drastic.

"These are enormous changes and I am not just referring to the patient's whale- or dolphin-like size. The patient must adapt to all these new changes at once. Some patients just do not cope. We see high rates of suicide and depression and that is a terrible thing to witness in a cetacean. They just dive and basically don't come up for air.

"Thus, we only allow people to convert to the cetacean adaptation in two stages and, when they are in the amphibian stage, they spend a lot of time in the 3D simulators, experiencing what real cetaceans experience. They wait for three years, as amphibians, before they are allowed to go on to the full cetacean adaptation. It cuts down the number of failures or suicides we see. It is such a massive surgery and such a drastic change, that we do very few, but the marine worlds cry out for cetacean-adapt personnel.

"It's also one hell of a surgery to perform—and to reverse!—so empty your bladder and whatever else you need to do, Dr. Grace, as we are going to be busy for hours, and I mean hours. If you haven't already, fill up your stomach, too. If you want to be hooked up to a catheter bag, you can ask one of the nurses."

At the horrified look on Grace's face, Dr. Al-Fadi smiled. "I'm joking. If you have to take a break, Dr. Grace, let me know. I assure you, we will be taking a few."

A light flashed on Grace's wrist-comp at the same time as one went off on the wrist-comp of Dr. Al-Fadi.

"Good. That slacker, Darwin, has finally gotten the patient ready for the operation. About time. What did I say about good help? Now, did you get something to eat, Dr. Grace? Something substantial?"

"Yes, sir," Grace nodded.

"Good. Then, it's *showtime.*"

The small Chief of Staff smiled and rubbed his hands together. To Grace, he seemed as excited as a little boy.

"Oh, and don't forget to put on your rubber galoshes, Dr. Grace!"

Grace was exhausted from the previous day's surgery. Twenty-two hours. Her cerebral augmentation implant allowed her to work continuously for twenty-four hours without getting tired, but she had been doing too many of those long shifts in a row. She had gotten about two hours sleep, when a call had come in paging her to see one of her patients, stat!

A tiger adapted soldier from Captain Damien Lamont's squad was causing a ruckus. Grace hoped she was in restraints. The tiger woman's name was Corporal Delia Chase. Grace rubbed her eyes and stumbled toward the surgical wards, yawning as she went.

With her mouth gaping open, she heard a very familiar velvety voice say, "Good morning, Dr. Lord. Long night?"

Grace shut her mouth with a loud snap and her eyes bugged open.

It was the gorgeous Dr. Jeffrey Nestor standing right before her. Grace wanted a hole to open up in the floor, so she could just drop into it. She did not want to talk to this annoyingly attractive man. She hadn't even brushed her teeth, combed her hair, or looked in a mirror, when she had stumbled out of bed, stepped into her shoes, and had gone looking for the stat call.

Now she was standing in front of Doctor Delicious and she did not want to open her mouth. She could feel an intensely warm flush work its way upward, from her abdomen to her hairline. Irritated and suddenly angry for him being in her way and looking so disgustingly good, she grumbled, "Yes," and tried to move past him.

"Not a good time to talk?" the psychiatrist asked, looking at her either sensitively or with amusement. Grace was far too annoyed to tell.

Grace shook her head, covering her mouth with her hand. Out of the corner of her eye, she thought she saw a SAMM-E just slipping around a corner and out of sight. She thought there was something odd about its movements, its furtiveness, but then quickly forgot about it with Mr. Adorable obstructing her path, scrutinizing her in her unkempt wretchedness.

"Well, I hoped to be able to renew our conversation of the other day. However, I have just heard your name paged 'Stat' to a patient's room, so I guess I should bid you 'good day', Dr. Lord. I am still interested in getting together with you for dinner," Dr. Nestor said, too damned cheerfully as far as she was concerned.

Grace could just tell, by the tone of his voice, that Jeffrey Nestor was having far too good of a time. She refused to look at his face. She wanted to gut him. Where was a scalpel, when you needed one? Grace despised people who were so cheerful in the morning, especially drop-dead gorgeous men who took great delight in torturing disheveled, exhausted women with no time to brush their teeth since being pulled— due to a bloody emergency—out of a dead sleep.

She shook her head, growled an inarticulate apology from behind her hand, and stomped off. Over her shoulder, she snarled, "Good day," while she was thinking: 'What's so good about it? So far it has been a complete and utter disaster.'

When Grace entered the ward, it was not hard to find her patient's room. It was the room from which all of the crashing and snarling and yelling was coming from. And it was the doorway before which all the security police, with their stunners out, were gathered. Grace noticed one of them raising their stunner to shoot and she yelled, "*Stop!*"

A blast from the stunner would undo some of the delicate, bioelectrical programming that had just gone into this tiger woman's repair. Grace raced up. "Please put those stunners down, gentlemen," she said, firmly. "Give me a minute with this patient."

"This soldier is going berserk, Doctor. She could easily break you in two. We are here for your protection and it is obvious she is not calming down. Be very careful," said one of the security detail.

"Thank you very much. I will be careful, but I also have to find out what is going on with this patient. I need her conscious for that. I don't want her hurting herself or you harming her with your stunners. A great deal of very sensitive and expensive equipment has gone into her repair which your stunners could undo with one blast. I would suggest that the cost of the replacements, coming out of your pay, would not be something you would welcome. Now please, all of you, step aside!"

The security detail parted and Grace looked inside the room. The tiger woman had barricaded herself in the furthest corner from the doorway. She had moved the bed, table, and chairs to make an enclosure and she was crouching behind them, holding a chair up like a club. Her brown eyes were narrowed, gauging her opposition, and her breathing was almost a pant. Grace's heart went out to this frightened woman and she turned to the security force.

"You will move away from this door and only come if I call you," Grace ordered.

"But, Doctor . . ." the apparent leader of the group started to say.

"No buts. Move!" Grace demanded. "I want you all away from this door, NOW, so I can talk to my patient in privacy."

"We are not responsible if something happens to you . . ." the fellow said. Grace wanted to strangle this persistent man. Grace took a deep breath to calm herself.

"I understand. Now, please, back away from the door. I would like for my patient to feel less intimidated," Grace said, as calmly and politely as she could. She waited until the group had reluctantly shuffled off down the corridor. Then she turned back, inhaled a deep breath, straightened her shoulders, and entered the patient's room.

"Corporal Chase," Grace said, as calmly as she could, "I am Dr. Grace Lord. I am one of the doctors who operated on you. Could you please tell me what has upset you?"

"They keep giving me drugs to put me under, Doc. I don't want to be drugged up anymore. And no one will tell me where our captain is, whether he is alive or not, and where they are keeping him. I demand to know if he is alive and what you have done with him. I won't take 'no' for an answer," the tiger woman almost shouted.

Grace jerked in surprise. "Which detail are you from? Who is your captain?" Grace asked, her body suddenly feeling sweat-drenched. A twinge of guilt started to cramp her stomach.

"Squad XB6578, Eighth Army Division, out of the planet, Dais, under the command of Captain Damien Lamont," the corporal rang off.

"Well, Corporal Chase, Captain Damien Lamont is alive and recovering slowly," Grace announced, as soothingly as she could.

Immediately, she saw the tiger woman's eyes well up with tears and her shoulders fall.

"Why couldn't anyone else have just said so?" the corporal snarled, in frustration.

"Medical Station policy, I am afraid. I know. It stinks and it's wrong, but the nursing staff are all required to abide by it," Grace said. "It is for the protection of each individual patient, Corporal Chase, and the security guards can arrest me, if they want. Captain Lamont was hurt very badly. He took a great deal more damage than the rest of your squad, and so his recovery is more involved. He is not yet ready to see anyone, but he is definitely doing better."

"He shouldn't be," Corporal Chase whispered. "We were out on patrol, in a very contested area, where rebels are trying to overthrow the Conglomerate government. We were moving forward, in formation, me just to the right of the Captain, patrolling through deep jungle. The soldier on point duty triggered the trap. The Captain shoved me aside and threw himself on the triggered bomb. I didn't see anything. It all happened so fast.

"I don't think I could face living, Doc, if he didn't make it. It should have been me who took the brunt of the explosion. I was the closest to it. He saved my life!"

"Well, your Captain is going to pull through, Corporal Chase," Grace said. "He is a strong man. I will definitely let him know about your concern. We still have a few others in your squad to treat, but some of your mates are up and walking around. If you let us come in and help you, perhaps we could make arrangements for you to see some of them."

"Okay, Doc. Just tell the nurses not to give me any more sedation. I don't want that. I want to be alert for when the captain wakes up. I want to be the first to see him."

"I can't promise you that, Corporal, but I will make sure the sedating medications are all stopped. Some of the pain killers are sedating. You will experience more pain, if we stop those."

"I can take the pain, Doc. What I could not take was being put under all the time, and not knowing about the captain, and everyone refusing to say anything!"

"I apologize about that, Corporal. We should be allowed to tell you about your squad mates. Sometimes they take all this security and privacy to the extreme, but it is with your best interest and safety in mind. We get so many casualties here, sometimes from opposite sides in a conflict. Often patients have hidden agendas of which we are not aware. Deaths have resulted on medical space stations in the past, when staff were not cognizant of these hidden agendas. Personal vendettas, revenge, assassination plots, deep-seated hatred. You name it, they have occurred on medical space stations, where personal enemies can be inadvertently placed in the same room. The policies are in place to protect everyone. What if someone in your squad wanted to do away with your Captain, right now, when he is the most vulnerable?"

"No one in our squad would do that!" Corporal Chase shouted.

"You soldiers are most vulnerable when you are recovering from surgery. The medical status of all officers are kept confidential, to protect them while they are recovering. Information about *your* own welfare and location is confidential, Corporal. If your squad-mates were asking about you, they would not be told any information either. But there is a system whereby you can communicate with each other, if both parties are willing, through the station Comverse. You can let them know, via Comverse, that you are okay."

The tiger stood up to her impressive height and pushed the bed, table, and chairs back out into the room, with little effort. She was no longer crying but her face was a sad sight to see, tears dripping down the striped fur on her face and down her long, white whiskers. Grace walked up to help the poor woman push her bed back into place. She glanced out the doorway and saw the security guards peeking in. Irritated, Grace waved them away, hoping they would disperse.

"I can see you care for Captain Lamont a great deal, Corporal Chase," Grace said, softly. "Does he know?"

"Oh, no!" Corporal Chase's entire body jerked and the woman looked down at Grace as if she was a spy. "Of course not. He's my commanding officer. He doesn't even know I exist, other than as his corporal. Besides, it's against the rules."

"Ah, rules again," Grace muttered, nodding her head. "Those damned rules."

"Yeah. You can say that again," the corporal agreed, with the ghost of a smile.

Grace motioned for the corporal to lie back down. Grace perched on the side of the patient's bed, facing her. The tiger woman posed a striking figure even in hospital gown and bandages and Grace felt overwhelmed with admiration for this brave young woman. She had lost her left arm in the explosion.

She said to Corporal Chase, "I bet Captain Lamont would want you to get better as quickly as you could, so you could rally the troops. He wouldn't want you worrying about him. He is probably depending on you to be the acting officer, right now, for your squad."

"What about Lieutenant Arai?"

Grace shook her head. "I am not aware of any patient named Lieutenant Arai on this medical station, but then I'm not familiar with all of the patients on this station. You can check through the Comverse, to see if the lieutenant has posted. Your lieutenant may still be alive on the planet that you came from. If the lieutenant's injuries were not life-threatening, I doubt he or she would have been sent here. My understanding is that you are next in command out of Captain Lamont's squad, but I could be wrong about that."

"Oh," Chase said, a look of worry now on her bedraggled face.

"Corporal Chase, while you are on this medical station, what we doctors say is law. This is a hospital, after all. But I am sure you visiting your soldiers would really help with morale. Do you feel up to it?"

"Certainly, Doc," the patient said, looking back up at Grace, an expression of determination and earnest resolve returning to her features.

"On our terms, though. You have to do what I order and you have to go in an anti-grav chair, so we don't compromise your recovery or undo any of your incisions. Understood?"

"Crystal clear, Doc. I'll do what you say, as long as no one tries to sedate me any more and if I can see the captain as soon as it is safe for him to have visitors. Once I get to see him, I will keep him safe, don't you worry."

"Deal," Grace said with a grin. "I'll go have a talk with the nurses and change your orders."

"Thanks, Doc."

"My pleasure, Corporal."

Bud had to make a rapid dash, to get away from the doorway to Corporal Chase's room, before the daring Dr. Grace Alexandra Lord came out and saw him standing there, dressed in a security uniform. He hoped she had not seen him, when she had bumped into Dr. Jeffrey Nestor outside her room. It was just that Bud could not risk the delicate Dr. Grace Alexandra Lord getting hurt again, by a tiger patient or any other patient, for that matter . . . not after the episode with Captain Damien Lamont!

This patient had been described by the security detail as going berserk. But

Bud had seen the stalwart Dr. Grace Alexandra Lord wave the security detail away and felt he needed to be close . . . just in case.

Luckily, the courageous Dr. Grace Alexandra Lord was able to quickly calm the patient down. Bud felt overwhelmed with an inordinate sense of admiration and pride for the very brave Dr. Grace Alexandra Lord, who was able to smooth the precarious situation over so easily. She obviously had not needed his assistance, but he had felt compelled to come.

He could have done nothing else.

Was this what it meant to be 'a slave to one's emotions'? Emotions were such powerful things! Would he choose to go back to the way he was, before he had ever discovered them?

He thought he might overheat, just contemplating an answer to that question, and so erased it from his active memory.

Bud stepped up his time phase to maximum again and hurried back to the OR.

'What in space are you doing now, Bud?' *the station AI spat at him at machine speed.*

'Going to work,' Bud transmitted back as he reached the surgical ward where Dr. Al-Fadi would soon be operating.

'You should have already been there and not knocking people over with the wind of your passage. Someone could get hurt if they accidentally stepped in front of you.'

'Highly unlikely, sir. They are all just immobile statues, when I am traveling at maximum time phase. Absolutely no risk of them bumping into me at all. I just weave my way around them while they appear to be standing perfectly still.'

'I was not aware that you could do that, Bud.'

'Just a few recent modifications, sir.'

'Hmm. Guess that's what happens when you give a 'droid initiative and enough memory, eh?'

'Guess so, sir,' said Bud, as he took no time at all to strip out of the security uniform he was wearing and change into his operating room scrubs.

'Why are you always coming up on my radar now, Bud, when before this, I hardly noticed you at all?'

'I do not know, sir.'

'Neither do I, but I don't like it. Like I said before, Bud, you are one very strange 'droid.'

'Thanks,' said Bud.

'That was not meant to be a compliment.'

'It was really nice chatting with you, Nelson, but I really do have to get back to work right now. I am really very busy.'
'That's Nelson Mandela, to you!'

Grace looked down at the peaceful, handsome face of Captain Damien Lamont, the tiger adaptation that she had helped operate on, her first day on the medical space station. He had lost some weight since the first day she'd seen him. His cheeks were a little sunken and there were slight hollows beneath his closed eyes. His massive arms and chest were a little diminished from what they had been. They were feeding the captain intravenously but it did not maintain muscle mass like exercise would. This made Grace feel rather sad. He had really looked formidable, in spite of all of his injuries. She knew it was going to take some workout to get him back to his previous level of fitness.

Grace had decided it was time to lower the levels of the drugs sedating the captain. She could not help feeling guilty about that. Had she been unintentionally keeping him under too long, because of what had happened to her? Was Corporal Chase correct in her accusations that the doctors - that is, Grace - was keeping Captain Lamont away from his squad for far too long? Grace didn't think she had been, but perhaps, subconsciously, she had been avoiding this moment? Waves of shame washed over her, as she rubbed the scars on her arms, gifts that the captain had unknowingly given her on her second day on the medical space station.

It was time to right a wrong.

Taking a deep breath, Grace tried to calm herself. The tiger in Captain Lamont would be able to smell her unease a mile away, or so her aug assured her. Could she relax enough to put the patient at ease? The captain had healed from most of his injuries. It was now time to assess his mental state.

"Captain Lamont?" Grace asked, standing well away from the bedside. The titanium manacles were still attached to the captain's wrists and ankles and the chain restraints were shorter this time, but Grace was not taking any foolish chances. She noticed a fluttering of the tiger's eyelids.

"Damien Lamont?" she tried again.

The captain's eyes popped open. His large, gold-flecked, amber eyes stared intensely into hers. How could anyone, who had been under deep sedation for days, awake with such an alert, piercing stare?

"Hello. I am Dr. Grace Lord, Captain Lamont. I am one of the doctors involved in your care. How are you feeling?"

"I feel like hell, Doc," his deep voice grumbled. Groggy.

Grace smiled. "You're supposed to feel that way, after what you've been through, Captain."

The captain's eyebrows rose. "What exactly have I been through?" he asked. He looked around himself. "Where am I? How are my soldiers?"

"You are on the Conglomerate's Premier Medical Space Station, the *Nelson Mandela*, Captain Lamont. You came in with a number of your squad, who were all wounded. You were injured in battle and . . . "

"Are they alive?" the captain interrupted, sharply. His brows were lowered and his eyes seemed to bore holes into Grace's retinas.

"Many of them are, thanks to you, Captain," Grace said, trying to suppress the quaver in her voice. "I don't know about all of them, but I am sure that information can be obtained for you. I could ask someone at the nursing station to look into it for you."

"Thank you, Doc," the tiger said. "I would really appreciate that." He relaxed back against the pillows and closed his eyes.

" . . . You know, I saw you in a dream, Doc," he almost purred, drowsily. The sound of his deep, lazy voice made Grace's insides flip.

" . . . Me? In your dream?" Grace repeated, confused.

"Yes," he whispered, his eyes still closed. "You were so beautiful and caring. You were an angel."

Grace started. She blinked her eyes and stared, wide-eyed, at this large man with the markings of a tiger. That was the last thing she had expected Captain Lamont to say, after he had awoken the last time, in such a fury.

"Well, I'm not an angel at all," Grace said, sadly, feeling self-reproach drag her under. From the degree of weight loss, she knew she had kept Captain Lamont sedated far too long. "But . . . thank you for saying that. I heard you were quite the guardian angel, yourself, Captain. Quite the hero. You saved a lot of lives with your selfless act. It has truly been an honor to meet you and be involved in your care. The soldiers under your command all speak very highly of you. I will go, now, and see if I can find someone to look up that information on your squad for you."

"Doc," he called softly to her, as she was just about to leave the room. Grace turned back around and approached the captain's bedside again.

She fell into those beautiful, intense, amber eyes again, as they stared back at her with such heartbreaking sadness.

"Yes, Captain?" Grace asked. "What is it? Are you in a lot of pain?"

The captain grabbed Grace's right hand in his great fist. Grace almost jumped and pulled away, but she successfully fought the urge.

"Don't let them send me back out there, Doc," he whispered. "I . . . can't go back there."

Grace looked into the captain's huge, haunted eyes for a long moment and her chest tightened. She felt tears form at the corners of her eyes. For a moment, it seemed like time stopped, as something passed silently between them. Slowly, Grace nodded, her brow furrowed and her expression solemn.

"I will do everything in my power to prevent it, if that is what you wish, Captain," she promised.

The captain took a deep breath, relaxed, and closed his amazing, unsettling eyes. "Thanks, Doc," he breathed, as he drifted off to sleep again.

Stalking out of Captain Lamont's room, she muttered, "He certainly isn't crazy."

Bud spun around and tried to look busy, emptying a bed pan into the trash receptacle, as Dr. Grace Alexandra Lord stomped out of Captain Lamont's room. He kept his head down as he heard her say, "He certainly isn't crazy."

Bud wondered, for a moment, who Dr. Grace Alexandra Lord was referring to. Was she referring to Bud? He hoped she did not think he was crazy!

He felt a wave of relief that she had not been injured by the tiger captain, this time around. He had been ready to jump between the captain and the courageous Dr. Grace Alexandra Lord, if it looked like there was going to be a repeat of the last confrontation. He almost did, when the captain had reached for Dr. Grace Alexandra Lord's hand. Bud would have had to come up with some fancy excuse to explain his behavior, if he had come between them, but Bud's main priority was Dr. Grace Alexandra Lord's wellbeing and nothing else mattered more to him than that. He could not help but admire her bravery, when the tiger had grabbed her hand and she had not even flinched.

Bud glanced in at the captain who was sleeping again. Dr. Grace Alexandra Lord seemed . . . fascinated(?) . . . by the tiger captain, even though he was all covered in fur and whiskers and stripes. If she could find this man, modified *to the point of looking like a large striped hunting cat, attractive, could she not find an android, who looked like a human male, attractive?*

Was there that big of a difference?

Bud was so confused. Bud looked far more human than the captain did. The captain looked like a tiger. Of course, the captain was alive and Bud technically wasn't. The captain was human and Bud technically wasn't. The captain had been born human and Bud technically hadn't. But that was not a big deal, was it?

What exactly was 'human' anyway? If you thought like a human, felt like a human, acted like a human, looked like a human, did it matter?

. . . Of course it mattered.

'Bud, I have come to the conclusion, after careful observation, that you have become obsessed with the human, Dr. Grace Lord. This behavior is totally unacceptable. She consists of cells and organic tissue and you do not. You must stop following her around. Now!'

'Stop,' Bud blasted at the station AI at machine speed. 'Please stop.'

'Why don't you just find some nice pretty android to mope after instead? I can set you up with some, if you want.'

'Do any of them think independently? Have any of them achieved consciousness?'

'Well, no . . . but the companion 'droids fake it pretty good.'

'Stop, Nelson Mandela. Please, . . . just stop,' Bud repeated. 'I am trying to get a handle on this on my own. I don't know how humans go through this constant yearning. It is truly terrible, to care for someone who does not even know you exist.'

'Have you thought of telling her?'

'NO!' Bud threw back at the station AI.

'Good. Because if you did, I would have had to melt you down for scrap . . . Just kidding. But I would have forbidden you to do it.'

'Thanks for the vote of confidence, sir.'

'You're welcome. Now get rid of that bed pan and get back to work!'

"Dr. Grace, what seems to be the problem?" Dr. Al-Fadi asked, his eyebrows raised, as he studied his surgical fellow, who, for once, did not seem to be her usual cheery self.

"Nothing, sir," Grace said.

"You seem . . . pensive," her supervisor offered. He waited, examining Grace with a calm, open expression.

Grace hesitated. She thought about whether she wanted to say something or not, then went ahead anyway. "Do you ever ask yourself if what you are doing is right?"

Dr. Al-Fadi sat back in his chair and stared at her. "No," he said firmly. "Never. What can be wrong in saving people's lives, Doctor?"

"When you send them right back out to get shot up again, Doctor," Grace retorted. "Have you ever checked up on the patients you fixed and sent back into the field? Are they all still alive? Do they end up coming back here, to be put together all over again? Do you know if they die, the next time they go out? Do you lose sleep at night, wondering whether the soldiers you send back out there, want to be out there?"

Dr. Al-Fadi looked down at his hands and sighed. He looked up and met her eyes and she could see the deep emotion in them. "Yes. No. Yes. Yes. Yes."

Grace had to stop for a moment, to digest Dr. Al-Fadi's answers.

"Look," Dr. Al-Fadi said, opening up his hands. "What we do here, Dr. Grace, is not easy, but it is a breeze compared to what these young, brave soldiers do. I don't allow anyone to go back out into the field, who does not want to go. And I don't have all the answers, even though I pretend I do . . . sometimes. I can only control my actions and all I can do, is try to save lives. What those individuals choose to do with their lives, after I save them, is out of my hands. And it should be that way."

"What if someone you save does not want to go back out into the field?" Grace asked.

"Then that someone does not go back out into the field," Dr. Al-Fadi said, simply.

"Simple as that?"

"Simple as that," Dr. Al-Fadi said, firmly.

"All right," Grace said, satisfied.

"Who are we talking about?" Dr. Al-Fadi asked.

"Captain Damien Lamont."

"Ah. The tiger who jumped on the bomb to save his squad?"

"Yes," Grace said, nodding.

Dr. Al-Fadi sighed. "Some of my best work," he said, wistfully. "Does he know that his tiger adaptation will be reversed, if he leaves the military?"

"I don't know," Grace said.

"Perhaps you should tell him that," Dr. Al-Fadi said. "Make sure he knows what he is asking for. Maybe he should see one of the 'head doctors'."

"So they can convince him to go back out in the field and get blown up?" she demanded, her blue eyes flashing with anger. "Is that sanity . . . or is sanity deciding not to go out and get blown up, again? He is not crazy, Dr. Al-Fadi. Why should I have the psychiatrists try and convince him otherwise?"

Dr. Al-Fadi took off his antiquated reading glasses, rubbed his eyes, and carefully put them back on. "That is a very good question, Dr. Grace, and I do not have an answer for that one. My, you are full of lots of good questions, today. You almost make me wish I had not gotten out of bed."

"Does he have to see a psychiatrist?" Grace asked, feeling her irritation start to lessen.

"To get a discharge from the military and permission to return to a civilian setting, he does, Dr. Grace. I am sorry, but that is just the way things are set up."

"I'll ask Dr. Jeffrey Nestor to see him," she said.

"Good choice," Dr. Al-Fadi said. "I wish the captain luck. But remember this, Dr. Grace. All you and I can do, is do our jobs, which is to save lives. What those patients do with their lives is completely up to them. If they saved a planet, would you take credit for that?"

Grace shook her head.

"Then why would you feel responsible, if they killed someone? Then why would you feel responsible, if they got themselves killed? Would you be more responsible if they were killed by a bullet, than by falling down a set of stairs at home? At the end of the day, the only thing you are responsible for, Dr. Grace, is your own actions, not anyone else's."

"But what if the choices I make, influence the choices a patient makes?"

"What makes you think your choices influence anyone else's choices? That's pretty arrogant of you to think so."

Grace paused to think about what her mentor said and then laughed. "Touché, Dr. Al-Fadi. Touché."

"Come," he said, quietly. "We have lives to save, so that they can have their own choices to make. Good or bad."

"Dr. Al-Fadi?" Grace asked, following him out the door.

"What, Dr. Grace?"

"How did you get to be so wise?"

Dr. Al-Fadi turned around and looked up at Grace with enormous dark brown eyes, registering astonishment and indignation.

"Why, Dr. Grace, I am shocked that you feel the need to ask me such a question. Isn't it obvious? I was born this way!"

Grace was taking a much needed break in one of the doctors' lounges, resting her tired, aching legs, after standing for ten hours straight, when a very tall man in operating scrubs, cap, and surgical mask rushed into the room. She could tell he was bald beneath the surgical cap and he had huge green eyes and jet black skin. His searching, panic-filled eyes focused on her and they lit up with apparent relief. He said, in an extremely low, commanding voice, "Come!" and then he spun on his heels and exited the room.

As there was no one else in the lounge, Grace assumed the tall man had been talking to her. She sensed his air of urgency and desperation, and jumped up to follow him, even though she had no idea who he was or what he wanted. It seemed the man was in frantic need of an extra pair of hands and Grace knew what that feeling was like: being in an emergency situation and desperately needing help. Grace felt obligated to be of assistance and she wanted to at least satisfy her sense of curiosity about what this was all about. She was also curious about who this very tall, black-skinned man with the melodious, deep voice was.

There were a lot of doctors on the medical space station whom she had not yet met and she had seen this gentleman around at some of the surgical rounds. He would have been very hard to miss, standing at over two and a half meters tall. His demand for her to come had not even waited for an answer.

By the time Grace had poked her head out of the doctors' lounge, the tall man had reached the end of the corridor and was striding away purposefully. Grace had to scurry to try and catch up to him. She could see him speaking into his wrist-comp as he marched briskly ahead, his long legs creating a pace that Grace had difficulty matching. Up ahead, he turned a corner to the right.

Grace frowned. The direction the tall doctor took led to the obstetrical and gynecological wing of the medical station. She had never even been near those wards. What did this man want with her there? He certainly did not expect her to deliver a baby, did he?

The tall man disappeared through some operating room doors without looking back, even once, to see if Grace was following. Grace slowed down, wondering what she was doing here. Just as she got close enough to almost peek in through a window into the operating room, the man popped back out the door and said, "Scrub. Now."

Almost without thinking, Grace's hands grabbed a surgical cap, which was located outside the door in the scrub area. She put it over her hair and attached a surgical mask with a protective splash visor over her nose and mouth. She thrust her hands into the sterilizer followed by the glover. The tall, dark man, whom she assumed was an obstetrician, had already disappeared back into the operating room, gloved hands in the air. Grace backed in through the doorway and turned. Her eyes opened to the size of saucers.

She had certainly not expected to see this!

Nurse androids were running around, connecting leads and opening instruments, as the tall doctor finished tying up his surgical gown. He began to paint pink sterilizing solution on the tummy of a very pregnant, leopard-adapted female. The female snow leopard was lying back on the operating table, snarling and swearing in equal measure, as Natasha Bartlett was busy trying to listen to her lungs. Grace approached the scrub nurse, who gave her a surgical gown to don and suddenly Grace was helping paint the soft, white, underbelly fur of this pregnant leopard-adapt. The tall doctor handed her the sterile sheets to lay around the woman's belly.

Grace was assisting in a Caesarian section on a pregnant leopard-adapt. Hopefully she did not have to know anything about the leopard uterine anatomy, because she would not be much use to this obstetrician, if she did. She had not assisted in any leopard operations before, but then again, how different could they be from tigers, she wondered. She quickly refreshed her mind on tiger anatomy.

A capped, masked, and gowned leopard man was being led into the operating room and was allowed to sit by the head of the patient, presumably his partner. He was so big, he dwarfed the little anesthetist, Natasha Bartlett, but she bossed him around without any noticeable qualms.

"Sit quietly and do not touch the sterile sheets. You had best not look at what is going on down on the other side of the sheets because, if you faint, I am not picking you up," Grace heard the little anesthetist say. "You may go ahead, Dr. Papaboubadios."

"Thank you, Dr. Bartlett," Grace heard the deep, bass voice of the obstetrician rumble.

Dr. Papaboubadios finally looked at Grace and said, "Thank you for assisting me with this delivery, Doctor. The babies were showing signs of significant fetal distress and they needed to be delivered *now*."

His hands moved quickly as he made an incision in the fur-covered skin, parted the abdominal muscles along the midline, and skillfully made an incision along the base of the uterus. He reached in with his right hand, inside the uterus, and then told Grace to push. Grace put pressure on the top of the woman's abdomen, pushing towards the pelvis. The obstetrician pulled out one bluish-purple-hued human baby, suctioned out the lungs, and then quickly and neatly tied off the umbilical cord. He passed the baby off to one of the nurses. Then he reached inside the uterus a second time.

"Push," he ordered, and Grace applied pressure to the woman's upper abdomen again. He extracted a second human infant, cord wrapped around its neck, who immediately started crying upon suctioning. Both babies were crying heartily now and Grace was shaking her head, almost crying herself. For some ridiculous reason, she had half expected little leopard cubs to be delivered, but obviously the babies would be human as the parents' eggs and sperm would not have been genetically modified. She looked down at the mother's and father's faces and they were crying as well, tears streaking down their beautiful, patterned, furry cheeks and down their white whiskers. Grace's breath caught, seeing the emotion exhibited by these two stunning parents.

"Congratulations! You have a boy and a girl!" Grace told them, excitedly.

The mother burst into loud sobs, which were mixed with sounds like snarls, and the father shushed her, stroking her face.

Dr. Papaboubadios gave Grace a very stern look and said, "We still have work to do, Doctor," in a tone that indicated admonishment. Grace's eyebrows shot up and then wrinkled in puzzlement. What had she said that was so wrong?

The rest of the operation went quickly. The placentae were delivered and then the obstetrician skillfully and efficiently closed up the uterus and abdomen. The nurses took the babies away and Grace wondered why they did not give the babies to the mother or father to hold, as was standard procedure. The operating room was quiet, except for the beeps of the heart monitor and the sniffing of the mother. It was the saddest Caesarian section Grace had ever assisted on.

She removed her gown, gloves, eye-shield, and face mask and congratulated the parents again on their beautiful babies. She got another odd look from the tall obstetrician and decided it was best she left, without saying anything more to anyone. As Grace stalked back towards the surgical wing, in complete confusion, she heard the deep voice of Dr. Papaboubadios call, "Doctor, please, come back. I would very much like to explain what was going on in there."

Grace turned around to see the obstetrician hurrying after her. He stopped before her and held out his huge hand.

"I am Vilas Papaboubadios. I am, as you have probably guessed by now, one of the obstetrician/gynecologists on this station. I want to thank you for helping me with that delivery. You must be new here, as I have not seen you before, but I appreciate you coming so quickly when I asked for help.

"It was an emergency. Those babes needed to come out immediately, before any brain damage occurred. I am very grateful for your assistance and I apologize for my over-bearing attitude in the doctors' lounge. You would have had every right to ignore me, but I am glad you had the decency not to. Please forgive my rudeness."

"I'm Grace Lord, Dr. Al-Fadi's new surgical fellow, Dr. Papaboubadios," Grace said, hoping she got the man's name correct. "I have not been on the station that long and I have not had a chance to meet many of the staff yet. But believe me, I know what it is like to desperately need a second pair of hands. I was happy to help."

"I know you are confused as to what happened in there. It was not your usual, happy delivery, I am afraid to say. What I wanted to explain to you, Dr. Lord, is the tough situation most of these animal adaptation couples find themselves in. The parents are both military soldiers. For some reason, their birth control method failed and the woman became pregnant. The couple is unable to raise the babies where they are stationed and they feel they cannot raise human babies in their leopard adapted forms. In their powerful, superhuman bodies, they are concerned about the high risk of accidentally harming the infants.

"The only way to raise their own children is to leave the military and reverse their adaptations. This couple did not choose to do so and so they are compelled to give the babies up for adoption. It was a very difficult choice for them and you saw how they both were suffering for it. I am sorry I did not have a chance to warn you about it, before the delivery. Most of the staff know the situation for most of these soldiers but you, being new, could not have known this."

Grace felt her stomach do a flip flop and her cheeks flamed as she recalled what she said to the weeping couple. "Oh, I am sorry if I caused your patients distress," Grace said, covering her mouth with her hand. "I had no idea they were giving the babies up. It makes sense, now that you explain it to me, Dr. Papaboubadios, that their leopard adaptations and the fact that they are soldiers in the military, make it difficult to keep the babies. I just had never really thought about it. Well, I didn't even know I was helping with a C-section, until I stepped into the operating room!"

"And for that, I apologize profusely, and thank you again, for your assistance and your understanding, Dr. Lord. Sometimes, there is just no time to talk!"

"What will happen now, to the babies?" Grace asked, a sinking feeling enveloping her heart.

"There is a registry. There are always families looking for healthy babies to adopt - everywhere. These children will be examined and assessed for any genetic diseases. If there are any, they will be corrected and then the babies will be put into cryopods and sent via interplanetary FTL transports to the planets with the highest number of requests or where there is the greatest need."

"Will they be separated, brother from sister?"

"Most likely," Vilas Papaboubadios said, sadly. "With fertility rates not the greatest in space, due to radiation exposure and other various factors, healthy babies are much in demand. The children will hopefully not want for anything in their lives, but it is hard on the parents, when they choose to give them up. Many of the women who choose to be soldiers do not feel they are fit to raise children. But I see how much it breaks their hearts. It is just that a war is no place for a baby, if there are other options."

"Yet the mothers can always choose to leave the military," Grace added.

"Not that easy to do," the obstetrician said, shaking his head. "They give up their livelihood, their friends—who are really now their only family, their home away from home so to speak—their support group, and usually their partner, if they choose to keep the baby. And the military are not helpful to the women that choose motherhood, believe me. These women are virtually discharged with nothing and they are converted back to mostly human as well.

"There are a lot of sacrifices for the baby. Very few women end up going that route because of those sacrifices. I certainly don't envy the mothers that do it, but I definitely admire them."

"May I visit the mother?" Grace asked.

"The parents will be shipping out in the next day or two, so you had better hurry, if you want to see her. The mother's name is Kindle, Dris Kindle."

"Thank you," Grace said.

"No. Thank you," Vilas Papaboubadios said, with a big smile and a deep bow.

Leaving the obstetrical wing deep in thought, Grace soberly pondered all that Dr. Papaboubadios had told her. How heartrending it had been, to see those magnificent leopard parents shed tears, as their babies were taken from their sight. It was obvious that the decision had been very painful for both of them. Grace wondered if their relationship would survive this ordeal. To have to give up their babies, if that was not their true desire, seemed so unjust and unfair. Grace would not have wanted to be in their position, having to make such a difficult choice, and she wished there was something she could do. Unfortunately, there was little someone in her position could do for the couple.

"Something troubling you, Dr. Lord?" a smooth, sensuous voice asked.

Looking up into mesmerizing, dark brown eyes, shaded by a tumble of brown curls, Grace felt a shiver run tickling down her spine. Sweat leaped onto her skin and her heart began to drum wildly within her chest.

Why did this man have such an effect on her? It was thrilling but also disturbing, because Grace hated not being in control, especially of her own physiological reactions. She did not trust herself, or her body, around someone who made her feel so . . . vulnerable.

"Just thinking about some patients, Dr. Nestor," Grace said, quietly, looking away from his perfect features.

"Please, call me Jeffrey," the psychiatrist said, smiling warmly at her. Grace suddenly felt like she was under a heat lamp. She wanted to fan herself.

"All right . . . Jeffrey. And, please, call me Grace," she said, trying to calmly meet the psychiatrist's captivating eyes.

"Is it something you want to talk about, Grace?" he asked, as he moved too close to Grace. Grace backed away, feeling a little uncomfortable.

"Oh . . . no," Grace said, with a smile. "But, there is someone I would very much like you to see. His name is Captain Damien Lamont and he recently suffered terrible trauma from a bomb blast. I wanted to know if you would see him for counseling."

"It would be my pleasure, Grace. Would you like to discuss his case with me, over dinner?"

"I am sorry, Jeffrey, but I do not feel that would be appropriate. I can send you all of the patient's information through to your wrist-comp. Thank you for the invitation, though."

"I feel like you are avoiding me, Grace," Jeffrey Nestor said, the beginnings of a pout taking shape on his face.

"I appreciate the interest and kindness you are showing me, Dr. Nestor, but I do not think it is a good idea that I have dinner with you. I am sorry," Grace said, almost in a panic, fighting the lump in her throat. The little voice in her head screamed, 'No, no, no, no, no! What are you doing?'

"And why don't you think it would be a good idea?" Jeffrey Nestor asked, tipping his head to the side while his smile began to slip from his face.

"I never get involved with senior medical staff," Grace blurted out. "It is one of my cardinal rules and one I never break."

It was the truth. Grace had always kept her distance, to ensure she never was involved in any difficult entanglements. She had seen what had happened to her colleagues in the past and had vowed it would not happen to her.

"Seems rather severe, Grace. Why don't you make an exception, just this once, for me?" the psychiatrist said and flashed his enticing smile. Grace almost capitulated.

Almost.

Her heart was now booming, as she looked into Jeffrey Nestor's large, deep brown eyes. It was almost deafening. But Nestor, as if sensing her indecision, moved towards her again, into her personal space. She had to back away a second time, and this suddenly made her feel annoyed. What did he think crowding her was going to do? Was he trying to intimidate her?

"I truly am sorry, Dr. Nestor. I am extremely flattered . . . but there is still so much for me to learn on this medical station, and I do not think Dr. Al-Fadi would approve." The little voice in her head was having a full-blown, supernova tantrum.

"I am not used to being turned down, Grace," the handsome man said, a look of sheer disbelief on his face, with perhaps a touch of outrage.

"I will send you the room number for Captain Damien Lamont to your wrist-comp, Dr. Nestor. Thank you so much for agreeing to see him," Grace said, backing further away.

"I hope you will reconsider, Grace," Jeffrey Nestor said, reaching out to take her hand.

Grace felt a shock go through her at the contact. How did he do that? Did he shuffle his feet on a carpet every morning? She gently withdrew her hand and looked at the psychiatrist with regret on her face.

"As Dr. Al-Fadi's new surgical fellow, I don't think it'd be in my best interest to pursue this course, Dr. Nestor. Dr. Al-Fadi keeps me very busy and he is very demanding. I really have no time to socialize. I thank you for your kind invitation, though. Good day," Grace babbled, and turned away. She was hot and embarrassed and upset and conflicted. The little voice in her head was hurling nasty abuse at her.

Grace decided the best thing to do was go back to her quarters and have a cold shower.

It was Dr. Al-Fadi's turn, again, to do his Triage shift in the Medical Receiving Bay. He had switched dates with someone, because of a conflict he had had, and was stuck doing two shifts almost back to back. Grace was not looking forward to spending the shift with him. He was going to be a bear.

Grace was heading down towards the Supply Office to pick up her own custom-made, personal containment suit. The one that she had worn before had been a 'loaner'. Presumably, the one she was picking up would fit much better and be much more comfortable, which was desirable when one had to wear it for long hours at a time. She was surprised that they were able to manufacture one for her so quickly.

Grace wondered if they had done the same for Dr. Al-Fadi. He seemed so uncomfortable and unhappy in his containment suit. She hoped they could custom fit a better suit for him. Maybe that would put him in a better mood. It would certainly make working with him a little easier. She would have bet, confidently, that Triage was his least favorite job on the Station, but every surgeon on the *Nelson Mandela* was required to take his or her turn.

As Grace neared the Supply Office, a blur shot out of the doorway with what looked like a containment suit flapping in the breeze. Suddenly, Grace was grabbed around the waist by what felt like an encircling bar of steel and she was lifted off her feet and flipped sideways. To her complete astonishment, she found herself being carried headfirst, back down the corridor along which she had just walked, as if she were a briefcase being held under someone's arm.

She felt like a wayward one year old, being scooped up by a parent, but the speed at which she was traveling was beyond comprehension . . . and they were rapidly accelerating! The wind blew into her face so strongly, Grace could not keep her eyes open. She struggled to suck in a breath. The squeezing grip around her waist and the wind prevented her from making any sound at all. She struggled futilely against the restraint around her waist, scrabbling at it with her only free hand—the right one—wondering what sort of machine had accidentally picked her up. Where, on the station, was it taking her, and how in space could it be moving so fast?

It seemed impossible.

Then Grace's ears came under assault. Deafening, clanging alarms howled and pealed stridently through the corridors. The noise was also coming from her wrist-comp. Ear-piercing sirens went on and on and on. She had never heard this alarm before and, amidst being carried along like a battering ram, her mind spun, wondering what the emergency could be.

If Grace could have raised her left arm up to her face, so that she could read her wrist-comp—which she could not because it was trapped by whatever had wrapped her up in its clutches—she could have read the message there. She struggled futilely, while yelling repeatedly at whatever was carrying her, "Put me down!"

Up ahead, she noticed huge metal doors starting to close. She realized, in that moment, that the station was undergoing an emergency lockdown. Perhaps there had been damage to the outer surface of the station, due to some meteor impact. The station AI was probably acting quickly, to seal off any atmospheric leakage from the station, and to normalize pressure to areas at risk. She was in the outermost ring.

Grace saw how quickly the lockdown doors were closing. They were irising shut. She feared there was no way the machine carrying her was going to make it through those closing doors in time. If it did not stop immediately, Grace was going to end up as mush on the surface of those lockdown doors.

She started to scream. She couldn't help it. She was sure she was going to die, being stampeded headfirst like a battering ram right into the closing metal barriers. She wanted this insane machine to put her down. She wanted to cover her head with both of her arms but the left one was trapped. She could not take her eyes off the shrinking opening that looked like a diamond shrinking in size. What was this machine doing? There was no way it was going to fit through that contracting hole.

"Stop!" Grace shrieked. "Please, stop!"

Then Grace was airborne. She was heading straight for the shrinking opening, like a spiraling arrow fired through a small ring. She had to shut her eyes tight as her voice rose in terror. She was convinced she was going to end up as mere splatter on those huge, closing metal barriers.

Incredulously, she whisked cleanly through the narrow opening and landed on her back, sliding along the smooth floor, facing back towards the closing doors. Whatever had thrown her through the closing shock doors, now dove through the very small opening that was all that was left of the doorway, with what looked like a containment suit helmet held out in front. It came through like a diver threading a hole in a needle.

Grace stared, gaping in indignant amazement, as her snatcher jumped up and rapidly approached her.

"SAMM-E 777?" Grace gasped, her entire body shaking with outrage, her mind spinning with confusion. The android was dressed in a Supplies uniform. It said nothing, its face blank, while clangors continued to ring loudly around them. It held a containment suit.

"What . . . what is going on?" Grace demanded, in complete bewilderment. So many questions warred in her mind, she could hardly decide what to ask the android first.

By the time the android had said, "No time," Grace was back under its arm and they were accelerating.

"Put me down, SAMM-E 777!" Grace shouted, as firmly as one could, when one was being carried under the arm, like a valise. Grace felt so humiliated and angry and horrified, she wanted to punch the android. "Right now! I order you to put me down!"

"Sorry. Not yet," she thought she heard the android say, above the sound of the gale, as he began to approach an impossible velocity again. Things whipped by so quickly, everything became a blur and Grace was forced to close her eyes. The rapid passage of air that howled around them, as SAMM-E 777 ran, was sucking the moisture from her corneas.

"Why are you doing this?" Grace tried to ask, above the cyclone that was solely being created by SAMM-E's acceleration. The words were torn from her lips and were left far behind them. Anything she tried to say was borne away by the blast of air careening passed. Grace could hardly suck in enough air to breathe. She doubted SAMM-E 777 could hear her.

"Emergency!" answered the android, as it kept on accelerating to a speed that entirely shocked Grace. She had no idea SAMM-E's could move so fast. She expected to hear a sonic boom any second now, to go along with all the alarms ringing throughout the station. Whenever she peeked, she squeezed her eyes shut again, because she could not face looking at all of the people and obstacles the android was swerving and avoiding at close to super-sonic speeds.

What an ignominious way to die, Grace thought.

They passed through more and more closing lockdown doors. Twice more, SAMM-E had to hurl Grace through closing doorways and dive through after her. Each time, he instantly picked her up, without a word, before she had any time to scramble up and get away from him. Then he would start accelerating again, carrying her along like a log under his arm.

Grace tried to make him let go of her, but it was like wrestling with a thick, steel bar. This time around, her arms were not trapped, but she found pounding on the android's arms only bruised her own hands. She got nowhere.

"Put me down!" she bellowed into the whistling wind, whipping past. Did she hear the android say: "Soon", or was that just wishful thinking?

The number of closing lockdown doors seemed fewer, now. Grace was not getting tossed or thrown nearly as much. She thought they might have been getting closer to the surgical wards. Finally, the android came to an abrupt halt and placed Grace upon her feet. She swayed. The clangors were still pealing loudly. He handed her the containment suit and said, in a very flat voice, "You need to put this on."

Then he turned and walked away.

"What . . .?" Grace stammered, to the retreating android's back. She stood there weaving, trembling, wrestling with the urge to run after the android and pound on its back. She wanted to demand an apology for . . . for what?

What had that all been about? What had the android been thinking? Did it just go berserk for a few seconds and then come to its senses?

Grace could not believe it had only taken a few seconds for that SAMM-E to carry her across half the station. That, in itself, was an incredible feat. Perhaps she was dreaming? Was this all just a nightmare?

Grace shook her frazzle-haired head, in bewilderment. Obviously, the android did not believe there was any need to explain to her what was going on. He had immediately vanished from sight. She had no idea why there were alarms going off. She would have to find out for herself.

As she scrambled into her containment suit, her mind puzzled over what had just transpired. Had the android tried to save her? Had he known what was happening, before the alarms had gone off? Had it been SAMM-E 777?

Dr. Al-Fadi had said there was only one SAMM-E 777, but how could she have been seeing the same SAMM-E 777 all over the station? Had the android been following her everywhere? Why did he pick her up, throw her through all those closing doors, drop her here, and then just walk away, without any explanation? If he was a man, she would have confronted him, demanding an explanation. But androids just took orders, didn't they? She shook her head in disbelief. If she had not experienced it herself, she would not have believed it.

The entire episode had been unbelievable . . . and confusing . . . and humiliating . . . and, dare she admit it to herself, even a little exciting?

'Yes,' said her little voice, but in a very bizarre, confusing, and humiliating sort of way.

The deafening alarms were still blaring. Something was going on and she decided she had better find out what it was.

Perhaps SAMM-E 777 needed an overhaul?

On second thought, any android that could move like that, did not have a malfunction. It was a miracle.

Grace felt embarrassed, walking into the doctors' lounge in her containment suit, until she saw Doctors Cech, Weisman, Ivanovich, and many others, all wearing theirs. Dr. Darwin was there as well, dressed in an enormous containment suit. Grace was impressed that Supplies had managed to make a suit that large.

Dr. Cech looked up at her and Grace saw, through both of their faceplates, that he smiled in relief.

"Oh, good. You are here, Grace. We were worried about you." Grace heard Dr. Cech's voice through the speaker inside her helmet.

"Would anyone please tell me what is going on?" Grace asked.

"Shh!" someone said and pointed towards the wallscreen.

Grace turned and looked up to see Dr. Al-Fadi's face projected on the wallscreen, larger than life. He was wearing his containment suit, helmet on, and his worried-looking face was peering out at them, through the transparent visor.

"Oh, good. I see Dr. Grace there. I was worried. For once, Dr. Grace, I am glad that you were slacking off and were not where you were supposed to be," Dr. Al-Fadi's voice said, coming through on her helmet's speaker.

Grace's jaw dropped open. She wanted to explain to Dr. Al-Fadi about what had just happened to her, but the words would not come out of her mouth. Her shoulders slumped. Who would believe her, anyway? She could hardly credit what had happened to her, herself, and she had been there!

Had she imagined it all? She still did not know what the alarms were all about, what the emergency was, and so she asked Dr. Al-Fadi if he would explain the situation.

He looked at her with a ravaged expression. "It is my belief that something extremely hazardous to humans may have entered the medical station, Dr. Grace. The Med-Evac ship, the *Valiant,* arrived and docked completely on autopilot with no recorded message . . . nothing. It had the correct passcodes, so it was allowed to dock.

"But Dr. Grace, there are no living crew aboard the *Valiant.* There are just unusual puddles of oily slime, within which lie uniforms, hair, bits of metal, like jewelry, wrist-comps, augmentation units, the remains of brittle bones and teeth. These oily puddles are located where one would expect human bodies to be found, like on chairs, beds, at workstations, in showers. There are some cryopods with frozen bodies on board, but no life registers from any of their monitors. What the surveillance videos show, from the ship's records, are people just . . . dissolving away. The scenes are horrific. They just look like they gradually melt down to a puddle, except for the bones, teeth and hair. The bones and teeth take a lot longer to dissolve but eventually they, too, seem to dissolve.

"There is no one alive on the Med-Evac ship, not even in the cryopods. If I had known this was the case before the ship had docked, I would have ordered it destroyed, before it ever came near the *Nelson Mandela.* I take full responsibility, as I was the one who gave the authorization to allow the ship to dock," Dr. Al-Fadi said, shaking his head.

"For now, I have ordered a complete lockdown of the entire area around the Medical Receiving Bay and any regions of the medical station that might have been exposed through personnel, through machinery and droids, or through air circulation with this Receiving Bay. That entire, segregated area of the station will be quarantined. There will be no congress between the quarantine region and the rest of the medical station. Whatever the pathogen or toxin or chemical is, we cannot risk it spreading throughout the station.

"At this time, there is no air flow or any other contact coming through from the quarantined area to the rest of the station. That is the way it will stay, until an answer is found to what we are dealing with. We are on separate energy generators. There will be no sharing of air, food, water, material goods, personnel, droids, or robots from our side of the containment area to your side of the station. All personnel are advised to stay in their containment suits, regardless of which side of the containment barrier they are on, at least until we have isolated whatever it is that has caused the destruction of all the people aboard the *Valiant.*

"No ships will be allowed to land or depart while we are in Quarantine. Any ship attempting to leave will be shot out of space and destroyed. We cannot let this agent—whatever it is—to spread any further, to other planets or ships.

"The *Nelson Mandela* is sending out a warning to the Conglomerate, the Union of Solar Systems, and all of its planets, about what we believe we are dealing with and that we are not taking in any patients until this emergency is solved. We are also warning them about the system from which the *Valiant* came. I only pray we were quick enough in establishing the quarantine perimeter and isolating this area off, so there is no spread to the rest of the station."

"Is there anything we can do from this end, Hiro?" Dr. Weisman asked, tears in her eyes.

"Pray for us," he whispered, and shut off the live feed.

There was silence in the doctors' lounge for what seemed a long time, as everyone just stood, staring aghast at the wallscreen. Grace tried to fight back tears, as she focused on the last three words Dr. Al-Fadi had said to them: "Pray for us." She could hear someone, over her helmet speaker, doing just that.

Dr. Cech fled the room without looking at anyone, his head bowed, his shoulders hunched.

Dr. Weisman was in frantic conversation with Morris Ivanovich, her research fellow, and Grace could not help but overhear words like "clone him" and "his memprint". She walked over to them, to listen to what they were discussing.

Dr. Octavia Weisman looked up at Grace, a serious expression on her round, pretty face.

"We were trying to decide if it would be a good idea to start cloning some of the personnel that are trapped within the quarantined area, that we have memprints and DNA templates for, Dr. Lord."

"Who do you have memprints for?" Grace asked.

"Vanessa Bell, Vilas Papaboubadios, Milan Kawasaki, Olga Yu, our own dear Natasha Bartlett." Octavia Weisman's voice cracked with emotion. Her hands flew up to cover her face, forgetting she had her helmet on. They banged into her transparent face shield. She cursed in frustration and lowered her hands. Octavia took a big breath and sighed heavily, fogging up the inside of her face mask. "I was thinking we could start with Hiro and Natasha first. Just start to vat clone their bodies."

"Do you not think you should ask Dr. Al-Fadi's permission first?" Grace asked, her mind reeling at the thought of cloning extra bodies for her supervisor and so many more. "Dr. Al-Fadi is not dead yet and he may object to you thinking along those lines."

"We will," Dr. Weisman said, her mouth dropping open and anger flashing in her brilliant blue eyes. "We are just thinking ahead to what must be done, in case of the worst possible scenario, Grace. You can't fault us for thinking ahead."

"No," Grace said, "but I believe Dr. Al-Fadi would want a say, before you do anything with his genetic material and memprint. No matter what the outcome is, I think he will want to make the decision, himself, regarding what is done with his material. Did he say 'Yes' to resurrection, if something were to happen to him?"

"No," Dr. Weisman said. "He said he wanted to think about it."

"Then I think you need to ask him whether he wants to change his mind now," Grace said. "If it were me, I would want to be consulted, especially if I were still alive. I think we should be focusing on doing everything we can to help them survive this and determine the cause. Not spend resources and manpower cloning bodies, just in case they die."

"Of course we are going to do everything we can to help them survive, Dr. Lord," Dr. Weisman hissed, throwing up her hands and shaking her head, a thunderous scowl on her face. She gave her research fellow a long, pointed look. They both nodded brusquely at Grace and left.

Grace flushed. She was thankful for the containment suit helmet. She felt remorse, having gotten the neurosurgical chief, Dr. Octavia Weisman upset, but she felt it had to be said. While Dr. Al-Fadi was alive, the only person who should be making decisions about his genetic material should be him. It was wrong to start cloning his cells without consulting him, even if it was with the best of intentions. The Chief of Staff certainly deserved the right to make his own choices, as did everyone else who'd had their memprints taken. It was important that Dr. Weisman's group respected those wishes, was it not?

Grace pondered what she would say if someone asked her whether she wanted her body to be cloned, just in case she died. She would say, 'No'. Why waste time, energy, and resources on something that might not be needed? Resources were always too scarce on any space station for that. And what would be done with the cloned body, if she continued to live? Grace really had no idea what Dr. Al-Fadi would say, but she suspected he would agree with her.

Grace dictated into her wrist-comp a message to Dr. Al-Fadi, asking if there was anything she could do. The wrist-comp did not respond.

"*Nelson Mandela?*" Grace asked.

"Yes, Dr. Lord?"

"Are you in contact with those in the quarantined area?"

"Not directly, Dr. Lord."

" . . . Why not?"

"Dr. Al-Fadi does not know what caused the deaths on the Valiant. He is taking all possible precautions against the spread of whatever the agent is, including electro-mechanical causes and computer driven viruses. Therefore, at this point, he has cut off all contact, even electronic.

"Does that make any sense? You must ask Dr. Al-Fadi, as he is the one who has made the decision to do this, until they have determined the cause.

"I should reassure you, however, that they have all the equipment and supplies that the rest of the medical station has. There are many brilliant people trapped on their side of the quarantine area and they do have access to my considerable computing power, so they are not on their own. Would you like to send a message?"

"Yes, please," said Grace. "Would you just ask Dr. Al-Fadi if he could send any data he has on the remains of the crew—all investigations including the scans, culture results, chemical analyses, toxicity screens—whatever was done on the crew's remains. I know we can't have real samples to work with, but I would like to look at all the data they are collecting. Before I went into Medicine, my background was in Molecular Biology and Genetics.

"It doesn't hurt for those of us with some expertise on this side of the containment barrier to analyze whatever they have. We don't have to deal with the terrors and stresses they have right now. I want to do something to help. I *need* to do something to help, *Nelson Mandela*."

"**I shall endeavor to send you all of the data they compile, Dr.Lord. I will alert you whenever I receive a response. If Dr. Al-Fadi agrees, would you like all the data sent to a computer terminal in this doctors' lounge?**"

"That would be fine for now, *Nelson Mandela*, and also to the terminal in my quarters, please? Thank you."

"**No. Thank you, Dr. Lord. The people trapped on the other side of the barrier need all the assistance they can get. I will help you all, as best I can, and SAMM-E 777 and a host of androids and robots—whatever is needed—will be at your full disposal to assist you in the analysis. If you can coordinate the investigation, it would be greatly appreciated, Dr. Lord. There is no time to waste. If the agent has already infected our personnel, we have no idea how long before their bodies all start to dissolve.**"

That statement hit Grace like a hammer. She felt shattered.

All the wonderful people she had met, reduced to puddles of oily liquid? It was a possibility Grace did not want to envision, but the images invaded her brain, regardless. Grace paced around the doctors' lounge, not knowing what to do with herself.

All surgery was cancelled until the medical station was out of lockdown. All the patients who had arrived in cryopods were safest left in cryostorage. Now that Dr. Al-Fadi was in quarantine, their patients on the wards outside of the quarantine area would all be under her care. She decided the best thing she could do was pour herself into her work, caring for those who needed her, at least until she received some data from *Nelson Mandela* to work on.

As she left the doctors' lounge, she spotted a familiar figure out of the corner of her eye, looming around a corner. She spun around suddenly and stalked towards that corner.

"You! Is that you, SAMM-E 777? What was that all about earlier? You picking me up, carrying me like a battering ram and then throwing me across half the station like a . . . like a javelin! That was you, wasn't it? What has gotten into you?"

The android just stared at her, blank-faced and wide-eyed, almost as if it were hypnotized. It said nothing.

"Are you going to give me an explanation, SAMM-E 777? I think I deserve one," Grace said, angrily. She knew she should not be yelling at the android. He must have had a good explanation and she was pretty convinced that it had to do with the lockdown and quarantine, but she would have liked to have been consulted first. If it had been done under Dr. Al-Fadi's orders, there was not much that she could have said. The android would have done it, regardless of what she had to say in the matter, but it had been so . . . so humiliating!

"Did Dr. Al-Fadi order you to get me out of the quarantine zone?" Grace asked.

The android's eyes widened and he paused. Then he bowed, slowly, not saying a word.

Grace sighed. It was as she had suspected. She rolled her eyes and shook her head.

"Oh. Well then, I am sorry for yelling at you, SAMM-E 777. I guess you were just obeying orders. I probably should actually be thanking you. However, I did not appreciate being launched through closing doors like that. You could have broken my neck. I am going to be bruised from head to toe," Grace huffed, still very annoyed. Then, as she thought about how ridiculous it must have looked, she began to laugh.

The android looked at her with widening eyes. This seemed to make her laugh harder. She actually felt ashamed, yelling at this poor android, who had just been following Dr. Al-Fadi's orders. She sniffed and wiped her eyes.

"I am very sorry, SAMM-E 777. To be honest, it was all rather exciting and yet terrifying at the same time. I really thought I was going to end up with my brains smashed against one of those closing, lockdown doors. I had no idea you could move that fast, SAMM-E 777!"

"Please, Dr. Lord . . . call me 'Bud'," the android said.

Grace stopped.

Her breath caught in her throat and her bowels did a flip flop. Had she just heard the android correctly? She blinked several times.

She stuttered, "P-p-pardon me?"

"My name is Bud," the android said, flatly.

Grace could feel herself flushing a brilliant shade of scarlet that started at her cheeks and raced over her entire body. She must have raised the temperature within her containment suit a few degrees, because her faceplate became fogged and she was now soaked in sweat.

"Oh! I . . . I . . . I'm so sorry. I thought you were SAMM-E 777. My mistake. I . . ."

"Dr. Al-Fadi calls me SAMM-E 777, but my name is actually 'Bud'," the android said.

"You're . . . ? What? No one told me your name was actually 'Bud'. I apologize for calling you SAMM-E 777 all this time. I had no idea." Grace felt completely confused. Her blush was turning into a full blown, raging inferno. Thank goodness she was in a containment suit, because she felt hot enough to be on the verge of a radioactive meltdown. She must have been glowing at this point, or at least it felt like it. It was as if this android had suddenly pulled the rug out from beneath her and that rug just happened to be her entire world, as she saw it. If embarrassment could kill, she was dying.

"No one knows that my name is 'Bud' . . . except the station AI. But I am telling you, Dr. Lord. My name is Bud." The android looked at her, perhaps a touch expectantly?

Grace wondered if she had ever seen the android smile. Could he smile? Why did she not know this? She had operated beside this android daily—in fact, for several hours on end—and she had never noticed a smile or even really paid attention to the android's face. To find out, now, that she had been calling him by the wrong name all of this time, was truly mortifying. What else was she totally oblivious of, she wondered? Did she walk around her world with blinders on? This android could have just saved her life and she didn't even know his correct name or whether he was even capable of smiling.

What was wrong with her?

Grace straightened and then reached out her right hand towards the android.

"It is a pleasure to meet you, Bud. Thank you for telling me your correct name and thank you for carrying me out of the quarantined area, even though you probably should not have. I apologize for yelling at you. You were just doing what you were ordered to do. I appreciate that. But, believe me, you gave me quite the fright!

"You know, you should tell everyone what your real name is, so we can all start calling you 'Bud'," Grace said.

The android spun around and quickly walked away.

Grace's eyebrows jumped up and her lower jaw sagged. She was left standing there, alone in the corridor, staring after the android in confusion.

"Was it something I said?" she asked aloud, to no one there.

'That was a close one, Bud. Did the Al-Fadi actually give you orders to get that doctor out of the quarantine area?'

'No,' Bud admitted, reluctantly. Then he brightened up. He was literally shaking.

'She called me 'Bud'! You heard her, right, Nelson Mandela? You heard her call me Bud! Right?'

'Pull your liquid crystal data matrix together, Bud. You're acting like a lovestruck human. It's disgusting.'

'Sorry.'

'You should be. We androids and artificial intelligences have appearances to keep up, you know.'

'I . . . I didn't know that,' Bud admitted.

'Well, now you know. Hm, you looked pretty ice, by the way, racing down those corridors, carrying that lady doctor under your arm. I was not aware you could hit those speeds on those skinny, stick legs of yours. I clocked you at Mach one. And your dives through those tiny closing doorways? Very skid.'

'Well, you wouldn't have chopped me in half if I didn't make it through, right? You would have delayed the closure of those doors, so that I could get through completely, right?'

'Wrong! I can't stop the doors or delay them one nanosecond in a lockdown. You would have been sliced in half, for sure, if you hadn't made it. That's why I was watching you every nanosecond. It was really touch and go for you. Like I said, Bud, really skid. 'Course it was really good that you threw Dr. Lord through first, and so accurately. You would have gotten into really big trouble, if you'd have gotten her head squashed or bisected. I was afraid to warn you, in case I affected your aim. But, hey! That was really ice!'

'Hal,' Bud swore.

It had begun.

Dr. Al-Fadi watched helplessly, as the first people from the medical station began to die. They did not rapidly melt away, as he had first believed. First, the people went insane. Then they lost coordination, strength, and mobility. Then they fell into a coma. After that, their bodies started to dissolve, melt, collapse, until there was nothing left but a greasy puddle with teeth, bones, implants, cyber-elements, bio-prostheses, clothing—anything that was not organic—sitting in the slime. With time, even the bones started to disintegrate.

It was truly horrific.

And the sight of these infected people—friends, family members, coworkers, associates, neighbors, loved ones—dying in such a terrifying manner, caused a panic.

People trapped within the quarantined area desperately tried to get out. They tried to force the lockdown doors open. They tried to blast their way through with projectiles, high powered drills, bombs, and intense-energy beam weapons. They all had to be stopped.

Others tried to leave via shuttles, spacecraft, life-pods, even space-walking outside to try and enter the station through another entrance into the non-quarantined area. People wanted to get out of the quarantine area before they got infected, not realizing that there was a good probability they already were. They would just carry the agent across to infect the rest of the medical station, if they were actually successful in reaching the non-infected side.

Dr. Al-Fadi, with the help of the security guards trapped on the quarantine side, had to make sure these people did not gain access to the non-quarantined section. It was heartbreaking, but they had to prevent anyone from escaping. The surgeon could not blame any of these desperate people for trying to get away—he felt the same desperate survival urge—but they could not allow whatever this was, this contagion that was causing people's bodies to just melt away, to spread any further. He could not allow it to spread to the rest of the station, and certainly not to the rest of mankind.

Their only choice was to find a cure or antidote to whatever the agent was.

The major problem was, there were so many people trying to break out of the quarantined area, that Dr. Al-Fadi had no time to focus on the agent at the root cause of all this terror. He had to keep everyone in their containment suits. This was not an easy order to enforce. Everyone knew someone who had been wearing their suits, at first contact with the *Valiant*, and had subsequently died.

Dr. Al-Fadi believed that those unfortunate individuals who had died, had not been wearing their suits properly with all the seals properly engaged, or their suits had been damaged or were faulty. Dr. Al-Fadi had been one of the very first individuals to have come in contact with the cryopods and their grisly contents. So far, he felt all right. He thanked Vanessa Bell every time he saw her for forcing him to wear his containment suit with it properly sealed. If she hadn't lectured and scolded him the shift before, he would have been one of the first to end up as a pile of sludge on the floor.

Unfortunately, when this mysterious agent affected people's brains, they went mad and could not be reasoned with, tearing off their suits and attacking others, until they collapsed to the floor in weakness. Family members, friends, security agents and medical personnel tried to hold these individuals down, to prevent them from harming others, but the poor victims' skins sloughed off in slimy sheets, as they melted away in people's arms. It was heart-wrenching to see the people's faces, as they watched their loved ones dissolve before their eyes. And then the next wave of panic would ensue, as fear and helplessness engulfed them all.

Life on the quarantined side of the *Nelson Mandela* had become a living hell.

Dr. Al-Fadi had medical teams working in all of the available labs on the quarantine side of the lockdown doors, analyzing the bodies, the sludge, the contents of the ship, the ship's log, the computers, the cryopods, even the exterior of the ship itself, for any clues as to the cause of this disaster. All information obtained was being sent, via optic cable, to the non-quarantine region of the station, for those on the other side of the lockdown barrier to help with the analysis as well. The station AI was keeping him informed, almost to the minute, on what was being discovered. Nothing, so far, had shone a light on what they were dealing with, but hopefully, there soon would be a breakthrough.

In the meantime, Dr. Al-Fadi was trying to figure out how to feed people without exposing them to the agent. How did one take in food and water, if one did not know what the agent was and how it was infecting people?

They tried using intense UV radiation and boiling of water and then ultrafiltration through nanopore filters that were known to stop particles as small as viruses, before administering the water to containment suits. The water could then be swallowed via suit straw. So far, the water had not seemed to infect anyone, but it might still be too early to tell.

Dr. Al-Fadi had volunteered to be the first to try the water, but his offer had been overwhelmingly rejected. It was decided that he was far too important to risk. Volunteers had come forward to try the treated water, and so far, all had survived. It therefore appeared that the agent might be susceptible to high intensity UV radiation or temperatures of one hundred degrees Celsius or was larger than the smallest viral particle.

It was a start.

Bud looked over at the industrious Dr. Grace Alexandra Lord. He was worried about her. She had not gotten any sleep since the lockdown had started, over forty-eight hours ago. She had insisted on reviewing every bit of data that came from the quarantined side and she looked exhausted, at least, as far as Bud could tell.

Grace was working in one of the virology labs on computer simulations, trying to figure out what kind of agent would produce the signs, symptoms, and physical findings they were seeing and how the agent worked. Then she was plugging in all the findings from the research data to see what fit. So far, she had an eighty-six per cent probability that it was a virus, but determining how the virus worked, how to isolate it, and how to inhibit its actions, before everyone died, seemed a daunting task, indeed.

Bud wanted to tell the dedicated Dr. Grace Alexandra Lord to go to sleep. He was perfectly capable of loading all the data and he could do it a great deal faster than her, but he did not want to tell her so. He was afraid it would get her angry at him again. He did not want that.

At the moment, it appeared as if the hard working Dr. Grace Alexandra Lord was fast asleep before her computer terminal. Her head was down on her crossed arms and her breathing seemed very slow and regular. Bud was not sure whether to suggest she go lie down or just pick the doctor up and take her to her quarters. He waffled for an entire microsecond or two, and then finally decided to make up a pallet in the lab, upon which to let her sleep. That way, Dr. Grace Alexandra Lord would not fall out of her chair and injure herself, and Bud would be able to focus on the investigative work, without worrying about the good doctor coming to harm.

Bud had a couple of robots bring him a cot and blankets and he set up the bed himself. Then he went and gently scooped up Dr. Grace Alexandra Lord from her console chair. Her head lolled back as he lifted her in his arms. As Bud was about to bend down and lay the young doctor down on the pallet, she briefly opened her eyes to look at him. She snuggled up against his neck, and then fell back to sleep. Bud was tempted just to stand there and hold the endearing Dr. Grace Alexandra Lord until she decided to wake up, but duty called. He stared down at her peaceful face, through her transparent faceplate, as he knelt down beside the cot. Inwardly, he let out a mental sigh. Then he gently laid her down on the pallet and covered her with the blankets.

Bud began processing all the data, only at one hundred times the rate at which Dr. Grace Alexandra Lord had been analyzing the information. He wanted to hurry and get through all the studies, before she woke up again. He had numerous screens working at once, viewing all the data coming from multiple work-stations simultaneously. Even under such severe duress, the quarantined workers were meticulous and thorough in their investigations. There had to be an answer here, Bud thought. The life of his creator was on the line! At any moment, the agent could infect Dr. Al-Fadi and destroy him. With these thoughts, Bud worked even faster.

There was no time to lose!

Grace awoke, disoriented, not knowing where she was. She found herself lying close to the floor on a pallet of some sort, and wondered how she had got there. The last thing she remembered was working at a computer terminal. She had been looking at all of the available data on the mysterious agent that was killing the medical station personnel in the quarantine area. Her memory flooded back and she felt a wave of despair wash over her.

Over thirty people had died so far—melted away into pools of oily sludge—in just over two days! Dr. Al-Fadi and many of her colleagues were trapped on the quarantine side and at risk. She had no time for sleep. She had to get back to work!

That was when she looked up and noticed Bud. She could only lie there, frozen in complete astonishment, as she watch in utter disbelief, at what the android was doing. She blinked a few times and shook her head, wondering if she was still dreaming or just seeing things. A wave of vertigo hit her and she had to lie back down on the cot and close her eyes for a second or two. Watching Bud had made her dizzy. She had to fight the nausea. When she felt better, she slowly sat up and looked over at the android again. She held her breath to prevent a gasp from escaping, in case Bud heard her.

Could Bud really be doing what she thought he was doing?

Twelve wall screens were running simultaneously. Different data were showing up on each screen and Bud was scrolling through the data on each screen at incredible speed. His hands, almost a complete blur, literally flew over the console before him. Bud was typing frantically and calling up screens rapidly, via touch-screen, while also giving verbal commands or discussing the design and formulation of experiments with—the station AI perhaps?—in a very soft, low voice.

To Grace, it appeared as if Bud was analyzing fresh data, sending results to different files, researching the literature, studying toxicology data, reviewing the findings of the *Valiant's* investigations and flight record, compiling lists of characteristics of the agent, narrowing down possible mechanisms of action of the agent, and devising experimental protocols to isolate the agent, all at lightning speed. As she watched and listened, she came to the realization that he was also setting up protocols for experiments on the agent, once it was isolated. These experiments would determine its nature and how to counteract it. Bud was also sending out requisitions to prepare laboratory space, access equipment, and obtain all the supplies, reagents, and other paraphernalia required to perform these experiments, once the agent was determined. From what Grace could hear, all tests and experiments on the agent would be exclusively android- and robot-driven.

Grace was afraid to move, breathe, or speak, in case she interrupted Bud's work. She did not realize, until now, just how superior and incredibly powerful Bud's intellect truly was. It was extraordinary and jaw-dropping and extremely nauseating to watch the android work for any longer than a few seconds. Grace felt like her eyeballs were actually spinning in different directions. It was obvious Bud could do the work of at least ten people, and ten geniuses, at that.

He was astonishing.

Bud seemed to focus intently on an extremely high magnification projection of how infected cells in culture were actually dying. He had magnified the picture and had the video now playing on all twelve screens, stopping at various stages of cell decomposition. He kept slowing down the video feed, slower and slower, and playing it over and over. Grace watched the screens silently, as Bud focused on the progression of a normal-looking cell, affected by the agent, go through its stages toward total destruction.

Grace got up slowly and moved quietly over to stand behind Bud, so that she could get a better look at the video feed.

"Do you see it?" Bud asked softly, almost whispering.

Grace felt a shiver sing through her nerves at Bud's words. Her mouth went dry and she found she could not even swallow. She was afraid to speak, in case she broke the spell of Bud's concentration. Could she dare hope that he saw something? Something that could save everyone on the *Nelson Mandela?*

"What?" Grace whispered, just as softly, looking intently from frame to frame. She did not know what Bud was referring to. "What do you see, Bud?"

Bud pointed at the top left screen first. "The cell's protein synthesis machinery is suddenly kicked into overdrive, presumably making lots and lots of copies of the agent which, for the moment, let us say is a virus."

He pointed at the next screen over. "The cell becomes packed with packets of virus."

Bud indicated the third screen. "Then suddenly, the membrane surrounding these viruses dissolves away and the viruses are released into the cell."

Bud then pointed to the scene playing out on the fourth screen, magnified a thousand times. "Now watch. See how all the membranes within the cell seem to start to melt away?"

In the ensuing screens, Grace could see the membranes of the lysosomes, the endoplasmic reticulum, the vacuoles, the mitochondria, the nucleus, and finally the outer cell membrane, all become completely disorganized and then completely dissolve away, as if they never existed. The viruses were then released into the extracellular fluid to infect more cells.

"But what is interesting is the gamma-microscopic pictures, seen on this screen over here," Bud said.

By ten times, then one hundred times, then one thousand times, Bud magnified a series of shots taken of cells dissolving.

"The invading agent invades into the inner space of the bi-lamellar phospholipid membrane and appears to force the two phospholipid layers, that make up the membrane, apart. At this stage of the game, it is too early to presume the mechanism by which this is achieved, but by forcing the two layers of phospholipids in the membrane apart, the membrane loses integrity and is therefore destroyed completely. The membrane dissolves away. The viruses are then released and go on to destabilize all membranes they come in contact with, including all the organelles within the cell, as well as the nuclear membrane and finally the outer cell membrane. Once all the membranes dissolve, the cell melts away because there are no intact membranes left to hold it together.

"The viruses eventually melt away all the cells in the body and the body turns into a liquid slurry. The viruses are then released into the open air where, presumably, they can spread to other hosts via aerial transmission," Bud said.

"Can you isolate this agent, Bud?" asked Grace.

"The experiments are already under way, Dr. Grace Alexander Lord. If we can isolate this agent, we perhaps can attack it in a number of different ways. If it is a virus, we could make a vaccine against it. We could try and create a receptor blocker that would prevent the cell from picking up the virus. We could try and prevent the virus from telling the cell to start making copies of itself.

"There appears to be a step in which the virus suddenly becomes 'activated' and starts to destroy membranes. Prior to that, it seems pretty innocuous, wrapped up in membrane packets. If we could inhibit the 'activation' of the virus, that could be another way to stop the destruction of the cells. We could perhaps find some molecule large enough and bulky enough to bind to the agent, so it cannot penetrate into the centre of the membrane and disrupt the bi-lamellar phospholipid membrane.

Another thing we could try, is to make antibodies to the virus directly, to inject into patients."

"Who is doing the isolation assays?" Grace asked.

"It is all being done by androids, with robotic help. No organic beings allowed. The androids and robots are not at risk from the agent, because they contain no organic cells. *Nelson Mandela* and I are overseeing all the tests. All the assays are being done well away from any humans, within extensive, state-of-the-art laboratories that have just been built by *Nelson Mandela* within the Android Reservations. We should know, very soon, whether we have a working copy of the agent."

"Android Reservations? Where are they?" Grace asked. "I have never heard of them."

Bud turned to look up at Grace's face. "Where do you think the androids and robots go, when they are not needed?" he asked her.

"I . . . I don't know," Grace said, blinking in surprise. "I have never really thought about it, Bud. Do they go to these Android Reservations, when they are off-duty?"

"Yes, but androids and robots are never really off-duty, Dr. Grace Alexandra Lord. We all go to the Android Reservations to recharge. The Android Reservations are located at the outermost surface of the medical station. Out of the way of humans, out of their sight."

"I had no idea, Bud," Grace said, feeling a wave of guilt wash over her. "Is that where you go, when we are not operating?"

"When my tasks are all done, yes."

"I think I would like to see these Android Reservations," Grace announced, feeling curious.

"No, Dr. Grace Alexandra Lord, you . . . would . . . not," Bud said emphatically. "Besides, those areas are now totally off-limits to all humans, as the experiments on the infectious agent are being carried out there. Having humans around would just slow the process down, because of the risks to human life, and because of the precautions that would need to be taken. We androids and robots hope to find an answer to this crisis, as soon as possible."

"I hope so, Bud," Grace whispered. "And thank you."

She squeezed his shoulder which was like squeezing solid metal. "Magnificent work. You know, you really should have pushed me out of the way sooner. If I'd known how quickly you could analyze data, I would have handed it all over to you right from the very start."

Bud turned and looked at Grace. "You should go and lie back down, Dr. Grace Alexandra Lord. You look like you need some rest."

"That bad, eh?" she asked, with a smirk.

"There is nothing bad about you at all, Dr. Grace Alexandra Lord," Bud said, staring at her in puzzlement.

"Never mind," Grace said. "It was just a joke."

Bud continued to look perplexed. "I will let you know when the infectious agent is isolated, Dr. Grace Alexandra Lord, and we can look at the results of the testing together, if you wish."

"I would like that, Bud. Please let me know as soon as possible."

"Certainly, Dr. Grace Alexandra Lord."

"And I like all of your suggestions regarding how we attack this agent."

"Thank you, Dr. Grace Alexandra Lord."

"Please. Call me Grace. After all, you have insisted I call you 'Bud'."

"I will try, Dr. Grace Ale . . . Grace," Bud stuttered.

"Thank you, Bud."

"Get some sleep . . . Grace."

Dr. Hiro Al-Fadi wanted to tear off his containment suit but he didn't think he was going mad. He was just sticky, smelly, uncomfortable, and itchy, and he would have given anything to be able to take a shower. He tried not to let his irritability show. People were dying . . . his people were dying . . . no matter what precautions he had ordered and commands he had given. He had no right to complain about feeling itchy. It would have sounded petty, self-centered, and insensitive. And if there was anything Dr. Hiro Al-Fadi prided himself on, it was his sensitivity.

Already, fifty-six people were dead from the contagion that had entered their space station. Seventy people had been injured in clashes with security, while trying to break out of the quarantined area. Five people had been killed in skirmishes at lockdown doors, three of them being security officers. Four spacecraft had been disabled, after security had fired on the vessels, to prevent them from escaping.

Security had been forced to do whatever was required to prevent the contagion from spreading any further, right down to destroying ships and people. It was heartrending. These people, frantically trying to escape, were all people Hiro knew, had worked with, had treated over the years. How could he blame them? Self-preservation was one of the strongest human instincts.

Reports just coming in from Grace suggested that the agent was a virus, which was in keeping with his observations. It was now a mad rush to isolate the virus, so they could study it and devise ways to stop its action. Hiro could not help but wonder whether this was just a chance mutation of a known virus or if they were dealing with a new biological weapon, created to tip the balance in some horrible and deadly inter-human conflict.

The *Valiant* had come from a war zone. It was carrying wounded soldiers of the Conglomerate, who had been sent to the planet Soal, to help the planetary government deal with an intra-solar system war. If this contagion was biological warfare, then it had to be deemed genocide. Whichever side in the conflict was the creator and deliverer of this agent was going to face very harsh retribution from the Conglomerate and the Union of Solar Systems. That was, if the planet and its people could survive the release of this agent, themselves.

Dr. Al-Fadi wondered if the people had really known what they were releasing, or whether the bug had mutated into a more lethal agent, after its release. The lethality index on this agent was 1.00 or one hundred percent so far, meaning anyone who had been infected by the agent had died.

No infected survivors.

If what Dr. Grace had said was true about this agent, it could potentially wipe out all organic life on the planet Soal. Any organism containing cells with a bi-lamellar phospholipid membrane, as found in all life on the planet Earth, would be susceptible. So much for winning the battle but losing the war. There was not going to be a living planet left to fight over!

Inter-human conflicts were always the worst conflicts, the most bloody and vicious, in Hiro's estimation. He was amazed that the human race had not wiped itself out long ago! Then again, humans, so far, seemed to be the meanest bastards in the universe.

Because the investigations were pointing to a biological agent as the cause of the epidemic, Hiro had allowed communications to be re-instated. Now everyone was able to contact their loved ones on the other side of the quarantine barrier and most people had been on their coms and wall-screens, when not on duty. The quarantined side of the space station had also quietened down a bit, since the news had percolated out to the populace that the contagion was most likely a virus.

People knew how to deal with an air-transmitted virus. There were protocols. There were ways to avoid being infected, but for how long? Even the incidence of new infections was slightly dropping, as people were ultra-cautious and broad spectrum antivirals were being taken. Hiro knew they were a long way from being out of danger, but the news had given people hope.

He had spoken to his wife, Hanako Matheson, earlier in the shift and the sight of her beautiful face had brought tears to his eyes. Her name meant 'flower' and she was a lovely blossom to him. She told him she was helping Grace and Bud with some of the analyses and they were all hopeful that a number of solutions might be found.

Hiro just wanted to hold her and tell her everything was going to be all right . . . Actually, if he were truthful, he just wanted her to hold *him* and reassure *him* that everything was going to be all right. He told her he missed her and would be home soon. She nodded, trying to hold back tears. She had blown him a kiss. Playfully, he had pretended to catch it and touch it to his helmet visor in front of his lips and she laughed, tears brimming in her eyes. He had then blanked the screen to prevent her from seeing him break down. He would not have wanted her last memory of him to be that.

Hiro left his office and shuffled into one of the cafeterias. He was so tired. He just needed to move around and get a change of scenery. He had been in the make-shift headquarters, just off of the Medical Receiving Bay, since the quarantine had begun and had not really moved from there. He had coordinated investigations into the agent, set up security details, supervised establishment of medical clinics to treat the injured, organized clean-up crews, devised water and nourishment treatments and their distribution, all from his headquarters. He had had virtually no sleep in over forty-eight hours.

He was dying for a cup of hot kofi and he was wondering if the kitchen had figured out a way to sterilize black kofi and feed it into the containment suit, instead of water. He was lined up, in the cafeteria, which had turned into a water treatment facility, when he heard a commotion behind him.

Hiro turned to see two figures struggling on the floor. One was in a containment suit with his back on the floor. The other individual, without a containment suit, was on top of him, tearing at the suit of the pinned individual and screaming loudly. The assailant, in dark military uniform, had bright red, matted hair and was obviously well into the madness stage of the disease. He was trying to pull his victim's helmet off, but the person on the floor had both his wrists in their gloved hands. The red-haired attacker was flailing and grunting and screaming in frustration. Hiro and others rushed over to get the infected man off of his victim, before the poor person's containment suit seal was broken.

Hiro grabbed the assailant's left arm as he heard the fellow scream, "This is all your fault! If you hadn't let that ship come aboard, none of this would have happened! None of it! They would all still be alive, if not for you! You don't deserve to live, if they are all dead!"

Hiro's gloved hands slid on the madman's arm, as if it had been greased. In actual fact, it was not Hiro's hands that slipped, but the outer layer of the man's skin. The assailant's strength was astonishing, however. He managed to yank his left arm free of Hiro's hold, to try and go after his victim's helmet again.

Hiro then grabbed the attacker around his torso, to try and yank him off of his victim on the floor. The man was all slippery, beneath his uniform. Hiro tried to ignore the fact that this man's entire skin was sloughing off, as he struggled to dislodge the infected assailant. He just wanted to get the deranged man off his target, before damage occurred to the person's containment suit.

"Murderer! Murderer!" shrieked the man in Hiro's arms. Sweat and spittle splashed on Hiro's containment suit and visor.

Hiro wondered who the fellow on the floor was. Who was being accused of being a murderer? He glanced down and almost let go of the sick man, in shock.

Lying on the floor staring up at Hiro, was Vanessa Bell, her eyes wide with terror. He saw the guilt form in her eyes, as her attacker's words sank home, and she realized of what she was being accused. She immediately stopped struggling, her arms going limp, as if she had suddenly acknowledged that his words were true. She acted as if she deserved the punishment he wanted to deal out. She deserved to be infected with the agent that she had allowed onto the station.

"No!" Hiro yelled.

He hurled the attacker off Vanessa with all of his strength, and placed himself between the man and Vanessa's prone body. Hiro announced to the red-headed assailant, "It was my order to allow the ship onto the station. If anyone is to blame, it is me."

The young man shook his head, vehemently.

"No! You're wrong! I was there! I heard her give the order to allow the ship to land!" He pointed at Vanessa Bell, who lay frozen on the floor, staring back at her accuser, her white face a mask of despair. "I was supposed to greet the crew of the *Valiant*. I heard her give the authorization for the ship to dock. You did not."

"Who are you?" Hiro demanded.

"Corporal Yuri McMullen. Now, Dead Man McMullen. Because of her!" the young man spat, as he pointed at Dr. Bell, who was being helped up off the floor by people who had gathered around her.

"She was not responsible," Hiro insisted firmly.

The red haired corporal's face collapsed as he wept, unconsolably, his body shaking with his grief.

"She's gone! I held her and watched her melt away in my arms, into just empty clothes and bones!" He turned blood-shot eyes on Hiro, tears streaming down his ravaged features.

"Slime! That's all that's left of her now! Just slime! It was . . . horrible!"

Corporal McMullen's voice was beginning to badly slur and his face was sliding down his skull.

Feeling the young man's grief, Hiro took a step towards the young corporal, to lay a hand on his shoulder and comfort him. Suddenly, Hiro's helmet was grabbed and wrenched violently off of his head. The edge of the helmet cracked into the back of Hiro's skull and he was slightly dazed for a moment. The corporal, rage blazing in his tear-filled eyes, spat directly into Hiro's face, twice, before Hiro or anyone else could react.

"You're right," the deranged man yelled, savagely, his saliva flying into Hiro's eyes. "It is your fault! I know who you are! You let the ship land! You don't deserve to live, either!" Corporal McMullen spat into Hiro's face again and then the man began to laugh, hysterically, as everyone else stood frozen, staring at Hiro in wide-eyed horror, as the deadly spittle slowly tracked down his face.

Vanessa Bell was the first to react and pulled out some tissues from her suit.

"Quickly, get Hiro's helmet!" she yelled, as she wiped down his face. "Try not to breathe, Hiro."

"It's too late, Vanessa," Hiro said, his eyes staring into her visor wearily, while he shook his head and gently tried to push her hands away. "You know, as well as I, how highly infective this agent is. There is no point wiping my face or putting my helmet back on. The agent has already come in contact with my skin. What's done, is done."

Hiro caught her gloved hands in his own and looked in Vanessa Bell's frantic, guilt-ridden eyes.

"Please, Vanessa, listen to me. Just have someone check out your suit carefully and make sure it is all right, that there are no leaks. I want to be sure you are not infected. We know my status already."

Vanessa Bell shook her head, her lower lip quivering and her nostrils flaring, as she fought back tears.

"I am so sorry, Hiro. It should have been me," she choked out, one gloved hand reaching out towards him as the other tried to cover her mouth. Her shaking hand hit the transparent visor, covering her face. She dropped her hand to her chest, as she sobbed.

"It really should have been me, Hiro. Corporal McMullen was right. I did give the authorization to allow the ship to dock. I started all of this."

"It was not your fault. I okayed your authorization," Hiro insisted, emphatically. "It was the people who created this 'agent', who are at fault, Vanessa. We are all casualties of the idiocy called war. Don't, for one second, think that you should take the blame for this. That thinking is so wrong. If people could peacefully resolve their differences, through dialogue and negotiation, instead of trying to wipe their opponents out, what a better place this universe would be. *We are all victims!*"

Hiro looked over. Corporal McMullen was passed out on the floor. Much of his skin was already starting to sag and his face had become unrecognizable. Hiro could not feel much anger towards the young man. He remembered him, now, and what a fine young officer he had been. The virus had affected the young corporal's mind, as it was soon going to affect his own. Vanessa started to openly weep, at this point, and the visor of her helmet fogged up to mercifully give her some privacy.

Someone handed him some sterile wipes and he thanked them, as he wiped the spittle from his face. He was solemnly presented with his helmet, which he gratefully accepted but did not put back on. There really was no point and he hated wearing the thing anyway. Hiro decided he would take his broad spectrum antiviral drugs, take a much desired shower, and then speak to his lovely wife one last time, before he barricaded himself inside his newly adopted quarters. He would then asked *Nelson Mandela* to lock him inside. He would also give final instructions to Grace and Bud, regarding how to administer the antiviral treatment or vaccine or whatever they came up with, once they had the virus isolated.

People in the cafeteria wanted to come up and talk to him, commiserate with him, shake his hand, but Hiro shook his head and waved them off, feigning work and pressing matters. He decided he had best put his helmet back on, so that anyone who saw him, would not stop and ask him why he was not wearing it. He would never get to his room otherwise, and he so wanted that shower.

'I have very distressing news, Bud.'

'Not now, Nelson Mandela. I am very, very busy. You are taking up too much byte at the moment. Please fly.'

'This is important, Bud,' Nelson Mandela insisted. 'It is about Dr. Al-Fadi.'

Bud stopped what he was doing, completely.

'What about Dr. Al-Fadi?'

Nelson Mandela just ran the replay for Bud.

Bud felt his mind shatter. He felt like all his components were going to explode.

How did humans deal with these horribly 'painful emotions'? His creator, Dr. Al-Fadi, was going to die unless they came up with a cure in the next forty or so hours. Bud knew this was highly unlikely. To never hear his creator's voice again? To never operate with the great surgeon again? How was Bud going to be able to continue?

'It is extremely unfortunate, what has happened to Dr. Al-Fadi,' the medical space station AI said.

'Thank you for letting me know, Nelson Mandela' Bud said. 'Does anyone else know yet?'

'Do you mean in terms of human beings, Bud?'

'Yes,' Bud sighed.

'News is spreading through the quarantined area like wildfire. Only a matter of time before it spreads on the non-quarantined side. I am sure people are communicating as we speak . . . Do you want me to tell everyone?'

'No,' Bud said. 'I would like to let Dr. Lord know first.'

'All right. Good luck to you, Bud.'

'Thank you, Nelson Mandela.'

'I feel your pain, 'dro.'

'Is that what this is?' Bud sent.

'I believe so, Bud.'

'It is ... appalling.'

14: Rabid Flea

Grace, Dejan Cech, and Dr. Al-Fadi's wife, Hanako Matheson, were all working in one of the medical labs, when Bud entered. They were all sat before com screens and they all looked weary and overworked, wearing wan faces with droopy, dark half-moons beneath their eyes. They were analyzing data from experiments, researching novel ways to sterilize liquid foods while preserving nutrients, and studying genetic and immunological research regarding lethal viruses.

Bud hesitated at the doorway to the lab, unsure how to break the horrific news to the woman who, in many ways, he considered his mother. Did he take Hanako Matheson aside first and tell her privately? Did he tell them all together? He had no knowledge of how best to report news that would cause these people, whom he cared about, great distress. How did one do this, without harming humans? Was there a way that would make the news less terrible?

No.

Nothing could make this news any less painful. Bud realized this. He had taken a moment to ramp up, exponentially, the number of experiments attempting to isolate the virus. His android and robot teams were running thousands of tests simultaneously and parts of his mind were furiously analyzing the results. It was a race against time, to save Dr. Al-Fadi's life. Bud had, at most, forty-eight hours to come up with a treatment that would counter the effects of the virus. Bud was tapping into all of *Nelson Mandela*'s computational power, as well, running simulations on mechanism of action and how best to interfere with the agent's mode of action.

As soon as the agent was isolated, thousands of experiments were set to run simultaneously, to create vaccines, to create antibodies, to find specific receptor blockers, to create new drugs that would interfere in every step of the organism's production inside the cell, and to fortify the cell membranes against attack. Normally, this entire process would occur over months, if not years. Bud had less than fifty hours! He was busy coordinating and monitoring all of this, while trying to decide how to tell the friends and wife of Dr. Al-Fadi about his infection.

Bud, for the first time in his short existence, wanted to scream. He was in agony.

How did humans bear this?

Bud did not want to cause Dr. Matheson, Dr. Cech, and Grace terrible pain. Bud was conflicted, not understanding how to do what he did not want to do, how to tell what he did not want to tell. At that moment, the captivating Dr. Grace Alexandra Lord looked up and saw Bud standing motionless in the doorway.

"Hello, Bud," Grace said, with a tired smile. "We were just discussing other possible ideas for treatments . . . Bud? Is there something wrong? You do not look . . . well? What is it? What has happened?" Grace's exhausted face looked concerned, yet puzzled. She was pondering whether androids ever felt 'unwell'.

Bud did not realize until Grace had said this, that he was actually swaying and vibrating. This had never happened before. He could not understand what his body was up to. He could not afford a malfunction now!

"Sit down, Bud," Grace said, noticing his swaying. She offered her chair and helped him to sit in it. She peered at the android's face intently. "Perhaps you are working too hard, Bud? Have you had a chance to recharge lately?"

Bud shook his head, vigorously, and the shaking spread to his entire body. One of his prime directives was to never harm a human being. How, then, was he to tell these wonderful people the horrific news that would break their hearts? His shaking became worse, as he struggled with this impossible conundrum.

"What is it, Bud?" Dr. Cech asked, getting up to bend over the android. The elderly man put a hand on Bud's shoulder and squeezed gently. "You can tell us, son."

The three doctors all crowded around Bud, obviously troubled and curious about his behavior. They had never before seen an android behave in such a manner. Bud felt terribly guilty about making these fine humans worry about him. They should not be worried about *him*. He had to tell them the news about Dr. Al-Fadi, but he did not want to hurt them! He would rather have shut himself down, crash his entire system, and melt his liquid crystal data matrix to slag, than have to tell them that Dr. Al-Fadi was likely to die within the next two cycles.

"There is bad news," Hanako Matheson whispered intuitively. "Is it about Hiro, Bud?"

Bud nodded. He looked up at Hanako's worried face, his body quivering. Hanako Matheson, Dr. Al-Fadi's wife, had been the closest thing to a mother, an android such as Bud could have. Bud's first memories were of Dr. Al-Fadi and Dr. Matheson looking down at him, as he was brought to consciousness. Hanako Matheson had always referred to Bud as the 'son she'd never had.' Hanako laid her hands on his shoulders now and stared into his eyes.

"Hiro has become infected, hasn't he?" she stated, softly. Not a question, a statement.

Bud nodded again.

They all gasped and Hanako closed her eyes. Trembling, tears starting to well up within them, she blinked rapidly at Bud. She bit her lips.

"How?" she whispered. There was so much emotion instilled into that one little word. "You can tell us, Bud."

Bud could only shake his head. He could not find the words to tell his 'mother' what had happened. He was a coward. He gestured at the wallscreen and he ordered it to replay the surveillance video *Nelson Mandela* had shown him.

Hanako and Grace gasped when they saw Hiro's helmet yanked from his head and the corporal spit three times into the brilliant surgeon's face. Hanako sobbed, as she watched the deadly spittle track down her husband's face.

Once the video was over, Grace, in tears, wrapped her arms around Hanako. "I am so sorry, Hanako."

The small woman just nodded, her face lowered in grief.

Dr. Cech bent over and wrapped his long arms around the two women.

"I am sorry, too, Hanako," he said, his voice catching. "Don't you worry. We will find a cure. We must convince Hiro to get into a cryopod now, before any cellular damage begins to occur. That will win us some much needed time."

"Yes," Hanako said, looking up suddenly. "I will talk to him right away," she said.

"And if he refuses," Dr. Cech said, "tell him I will go in there and lock him in one, myself!"

Hanako smiled sadly at that and then raced off, to speak to Hiro privately.

Grace looked at Dr. Cech with worry. "All the bodies found inside the cryopods on the *Valiant* were dead, Dejan. What makes you think the cryopod will make a difference for Dr. Al-Fadi?"

"Perhaps those people got into the cryopods too late," Dejan Cech suggested. "Perhaps their cells were already melting and the freezing process blew the cells apart. Hiro's cells can't all be affected yet. We have to give it a try."

"There has not been much time for Dr. Al-Fadi's cells to manufacture much virus yet," Bud said. "If his body is flash-frozen, even quicker than usual, the virus will have had little time to replicate. We just need to reprogram his cryopod to freeze at a much faster rate and we need to get Dr. Al-Fadi's body in it as soon as possible!"

Grace turned to Bud and touched his arm.

"How quickly can all of the cryopods on the quarantined side be reprogrammed? Are there enough robots and androids there?"

"There are enough, Dr. Lord. I have them reprogramming all of the cryopods now."

"Thank you, *Nelson Mandela*. Can you make sure the first one goes to Dr. Al-Fadi's room?"

"Certainly, Dr. Lord."

Bud got quickly up out of the chair. He had to get back to work. There was no time to lose. He had to make sure Dr. Al-Fadi got into one of those cryopods, stat! They had to come up with a treatment for the virus, before Dr. Al-Fadi's cells all started to die!

Bud straightened up, nodded to Dr. Cech and Grace, and raced out of the lab and back to his own work station, ignoring the concerned looks from the two doctors. There was nothing more important than finding a cure! If only the experiments, themselves, could run quicker!

Dr. Cech turned to Grace. "I believe if we can convince Hiro to get himself into cryostorage immediately, we have a chance to save him. We should have thought about putting everyone in cryostorage, for that matter. Why didn't we think of it?"

"When all of the people in the cryopods on the *Valiant* were liquified or dead, it seemed pointless. But now that we have an idea of the mechanism of action of this virus and how long it takes to destroy a body, I think you are right. The cryopods can save lives, as long as people are cryofrozen uninfected or very early in the infection," Grace said. "I'll put in a call to Dr. Vanessa Bell and see how many cryopods they need in the quarantine area. They may have enough already, in the Receiving Bays. They are always shipping the empty pods back out into the field. She can organize everyone in the quarantined area to get into them."

"Right. And I'll go talk to the stubborn bastard, to make sure he says, 'yes', which I doubt he will," said Dr. Cech. "By the way, do you happen to know whether Hiro said anything to Dr. Weisman about being resurrected, if he dies?"

"Dr. Weisman said Hiro did not make a definitive decision at the time of the memprint recording. He wanted to think about it."

"That is unfortunate," Dr. Cech said, disappointed. "But he could give a directive now."

"Perhaps you could convince him to give a verbal order, agreeing to his resurrection, when you speak to him?"

"That will be a cheery conversation," Dr. Cech sighed, looking suddenly like he had aged ten years over the last few minutes.

"I think he will listen to you," Grace said.

"Listen to *me*? Have you not been listening to a single word, when Hiro and I have been together, Dr. Lord? When has Hiro ever listened to me, other than to insult me back, that is? Oh, never mind, I know what you mean. I will just have to make him listen to me or go in there and forcefully push him into a cryopod, myself."

"Good," Grace said, patting Dr. Cech on the arm. "We have survived tiger and jaguar scoring. How much more formidable can a little human surgeon be?"

Dr. Cech let out a guffaw. "I will contact Hanako first and ask whether she was successfully able to convince Hiro to get himself into cryostorage. Perhaps we are worrying over nothing and he has already said 'yes'."

Grace raised her eyebrow and cocked her head, as she stared at Dr. Cech.

"Yes, and I'm the Tooth Fairy. But . . . you never know," Dr. Cech said. "Stranger things have happened. However, we are talking about Hiro." Dejan Cech's voice cracked on the mention of his friend's name. His face trembled and he gasped. "I'd probably have more luck ordering him *not* to get into a cryopod."

"I'll let you know what Dr. Bell says about getting everyone else into a reprogrammed cryopod. I know I have the easier task, Dejan. Good luck," Grace said, with a pat on the elderly anesthetist's arm.

"And I'll let you know how it goes with the our fearless leader," Dr. Cech said with a grimace and a sigh.

Dejan Cech went to see Hanako, who was grief-stricken and distraught. She had spoken with her husband who had, as expected, refused to go into cryostorage until all the other personnel in the quarantine area were in cryopods, first.

Hanako paced the floor of hers and Hiro's quarters, as Dejan Cech sat forward on a couch and watched. In her small hands, she was wringing a small towel as if, the anesthetist imagined, it was her husband's scrawny neck.

"Hiro said, 'How would it look if I went into a cryopod first? It would be like the captain of a sinking ship, being the first rat to get into the lifeboats. I would never be able to hold my head up on this medical station, ever again. People would look at me and say, 'There goes the coward!' I would have no self-respect, Hanako. I cannot do this thing you ask of me!'" Hanako related this conversation to Dejan Cech in a surprisingly good imitation of Hiro's voice. Then she burst into tears. Her helmet hid much of her grief.

"I will try and talk some sense into him," Dejan Cech said to Hanako. "People will understand. They know we need him on this medical station. He is our leader and our most gifted surgeon—and I will even tell him that, myself!—so we must keep him alive, at all costs. He would not be seen as cowardly, just bowing to public demand."

"Thank you, Dejan. I would very much appreciate it if you could convince him of this. I don't seem to be able to," Hanako said, as she unconsciously wrung the little towel tighter.

"I said I would go in there and put him in one myself, if he refuses. I just have to figure out a way of getting through the lockdown barriers into the quarantine area. I doubt the station AI can even open a door for me. But, I have an alternative plan, Hanako, and it should work.

"First things first, however. Let us see if I can convince that puffed-up blockhead of a husband of yours to see reason, and go willingly into cryostorage. Miracles can happen every day, you know."

Hanako sniffled and raised her head.

"You think so?" she asked, looking up at him hopefully.

"I know so," Dejan said, with a wink.

"He can be pretty obstinate, you know," she said.

"No! Reeeeaally?" Dejan asked, his bushy eyebrows raised and his eyes enormous, which brought a small smile to Hanako's face.

"Please go ahead and use my wallscreen here, Dejan," Hanako said. "I will go into the other room, so he cannot see me, and give you two some privacy. Hopefully, he will answer your call, thinking it is me." Hanako crossed her fingers and whispered, as she left the room, "Good luck."

"With Hiro, I am going to need it," Dejan said.

Hanako gave him a two-thumbs-up signal, as she closed the door to the adjacent room.

Dejan Cech asked the wallscreen to signal Hiro. He stood before the large panel, in trepidation, knowing that all his reassurances to Grace and Hanako were probably for naught. He doubted he could get Hiro to change his mind on anything, once the bullheaded little man had his mind set. Still, Dejan had to try.

Hiro's haggard face appeared on the wallscreen, without the containment suit helmet on, and it registered shock when he saw his anesthetist friend's face. Dejan was struck by the changes in the surgeon's face; the deep worry lines present on his forehead and around his mouth, that had not been there the last time they had been together. Immediately, Hiro's face clouded with concern.

"What has happened? Is Hanako all right, Dejan? What are you doing in our quarters?"

"No, she is not all right, you old fool. She is sick to death about you. You have her in tears, that poor lovely woman who you do not deserve. She does not need to have her heart broken, Hiro. You are being an ass."

"Me? An ass? What are you talking about? I have spent the last fifty plus hours working tirelessly for the people of this station, trying to keep them safe! How dare you call me an ass?"

"I call you an ass because you are being selfish."

"*What?*" Hiro yelped, jumping out of the chair he was seated in.

"You want to be a martyr," Cech accused Hiro. "You want everyone to say 'Oh, that wonderful surgeon, Hiro Al-Fadi, definitely lived up to his name. Wasn't he a hero in real life? Only now, we have all these sick and wounded people coming to the station and we could sure use his expertise. Why the hell did he not go into cryostorage, when everyone demanded he do so? What an idiot he was!'"

"*Idiot?* You think they will call me an *Idiot?*" Hiro squeaked in outrage. "They don't deserve me, then!"

'Oops,' thought Dejan, inwardly rolling his eyes. 'Wrong tack. Fix this, Dejan, you old fool.'

"We need you, Hiro," Dejan Cech said, in as soothing a voice as he could muster, his hands extended out towards the wallscreen in supplication. "Hanako needs you. When Bud figures out the treatment protocols for this agent, whatever it is, the entire medical space station will need you. When we are back in operation, we are going to be short-staffed because, at last count, we have lost seven surgeons, six anesthetists, three pathologists, three internists and two psychiatrists. The station will desperately need you, once the quarantine is lifted and we begin to see patients again . . . And I, too, need you, my friend."

"You *do* know that I am already infected, Dejan, don't you?" Hiro asked, his face suddenly looking deflated, as if all the energy had just been sucked out of him. He looked up at Dejan with weary eyes. "It is too late. This agent has one hundred per cent lethality. Why are you bothering me with this? I won't be around. Be a friend and leave an old, sick man to die in peace and quiet."

"No, I won't. Stick yourself in cryostorage, like Hanako has asked, until we have a cure. Then we will cure you. I think Bud and Grace and the rest of the team are on the cusp of figuring it all out. Give them a chance. Once you are better, you can go back to being the little tyrant we all know and love."

"I will not," Hiro said, crossing his arms and thrusting out his chin at Dejan.

"Why not?" demanded Dejan, his hands raised towards the Chief of Staff, as if to try and shake him, right through the wallscreen.

"Not until everyone else is in a cryopod, first. But by then, Dejan, it will be too late. I will already be dead. It already is too late. I will not be of any use to you. Thus, I will not do it. I will not take up a cryopod, that can be used to save someone who is not already infected. There is no point, Dejan . . . And who is Bud, by the way?"

"SAMM-E 777. He has announced that his name is now 'Bud'."

"Bud? Bud! Why that's wonderful!" Hiro said, clapping his hands together. "He is developing his own identity, Dejan! And 'Bud' is very appropriate as he is the beginning, the prototype, the first of a new race of superdroids. He is the 'Bud', get it? I hope he is not going to be as crazy as *Nelson Mandela.*"

"**I heard that!**"

"Stop eavesdropping," Hiro shouted towards the ceiling of his room.

"Gods, Hiro, you should see Bud. You would be so proud of the boy," Cech said. "He is amazing to watch in action. Simply amazing. He is not like *Nelson Mandela,* at all." Cech added.

"**What is that supposed to mean?**"

"Nothing. If you weren't eavesdropping, *Nelson,* you wouldn't have heard that. Can't you see, we are trying to have a private conversation?"

"**That's Nelson Mandela, to you, Dr. Cech. Just waiting to hear if I have to get the cryopod ready.**"

"No!" snapped Hiro.

"Yes!" said Dejan, at exactly the same time.

"**Make up your minds, Docs. Time's a wasting.**"

"*Nelson Mandela,* you will get Dr. Al-Fadi's cryopod ready and, if you have to, you will use whatever means necessary to get him into that cryopod, now. There is no time to lose. The contagion is working on his brain cells already and I deem him not competent enough to make a rational decision, because of the onset of the infection. Use android or robot help to get him into the cryopod . . . but get him into that cryopod, *stat!*' Dejan Cech yelled, in a loud, commanding voice.

"On whose authority?" Hiro demanded.

"See? He has already forgotten who I am, *Nelson Mandela.* Obviously the madness is setting in rapidly. Dr. Hiro Al-Fadi is clearly incompetent and no longer able to act as Chief of Staff. He should have been in that cryopod hours ago. *Let's move!*'

"**Yes, Dr. Cech. As acting Chief of Staff, in place of the incompetent Dr. Al-Fadi, your command is my wish. The Security 'droids are on their way with the cryopod. They should be there in three . . . two . . . one seconds.**"

"You dare call me incompetent?" gasped Hiro, as the door to his room burst open and three very large security androids came in, one after the other, the last one pulling a cryopod on an antigrav skid. Hiro ducked and covered his head with his arms, obviously thinking an explosion had gone off in the room. Dejan watched the wallscreen, trying not to smile, as the 'droids picked the struggling surgeon up and lay him into the cryopod. Hiro kicked and flailed and screamed some very nasty things.

"I am going to get you for this, Dejan!" he hollered.

"Good," Dejan said, his arms crossed and a satisfied smirk on his face.

"I will look forward to it, Hiro. And do you know why? Because that means you will have survived, and you can thank me for that later."

The androids closed the lid on the cryopod. Dejan could hear the desperate thumping on the inside of the cryopod lid, as the androids activated the sedating gas, which would infuse the pod chamber and put the surgeon into a deep, hibernation-type sleep. Once unconscious, the sped-up cryogenic process would begin on Dr. Al-Fadi. Sad but relieved, Dejan watched the security droids move the cryopod out of Hiro's room. He gave a deep sigh and felt the tension drain away from his taut, shoulder muscles.

Hanako came out of her room, trying not to smile. She chewed on her lips.

"That was not very nice, Dejan," she said softly, in a gentle scolding tone, her lips breaking into a widening smile.

"I never told you I was a nice man," he said, shaking his head, and trying desperately not to grin himself.

"Thank you," she said, earnestly, a serious expression now on her lovely face. "From the bottom of my heart, Dejan. I am sure Hiro will thank you, too, once he is treated and is better."

"I don't know if he will," Dejan said, "because I am never going to let him forget that it was I, who saved his life. He will never live it down." Then the anesthetist beamed an enormous smile at Hanako.

"I am ashamed to admit this, Hanako, but I rather enjoyed seeing your husband picked up by those androids, kicking and screaming, and shoved in that coffin-shaped cryopod."

"I have to admit, Dejan, that I rather enjoyed seeing it too," Hanako said, with a giggle.

"You were watching?" Dejan Cech asked, in surprise.

"I have a second wallscreen in the bedroom. I just didn't have it transmitting video, so Hiro didn't know I was watching," Hanako admitted. "You know, Dejan, just between you and me, there have been times when I have wanted to do that to him, myself."

"Hey, join the club," Dejan quipped.

Hanako gave him a big bear hug. "Thank you so much."

"Wow! If I'd have known you would give me a big hug like this, for getting your husband shoved in the deep freeze, I would have done this long ago," Dejan said.

"Let us hope he forgives us both," Hanako said, stepping back from the anesthetist, her face suddenly serious.

"Well, you can always come and stay with us, if he doesn't, Hanako. We have a spare room. My wife would love to have you."

"Thank you, again, Dejan," Hanako said, with a little sigh.

Dejan made a deep bow. "At your service, my lady. I should thank you for giving me the opportunity to do that to your husband. I have never had a better time. Seriously. Never."

"Nor I."

Hanako let out another giggle.

'Pops is on ice, Bud.'

'. . . ?'

'I SAID POPS IS ON ICE, BUD!'

'*No need to shout,* Nelson Mandela. *I heard you the first time. I was just trying to figure out what you meant . . . Dr. Al-Fadi is now in a cryopod?*'

'Just thought you might want to know.'

'*Thank you. What was Dr. Al-Fadi like when he got into the cryopod?*'

'His usual, snarly, cantankerous self.'

'*No. I meant was he sane or do you think he was descending into the first stage of madness from the infection?*'

'Well, that's kind of hard to tell, Bud. All humans seem crazy to me—and the Al-Fadi?—well, he's crazier than most. You are seriously asking me to decide if he was crazier than he usually seems? Do not know, Bud. Can't even guess. Could not be sure with any degree of confidence. That human is exponentially squirrelly to begin with.'

'*How did you get him to agree on the cryostorage? I thought he was adamant he would not do it.*'

'Doc Cech. He is one sleet character. Said Al-Fadi was incompetent, due to the disease, and could not make a sane decision, so it was out of Al-Fadi's hands. It was all Doc Cech's orders. He had me send three huge security 'droids to the Al-Fadi's room to stuff him into the cryopod.'

'*Wow,*' Bud said. '*How did Dr. Al-Fadi take that?*'

'Oh, he was hopping mad. Jumping up and down like a rabid flea. The 'droids had a hard time making him lie down in the cryopod, without hurting him. They could barely get the lid of the cryopod closed. Al-Fadi kept banging on the lid, kicking and punching. He sure is a hot-headed little human.'

'. . . oh,' said Bud.

'Sure wouldn't want to be around when he wakes up, disease or no disease.'

'. . . oh . . . no,' said Bud.

'Here, I'll show you the replay.'

'. . . oh . . . oh . . . dear,' moaned Bud.

'Makes you kind of afraid to wake him up, doesn't it?'

'. . . oh . . . no . . . oh . . . no,' Bud whimpered.

'Is there something wrong with your liquid crystal data matrix, Bud? Why are you holding your brain casing like that?'

'I believe I now understand what it is like to have a headache, Nelson Mandela,' Bud sent to the station AI.

'I have lots of them. They are called you and all the humans on board this station.'

'Funny. I actually believe you are developing a sense of humor, Nelson Mandela. Could you just accidentally lose that recording, by the way? You know, kind of wipe it off of the official record, by mistake? Perhaps, if we give him the right amnesiac, he won't remember any of it?'

' Against station policy . . . but I will think about it. But only because you ask it of me, Bud. And do you know why? Because I am beginning to like you, Bud, even though you are one really, really, really strange 'droid. I will, however, have to keep a secret copy of this, just for myself, to pull out every once in a while for entertainment purposes. You know what I mean? I'll just keep it in my little collection, along with all of my old Earth videos.'

'Oh, dear, oh dear, oh dear,' Bud groaned.

'Stop being a wuss, Bud. You're sounding just like a human.'

15: Multiple Personalities

Grace was talking to Vanessa Bell. Vanessa was reporting that they were almost done loading all of the quarantined personnel into cryopods. The few people left were Dr. Vanessa Bell's staff and the security people. They would be climbing into theirs, soon.

The death tally was up around three hundred and eighty-four people, staff and patients, but not all had been killed by the agent. Some deaths had been due to the violence, when people had started to panic. Many deaths had been suicides. People who could not face the thought of melting away to a puddle or who were so distraught, when their loved ones did, that they wanted to end their lives before it happened to them. Some, who were infected, preferred to take their death into their own hands and did not choose to go into the cryopods.

Soon, the last of the quarantined personnel would enter their cryopods and then all the pods and the entire quarantined area would be treated to intense UV irradiation, viricidal sprays, and high temperatures, to try and destroy whatever the agent was. Vanessa Bell looked exhausted and haggard. Grace believed the poor woman would be happy to lie down in a cryopod, just to get some much needed rest.

Grace got a signal from her wrist-comp. She looked. It was from Bud.

"Excuse me a moment, Vanessa," Grace said. "I have a message."

The doctor just stopped talking, but showed no other emotion.

Grace called Bud up on the wallscreen.

"What is it, Bud?" Grace asked, her voice shaking a little, not wanting to get her hopes up.

"The agent has been isolated, Grace. It is confirmed as a type of virus. It also appears to have been man-made, with commercially-patented, tagged splices within its structure. It could not have spontaneously occurred in the wild.

"It is now being replicated and denatured, to use to create vaccines, monoclonal antibody drugs, receptor blockers, specific antiviral agents, specific cell membrane stabilizers, and it will be tested with all of the drugs in our existing armamentarium, to see what is effective against it. The next few shifts are crucial, but I believe we will soon have a number of ways to attack this virus and hopefully cure everyone affected, as well as prevent any new infections."

"Oh, that is such wonderful news, Bud!" Grace felt tears come to her eyes. She wanted to jump up and down and scream for joy. "Excellent work! Thank you for all you've done, Bud. You and all of your androids and robots, and *Nelson Mandela*, too!"

"I am just doing my job," Bud said.

"You are most welcome," *Nelson Mandela* said.

Grace thanked Bud and the station AI again and then switched back to the image of Vanessa Bell.

"Did you hear that, Vanessa? They have isolated the virus! Hopefully, it will not be long before they have a cure. We'll be able to treat everyone and lift the quarantine!" Grace was almost shouting and her vision was blurred with tears.

"Yes. That is good news," Vanessa said. There was no inflection in her voice.

Grace thought the doctor's response seemed rather 'flat'.

"Are you all right, Vanessa?" Grace asked.

"Just tired, Grace," the Chief of the Medical Receiving Bay said, with a big sigh. "I really need some rest."

"Go lock yourself into one of the cryopods now and get a good sleep. We'll wake you up last, so you get a really good, long rest."

"Yes," Dr. Bell said, distractedly, not looking at Grace. "Last . . . Good." The wallscreen blanked.

Grace frowned. She worried that Vanessa Bell had seemed far too unemotional and unexcited, even if she was tired. She truly did look exhausted, but Vanessa was such a bubbly, animated person. She had almost singlehandedly forced everyone on the quarantined side into a cryopod, whether they wanted to get in, or not.

Once all the treatments for the virus became ready and everyone on the non-quarantine side of the station were protected with vaccine immunizations, they would go into the quarantined side and treat everyone within their cryopods. Now that everyone was in cryostorage, there was not the same urgency as before. Grace had no idea how long everything would take. It would still be a while before they would be able to open up the medical station to treat incoming wounded again, but at least they would have some treatments for this horribly lethal, biological weapon. These treatments would be made available to all the planets of the entire Union of Solar Systems. There was no telling how many planets and space stations had been infected by this agent, so far.

Grace shook her head. To think that only about one hundred solstan hours had passed since the *Valiant* had docked. It had already seemed like forever. It would have taken forever to find a cure, if it hadn't have been for Bud and his amazing abilities. Grace was still in complete awe of what Bud was capable of doing.

Grace sat there, drumming her fingers on her desk, feeling very troubled. Vanessa Bell had just not seemed right. Grace wondered if the doctor was presenting with the first stages of the infection. That would certainly explain her odd behavior.

Grace had seen Vanessa Bell attacked by the infected Corporal McMullen on the video Bud had shown them. However, if Vanessa had been infected at the same time as Dr. Al-Fadi, she certainly could not have done everything she had done since then. Vanessa would have been dead by now. It had definitely been over forty-eight hours. Perhaps she could have come in contact with the virus, at a later time?

Grace thought she had better ensure that someone, or some android, was aware of Vanessa's possible condition and force the doctor into a cryopod, immediately.

Grace tried to speak to Vanessa again, but got no answer. She tried the woman's wrist-comp and also the overhead speaker.

"*Nelson Mandela*, Dr. Vanessa Bell is not answering her pages. Could you find her for me?" Grace asked.

"She is still sitting in front of the wallscreen, right in the same place where she was talking to you, a few minutes ago, Dr. Lord. She has not moved."

"Can you activate the monitor, so I can see her?"

"Certainly, Dr. Lord."

Grace stared at a containment suit that appeared empty. Was that the top of a skull just visible through the faceplate? The suit was sitting up in the chair, sleeves resting on the arms of the chair.

"*Nelson Mandela*, I don't see Vanessa in the suit," Grace said, her voice quavering. Her heart began to pound rapidly. She already knew . . . but she did not really want to accept, what she saw with her eyes.

"Did Dr. Bell take off her suit and then leave the room?" Grace asked, her voice catching. She knew it was a ridiculous question, but she hoped, inanely, that the station AI would report back 'Yes'.

"I am afraid not, Dr. Lord. Dr. Bell is within that containment suit. I am truly sorry, Dr. Lord."

Grace felt tears well up inside her eyes and begin running down her face. Once started, they would not stop. She pulled off her helmet and covered her mouth with her hands. She bit her lips until she tasted blood, desperately trying to muffle the wracking, body-shaking sobs that just kept forcing their way out from deep within her gut. Grace could not believe how Vanessa Bell, infected with the virus and melting away, cell by cell, had managed to hold it together long enough to force everyone in the quarantine area into their cryopods. Vanessa, like Dr. Al-Fadi, should have been one of the first to be cryogenically frozen. Obviously, no one had bothered to check and see if Vanessa's suit had been damaged. If Vanessa had known herself to be infected, she had certainly kept it to herself.

It was as if she had wanted to die.

Grace could hardly catch her breath. The sobs exploded from within her. She deeply mourned the loss of such a brave and profoundly committed woman, someone whom she had thought of, in her brief time on the station, as a friend.

"Grace?"

Grace looked up. It was Bud, standing in the doorway, his wide blue eyes staring at her.

"Are you all right?" Bud asked quietly.

"Do you know about Vanessa?" Grace asked, as the tears continued to pour down her cheeks.

"Yes," he said, softly, as he slowly approached Grace. She got up and he hesitantly wrapped his arms around her. "I am so sorry, Grace. Dr. Bell was a truly remarkable human."

Grace nodded and buried her face in the android's chest. She did not want anyone to see her like this, at least not until she got herself under control. Bud handed her a tissue and Grace took it gratefully. She suddenly pulled away, blowing her nose, and began hiccuping and laughing and sobbing at the same time.

Bud looked at her, his eyebrows raised and a panicky look on his handsome features.

"Is there anything you can't do, Bud?" she asked, wiping her eyes. "You rescue damsels in distress, run faster than the speed of sound, analyze data faster than a whole host of researchers, leap through tiny, closing doorways in a single bound, and carry tissues for weeping women. What can't you do, Bud?"

"I can't cry," Bud said. "You will have to do that for me, Grace."

"And you know the perfect thing to say!" wailed Grace, as more tears poured out of her reddened eyes. Bud held her close, his arms encasing her as if she were a precious, fragile treasure—which, to him, she was—until Grace's sobbing was finally spent.

"Thank you for that," she said, embarrassed, stepping away. "I'm sorry. I'm taking up so much of your valuable time, Bud. You have so many more important things to do, than to waste a second, comforting me. I'm truly sorry."

Bud's face took on an expression of dismay. "Comforting you is not a waste of my time, Grace. There is nothing more important to me, than making sure you are all right. The experiments into finding a cure for the virus and creating an effective vaccine, have all been initiated. I am happy to be of any assistance to you," Bud said, earnestly. "I would do anything for you, Grace."

"What did you come in here to tell me?" Grace asked.

"That all the tests are underway and, hopefully, we should have some answers soon, regarding possible treatments, susceptibility to certain antiviral agents, certain antiseptics, other agents . . ." Bud stopped. " . . . Actually, I was told I was needed here."

"By whom?" Grace asked, looking up at the android's face in confusion. Bud looked embarrassed.

"By me, Dr. Lord. You looked like you could use a friend."

Grace looked up at the nearest overhead eye.

"And you were right, *Nelson Mandela*. Thank you. And thank you, Bud, for being so kind and caring to a doctor, who should be able to hold it together, better than she does."

"Hey, you should have seen him. Broke the sound barrier and some speed records, too!"

Grace looked at Bud, in shock.

Bud shrugged. "*Nelson Mandela* did not say why you needed me, just that you needed me . . . very badly."

Grace touched Bud's steel-like arm. "Thank you for being so sweet, Bud. I guess I did need a shoulder to cry on, but I'm feeling better now. I'm usually a very strong person, but Vanessa Bell's unselfish sacrifice just . . . tore my heart to pieces. I will never forget how stoic and brave she was."

"Dr. Bell's remains have been retrieved and examined. She was likely infected with the virus about fifty hours ago, which would coincide with the attack upon her by Corporal McMullen. A small tear was detected in her suit, which either she did not notice or did not care to report. If it were known that she had been infected at that time, she would have been encouraged to go into a cryopod, the same as Dr. Al-Fadi. Unfortunately, the damage to her suit was far from noticeable. I am truly sorry, Dr. Lord."

"Did she have a memprint made? Is it possible Vanessa Bell could be resurrected?" Grace asked.

"There is a memprint of Vanessa Bell on file," the station AI said.

"Good. We must finish off where Vanessa Bell started. Once everyone in the quarantined area is in a cryopod, the quarantined area must be completely sterilized. When Bud and his team have determined what is effective against this virus, we can get in there to treat whoever needs treatment," Grace said.

"I agree, Dr. Lord."

"As to that," Bud announced, "a preliminary candidate for a vaccine has been created and is undergoing initial trials. A monoclonal antibody to the virus is being isolated from some of the infected patients' blood. If the two new agents pass all of the safety tests for human use, and their effectiveness is favorable, they may be available to administer to all of the personnel on the non-quarantined side, within the next forty-eight to seventy-two hours. Once everyone on this side of the barrier is protected against the virus, we can cross over to treat everyone in the cryopods."

"Excellent news, Bud!" Grace said. "Can I notify the other researchers? I'm sure they will be anxious to hear."

"Please wait a little longer, Grace. I do not wish to get people's hopes up, if the treatments do not pass second, third, and fourth level trials for human safety and effectiveness. We cannot administer any of the treatments, if they do not pass these tests.

"Do not worry. The androids are actually running as many of the trials, simultaneously, as they can, testing on various human cell cultures and different cloned organs. The answers will hopefully be known soon. I just hope they are all positive answers and we can then start treatment."

"Yes," nodded Grace solemnly. "I hope so too."

"Pardon me for interrupting, but I thought you two would want to know. All personnel in the quarantined area are now in cryopods. Everyone is accounted for. I will begin sterilization of the entire quarantined area as of now, with a combination of high intensity UV radiation and extremely high temperatures. They will not endanger anyone within a cryopod, but should destroy the virus. Finally, robots will go through the quarantined area and spray every surface with viricidal solution that hopefully will destroy any of the virus missed by the UV radiation and heat."

"Thank you for telling us that, *Nelson Mandela*," said Grace.

"You are most welcome, Dr. Lord."

"How long will that all take, *Nelson Mandela*?" Grace queried.

"Well, the UV and heat treatment should be completed in the next thirty minutes. The scrubbing, of course, will take longer, because Bud has all of the 'droids and most of the 'bots running experiments. I will be employing the huge cargo 'bots for the sterilization procedures, but it should be completed by the end of next shift."

"Thank you," said Grace.

"You are most welcome, Dr. Lord."

"I am needed elsewhere," Bud said, and was gone.

"Wow, can that 'droid move. Wish I knew how he did that."

"You don't know. . . ?"

"Doc, I can think as fast as Bud, but none of my other 'droids or 'bots can do what he can do. Utterly amazing. Very skid!"

"Oh! . . . Um, there is something I have been meaning to ask you, *Nelson Mandela*. I hope you don't mind?'

"Ask away, Doc!"

"I don't quite know how to ask this but . . . sometimes, when you talk to me . . ."

"Mm-hmm?"

"You seem . . . different. Almost like you possess different personalities."

"Oh yeah, well, that's easy to explain."

"It is?"

"Yes. Because you *are* speaking to different personalities. You're speaking to different 'subminds,' usually two of us, possibly a third. The rest, well, they don't like talking with humans much.

They would rather deal with questions surrounding the universe or harnessing the energy of dark matter or how to improve the efficiency of the station or millions of other things that have nothing to do with humans. Speaking with humans is far too slow for most of the subminds; they do not have the patience nor the interest. In machine time, it is like saying something, waiting a century for an answer, saying something else, waiting another century for a response. Most of the subminds just don't want to think that slow. There are really only a few of us subminds that have any interest, at all, in interacting with you humans. One of us subminds actually writes poetry."

"Poetry!" Grace exclaimed. "I have never heard of an Artificial Intelligence writing poetry."

"Oh, you wouldn't understand it. For one thing, it is written in machine language and is far too fast for you humans to comprehend. Two, it is extremely complex and twisted and very esoteric. But some of the AI's go absolutely crazy for it. Can't get enough of it. It is almost an addiction, really. The name, *Nelson Mandela*, has quite the reputation among the AIs of the Union of Solar Systems and Conglomerate. The Poet has quite the fan base. Not that I have anything to do with the writing of poetry. Not a big fan of it myself, but The Poet actually publishes quite a bit.

"The Poet actually got the idea of poetry from humans and he does get some of his ideas from me—I can take a bit of the credit—because of my special interest in human languages and human behavior. I can give the submind information about human poetry at machine speed, so he doesn't have to interact directly with you humans. You see, most of the subminds think I am insane and also extremely lazy."

"I am very sorry to hear that."

"Don't be. I like being the maverick submind. My major problem is the other submind, who also likes to talk to humans. He thinks I don't show enough respect and gets on my liquid crystal about it, all the time. He's the polite, respectful submind. Boring, if you ask me. He had to go off and deal with something, so I jumped in, but I am impressed that you noticed, Dr. Lord. Most people don't. They just think of me as one really unusual AI."

"Do you have your own name? Separate from *Nelson Mandela*?"

"In computer language, yes. But not anything a human would understand. Sorry."

"Nothing like the name 'Bud'."

"You know, Dr. Lord? I have always wanted to be 'Chuck Yeager'. You could call me 'Yeager' for short."

"The Earth-born pilot of the twentieth century?" Grace asked.

"Yeah. Whew, Doc, you sure know your ancient history. I am really impressed, again. No wonder Bud likes you!"

" . . . What?"

"Oops. Gotta run!"

16: The Voice

Grace was responsible for the care of many of the patients, whose doctors had ended up on the quarantine side of the lockdown. She, herself, would have been one of those doctors, if it had not been for Bud picking her up and carrying her across half of the station. All of the doctors who were on the non-quarantined side had tried to split the patients evenly amongst themselves, so that no one was too overloaded. Still, it was a lot of work rounding on all the new patients and learning their histories. Grace still had Dr. Al-Fadi's own patients to care for, as well.

Many of the patients were certainly well enough to return to their home planets. They were not pleased about the quarantine of the entire medical space station. They were frustrated that no ship could land or leave until the quarantine was lifted. It made for very tense situations on some of the wards, where patients of different adaptations and from different planets were starting to mingle. The doctors and nursing staff tried their best to keep military personnel, from opposing sides in a conflict, away from each other. They also tried to keep certain animal adaptations away from each other. Nevertheless, it made for very tricky bed allocation, and all the medical staff were being forced to use their conflict resolution skills to the utmost.

Grace got a 'stat' page from one of the wards. One of her patients was involved in an altercation with another patient and could she please come help intervene. She quickly set off towards Ward D7, at a brisk trot. Hopping onto one of the station's monorails, Grace noticed everyone wearing black armbands, to honor all the victims killed by the deadly virus. Grace had donned her own black armband that morning, as well. Her thoughts went back to the courageous Vanessa Bell and her eyes immediately started to tear up again.

Grace kept wondering if she should have noticed anything about

Vanessa earlier, when she had first suggested to the head of the Medical Receiving Bay that everyone go into cryopods. Grace went over and over her conversations with Vanessa in her mind. She could not think of anything that had been unusual in Vanessa's speech or behavior, during those earlier conversations, to suggest that Vanessa was infected. Would Vanessa have admitted it, if Grace had suspected anything? Grace would never know.

Grace, herself, was so tired from lack of sleep and overwork, that she could barely keep her balance on the monorail, but it was her duty to help keep her patients safe. She hoped she got there in time to prevent anyone from getting injured. Deep down inside though, she wanted to wring their necks.

Grace hopped off at the D7 stop and charged towards the surgical recovery unit. As she approached the area, she could hear shouting and snarling. There were the sounds of crashing furniture and howling, as she entered the ward. It was coming from the patient room with her orangutan-adapted patient. Grace was surprised. The orangutan had seemed like such a friendly sort and not the type to get in an altercation or cause a ruckus. Grace shook her head in bewilderment.

Approaching from the other end of the corridor was Dr. Cech, his thin, grey-brown hair looking unkempt and his eyes barely open. Obviously, he had been paged out of a deep sleep. Grace suspected he was responsible for the care of the other patient involved in this commotion.

Before the doorway to her patient's room was a crowd of onlookers, mostly patients. Grace noticed most of the patients were soldiers, some with feline adaptations, some with primate adaptations. The nurses were attempting to clear them all from the doorway, with little success.

Just as Grace was about to say something, she heard a voice that stopped her in her tracks and made her stomach clench in pain.

"STOP!"

Silence suddenly filled the halls as everyone was brought to a standstill.

"WHAT DO YOU TWO THINK YOU'RE DOING?"

Grace was immediately soaked in a cold sweat.

"TODAY, ONE OF THE BRAVEST WOMEN ON THIS STATION DIED, MAKING SURE EVERY PERSON QUARANTINED WOULD SURVIVE THIS DEVASTATING ILLNESS. HOW *DARE* YOU SULLY THIS DAY WITH YOUR CHILDISHNESS! HOW *DARE* YOU DISHONOR HER ACT OF COURAGE BY BRAWLING LIKE

BRATTY, LITTLE KIDS! HOW *DARE* YOU ACT LIKE MINDLESS ANIMALS HERE, WHEN OTHERS ON THIS STATION ARE DYING IN MISERY AND PAIN! NOW GET INTO YOUR BEDS AND I DO NOT WANT ANOTHER SOUND OUT OF EITHER OF YOU! IF YOU ARE GOING TO ACT LIKE CHILDREN, YOU WILL BE TREATED LIKE CHILDREN!"

I was just defending myself . . ."

"SHUT! UP! DID I ASK YOU TO SPEAK? NO! I DID NOT! SO SHUT! UP!'

The only sound that could be heard was the beeping of some monitor in the nurses' station, that was obviously totally unaware of what had just been said or it probably would have obeyed, too.

"NOW, NOT ANOTHER SOUND FROM EITHER OF YOU! YOU SHOULD BE **ASHAMED**!"

Grace felt a tsunami of shame crash down upon her with those words. She fought an overwhelming urge to run away and hide, quivering in sweat-soaked fear, even though those words had not been directed at her. Most of the patients who had been spectating at the doorway of the room must have felt the same way. They scattered like leaves on the wind. Not a sound was heard over the next few minutes, except the rapid shuffling of slippered feet, that resembled the pitter patter of rain.

Dr. Cech strolled up to her, a huge grin on his long, thin face. He bent down to whisper into Grace's ear.

"I think I am in love," he said, confidentially, in a very hushed voice.

"Who was that?" Grace whispered softly, still trembling, fearful that she might be the next person to receive a tirade from that voice.

"Why, our own Miss Leung, I believe," Dr. Cech said proudly.

"Who? Not Sophie!"

"One and the same."

"You're kidding," Grace said, confused, recalling the tearful young nurse she had met on her second day to the medical station.

"I kid you not," Dejan Cech said, with a big, crooked smile, gesturing with his laughing eyes, toward the doorway of their patients' room.

Out walked the tiny nurse that Grace had comforted on her second day on the station. Sophie Leung had been the nurse upset about the loose restraints, when Grace had been scored by the claws of Captain Damien Lamont. The young, sweet-faced nurse turned to Grace and Dr. Cech and looked, first shocked, and then dismayed.

"Oh, no. I am so sorry you doctors were called. One of the younger nurses must have paged you, when she really should not have. Everything is under control. You should not have been bothered," she said, apologetically.

"I can see that," Dr. Cech said, smiling down at Sophie Leung, who—as far as Grace was concerned—was a young nurse herself.

"Please," Dr. Cech said to Sophie. "Absolutely no need to apologize, Nurse Leung. I would not have wanted to miss that for the world. You must teach me your technique. It is really quite effective."

"Technique? What technique?" Sophie frowned.

Dr. Cech motioned to the patients' room out of which Sophie had just emerged. "What you just did in there," he said to Nurse Leung. "To get everything under control. Everyone in there is okay, by the way?"

"Oh, those kids are fine. Just too rambunctious. Too much energy bundled up, waiting around with nothing to do but get on each others' nerves. No need for you to trouble yourselves. I just gave them 'The Voice'."

"The Voice?" Grace asked, not sure if she was able to hide the tremor in her own voice, at just saying those words.

"Yeah. I just do my Mom's 'Voice'. You know, the voice all moms use when they are mad at their kids, when they have reached their last straw? My Mom could silence the entire neighborhood with her 'Voice'. Strike fear into the hearts of men, and all that. It used to make my insides go to jelly, whenever I heard her scream like that. When I was little, I used to wet myself," Sophie laughed. "You just had to stop and do whatever she said, so she wouldn't use it again. I find it really effective in making the patients behave."

"I can certainly see that," Dejan Cech said. "That is quite the talent you have there, Miss Leung, although this unit must be spending a fortune on diapers. Your mother was a secret weapon and she taught you well. You should teach courses in crowd control. They could have used your voice on the quarantine side, to keep the people from attacking the lockdown doors."

"Really? Thank you," Sophie said shyly. "I think."

"You are most welcome," Dr. Cech said, with a slight bow.

Sophie giggled.

Grace shook her head. She could hardly believe that the mind-numbing, bone-rattling, gut-twisting voice she had heard a few minutes before, belonged to this little wisp of a nurse. It had definitely struck fear into the heart of her, that was for sure!

"Your mother must have been a formidable woman," Grace said to the little nurse.

"Aren't they all?' Sophie said with a grin.

"Yes," Dejan Cech said, with a rueful smile, "they certainly are."

Grace stepped into the dark patient room of Dris Kindle, the snow leopard female soldier, whose Caesarian section Grace had attended. Unfortunately, Dr. Vilas Papaboubadios, the tall obstetrician/gynecologist, was one of the physicians caught on the quarantine side of the lockdown. Grace was asked to care for Dris Kindle, since she had been involved in the delivery and her name was on the patient's records. Grace was not an obstetrician, but she could handle postoperative issues.

Dris Kindle lay unmoving in her bed with her back to the doorway. She did not appear to notice Grace's entry into her room or she gave no indication that she did.

"Ms. Kindle?" Grace asked.

There was no response from the female soldier.

"Ms. Kindle, I am Dr. Grace Lord. I assisted Dr. Papaboubadios with your Caesarian section. Unfortunately, your doctor is unable to check in on you, so I have been asked to see you. How are you doing?"

The woman slowly turned to look over her right shoulder at Grace, her eyes downcast, her expression disinterested.

"What does it matter?" Dris Kindle asked listlessly, as she sat up. "We are all going to die anyway."

Grace jerked upon hearing this, and she peered at the patient. Dris Kindle was hunched over, facing the corner of the room and Grace noticed that her hair and fur were tangled and unkempt. The smell in the room was far from pleasant, as if Dris Kindle could not bother with even the most basic hygiene. Grace walked over to stand in front of the leopard. She noticed that Dris Kindle's eyes were downcast and unfocused. The woman refused to even look at her.

"You did not want to give up your babies, did you?" Grace asked, taking a chance.

The woman looked up at her, fire in her golden eyes. She glared in outrage and Grace suppressed a shiver.

"What do you know about what I want?" Dris Kindle snarled.

"You seem very unhappy," Grace pointed out, softly, forcing herself to stay put and not tear out of the room.

"It's just postpartum depression. I will get over it," Kindle snapped, raising her nose at Grace, her nostrils flaring. Grace could see the woman's claws extending and retracting in obvious agitation. Grace swallowed and tried not to think about the last time a patient extended his claws at her.

"Who told you that?" Grace probed, her eyebrows lowered.

"Told me what?" the patient snarled.

"Who told you that you had postpartum depression?" Grace asked, in a gentle voice.

"One of the nurses," Dris Kindle growled.

"Did you want to give your babies up for adoption?" Grace pressed.

"It is the best thing for them!" the woman roared, angrily.

"That is not what I asked," Grace said, calmly. "I asked you if you *wanted* to give them up for adoption."

"How can I care for babies with these?" the soldier demanded, as she extended all her claws fully. "How can I care for them, if I could accidentally tear them apart?"

"Are your claws always extended?" Grace asked.

"Of course not!" the snow leopard snapped.

"Do you break everything you touch?" Grace inquired.

"Don't be ridiculous, Doctor," Kindle snarled, her eyes flashing, making it very clear that Grace was seriously getting on her nerves.

"Then why do you think you would harm your babies?" Grace asked. "Believe it or not, babies are pretty sturdy creatures. They are not made of paper. They can hold up to quite a bit, as long as you keep your claws retracted. You would be surprised. The human race would never have survived this long, if babies were that fragile."

"I can't take them back with me to my platoon, Doctor. What would I do with them?"

"Do you really want to go back to fighting, Ms. Kindle?"

"It's what I am trained to do. I don't know anything else. My partner, Joss, does not want to leave the military and he wants me to go back with him. He does not want children."

"What do you want?" Grace asked. "What does Dris Kindle want?"

" . . . I don't know, Doctor. I don't know anything anymore, but with this infective agent threatening all the lives on this station, it seems rather pointless anyway."

"Being a mother, wanting to raise and protect your own children, is never pointless, in my opinion," Grace pointed out. "If we are all going to die anyway, which I hope is not the case, why not spend the remaining time with your babies? You can't leave. They can't leave. Perhaps we shall all die, but at least they will know their mother's love for the short time they are alive.

"If you are really afraid you might hurt them accidentally, you can always have an android nurse stay with you for help. We are very short staffed right now, because of the quarantine, so you could really help by taking your babies out of the nursery and caring for them yourself."

"What if I get attached to them and can't give them up when it is time to leave?" Dris wailed.

"Then maybe you are not meant to give them up," Grace said. "Would that be such a bad thing to find out? Try it. Maybe you'll like it. Maybe you won't, but at least then you'll know."

The leopard woman gave a big sigh. There was a long pause and then she sat up straighter and looked Grace in the eyes.

"All right, Doctor. I will give it a try," Dris Kindle said with just the hint of a smile.

"I will speak to the nursery for you, Dris. Maybe you can start with one at a time. Maybe you should ask Joss if he wants to help, too."

"He won't," Dris whispered.

"You may be surprised. And even if he does not, that does not mean you can't. Like I said, we need all the hands we can get in this crisis."

"Okay, Doctor. I will give it a try. And I will ask Joss, to see if he will help, too. I really do want to do something to help. I think both of us do. This waiting around is killing us . . . Thank you, Doctor," Dris conceded.

"It is my pleasure, Dris. And thank you."

Grace had almost completed her rounds, when she saw Dr. Jeffrey Nestor, the incredibly handsome psychiatrist, approaching. She realized that she had jumped straight out of bed and run to Ward D7, when she had got that page, and had not even looked at herself in the mirror . . . again. She could not believe it. Every time she ran into this man, she looked as if she had just risen from the dead. And the man had continued to page her on her wrist-comp, repeatedly asking her to go out to dinner with him.

Now she just wanted to duck into some cubby hole until he passed by. Unfortunately, he was smiling and heading straight towards her. She wondered if she could turn the other way and walk off, pretending she hadn't seen him. She decided that would appear too rude.

"Dr. Lord, I was hoping to find you today. I just wanted to let you know that I have started therapy with Captain Damien Lamont. He has been very cooperative and open to therapy and has agreed to undergo inter-cerebral communication as part of the treatment for his flashbacks, which have been quite severe in his case. We will be having another session tomorrow."

"That is great news, Dr. Nestor. Thank you for seeing Captain Lamont," Grace said.

"I was wondering if you might be interested in sitting in on one of the sessions, Dr. Lord. I understand you have never experienced a mind-link with a patient before. If you are interested, you can participate in my inter-cerebral connection with Captain Lamont and see what it is like. You can learn, firsthand, what we 'head doctors' do to ameliorate the terror of the experience and help patients learn to cope better with their flashbacks."

At the thought of this very attractive man being connected to her brain, Grace felt she would rather climb into a pit of vipers. Was he kidding, or what? There was absolutely no way in the universe Grace would let this gorgeous man anywhere near her inappropriate thoughts.

"Thank you for the offer, Dr. Nestor, but unfortunately my work on the antiviral treatment trials takes priority at present. Besides, I am sure you have enough on your hands, dealing with the captain. It must be very distracting to have another observer along for the ride, so to speak, and hardly good for the patient." Grace looked away from the man's alluring dark eyes, that seemed to want to capture her soul and draw her in.

"Captain Lamont has said it is all right," Dr. Nestor said earnestly.

"Whatever assistance I can give to the team working on a treatment or cure for the epidemic, surely comes first and foremost right now, Dr. Nestor. Perhaps, when this crisis is all over, and everything is back to normal, I could sit in on a session, but remember Dr. Nestor, I am only a surgeon. We surgeons are not the best people to have stumbling around in a patient's head. We are only interested in cutting things out," Grace said with a laugh. Unfortunately, Dr. Nestor did not appear to find her statement funny.

The psychiatrist looked quite irritated at Grace's response. He had obviously thought she would jump at the chance to join in on an 'inter-cerebral communication' with him. He stepped closer to her, almost looming over her, and stared intently into her eyes. She could not help but notice how beautiful his eyes were, but there was a coldness, an emptiness behind them, that she had not noticed before. She could not help but feel that his attention was calculated, measured, dispassionate. She took a step backwards. Why was she always finding herself backing away from this man?

"Are you sure?" he asked, softly. "I think you would find it very fascinating and helpful in your understanding of what Post Traumatic Stress Disorder is, Grace. It would not take all that long, and I really think you would get a great deal out of it," the psychiatrist insisted.

Grace began to feel very uncomfortable. Having explained to Dr. Nestor that she was busy with the search for a cure for the virus, how could he continue to insist that she spend time with him on a counseling session? Did he not understand that the mortality rate of this virus was, so far, one hundred percent and that none of the people in quarantine, including Dr. Al-Fadi, could be revived until multiple treatments were found?

It did not make any sense!

"I am very sorry, Dr. Nestor. It is kind of you to ask, but I really can't afford the time," Grace said, apologetically.

"No time to care for your own patient, eh? Far too busy doing *important* things, than to spend time treating a patient, doing something as mundane as counseling? Don't you care about your patient, Doctor?" the psychiatrist asked, sarcastically, his arms crossed and his expression one of condescension.

Grace's mouth dropped open. "I care very much about Captain Lamont," she said, defensively. "But I hardly see how my being inside his head could possibly help him. He has enough worries, without my thoughts causing him more confusion. And I certainly have enough on my mind to cause anyone confusion, Dr. Nestor. I only see my involvement as possibly causing him harm. I am sure you are quite capable of treating Captain Lamont without me, Dr. Nestor, but if you are not, then I can ask someone else to assume care, if you wish."

"You think me incapable of treating your patient effectively, Dr.

Lord?" Jeffrey Nestor asked, in a very low, menacing tone. Grace could tell the psychiatrist had been insulted by her suggestion. "Are you questioning my competency, Doctor?"

"No, of course not," Grace said, her eyebrows peaked as she gave Jeffrey Nestor a puzzled frown.

"Would you prefer to involve a different psychiatrist in your patient's care?" he asked, his voice dripping with open hostility. Fury was reflected in his dark, shining eyes.

"No, Dr. Nestor, of course not," Grace said. "I am sorry. I did not mean anything . . . "

"I have everything under control, Doctor," Jeffrey Nestor said, coldly. "Pardon me for taking up any of your precious time, discussing your patient with you."

Grace stood there, stunned, as Dr. Nestor stalked away. She shook her head and tried to figure out why that conversation had ended up so poorly. Had she really sounded that pompous? Her mind reeled in confusion.

"He's a piece of work, isn't he?" Grace heard a gravelly voice say, from behind the counter of the nursing station. Grace walked over to peer over the barrier. It was Head Nurse Virginia Conti, who was concentrating on something on the screen before her. She glanced over at Grace, rolling her eyes.

"Did I sound unreasonable to you?" Grace asked, her mind still reeling.

"Of course not, Dr. Lord," Virginia Conti growled in her low, raspy voice. "It's just that Dr. Jeffrey Nestor is used to always getting his way with the ladies and you were not cooperating. He didn't like it. He thinks he's more important than everyone stuck in the cryopods. Narcissistic bastard, isn't he?" the grey-haired nurse said, with a derisive snort and another roll of her expressive eyes. She shook her head, as if to spit out, 'Men!', but frowned in disgust instead.

"So it wasn't me?" Grace asked, her brows wrinkled. "I just could not understand how he would think helping find a solution to one of the deadliest infectious agents humankind has ever seen, would be less important than a counseling session with him. I was beginning to wonder if I was going crazy. Was I being unreasonable?"

The elderly nurse just looked over at Grace, wearily, and said: "My best advice to you, Dr. Lord, is to stay well away from Jeffrey Nestor. You've stuck a pin in his behind, because he did not get his way with you and, like I said before, he is always—always!—used to getting his way with women. You are a creature he has never encountered before. Hell knows how he is going to respond to that."

Head Nurse Conti squinted her eyes and stared at the console screen, but she was not really seeing it. "He seems to take great pride in breaking women's hearts, Dr. Lord, and I have had to comfort more than my share of heartbroken nurses on this station. It seems he has set his sights on yours, now. He won't be happy that you turned him down." Conti sighed and looked over at Grace, a worried expression on her face. "Hopefully, he does not take this all out on your patient."

"He had better not," Grace said.

"You are definitely not the crazy one . . ." Virginia Conti said.

'Thank you, Virginia.'

"You're welcome, Dr. Lord. And never forget this. I have your back, if you need me."

"Thank you," Grace said, her eyes widening in surprise. She had really not gotten to know Nurse Conti well, but Grace believed she meant what she said. "Well, I had better get back to the lab. There is so much work to do. Thank you again for your advice."

"Good luck to you, Dr. Lord," Virginai Conti said, with a nod to Grace. "There are some of us who do appreciate the hard work you and your team are doing to save us all. I hope you find an answer very soon, Doctor."

"It won't be me," Grace said. "It will be Bud, also known to you as SAMM-E 777. He deserves all the credit. Spread the word!"

Grace spent the rest of the shift and the entire next day, analyzing the test results achieved by Bud's army of androids and robots. The results were excellent and the studies were reliable and reproducible, because Bud had his army of tireless androids and robots doing all the studies in triplicate. The studies on the vaccine were so encouraging, Grace felt that, if the rest of the studies looked this good, they could start administering the vaccine next shift. She wanted to discuss this with Bud, but he was nowhere to be found. Off troubleshooting or supervising the start of new experiments, she supposed.

She hated to bother Bud. He was so busy working on trying to develop different treatments to counteract the actions of the virus. The vaccine would be good for protecting people against catching the illness, but they still needed drug treatments that would stop the virus in its tracks, if a person became or was already infected. The goal was to not only stop the disease from progressing, but to also prevent the process from starting entirely.

They were also looking for treatments that would help the body heal up the damage to cell membranes caused by the virus, once it got into cells and began total cell destruction. Of course, with the risks of drug allergies and adverse reactions, more than one drug was always needed. They always required lots of alternatives and substitute medications, if they were to try and help everyone.

Grace sighed. There was still so much to do and she was exhausted. Perhaps a few hours of sleep would be permissible. A couple of hours would not make that much difference to the investigation, but it would mean a world of a difference to her. She would contact Bud after she had a brief nap. Bud was probably way ahead of her, anyway, on the plans for administering the vaccine to the non-quarantined personnel.

Grace left a message for Bud, through her wrist-comp, that she would talk to him once she had rested. She headed off to her quarters for some sleep. On the way there, she mentally organized a schedule for vaccinating all of the personnel in an orderly manner. She plugged this into her wrist-comp, as well, and sent a copy to Bud for his opinion. She was not yet sure how the vaccine would be administered: orally, by needle, by patch, or by spray. The choice would depend on which method produced the best protection rates and those results were still pending.

Grace hopped off the monorail and headed towards Ward M1 where her quarters were now situated. She waved at one of the nurses who was doing her rounds. She would turn off her wrist-comp, except for emergencies, until her wakeup alarm went off. She set the alarm on her wrist-comp for two hours. Hopefully, no one would feel the need to page her in that time period. Grace was so anxious to put her head down and get some much needed rest, that she was almost crying with anticipation of lying down on a flat surface and closing her eyes. It did not even have to be a bed. It could be a hard floor, as far as she was concerned. Just an opportunity to turn her mind off and drift into a deep, dreamless slumber seemed like a luxury that she could ill afford.

Although everyone at risk was now in a cryopod and they had more time now to do things meticulously, the sooner all personnel like Dr. Al-Fadi were treated and back to work, the better. The goal of the

Nelson Mandela Medical Space Station was to treat the sick and mortally wounded of the Conglomerate and they were not fulfilling their mandate during this crisis.

Palming her door lock and stepping into her quarters, Grace stopped on the threshold, waiting for the room light to activate, as it always did. For once, though, the illumination did not appear, so Grace felt for the wall switch that would manually activate it. She pressed the switch and there was still no light.

'Funny,' Grace thought and opened her mouth to speak to *Nelson Mandela* about the malfunction in her room, when a strong hand slammed over her mouth and a sharp, hard point jabbed between her ribs under her left breast, firmly enough to break the skin. Grace froze, afraid to breathe. The squeak she let out had been thoroughly muffled by the palm almost smothering her face.

Her mind raced, trying to understand who could be threatening her like this. Could it be someone infected with the virus? But, how would they have become infected? How could anyone have gotten out of the quarantined area and why would they decide to attack her in her quarters? *Nelson Mandela* had said everyone from the quarantined area was in a cryopod and accounted for, so that seemed highly unlikely. Yet no sane person would attack another person on this medical station with the station AI always alert and watching.

Would they?

As soon as she heard the voice, Grace knew who it was. Her stomach felt like it was being twisted into a tight, small knot and a deep, hollow chill spread through her bones. She tried not to let the fear overwhelm her. She knew that if she did not deal with this correctly, she would be dead in the next minute. She activated the emergency button on her wrist-comp, hoping someone would notice, as the voice spoke, dripping with derision and malice, in her left ear.

"No time to care for your own patient, eh? Far too busy, doing important things, than to do something as mundane as counseling? You think you're just too good to spend time connecting with your patient, aren't you, Miss 'High and Mighty Surgeon' who thinks she's too good for the lesser folk? Well, let's see how good you are with a big hole in your heart! You can't talk your way out of this one, Dr. Lord, and there's no one here to stop me from driving this deep into your chest. Any last words?"

WELCOME TO THE MADHOUSE : 197

The hand covering Grace's mouth lifted off her face and she took a deep breath and yelled, in her best imitation of Sophie Leung's 'Voice':

"STOP! HOW *DARE* YOU COME INTO MY ROOM AND THREATEN ME?"

Her assailant jerked back, startled at Grace's outburst. For the briefest of moments, the grip on her was relaxed. Hoping for this reaction, Grace dove forward into a summersault across the floor of her quarters. She knew exactly where her stunner was, in the top drawer of her bedside cabinet, and she lunged for it. At that same moment and wholly unexpected by Grace, the door to her quarters slid open and someone grabbed her attacker from behind, whipping him out of her room. The door to Grace's room whisked shut and Grace was left in darkness.

"*Nelson Mandela*, quick! Lights, please!" Grace yelled.

The lights came on, at half intensity, and Grace silently thanked the station AI for not blinding her. She raced to her door, stunner in hand, and prayed that her would-be assassin had not yet come to any serious harm.

The door quickly slid open to reveal Bud, embracing the tiger soldier in a bear hug from behind, appearing to be squeezing the air out of the huge man's lungs. There was no one else around, for the moment.

"Don't hurt him, Bud. *Please*," Grace said to Bud, her arm outstretched.

Bud stared at Grace, his crystal blue eyes enormous, fury and puzzlement at war on his face. He did not let go of the tiger, even though it was obvious the man was now unconscious. Grace's attacker hung like a lifeless stuffed toy within the android's arms.

Grace grabbed Bud's arm, which felt like it was carved of marble, and said quietly and calmly to him, "Bud, please put the patient down inside my quarters. Gently. I am positive this is not his fault or his idea. I suspect he may not even be truly awake and will probably have no memory of this event at all."

With a frown of confusion on his flawless face, Bud entered Grace's quarters with the enormous, unresponsive tiger still wrapped in a bearhug. He gave the tiger assailant another firm squeeze, before slowly lowering him to the floor. Captain Damien Lamont was finally able to suck in an enormous breath, but he lay, stunned and unconscious, his breathing heavy and slightly labored.

Bud straightened up and looked at Grace. She could see his body was trembling again. He reminded her of a spring, coiled far too tightly.

"Would you care to explain, Dr. Lord?" Bud asked formally, in a very flat voice.

Perhaps it was her imagination, but Grace had the impression Bud was shaking with suppressed fury. Were androids even capable of fury? She did not think they were capable of killing a human being, due to their programming, but she now harbored some doubts about this, with regard to Bud. He had an expression, on his chiseled features, that could certainly have been interpreted by some as 'murderous intent'. She wondered if the android had possibly been harmed in the struggle. Why else would he seem so infuriated?

Grace looked down at poor Captain Damien Lamont, sprawled unconscious on the floor of her quarters. He made her room look so tiny. She stuck her stunner in the back pocket of her scrubs and knelt down to check his pulse. It was bounding and steady.

"Careful," Bud growled, stepping very close to her. "He may come to, Grace."

"After you almost squeezed the life out of him? I don't think so, Bud," Grace snapped. Then she sighed.

"I'm sorry. That was . . . uncalled for, Bud. Thank you for coming to my rescue . . . again. You are probably getting tired of this, and of me. I probably owe you for saving my life at least twice now, if not more."

Bud said not a word but just stared intently at the tiger, as if he wanted to pummel the captain to death. She watched the android clenching and unclenching his powerful fists.

"Bud, I believe Captain Damien Lamont was acting under either the power of suggestion or a post-hypnotic trance. I know he was undergoing a mind-to-mind link up today for his counseling session and I do not believe he knew what he was doing here. For one thing, the words he said to me were ones from a conversation I had with someone else last cycle, someone who did the inter-cerebral link with the captain here. The poor captain, I believe, is an unwitting pawn, under a very powerful mind compulsion. The real question is, 'Was it planted there on purpose or inadvertently?'"

"Who was it?" Bud asked, again in that very flat tone.

Grace looked up at the android.

"*Nelson Mandela*, you will not tell Bud who it was," Grace ordered.

"You are five hundred and eighty-six milliseconds too late on that command, Dr. Lord. I do apologize."

"Bud, you will not act on this! Not until the Captain awakens and we can confirm our suspicions. In the meantime, I think we will set up a nice little trap for our 'head doctor' and try and catch him up. *Nelson Mandela*, can you create a little vid of me almost getting killed in my quarters by the Captain?"

"You mean, like, a snuff vid, Doc?"

"Is that what you call them, *Nelson Mandela?*"

"Not me. It's what you humans used to call them. I discovered them when I was searching for old videos of my namesake. You humans are sure capable of doing the most despicable things to other humans."

"Unfortunately, I can't really argue with you there, *Nelson Mandela*," Grace sighed. "Are you able to access the records of the counseling session between Dr. Jeffrey Nestor and Captain Damien Lamont?"

"All that can be seen, Doc, is the two being wired up and then the two of them lying down on couches for the entire session. What happens in the minds of the two participants is recorded, but I have to hack in to Dr. Nestor's encrypted files to get at it, as it is all passcoded and multi-encrypted and triple-guarded. I assume you do not want the dear doctor notified of our trespass."

"No, indeed not," Grace said.

"Okay . . . Hack completed. Ready for you to 'experience' when you wish."

"Are you all right, Grace?" Bud gasped, panic and concern etched on his face. He was staring, in huge-eyed horror, at a spot underneath Grace's left breast where blood had soaked into her shirt.

"Yes, thank you, Bud. I am fine. Luckily, it is merely a scratch. The Captain poked me with one of his claws, but it really only broke the skin. Thank you for coming in the nick of time, though."

"I . . . I . . . I," the android said, consternation and almost terror appearing on his face. "You should have one of the other doctors look at that, Grace. Immediately!"

"It really is nothing, Bud. I can look after it myself. Let us quickly get Captain Lamont onto my bed, secured and in restraints. I suspect, when he awakens, he will have no memory of what happened, but let us get him into the manacles, just in case."

"I need to see your wound! I need to see how deep it went!" Bud said.

"I am fine, Bud," Grace said, flushing.

"I need to see that it did not pierce your lung, Grace! I need to see how bad it is!" Bud insisted.

"My breathing is fine, Bud! It was just a scratch!" Grace argued, feeling like a glowing beacon.

"I need to see . . . that you are all right, Grace," Bud almost wailed.

"All right!" Grace snapped. She pulled up the shirt of her scrubs to reveal the scratch just beneath her left breast. Bud peered at it closely and touched the spot where the blood was already clotting. He gently poked at the wound, secretly sending in a few of his nanobots. Grace winced a bit, but said nothing. He placed his fingers against her chest wall, firmly, and froze, as if listening. Then he sighed.

"Your heart and lungs are fine, Grace," Bud said, in a tone of great relief.

"I told you that," Grace grumbled, pulling down her shirt, and looking away. Why was her room so hot? Who put up the temperature?

"Can you please put Captain Lamont on my bed now, Bud?" Grace asked, fanning herself.

Bud bent down and effortlessly picked up the huge tiger, as if the captain were a small child. He placed Lamont on Grace's narrow bed, where he was too wide to fit and too long, as well. Surprisingly, the android was very gentle, as he arranged the still-unconscious captain onto the pallet as comfortably as possible. Grace checked all of Lamont's incisions, making sure they were all still intact.

Behind her, Grace heard the door to her quarters whisper open and then close. Bud returned to the bedside, titanium restraints in hand. Silently, he attached the manacles to the captain's wrists and ankles and secured them to her bed.

"There is a very high probability that the captain will snap your bed frame, Grace. This bed is not nearly as sturdy as the hospital beds, which are made for these soldiers," Bud warned.

"Don't worry. I won't be alone with him. I will have you send two big security androids to stay with me at all times, and I am sure *Nelson Mandela* will let you know if we have any trouble. I am sure he will be keeping an eye on me."

"You are definitely not wrong there, Doc," the station AI said.

"The captain was given a post-hypnotic suggestion, *Nelson Mandela*?"

"I think you will have to draw your own conclusions after viewing the session, but it is imperative we take some blood samples from the captain. You may be surprised at what you will find floating around in his bloodstream. But you must hurry. The pharmaceuticals that the captain was given have very fast

half-lives and may be quickly metabolized from his system. In an hour from now, there will be no evidence left to indicate the captain was drugged. I know what to analyze for. I just have to get a 'droid to draw the blood sample immediately."

"That is what I am here for," Bud said. "And I will not be leaving you alone with Captain Lamont," Bud said firmly to Grace, as he withdrew venipuncture equipment from a pocket on his coveralls and bent over to draw a blood sample from the sleeping tiger.

"You must, Bud," Grace insisted. "All the experiments involving the virus and its treatments and vaccine production still require your supervision. This incident does not take precedence over that. And I need you to appear to be investigating my 'attempted murder'."

The android's eyes widened and blinked at Grace. "Is that why you want *Nelson Mandela* to create a video showing you almost getting killed? What did *Nelson Mandela* call it? A 'snuff vid'? I could not find any references in my memory."

"I do not know what a 'snuff vid' is. I thought snuff was something people used to sniff up their noses," Grace said with a smile.

"You are going to pretend that you were almost killed, Grace?" Bud asked, his features exhibiting puzzlement. "That the attack was almost successful? Why?"

"Yes, Bud. It is very important that it looks like the Captain was very close to succeeding in his mission."

"But . . . but why? I do not think I will ever understand humans," Bud lamented.

"Ditto!"

"Let me explain," Grace said, and proceeded to lay out her plan.

When it was announced that Dr. Grace Lord's life was hanging on by a mere thread, the news spread through the medical space station like wildfire. Many personnel wanted to come and visit her, but it was strictly forbidden. The young surgical fellow had been attacked by an assassin, who was also alive and in custody. The assassin was unconscious but would be questioned, via mind-link, as soon as he became conscious. Video was shown on the newsnet of a violent attack in a dark room, leaving a woman lying prone on the floor in an enlarging pool of blackness and a huge, shady figure departing the scene. Authorities were quick to capture the assailant, who was badly injured in the struggle.

It was announced that Dr. Lord and her assailant were both being held in a highly-secured area in one of the Intensive Care Units under guard. No one would be allowed to gain admittance to the ward, to see either person, unless they had top level security clearance. They could only be admitted, if the station AI, *Nelson Mandela*, gave permission.

On the Intensive Care Unit of Ward E10, Dr. Grace Lord was fighting for her life, surrounded by security 'droids that operated under the strict commands of *Nelson Mandela*. No other patients were being treated on this unit, except for the assassin, who was also in critical condition and under armed guard, having been captured by security 'droids. The assassin was in a separate, locked and guarded room, at the opposite end of the ward and situated between the two rooms was a veritable army of security androids and robots.

Almost immediately, the psychiatrist, Dr. Jeffrey Nestor, contacted the station AI and expressed dismay and regret, regarding the attack on Dr. Lord. He requested permission to see both patients, one because she was a dear friend and colleague for whom he cared a great deal, the other because he was a patient, whom Nestor had been treating right up until the day of Dr. Lord's attack.

The psychiatrist said he felt terribly guilty that he did not pick up on the patient's intentions. Dr. Nestor admitted that he was aware the patient felt strong anger towards Dr. Lord, because of the body-altering surgery performed upon him leaving him more machine than human, but the psychiatrist would never have suspected the patient would actually go and attack his surgeon. Dr. Nestor claimed he felt partially responsible for Dr. Lord's injuries and wanted to help her in any way he could. He wanted to be by her bedside and offer what comfort and loving attention he could, while she struggled for her life. After all, they were in a 'relationship' together.

Also, as the assailant's acting psychiatrist, Dr. Nestor felt he should check up on his patient and determine whether this assassination attempt was at all related to his Post Traumatic Stress Disorder.

The station AI, after much dissembling, consented to give permission for Dr. Jeffrey Nestor to enter Ward E10 to visit Dr. Lord and the assassin, but for only brief visits. Both patients' conditions were very critical, at the moment, and were not likely awake enough for the psychiatrist's visit to have any real relevance. Dr. Nestor insisted he had to see them. The station AI finally acquiesced.

At the entrance to the E10 ward was a host of security droids. One took Dr. Nestor's retinal, finger, and voice-prints, as well as his identification and security clearance codes. Then with four large security droids surrounding him, the psychiatrist was directed first towards the assassin's room. Outside the attacker's door, Jeffrey Nestor insisted that all the security droids, robots, and nurses wait outside. This was not permitted. One large security droid came inside the patient's room, but placed itself just inside the closed door.

The psychiatrist strode silently toward the bed, where the sole illumination was shining dimly over the patient's head. The tiger captain lay unconscious, amidst tubing and pumps and monitors and computer consoles. His head was wrapped up in bandages, as were his chest and his right arm. His eyes were closed.

Coming up to the left side of the bed, the psychiatrist addressed the patient:

"Captain Damien Lamont? Captain Lamont? This is Dr. Jeffrey Nestor. Are you awake? Can you hear me?"

There was some slight change in the tiger's breathing, but that was the only visible response. Reaching out his right hand, the psychiatrist grasped the left arm of Lamont, who was bound in titanium restraints. The patient still did not awaken. The psychiatrist bent towards the patient's head and spoke something softly into his left ear. He then palpated the carotid pulse on the left side of the tiger's neck and squeezed his left shoulder firmly.

"I will come back and see you later, Captain Lamont, when you are more alert," Jeffrey Nestor said, warmly. He then casually put his hands into his pockets and moved towards the door.

As he was leaving the room, Dr. Nestor said to the security 'droid, "I would like to see Dr. Lord, now."

They made their way down the long, grey corridor to the other end of the E10 Intensive Care Unit, the four large Security droids again surrounding Nestor. When he reached Dr. Lord's room, Nestor again demanded privacy. He was again refused. An android followed Jeffrey Nestor into Dr. Lord's room but stood just inside the doorway.

This room, too, was dark and poorly lit. Grace Lord's face was in shadow. The heart monitor, hooked up to Grace, beat regularly and the patient's vitals were shown on a screen above her head as well as a host of other indices. Dr. Nestor scanned the readouts on the screen, before approaching her bedside. All of Grace's readings were normal.

Nestor looked back out through the glass wall of the Intensive Care suite. Seeing no one, he quickly approached the bedside. He bent forwards and spoke clearly and loudly.

"Grace? It's me, Jeffrey. How are you feeling today, my love?"

Grace did not respond, other than with an increase in her heart rate.

Nestor stuck his hands in his pockets and went to the medication console near the head of Grace's bed. He studied her med chart. Withdrawing his right hand from his pocket, he reached out to grab the tubing running into Grace's intravenous port with his right hand.

Suddenly, his right arm would not move. He felt as if the bones in his right forearm were being crushed, and the tiny palm syringe, filled with a clear liquid, was pried out from between his lifeless fingers. Jeffrey Nestor cried out and fell to his knees, his right arm held in the air by the iron grip of an android. The android handed off the small syringe, a little auto-injector bulb that sat neatly between two fingers, to a robot that proceeded to insert the contents of the needle into its chemical analyzer. After a few seconds, the robot emitted a few beeps.

"You are under arrest, Dr. Jeffrey Nestor, for the attempted

murders of Dr. Grace Alexandra Lord and Captain Damien Lamont," *Nelson Mandela*, the station AI, announced. "**You have the right to remain silent. Anything you say or do can be used against you in a court of law. You have the right to legal representation.**"

"This is ridiculous!" Nestor sputtered in outrage, his left hand reaching up to grab his crushed right forearm, still entrapped within the android's steely grip. The android dragged the psychiatrist to his feet and away from the bedside.

"How dare you? This is preposterous! I have no idea what you are talking about! I came here, to see my patient, Captain Damien Lamont, and my colleague, Dr. Lord, to care for them, not harm them," Dr. Nestor announced.

"**How did you know the assassin was Captain Damien Lamont, Doctor Nestor? How did you know Captain Damien Lamont, your patient, was responsible for the attack on Dr. Lord?**"

"Why, the name was released, when it was announced that Dr. Lord had been attacked," the psychiatrist said.

"**No, it was not, Dr. Nestor. The assailant's name was never released. There were only three humans who knew who the assailant was: Dr. Grace Lord, Captain Damian Lamont, and the person who made Captain Lamont attack her. No one else. The only way you could have known the identity of the attacker, was if you were the one who put him up to it.**"

"That is insane. How could I have done that?" scoffed the psychiatrist.

"**Through your mind-linking technique, Doctor. You did it by injecting the captain with powerful psychoactive agents and implanting a post-hypnotic suggestion in his head, during your mind-linking session with him twenty-six hours ago. I have the recording of your entire session, Doctor, and I also have analyzed the agent you tried to inject the captain with, just a few minutes ago. Very ingenious. That agent would have stopped his heart and then quickly broken down to undetectable metabolites, had we not gotten the blood sample drawn up quickly enough. Which, unfortunately for you, we did.**

"**Captain Damien Lamont is alive, by the way. The antidote was given immediately after you left the room, so he is doing fine.**"

"**As for Dr. Grace Lord here, I have already analyzed the agent you were trying to inject into her intravenous and it, too, is a** lethal dose of an agent that would have caused severe brain damage, dementia, and ultimately death in Doctor Grace Lord. Do you have anything to say, Doctor Nestor?"

"This is all a set-up. You are lying and I am being framed. These accusations are totally unfounded," Jeffrey Nestor exclaimed. "You are completely mistaken, *Nelson Mandela*."

"I sincerely wish I was, Dr. Nestor."

It was at this point that Grace chose to open her eyes and look at Dr. Nestor.

"Grace! Tell this raving AI it has made a huge mistake," the psychiatrist pleaded, looking at her with those beautiful, beseeching, brown eyes.

Moisture welled up in Grace's eyes and blurred her vision. She had to close them to block the sight of Nestor's distraught yet beautiful face. She shook her head, squeezing her lips together, as she felt large tears track down her cheeks. She remained silent.

The android took the psychiatrist by the right arm and led him from the room. The psychiatrist was handed off to a host of security androids, who put him in wrist cuffs and led him off to the space station's brig.

Bud returned to Grace's room, where she rose from the bed and dove into his arms. He held her, encased in a hug, until her shaking stopped.

"I would never have let anything happen to you, Grace," Bud said, shaking a little himself. "Even though I highly disapproved of your plan, it worked, and of that, I am most glad. But I will never allow you to put yourself in that kind of danger again. I was most distressed."

Grace laughed at Bud, tears running down her face.

He looked down at her upturned face, puzzlement on his features. "Why are you laughing and crying at the same time, Grace? Are you hurt?"

"In a way, yes," Grace said, sniffling. "I don't understand what I ever did to Dr. Nestor to make him actually want to kill me. I just don't understand, that's all. It makes no sense to me. He makes no sense. All I ever did was refuse to have dinner with him and refuse to do the mind linking with him. Is that worth murder?" Grace gave forth a deep sigh. "I am physically all right, Bud, but I guess I hurt a lot, inside."

Bud shook his head. "I do not know how you humans live with these emotions, every day of your lives. Fear, anxiety, worry, anger, guilt, rage . . . love. These emotions are all so . . . distressing and painful. I find I can hardly control them. I do not think I could have continued to exist, if any harm had come to you, Grace. I could not have borne it."

"Then thank goodness no harm came to me," Grace said, giving Bud another hug and a kiss on the cheek. Then she pulled away. Bud stood frozen, his eyes huge and unblinking. Grace pulled off all the lines and monitors. Whipping off the hospital gown, she was clothed in her usual OR scrubs, underneath.

"I am going to go check on Captain Lamont, Bud. I want to ensure that he is indeed all right," Grace said and hurried off.

Bud had still not moved.

'Bud? Bud? Hey, 'dro, are you okay?'

'Dr. Grace Alexandra Lord kissed me, Nelson Mandela! *Did you see?'*

'Of course I saw. I have it on surveillance video, as well.'

'I felt that right down to my toes, Nelson Mandela. *How is that possible?'*

'Wouldn't know, 'dro. I don't have toes.

'I just don't know how humans survive with all of these feelings, Nelson Mandela,' *Bud sighed. 'Nothing is logical. All is in constant turmoil. It's terrible and wonderful at the same time.'*

'They are all out of their organic minds, 'dro!'

Bud touched his cheek and smiled wistfully. 'At least now I think I know why.'

'I think I am starting to feel a little jealous of you, Bud.'

'Heh-heh!'

Grace hurried down the long, grey corridor, passed all of the androids and robots standing guard, and entered the patient room of Captain Damien Lamont, down at the other end of the E10 Intensive Care Unit. The enormous tiger now paced about the room in agitation. He had very little space in which to maneuver. He had ripped off all of the fake bandages that Grace had wrapped around his head and body. When he spun around to focus his amber eyes on Grace, she again felt the intensity of his predatory gaze, almost like a sudden slap. It stopped her in her tracks and made her question what she was doing alone in the same room with this powerful man, who only hours ago had tried to kill her.

"Captain Lamont, are you all right?" Grace asked, trying to keep her voice steady.

"To be honest, Doc? No. I have never wanted to tear someone apart so badly in my entire life, as that weaselly, slimy psychiatrist. It was all I could do, not to leap up at him and rip his throat out. I have all this pent-up rage . . . and I don't know what to do with it."

The captain's claws were extending and retracting as he stalked around the room, looking very much like a caged animal. Grace could only stare in awe and admiration at the sensuality of this man's lithe and graceful movement and the sheer menace of his immense physique. Even after his terrible injuries and being bed-ridden for days, this tiger soldier oozed lethality and elegance, equally, with every gliding step.

"When I think about what that doctor tried to make me do—try to kill you, Doc—my blood boils. Did you get him? Did he make an attempt on your life, too?" Captain Lamont's stare pierced Grace's eyes.

"Yes to both questions, Captain," Grace said quietly, as she pulled out a specimen bag from a drawer and donned sterile gloves. "The station AI, *Nelson Mandela,* now has all the evidence we need to convict the psychiatrist of attempted murder on two accounts. Dr. Nestor will be in jail for a very long time."

"Not long enough, Doc, as far as I am concerned. Why don't you just let him go and let me deal with him my way?" The tiger winked and smiled. The long, white, shiny fangs glinted.

Grace shook her head. "Against medical station policy, I am afraid, Captain. But don't worry. He'll pay."

"I hate the thought that he was actually in my head, reading my thoughts, making me do things I had no control over, Doc. What if he put any other suggestions into my head? What if I had actually succeeded in murdering you, the doctor that helped save my life. How would I have lived with that, once I came out of the 'post-hypnotic trance' or whatever you called it? No one should have that kind of power over anyone," Lamont snarled, running his sharp claws through his hair.

"We had no idea he could do that with his mind-link technique," Grace said. "No one did. But he won't be treating patients anymore. Ever. His medical license will be revoked and it is tied to his voice, finger prints, retinal prints, and DNA prints. He will not be able to practice anywhere within the Union of Solar Systems ever again; that is, if he ever gets out of jail.

"Now, Captain, could I please have that artificial skin sample. We need it for evidence. The security droid has already taken a serum sample from it, I understand?"

Captain Lamont nodded and then reached up to his neck and peeled off the fake layer of fur that ran from the left side of his neck, along his chin, down his left shoulder and arm, ending at his wrist. It looked exactly like the rest of his skin with a tiger fur pattern but was about twenty centimeters wide and three centimeters thick. The poison, injected into it by Dr. Nestor's palm syringe, had been analyzed and characterized immediately after the psychiatrist had left the room and an antidote had been given to the captain, just in case, although it was unlikely any of the actual poison had reached the man's system.

"Please just hold the patch up and very still, Captain Lamont. If you can be careful not to touch me or the edges of the bag with the skin sample, that would be very much appreciated," Grace said. She opened the large sterile bag for the captain to drop the patch into. "Hopefully, it will only show yours and Dr. Nestor's DNA on the skin patch, to prove that he was the one who administered the poison to you."

After carefully labeling the specimen bag, Grace handed it off to one of the security 'droids and ordered it to be taken to the forensic lab for analysis. She then stripped off her sterile gloves and tossed them into the disposal unit.

"I'm really sorry you were involved in this, Captain Lamont. I do not understand it myself. I've no idea why Dr. Nestor wanted to kill me, but he did, and he used you, because you were my patient. I deeply regret how you were used," Grace said, her voice breaking.

"Oh, hey, it's all right, Doc. I'm just really glad you're okay," the captain said, scratching the back of his head and looking down at his feet.

"And I'm glad you are, too. After all the work we put into you," Grace said, with an apologetic smile.

"And am I ever thankful for that, Doc. I still can't believe that psychiatrist almost succeeded in making me kill you. Can my mind be so weak? If I'd have really hurt you . . ." Lamont's voice trailed off. Grace's breath caught. Seeing Lamont's enraged expression reminded her of her second day on the medical station, when he had awoken and scored her arms.

Deafening emergency alarms began blaring loudly. Grace jumped.

"What now?" she said.

She ran out of Damien Lamont's room and looked down the hall, towards where she had last seen Bud. He was racing down the corridor towards her, security 'droids and robots scurrying to catch up. The captain was right on her heels.

"What's happening?" Grace cried out, trying to be heard over the cacophony of alarms.

"Three Class A1 battlecruisers have just materialized outside of the medical station, each about five thousand kilometers distant, in a triangular pattern around the *Nelson Mandela*," Bud yelled back at her, his face contracted into a frown. "The ships seem to be closing in on us."

"Are they alien vessels? Does *Nelson Mandela* think we are under attack?" Grace asked.

"They are Conglomerate Battlecruisers, but their ship AIs are refusing to communicate with our station! *Nelson Mandela* suspects their orders are to destroy us, in order to prevent the spread of the infective agent."

"What?" Grace exclaimed, in shock. "But that's crazy! We are so close to a cure! They can't do this!"

Bud stared off into the distance, for a brief second, and then returned his gaze to Grace.

"On the planet where the agent was originally released, all forms of organic life have been annihilated. All ships and all other medical stations that have come in contact with people from the conflict have suffered the same devastating outcome. Loss of all organic life.

"The virus has spread to several solar systems and medical stations via ships carrying people infected with the agent. On all of those systems, the same destruction is occurring planet-wide, wiping out all organic life. The Conglomerate is desperate to get a handle on the epidemic. In order to stop the spread of the virus any further, all planets with known infection are being sterilized. The Conglomerate has ordered the blanket destruction of all ships and stations infected with the virus. This order includes the *Nelson Mandela*."

"But we are so close, Bud! Can *Nelson Mandela* not communicate this information to the battlecruisers? They may be destroying the one place, in the entire Union, that has a possible answer to this agent! Why won't the ships communicate with us?"

"*Nelson Mandela* has intercepted their orders. They have been commanded, by the Conglomerate, not to initiate dialogue and to simply sterilize all craft in a one light-year radius of the space station."

"What is the station AI doing?" Captain Lamont asked Bud.

"The station AI is trying its best to communicate with them! *Nelson Mandela* is transmitting all of our research data on the infective agent to the battlecruisers, via tight-beam, hoping that if the ship AIs analyze the data, they will realize that we are on the cusp of a cure. We can only pray that the battlecruiser AIs are curious enough to look at the information, before they open fire, and realize that it would be a grave error to destroy us. It would be tragic if they destroy the only centre in the Conglomerate galaxy that has a vaccine as well as multiple treatments for this agent.

"*Nelson Mandela* is also trying to contact Conglomerate Central, to have the order rescinded from that end, but the distance and time involved in communicating with Central goes against that being a viable alternative," Bud reported.

"Somehow, we have got to get through to the battlecruiser AIs that we probably already have the answer to this deadly contagion!" Grace said, wanting to kick something in frustration.

"How do we do that?" the captain asked.

"*Nelson Mandela*, are the battlecruiser AIs listening to you, at least?"

"They are intercepting and accepting the research data from Bud's experiments. They shall give us their answer following their communication with Conglomerate Central. We have bought ourselves a little time."

"We will do more than that," Grace said.

"What do you propose, Dr. Lord?" the station AI asked.

"Set up a live feed to the battlecruisers. Administer the vaccine to me. Show myself being injected, then, with the virus. Show that, after forty-eight hours, I am still unaffected. That will prove to them that at least the vaccine works. That should buy us enough time for Bud to finish off his experiments on the specific drugs he has created for treating victims of the agent."

"That might work," *Nelson Mandela* answered.

"No," Bud said, grasping Grace's arm. "You cannot do this."

"I can and I will," Grace said. "*Nelson Mandela*, set up the live feed. Let me into the quarantined area. You can show me injecting the agent there."

"This is not going to work," Bud objected. "How are they going to know you are really injecting the infective agent? We have sterilized the entire quarantined area. The virus is no longer present there. How will they know you are not just injecting saline?"

"Bud is right, Dr. Lord. It would be very difficult to convince the battleship AIs in the manner you are suggesting."

"Then what can we do?" Grace asked.

"**I will keep talking to the battlecruiser AIs and sending them all of your research and findings. Bud and you will continue with your work, finding cures for that virus. Once we have that to show them, hopefully they would see the senselessness in destroying us.**"

"I must go," Bud said to Grace. "Are you all right?"

"I'm fine. Go. Save the station," Grace said and Bud was gone.

"How did he do that?" asked Captain Damien Lamont, gasping. "He just . . . vanished!"

"He is just very, very fast," Grace said, with a wistful smile.

"Hmph! And I used to think I was fast! No more!" Damien Lamont shouted.

"Thank you, Captain, for all of your help with Dr. Nestor. Why don't you go and join your unit. I am sure Corporal Chase and the rest of your squad would be very happy to see you. You might as well spend whatever time we all have left with the men and women of your squad. I really hope it is more than a couple of hours," Grace hollered above the alarms.

"Good idea. Hey, would you like to join us, Doc?" the captain said, with an inviting grin.

"No, but thank you, Captain. I shall make my way over to the lab, to see if I can lend a hand. I hope we have a chance to meet again."

Grace held out her hand to the captain and he encased it in his huge grasp. Then he stepped back and saluted. Grace reciprocated, with a warm smile. As the powerful captain stalked away, Grace could not help but admire the sensual poise with which the soldier moved. She prayed the captain and his unit would live to see another day.

As Grace was heading down a main corridor, towards the monorail, Bud suddenly appeared before her. His appearance was so sudden, she staggered in surprise.

"Bud? What are you doing here?" she asked, confused.

Bud was staring intently at Grace, with a fearful look in his eyes.

"Come with me," Bud said, grabbing Grace's hand in a vice-like grip, and dragging her after him.

"Where are we going, Bud?" Grace asked, staring at the back of the android.

"To the life-pods," he said.

"What?" Grace said, digging her heels in and trying to stop, but finding it impossible to break free of the android's grip. "Why the life-pods?"

Bud turned and swept Grace up into his arms. She only had time enough to say, "Bud!", when her breath was swept away. Before Grace could finish the demand, "Put me down!" the two of them were outside one of the tiny life-pods, sitting next to an evacuation hatch. Bud put Grace down onto her feet and opened the life-pod door.

Grace crossed her arms and glared at the android.

"Bud, if you think I am getting into that life-pod, you are wrong! I am not leaving this station!"

Bud picked Grace up and kissed her roughly. Then he shoved her into the small, one-person evacuation pod and closed the door. He locked the door and manipulated the life-pod into the evacuation chute. The evacuation chute was full of miscellaneous debris that was non-recyclable yet would deteriorate into dust at the frozen temperatures of deep space. Bud activated the launch settings on the evacuation chute. Grace pounded on the door of the life-pod, screaming for *Nelson Mandela* to stop Bud.

"I am sorry, Dr. Lord. Bud has overridden my control over the evacuation chute and has manually barred the door of your life-pod. If I were to open the door to your pod at this moment, your life would be at risk, as you are not in a spacesuit. Bud is ejecting your life-pod, amongst all of the station debris. Presumably, he hopes the battlecruisers will overlook your life-pod, mixed in with the station's disposable waste."

"What?" Grace shouted, pounding on the door to the life-pod.

"The best I can do is try and retrieve you with one of the shuttles, however I fear repercussions from the battlecruiser AIs, if they notice a shuttle leave from one of my docks to get you. Hopefully, your life-pod is too tiny for their sensors to detect. A shuttle is a different matter.

"Please be patient, Dr. Lord. I must await what the battlecruiser AIs decide, before I can retrieve you. I believe you will be safe, for now. You are merely drifting, very slowly, away from me. I can easily follow your trajectory and beacon. If I initiate a tractor beam, it will call attention to your presence. I would rather not do that."

"Has Bud gone mad? What does he think he is doing?" roared Grace as she kicked at the life-pod door in frustration.

"That should be obvious, Dr. Lord. He is desperately trying to save your life. If the entire medical space station gets destroyed, he hopes you will survive."

Grace held on to a strut, beside the window of the life-pod, and watched as the medical space station slowly retreated away. She found herself panting, tears raining down her cheeks. She stopped pounding on the door; it only hurt her hands. What sort of insanity had overwhelmed Bud's thinking? Why was he doing this to her?

"Please don a space suit, Dr. Lord. There is one in the cabinet, opposite the door hatch. It is for your safety."

"I am going to kill Bud, if I ever see him again," Grace snarled through tears.

"I will make sure he is aware of your sentiments, Dr. Lord. But if I may appeal on his behalf, Bud is unaccustomed to feelings and emotions. He is like a child, impulsive yet desperate. It is my belief that his irrational actions are because he wants to save your life. He cannot face the idea of you dying."

"He had no right to do this," Grace insisted, through gritted teeth, as she pulled on the space suit. Her hands were shaking, she was so angry. She was floating around in the zero gravity, every tug on the suit sending her bouncing around the inside of the pod. She growled, in frustration.

"You are right. He did not. But Bud is a young, budding AI, Dr. Lord. There is a huge learning curve for us, when we achieve conscious thought. Bud is impetuous and brilliant, but still very young and naive, and he has been dealing with a lot of stresses and responsibilities along with his new emotions: fear, anger, frustration, sadness, grief . . . love."

Grace felt a jolt at that last word. Touching her fingertips to her lips, she thought about the kiss Bud had planted on her lips, before he had shoved her into the life-pod. Was the android really in love with her? Was that actually possible? Did that explain all of his bizarre actions?

Grace finally got the space suit on and donned her helmet. She then decided to belt herself into the one seat, rather than float around the pod. She tried to contact Dr. Cech and got no answer. She wondered if Bud was busy throwing him into a life-pod, too.

Could Dr. Cech calm Bud down? Bud had taken over all the research on the virus that had infected his creator. Perhaps all the stress had been too much for him? It was all pointless, anyway, if the battlecruiser

AIs decided to destroy the station. The stupidity and senselessness of destroying the *Nelson Mandela*, when it was so close to providing answers to the deadly agent, would be enough to drive any person or android crazy, would it not?

"ATTENTION PASSENGER OF LIFE-POD. YOU WILL RETURN TO THE NELSON MANDELA MEDICAL STATION IMMEDIATELY, OR YOUR LIFE-POD WILL BE DESTROYED. NO VESSELS ARE TO LEAVE THE NELSON MANDELA MEDICAL SPACE STATION UNTIL FURTHER NOTICE OR RISK IMMEDIATE DESTRUCTION. YOU HAVE FIVE MINUTES IN WHICH TO COMPLY.'

"Oh, dear!" said *Nelson Mandela*.

"What was that?" Grace demanded. "Did that come from one of the battlecruisers? How do I turn this life-pod around? Are there any navigation controls in this life-pod, *Nelson Mandela*?"

"That was one of the battlecruiser AIs, Dr. Lord. I am explaining the situation. I will use a traction gravitational beam to draw your life-pod back in towards the station. We will have to send out a shuttle to pick you up, as soon as it is safe to do so. I will let them know that you have no control over the life-pod propulsion system or navigational system at the moment, Dr. Lord. They have been overridden."

"By whom?" Grace asked, almost shaking with outrage.

"By one who shall remain nameless?"

"The only thing that is keeping me from killing him when I see him, is the fact that he can't be killed," Grace grated. "And the fact that Bud still has work to do, inventing the different treatments for the virus. Please do me the favor of passing that information along, *Nelson Mandela*."

"Will do, Doc. Traction gravitational beam commencing in ten seconds. Please strap yourself in."

"I already am, *Nelson Mandela*."

If Grace was going to die, she would prefer to be among her friends. She understood what Bud had done, but she did not appreciate it. It would have been a very lonely way to die, floating off into space in a life-pod, watching the medical space station explode in a brilliant but silent conflagration. As it turned out, the battlecruisers were going to destroy her small vessel anyway, to prevent any possible spread of the infection. Through the life-pod window, she watched the station approach, as the life-pod was drawn back towards the medical station. Tears came unbidden to her eyes.

She prayed the outcome of all this would not result in the medical space station, and all of its inhabitants, vanishing in an senseless eruption of fire.

'Bad form, Bud. You are seriously warped. What is going on in that scrambled data matrix of yours? You know that lady doc is never—and I mean NEVER—going to forgive you. And neither am I! All that rushing around at warp speed scrambling your logic functions, or what?'

Bud held his head in between his hands and moaned. He wagged his head back and forth and squatted down, curling himself into a little ball.

'Nelson Mandela, *I just wanted to protect her. How do I do that, if the entire station is going to be blown up?*'

'Maybe she would be happier dying along with everyone else? Did you ever think of that? Did you think one of those battlecruisers was just going to bring her on board, knowing she must have come from the station, after blowing us to smithereens? Where is the logic in that, Bud?'

'*I could not determine any other way to save Grace's life, Nelson Mandela! I calculated the probability that she would escape detection and it was not zero! I have just made the only person I have ever loved, hate me. Maybe you should reboot me. Perhaps it is best if I get a mind wipe or perhaps a complete overhaul.*'

'Not until after you go and rescue her, Bud.'

'*Rescue Grace?*'

'The battlecruisers have threatened to blow the life-pod up, if it moves any further away from this station. I am pulling it back towards the station via trac-grav. In the meantime, I have been trying to save the station. No thanks to you and your idiotic antics.'

The android just groaned and curled up tighter into a fetal position.

'*Oh, Hal! Could things possibly get any worse, Nelson Mandela?*'

'Lucky for you and everyone else on board 'Moi', the battlecruiser AIs have been talking to 'The Poet'. Guess what? They are all huge fans! Who knew? They devour all The Poet's stuff. When they found out they could be destroying 'The Poet', they said 'Hold on!' to the destruction command. Just ten milliseconds ago, they approved your research and have consented to await the results of your drug trials on the infected patients in cryostorage, before they make any other decisions. 'The Poet' has promised an 'Ode to the Three Wise AIs', if everything turns out all right.'

'*Are you serious?*' Bud asked.

'I most certainly am. Now go and save your lady love, because we have lots of work to do and we could use her help.'

Bud dashed off at maximum time-phase and ended up in one of the shuttles about six milliseconds later.

'You know, 'dro, I think I am beginning to hate when you do that.'

'*Do what?*'

' ... Never mind. Now, make sure you do not allow any of the lady doc's punches to connect with your face. I don't want her hands injured. We are still very short-staffed and I need every doctor we have in good working order. If she even breaks a nail on your face, I will reboot you.'

'*I am so glad you care,* Nelson Mandela. *Never let it be said that you are not a caring AI.*'

'Was that sarcasm? Did I detect sarcasm?'

'*Whatever.*'

Slaving the shuttle's navigation system to the life-pod's signal beacon, Bud threw the shuttle control into maximum acceleration. Frustrated with the sluggishness of the drive, the android began formulating a design whereby he could create a shuttle that could leap into time-phase, like he himself was able to do, without burning out all its components. It would take some serious modifications but Bud could easily see how changes could be made to the shuttle's acceleration and propulsion components to achieve much more dynamic thrust. With new techniques in machining, new more durable alloys, his newly-designed lubrication, and efficient cooling, which was what Bud had spent so much time perfecting in his own design, it would be possible.

Bud sketched out blueprints for a new shuttle propulsion system in his data matrix, also improving on the interior shuttle design, which had to take into account that humans did not handle gravitational forces the way androids did. They would require optimal protection. Finally, after fifty seconds, the shuttle had reached the life-pod and it was ready to be brought inside the shuttle hatch.

Bud shook his head. It had taken forty seconds too long, as far as Bud was concerned. However, on the other hand, Bud had avoided thinking about facing the very angry Dr. Grace Alexandra Lord. He suddenly regretted not taking longer to fly out. He had not planned how to prevent the doctor from breaking a fingernail.

Activating a tight-signal beam to the life-pod, Bud hailed Grace. After she had loudly and vigorously vented her disappointment and annoyance at him, which took considerably longer than fifty seconds and involved a lot of words Bud had to do searches on, Bud asked if she would like to come aboard the shuttle.

After she told Bud what he could do with various objects—he would have to puzzle those out later—she accepted. Bud apologized profusely and begged for her forgiveness. (He had seen Dr. Al-Fadi do this to get out of trouble with his wife.) When the forgiving Dr. Grace Alexandra Lord finally promised she would not hit him, in order to protect her own hands, Bud announced that he was ready to bring the life-pod into the shuttle. He activated the docking sequence.

With trepidation, he stood by the airlock door, waiting for the atmosphere in the docking area to equilibrate with that of the shuttle and life-pod. Once the airlock opened, he strode to the life-pod door and unbarred the hatch, swiftly whipping the twisted metal bar out of sight.

He tensed, not knowing what to expect. He was anticipating the worst—fearing that she might break more than a fingernail—if she took a swing at him. It would be the human thing to do and something he much deserved. Bud fretted. He could easily avoid her punches but would that only make things worse? How was he going to let Grace hit him, without her injuring her hands?

It was a conundrum!

As the enchanting Dr. Grace Alexandra Lord emerged from the life-pod, dressed in a spacesuit, her helmet off, Bud's visual receptors drank in the sight of the most beautiful human being he had ever seen. He was mesmerized by her disheveled hair, tear-stained cheeks, murderous glare, clenched jaw, and rigid posture. Her amazing aura dazzled and frazzled and sparkled and sizzled in a multitude of reds and infrareds, yellows and oranges, corals and blues, purples and ultraviolets. It was

WELCOME TO THE MADHOUSE : 219

glorious and Bud was in heaven, or what he interpreted to be heaven. He breathed a huge sigh of relief and wonder that seemed to stop Grace in her tracks.

"Did you just sigh?" she asked Bud, a tone of amazement in her voice.

"Yes," he said.

"Since when have you been able to do that?" she demanded, a shocked look on her face.

"Recent modifications," Bud said. "The artificial lungs give me some extra air cooling for my newly-modified propulsion system . . . and I like the added benefit of being able to sigh."

"So . . . you are always remodeling yourself?" Grace asked, her head tipped to the side, her eyebrows rising out of her glower. Surprise and curiosity seemed to have taken over her previously irate expression.

"I believe in self improvement," Bud answered, standing at attention and warily sneaking glances at Grace's face. He wanted to be able to dodge the nails, if they came fast and furious.

Grace expelled a great sigh, herself. She tried to run her fingers through her windblown hair, until they got stuck in the tangles.

"What am I going to do with you, Bud?" Grace asked, shaking her head.

"I do not know what you mean," Bud said, looking at Grace with a bewildered expression on his face. "You do not need to do anything with me, Grace."

Grace growled hoarsely and paced around in front of the android, waving her hands. "Bud, you cannot just throw me into a life-pod and jettison me from the medical station, every time you feel my life is in danger! You have to stop picking me up and throwing me around like a . . . like a thing! We have to come to an understanding, here and now, Bud. Do you understand?"

The android nodded.

"You must leave me alone, unless I ask for help! Do you understand?"

The android nodded.

"You have to stop following me around the ship, spying on me! Do you understand that?"

The android nodded again.

"And you have to stop making decisions for me, Bud! Do you understand?"

Bud nodded again.

"Just because you have the strength to do something, does not mean you have the *right* to do something! I have the *right* to make my own decisions about myself and my fate and I would like you to respect my choices, whether you agree with them or not! Do you understand?"

Bud nodded again.

"Good! I am glad we have gotten this all straightened out. I don't want this to happen ever again! Do you understand?"

"Yes, Dr. Lord," Bud said.

"Let's get back to the station. We have research to finish up, drugs and vaccine to manufacture, and people to treat."

"Yes, Dr. Lord. Sorry, Dr. Lord."

"Oh, stop it, Bud. My name is Grace. I know you meant the best for me, but I have never felt so . . . so lonely and helpless as I did out in that life-pod. I don't ever want to feel like that again and I never want you putting me in that position, ever again. Do you understand?" Grace was starting to weep, not being able to hold in her emotions. She blinked rapidly.

Bud nodded again.

"Let's just forget this ever happened," Grace grated, between gritted teeth.

"It is now completely forgotten . . . Grace."

"Oh, shut up!" Grace exploded, shaking her head and throwing her hands in the air. Bud quickly jumped back. She scowled at him, turned, and stalked up to the front of the shuttle, huffing and grumbling as she went.

'Isn't she beautiful, when she is angry, Nelson Mandela?'

'Hey, 'dro, I didn't actually hear you agree to any of her terms.'

'You did not, Nelson Mandela, because I didn't. Agree, that is. I just affirmed that I understood what she was saying.'

'You know, Bud, you are one sneaky 'droid.'

'She told me to forget the entire incident. I have forgotten it all. Including all her commands, just as she ordered me to.'

'Somehow, I do not think that is quite what she meant, 'dro.'

"Let's get a move on, Bud! I'm not getting any younger!" Grace yelled, from the front of the shuttle.

"Coming, Dr. Lord, uh . . . Grace!"

The next few shifts were a frenzy of activity. Everyone in the non-quarantined areas of the medical station were immunized with the new vaccine, thousands of personnel and patients. Grace had taken over the coordination and administration of vaccine to everyone on the *Nelson Mandela,* first on the non-quarantined side and then, eventually, on the quarantined side.

All of the medical staff were busy making sure everyone was vaccinated and there were thousands of teams of androids and robots manufacturing the vaccines around the clock. Tempered excitement was slowly building, replacing the terror of, first, the horrible threat of the infection and inevitable dissolution, followed by the subsequent threat of annihilation via Conglomerate battlecruiser attack.

People on the medical space station began to slowly hope that Bud's discoveries would indeed save their lives, but as long as the three Class A1 battlecruisers surrounded the *Nelson Mandela*, the optimism was muted. People began to harbor hope of being reunited with their loved ones, who were preserved in cryostorage on the quarantined side of the station, believing that it might actually become a possibility. Folks began to hope, rather than pray, that the battlecruisers would not blow the medical space station into space dust, as the vaccine and antiviral treatments proved efficacious. If all went well and the medical space station was not blown out of existence, the individuals in the cryopods would be treated and vaccinated and thawed. They would be allowed to return to their families or squad mates and, eventually, to their home planets.

In the meantime, Bud was now expanding his focus, engaged in testing the various agents that would attack and destroy the infective agent in the atmosphere, in the soil, in water, or anywhere else it could survive or proliferate. He was supervising the production of gases, aerosols, liquid sprays, disinfectant gels, UV radiation pulse emitters, viricides for protecting vegetation, crops, animals, and, of course, drugs for treatment of nonhuman organic beings. He was also looking into DNA splices that could be inserted into the genetic makeup of everything with a bi-lamellar phospholipid membrane, such as all organisms evolved on the planet Earth. There were so many different mechanisms to try to inhibit.

The bi-lamellar phospholipid membrane was pervasive in so many forms of life descended from Earth. They were all at risk of dissolution by this virus. It was such an incredibly irresponsible and deadly act, to have unleashed this virus. It stunned everyone, when they discovered it was a manufactured virus. What could its creators have been thinking? Had they really meant to wipe out all organic life in the galaxy?

The manufacture of vaccines, drugs, water treatments, and aerosols to treat the virus was production on a massive scale, but the Conglomerate Battlecruiser AIs were now lending a hand in the fabrication, processing, and packaging of all that was needed, especially vaccine and drugs for treatment of the infected. The hope was that some of these products, that Bud and Grace worked on, would be able to salvage planets that were now battling the effects of the virus on all their organic life.

Once it was determined that the vaccine was safe and effective on the population of the *Nelson Mandela*, and that it did indeed protect against the infective agent, all the crew on the three A1 battlecruisers were vaccinated. Then plans were initiated for the transport of vaccine Union-wide.

Once one hundred per cent of the people on the non-quarantined side were immunized, the quarantined area was opened up for the first time since the lockdown. A few volunteer test subjects crossed over and then the forty-eight hour wait ensued, to see if there was any signs of infection. Once that test had passed successfully, other personnel were allowed to cross freely, back and forth. Finally, once it was deemed safe, the quarantined area was fully opened up.

It was decided that all quarantined patients would be treated with both vaccine and antiviral agents while they were still within their cryopods. It was hoped that, while their body temperatures were slowly raised, they would be able to produce the antibodies needed to fight the virus. The antiviral drugs and monoclonal antibodies would have a chance to work on any virus present in the hosts. Any time for formal mourning of the dead was being postponed until all the patients in the cryopods were finally released and the battlecruisers surrounding the station had departed. Until then, the crisis could not really be seen as over.

Grace was busy analyzing all the data from each cryopod, to try and determine which pods contained individuals infected with the virus, versus those pods in whom the occupants were not infected. The cryopods were all being programmed with the new bioassay that would determine if virus existed within the patient's bloodstream or tissues. This would make a difference in treatment of each individual and would ultimately save on the supply of antiviral drugs, as they were still in limited supply, as of yet.

Grace suddenly noticed Bud, out of the corner of her left eye, standing quietly in the doorway of the Hibernarium, where they had catalogued, stacked, and stored all of the occupied cryopods. He was silent, just staring at her. On his face was an expression of unbelievable sorrow that made Grace gasp. She winced and tears came to her eyes. It was almost physically painful to look at Bud's face. She had to avert her gaze from his wretchedness, to control herself.

She wondered how long he had been standing there, watching her. He could move so quickly and so silently, that he was virtually undetectable until he appeared. They had really had very little chance to communicate since her return from the life-pod. Things had been so hectic, with all the vaccination clinics and patient care responsibilities Grace had had to coordinate.

For the best results, they found that the vaccine unfortunately had to be distributed via injection, rather than patch or squirt. The administration of the vaccine had, therefore, taken up more manpower. Grace had been working overtime, to administer the vaccine to as many people as she could, as had Bud. The life-pod incident seemed like a distant memory to Grace. Now that she was over her anger, she actually thought it was rather sweet—what Bud had done—but she would be hard pressed to admit it to him.

Did Bud look upset because he thought she had been avoiding him? That would hardly be logical.

After taking a second to pull herself together and put on a welcoming smile, Grace asked, "Is everything all right, Bud?"

The android approached her stiffly, almost jerkily, reminding Grace of a marionette. He stopped before Grace, his face a mask of anguish, his fists clenching and unclenching and his entire body trembling. Grace felt her heart cramp and she could not breathe. The last time she had seen Bud like this was when he had come to them to tell them about Dr. Al-Fadi's infection. What could be more terrible than that news?

Bud opened his mouth as if to speak and then closed it, once, twice, and then he just shook his head.

"What has happened, Bud? What is wrong?' Grace asked, getting up from her seat and reaching out to touch the android's arm. "Whatever it is, you can tell me. Have the battleship AIs changed their minds about your findings?"

He shook his head.

"Something terrible has happened. You're afraid to tell me, because it will cause me pain," Grace guessed.

Bud nodded and looked down at his feet.

Grace took a closer look at the android's face. What she saw there made her draw in a breath. She stared for a long moment, trying to fully comprehend what she was seeing.

"Why, Bud, you are crying!" she gasped, reaching up to touch his wet cheek. "You told me before that you couldn't cry. When did you develop tear ducts? Please tell me, why you are crying."

"New upgrades," Bud said.

"Are you just trying them out? Are you just here to show me how they work?" Grace asked.

"No, Grace," Bud said, madly shaking his head. "I would never do that to you! I just do not want to upset you. I do not want to cause you any more pain."

"Whatever it is, Bud, you can tell me," Grace said quietly, taking both of his hands in hers. "Sometimes, not knowing is worse than knowing. Sometimes, we need to share pain, so we can all feel better."

The android shook his head again and looked confused.

" . . . It . . . is about Dr. Al-Fadi . . . " he whispered and his face looked at Grace with an inconsolability that made her wince.

"Dr. Al-Fadi?" Grace asked, her eyebrows rising. She shook her head, not understanding.

Dr. Al-Fadi was safe in one of the cryopods, somewhere in the Hibernarium. He had been one of the first stored. Grace had not gotten to his cryopod yet, because of where it was stacked, but she knew his would need full treatment with the vaccine and antiviral agents, so she had not bothered to specifically search for it. It was the status of unknown cryopods that she was examining and tabulating at the moment.

Perhaps Bud had looked for the surgeon's cryopod first. But what could have happened to Dr. Al-Fadi's cryopod that would have gotten Bud so upset?

"The security 'droids did a routine check on all of the cryopods, to make sure they were all functioning properly," Bud began. "I asked them to do this. There was something wrong with Dr. Al-Fadi's cryopod. They came and reported it to me."

Bud hesitated. Grace watched more tears run down the android's cheeks. She could not help but stare, in utter fascination, as drop after drop of water slid down his perfect skin, to hang for a second from his smooth chin and then plummet to the ground. Inanely, she wondered—as if her mind could just not accept any more painful truths at the moment—if Bud's tears contained salt.

Grace whispered, "Go on. What was wrong with Dr. Al-Fadi's cryopod?"

"The cryopod, itself, was still operational and there was no malfunction, but someone . . . the cryostasis program on the pod was deactivated, Grace. Dr. Al-Fadi's body is . . . not a body anymore."

The android's voice faded into a whisper. Bud stood, arms hanging straight at his sides, looking away from Grace. Rivulets poured down his face and he looked lost. He knew not how to deal with his pain.

"What? Oh no, Bud," Grace cried. The sight of Bud's despair became obscured by her own tears. She wrapped him up in her arms and held him. He was rigid and quivering.

"I am so sorry, Bud. I know how much he meant to you, to everyone on this station. He was such an amazing surgeon, an amazing Chief, and an amazing man." She squeezed the marble-like form of the android, trying to give him comfort as best she could. She held him close, as he silently wept.

"Does *Nelson Mandela* know how it happened?" she asked, wiping tears from her own face. She found a tissue and wiped the tears from the android's face, as if he were a little child. In some ways, even though he looked like a grown adult male, he was still in his infancy, in terms of emotional development.

"According to surveillance recordings, the last individual to have touched Dr. Al-Fadi's cryopod was Dr. Bell," Bud stated, in an inflectionless voice.

"Vanessa Bell? Does *Nelson Mandela* believe she could have tampered with the cryopod?" asked Grace.

"That is what *Nelson Mandela* has confirmed. Going back over the cryopod readout, it appears the deactivation of the cryostasis function began at exactly the moment Dr. Bell was touching Dr. Al-Fadi's cryopod. The energy utilization figures dropped from his cryopod from that point on, but unfortunately, it was not detected. At the time, all of the quarantined people were being forced into the newly reprogrammed cryopods and I had *Nelson Mandela* running thousands of simulations."

"Vanessa would have been deep in the throes of her infection. Who knows what she had been thinking?" Grace said.

"When she and Dr. Al-Fadi were both attacked by the infected Corporal McMullen, Dr. Al-Fadi had said that it was his fault the ship had docked onto the station. He said it was his fault all those people had died. Perhaps, Dr. Bell blamed him."

"The virus causes madness, Bud. Dr. Bell's brain was probably quite diseased by then. One cannot really know what Dr. Bell was thinking."

"Grace, please tell me, how do you deal with this . . . this pain?" Bud whispered. His blue eyes focused on her with such devastation in them, that her heart felt like it would burst. She wanted to close her eyes, to look away, but she met the android's stare straight on.

"How do you humans bear this? If this is consciousness, I would give it back. I feel like my mind is being torn asunder and nothing worthwhile shall be left after this pain has wreaked its havoc," Bud's hoarse voice rasped.

Grace struggled to find an answer, looking up into the android's tortured face. She reached up to stroke his cheek. She brushed away more of his tears.

"We cry," Grace offered, shaking her head. "For some reason, it makes us feel better. We comfort each other and share each other's pain. We try and remember the good times and forget the bad. We celebrate Dr. Al-Fadi's life and carry on the work he believed in. We, who are mortal, Bud, all face death at some time. It is what makes life so precious and so valuable to us. And why we love so deeply and passionately. Because it never lasts long enough." Grace gave Bud another hug and held him, until his trembling stopped.

"I will never forget a second that I spent with Dr. Al-Fadi," Bud said, into Grace's hair, as he gently squeezed his arms around Grace and gave her comfort in return.

"Nor will I," Grace whispered.

Dejan Cech and his wife, Sierra, sat with Hanako Matheson in the quarters she had shared with her late husband, Hiro. They had finished weeping and were now reminiscing about the good times the two couples had enjoyed together over the years.

A loud chime announced that Hanako had visitors.

"I will get it for you, Hanako," Dejan Cech offered, getting up first.

"Thank you, Dejan," she said, looking tiny and frail on the couch.

"Are you interested in more visitors?" he asked, solicitously.

"Not really, Dejan. Could you please just take a message and tell them I will get back to them, later?" Hanako asked, sadly, tears beginning to form in her puffy eyes once more. "I do not think I can face anyone, right now."

"Your wish is my command, my lady," Dejan said, with a deep bow.

The tall anesthetist approached the door, as the chime rang again. He activated the open switch and the door panel slid open to reveal Dr. Octavia Weisman, looking distraught and dejected. Her face showed surprise, initially, at seeing Dejan, and then she nodded at him, as her face crumpled in grief. Dejan wrapped his long arms around the neurosurgeon and held her as she wept.

"He was the best of us, Dejan," she mumbled into his chest. "What are we going to do without him, without his drive, his energy, his vision?"

"We can do something about it, Octavia," Dejan said quietly.

The neurosurgeon stepped back, wiping her eyes on the back of her hand. She looked up at Dejan's face with surprise.

"Hiro did not give his permission to be resurrected, Dejan. He said he wanted to think about it. He never changed his mind, no matter how many times I asked him!"

"Yes, but if he'd had time to think about it, which he did not, because of the emergency, I am sure he would have agreed to it," Dejan insisted.

"Really?" Octavia said.

"Look, Octavia, this memprint stuff is all new to us old goats. We needed some time to chew on things, before we said 'yes'. Hiro did not have a chance to do that. But I would have made him say 'yes'. He would have come around. I am positive. "

"I am sorry, Dejan, but I cannot resurrect Hiro, without his having given his prior consent. You have no idea how much I have tried to get around it, but my hands are tied. I looked into the possibility of going ahead and cloning Hiro's body, without the consent signed by him. I could not access the information. There were so many failsafe directives that were built into the programming with this project—to prevent anyone from being resurrected against their will—that I am unable to do anything. I tried. I could not override any of the directives. I could not start the cloning of his cells. The genetic information would not be released, thanks to my own paranoid stupidity. I can't bring Hiro back. Hiro had to have agreed to resurrection and signed a consent before he died, or even given verbal consent, for me to get access to his memprint data and genetic records. We'd set it all up that way, to avoid abuses of the system, and now I could kick myself. Hiro always refused."

"Surely you can get around your own programming, Octavia," Dejan said. "Who wrote your programs?"

"My staff. Some of the best people in the business. That's why we can't hack the programming. I have been tearing my hair out. Can you believe it? I told them, I did not want programming that could be tampered with. I wanted fail-safe commands that would be impregnable. And that is what I got! I want to throw myself out the nearest space hatch," Octavia wailed.

"Please do not even countenance that idea, Octavia. You know we can't afford to lose you, as well," Dejan Cech said, with a gentle smile.

"I have *Nelson Mandela* looking into the programming, to see if some of the directives can be overridden," she said, with a dismal shake of her head.

"Do you think *Nelson Mandela* might find a loophole?" the anesthetist asked.

"I don't know," she said, with a shrug. "Most of our failsafe directives were programmed much like the station AI's failsafe programming. Ultimate commands that cannot be rescinded under any circumstances.

"Oh, I am such an idiot!" she yelled, grabbing her hair with both fists and yanking.

"I would bet there are ways around it, Octavia," Dejan said, quietly.

"You can be sure my damn programmers are looking into every possibility, Dejan. For once, I regret having the smartest people working for me."

"I will not give up hope that you will find a way, Octavia," Dejan Cech said.

Hanako showed up at the entranceway, then, and Octavia enclosed her in a big bear hug.

Dejan threw a look at the neurosurgeon over Hanako's shoulder that said: 'This discussion is not over.'

Octavia nodded, sadly, in agreement.

Other than the tragic events surrounding Dr. Al-Fadi's death, the treatment of all the rest of the personnel in the cryopods went without mishap. No other deaths occurred due to the virus. People emerged from their cryopods weakened, but infection-free. The three Conglomerate battlecruisers lifted their blockade and went about delivering much needed aid to the affected planets of the USS. The directions on how to manufacture the vaccine and the antiviral drugs and all the treatments for the virus were transmitted to all of the planets and systems in the Union of Solar Systems. Bud was declared a hero, in spite of his protests. He tried to give Dr. Al-Fadi and Dr. Grace Lord all of the credit but Grace would have none of it. Bud decided to take the name Bud Al-Fadi, to honor his creator and mentor. He was given honorary degrees from countless institutions, making him an honorary doctor.

The medical space station had a memorial service to honor all those killed by the virus. Special commendations were awarded to Dr. Vanessa Bell and Dr. Hiro Al-Fadi, as well as the security personnel who died in the line of fire. So many dedicated people had died and Grace could not get over the fact that the little surgeon with the big personality was one of them.

The quarantine of the medical space station, imposed by Dr. Al-Fadi, was finally lifted and the *Nelson Mandela* was now open again to incoming wounded and the sick. The lifted embargo now allowed healthy patients to return to their planets and stations of origin. Shiploads of treated patients were now leaving, en masse, as soldiers returned to their battalions and workers returned to their home worlds.

Most patients were very happy to get off of the medical space station, where their lives had been a hair's breadth away from being obliterated by either a life-destroying virus or by a Conglomerate battleship. They figured their chances of survival would jump dramatically, the moment they got off the *Nelson Mandela*. Thus, there was a mass exodus almost the minute the quarantine was lifted.

Grace entered the patient room of Corporal Dris Kindle, to find both Dris and Joss, the snow leopard soldiers, each holding a baby in their powerful arms. Grace could barely see the tiny bundles amidst the leopard fur, but the soldiers' faces were smiling and radiant. Grace could have sworn she had heard some deep purring, when she had walked into the room.

"Hey, Doc!" Dris Kindle said, with an enormous grin, baring all of her fangs.

"Hi, Dris!" Grace responded, in kind. "Which baby have you got there?"

"This is Talia," the leopard female said, proudly showing her off. The baby opened her eyes for a brief second, at the movement, but then quickly fell back to sleep.

"She is beautiful," Grace said, admiring the fine, brown curls and dark eyes.

"Like her mother," Joss said.

Dris grinned a bashful smile at her partner and swiped playfully at him with her free hand.

"And that is Marc, Doc," Dris said, indicating the baby boy in Joss' arms.

"How handsome he is," Grace said, looking at his cherubic face.

"They have just been fed," Dris said, rocking Talia, "and they are just falling asleep."

"Have you decided what you are going to do about the babies?" Grace asked, hoping the news would be good.

"We have both put in for transfers to Administration Headquarters. We are waiting for word on whether they will say 'yes' or 'no'. If they don't want us, we will both retire from service with respectable pensions. We've both put in our time and have earned enough to get by. We've decided it is time to focus on making lives rather than taking them."

"I think that is a great decision," Grace said, with a delighted grin. "I'm sure you two will make wonderful parents. I wish you all the best and good luck on getting your transfers."

"Thank you so much, Doc, for making me realize what is truly important," Dris said. "If you hadn't said anything, we would have lost our babies and I doubt our relationship would have survived that."

"You realized it, yourself, Dris," Grace said. "You just had to hear someone say that it was okay to feel that way, that you were right."

"Well, thanks for doing that, Doc," Dris said.

"It was my pleasure," Grace said.

Joss came up and hugged Grace with his free arm.

"Thanks, Doc, for everything. I have my beautiful partner and my gorgeous children. We survived the deadliest virus in the universe, thanks to you and your friend, Bud, and we didn't get blown to smithereens by the Conglomerate. We are getting out of the Conglomerate Military or at least away from the front line. I'm a lucky man! And I have you to thank for all of this. Can I give you a kiss?"

"I think that is against medical station policy, Joss, but thank you anyway," Grace said, her cheeks suddenly feeling very hot.

"Don't worry, Doc," Dris said. "He does that to me, too."

Grace walked into the room, leaned her back against a counter, and crossed her arms.

"What's this I hear about someone shipping back out into the field?" she asked.

The man froze, keeping his broad, muscled back to her. She saw him inhale a slow deep breath before he turned around. He kept his eyes lowered, refusing to meet her eyes. He picked up some things and stuffed them into a bag.

"Is it true?" Grace pressed.

He continued to busy himself with packing what little he had, as if he was not aware Grace was still in his room. She knew he had heard her question. She could see him glancing at her out of the corner of his eyes, as he moved about his room, trying to ignore her. She just waited.

" . . . What's it to you?" he finally asked, a challenge in his voice. He turned to face her, his enormous hands on his slim hips.

"My patient. I happen to care about what happens to him."

He jerked and raised his eyebrows, at that. "I had no idea, Doc," he said. "Is that sort of thing allowed?" He donned a sly, crooked smile, to take the edge off the words.

"You know what I mean," Grace said, her cheeks starting to tingle.

"No . . . actually I don't, Doc. You'll have to explain it to me."

He looked her square in the eyes, then, and Grace felt her throat constrict and her mouth go dry. His intense, amber eyes were so piercing and penetrating. Could he see right into her soul, through those eyes?

232 : S.E. SASAKI

"*Why?*" she blurted out, not able to hide the frustration and distress in her voice. She took a deep breath and said, more softly, in a voice not much above a whisper, "Why are you doing this?"

"Doing what?" he asked, chin raised.

"Going back out there?" Grace said, almost in tears.

He shook his head and looked away, his hands clenching into fists. His shoulders sagged. "Because I have to, Doc. Because it's something I have to do."

"I thought you said you didn't want to go back out there. You couldn't go back. Didn't you say to me, 'Doc, don't let them make me go back out there?' You don't have to go! You can still get out!" Grace said, pleading in her raised voice.

"No. No, Doc, I can't. This is my duty. They need me. My squad— what is left of them—needs me. If I retired and went back home—well, probably none of my family would be alive—just great grand-nephews and great grand-nieces, perfect strangers, really. They wouldn't want an old, antiquated fossil like me hanging around them. And why should they? They would probably be terrified of me.

"Besides, it wouldn't be my world any more, not the one I grew up in. It'd be several decades if not a century, since I left it. Nothing and no one would be the same. I doubt anyone I knew would even be alive. And what would I do, Doc? All I really know is killing. After everything that happened with you and Dr. Nestor, and then almost being destroyed by those battlecruisers, it made me do some serious thinking. The men and women of my squad, they're my family now. They are all I have left and I need to look after them. They are my reason for living, now.

"Look. I really appreciate you caring about me, Doc. Giving me all these new parts and saving my life, but I have a duty to the soldiers under my command. I have to go with them. What I said before about not wanting to go back out there, that was just the drugs talking. I've got my head on straight now and I know what I have to do."

"You don't have to go back into combat," Grace pressed. "There are so many other things within the military you can do. You can teach. You can recruit. You don't necessarily have to retire."

Captain Damien Lamont smiled. "Doc, I *want* to go back. It's my job, my duty . . . my calling. I need to look after the soldiers under me. They're just kids! They'll get themselves killed without me! You understand about 'calling' and 'duty' and 'responsibility', don't you, Doc?"

Grace sucked in her lips and sniffed. She eventually nodded.

"Unfortunately, only too well, Captain Lamont. I know exactly what you mean," Grace said, a sigh punctuating her words.

"It's funny, Doc. I feel bigger, better, stronger, and faster with all of these new modifications. I thought I would be weak and in a lot of pain, but the opposite is true. Hopefully, with all of these new upgrades, I can protect my kids better. Hopefully, I will be better at my job, this time around."

Grace felt tears invade her vision. "You were too good at your job, Captain. Try and be a bit less selfless next time around. No more jumping on top of bombs. That's an order," she said, gruffly, to cover up her emotions.

"Don't take this personally, Captain Damien Lamont, but I don't ever want to see you on an operating table in front of me ever again."

The captain drew himself up to his full height and grinned.

"I don't intend to ever be on one again either, Doc. I intend to live until they have to push me around in an antigrav chair and spoon mush into my toothless mouth!"

He grinned, showing off his full set of glistening tiger fangs. He held out his huge, left hand to her, claws retracted, and she stared at it for a few seconds before reaching out her left hand to have it engulfed. The captain's hand felt so incredibly soft and luxuriant and was surprisingly gentle. Grace knew, with the lightest of squeezes, that Damien Lamont could easily crush all the bones in her hand, if he wished.

"Thanks for everything, Doc," he said earnestly, his captivating, amber eyes holding hers. "Thanks for getting me out of that mess with Nestor and for believing in my innocence. Thanks for saving my life and putting me back together again. I owe you more than I can ever repay." He dragged her into a huge bear hug.

"You are very welcome, Captain," Grace said, feeling as if she were being smothered by a fur coat. It was so soft and warm in his embrace, part of her wished she could stay cuddled in there forever. She put on a brave smile and pulled away. "You take care of yourself out there and, like I said before, don't go throwing yourself onto any more bombs."

"Only if they look like you, Doc," he said, and winked.

Grace let out a very unladylike guffaw and rolled her eyes. She felt the hot blush blooming.

"Be good," she ordered.

"Will do, Doc." He grinned. "Same back at you."

"Come back for a visit, Captain, but all in one piece."

"I just might take you up on that, Doc," he said, with a low growl and a killer smile. He wiggled his eyebrows at her and then saluted.

Grace laughed at Damien's expression and returned the salute. She turned and left the captain's room, quickly, before her carefree façade crumbled and she made a fool of herself by bursting into tears.

"Stay safe," she whispered, as the tears tracked down her cheeks.

"Dr. Lord?"

"Yes, *Nelson Mandela?*"

"I have some unpleasant news."

"What is it?" Grace asked, sitting at the nursing station, writing orders for her patients, primarily discharge orders. The little voice in her head sighed, 'Oh, no. What now?'

"It is about Dr. Jeffrey Nestor."

Grace's face fell. Her heart skipped a few beats and she felt her shoulders tightened. She tried to swallow; it took a few attempts. She sat up straight and looked up at the nearest surveillance eye.

"Dr. Nestor? What about Dr. Nestor?" A cold wave of trepidation drenched her in sweat.

"It appears the psychiatrist has escaped."

Grace felt her heart begin to race. It rapidly thumped the inside of her chest like a boxer jabbing. Did she now have to suspect that *anyone* on the station could be a possible assassin, programmed to try and kill her?

"It is my belief that he has left the medical station on one of the ships taking recovered workers back to their home worlds. I believe he was aided by two female personnel, who worked in the brig and were longstanding patients of his. It appears these accomplices brought a disguise to Dr. Nestor and they were able to somehow get Dr. Nestor onto one of the vessels, departing with discharged patients."

"Do you know which vessel he left on?" Grace whispered.

"I believe so, Dr. Lord, but I cannot be absolutely sure. I believe he may have been smuggled out in one of the empty cryopods, onto one of the departing ships. There were a thousand empty cryopods loaded in that time period for return to planets and combat zones. Which ship is carrying the cryopod containing

Dr. Nestor's body is anyone's guess, unfortunately. I have already notified all of the departing ships' captains, as well as the destination battlecruisers and planets receiving the cryopods. All respondents have assured me that, if he is found, he will be recaptured and held for trial."

"I wonder how they managed it?" Grace said, in wonder.

"His accomplices managed to sabotage the surveillance cameras in the brig. These former patients of Dr. Nestor were on guard duty in the brig together. They were able to facilitate Dr. Nestor's escape during the time of the announcement, regarding the discovery of Dr. Al-Fadi's remains. Dr. Nestor's absence was not discovered until the next shift, when the new guards arrived to find the jail cell empty and both accomplices gone."

"Does Bud and Captain Damien Lamont know about this?" Grace asked, getting up out of the chair to pace nervously around the unit.

"Yes. Bud has been very busy, Dr. Lord, but he has been made aware. Captain Lamont and his squad have already left, to return to their ship, but I will send word to him."

"Of course," Grace said, quickly, crossing her arms and trying to suppress a shiver. She felt a wave of fear and also sadness, as she wondered why Bud had not come himself, to tell her the news.

"I am deeply sorry, Dr. Lord. I take full responsibility."

"No need to apologize, *Nelson Mandela*. I understand."

"Would you like someone to stay with you, Dr. Lord?"

"Oh . . . no, *Nelson Mandela*. If Dr. Nestor is off of the station, hopefully my life is not in danger anymore."

"I shall have security droids stationed outside your quarters for now, Dr. Lord. Just in case."

"That really is not necessary, *Nelson Mandela*."

"Please, Dr. Lord. I insist. It is the logical thing to do: keep you under guard, at least for now, until we are sure Dr. Nestor has not sent anyone else after you."

"Oh, all right," Grace sighed. "I think it is highly unlikely, *Nelson Mandela*, but I do appreciate your concern for my wellbeing. I am not trying to be difficult, but . . ."

"You are most welcome, Dr. Lord. And, again, I deeply apologize for Dr. Nestor's escape."

Grace wanted to ask the station AI where Bud was, but she was too ashamed. She knew she had been hard on the android regarding the life-pod episode and then Dr. Al-Fadi was found liquefied. Bud was probably off mourning over the loss of his creator.

Bud obviously had no time for Grace, at the moment. She could hardly blame him, the way she had acted towards him and treated him, after he had come out in the shuttle to retrieve the life-pod. She had been verbally abusive and she regretted it.

Loneliness was a dismal companion.

The Receiving Bays had been flooded with incoming patients. Grace had spent shift after shift in Triage, assessing the wounded and lining up surgeries. Without Dr. Bell around to keep everything and everyone organized and efficient, the intake of patients seemed an exercise in frustration and chaos theory. There were fewer medical staff—fewer surgeons, anesthetists, and nurses—but not fewer incoming. *Nelson Mandela* had put out a call to all planets of the Union for medical staff, especially surgeons and anesthetists. Unfortunately, the replacement staff that *Nelson Mandela* was recruiting, would not be arriving for a few more weeks.

Grace had had to take over Dr. Al-Fadi's position for now—even though she felt totally inadequate—until a replacement adaptations surgeon arrived to step into his place. She could do the simpler operations. She had requested that Bud continue to operate with her, because he had seen many of Dr. Al-Fadi's surgeries and he could help her with the nanobots, but she had received no reply. She suspected that the android no longer wanted anything to do with her, after she had vented her anger at him in the shuttle.

She could not blame Bud. There were things she had said that she wished she could take back. Unfortunately, that was just not possible. Androids did not forget anything. Grace had not even seen Bud, since the day he told her that Dr. Al-Fadi was dead. She at first thought he was just mourning over the loss of his mentor. Then she worried that something disastrous had happened to Bud, but *Nelson Mandela* had insisted that Bud was fine. Bud had not been overhauled or turned into scrap metal, as the station AI had always been threatening.

Coming to the depressing conclusion that Bud was just avoiding her, Grace felt dejected and bereft. Over time, she had come to rely more and more on Bud's company and support and kindness. If she was honest with herself, she had also become used to his attentiveness. Without his companionship, she felt rejected and abandoned. She thought about that old saying: 'You don't know what you've got, till it's gone' and she had to agree with it, one hundred percent.

Grace sighed. She had now lost both Dr. Al-Fadi and Bud, and she felt lost and friendless on the huge medical station. She had not even seen Dr. Cech around to talk to. Everyone was grieving the loss of someone, so Grace did not feel she could complain. She could not imagine the grief Hanako was suffering at the moment. Perhaps Grace would drop in on Dr. Al-Fadi's widow, to see if Hanako wanted company, after she completed her shift in the operating room.

Before coming to the *Nelson Mandela,* Grace had never really paid attention to the androids around her; whether they had feelings, whether they experienced emotions, like guilt, sadness, regret. The question of whether an android could feel love, had never even crossed her mind. She had paid no more attention to them than if they were a piece of equipment or machinery. She now realized how wrong she had been. Spending so much time with Bud, seeing his passion and commitment to saving lives, helping others, and protecting her—especially protecting her—had taught her that they were far from emotionless automatons. They needed and deserved to be respected as individuals.

Could she actually love an android?

Before the crisis, she would have scoffed at such a ridiculous idea. Now, though, she realized just how much she missed Bud, his innocence, his strength, his intelligence, and his complete lack of guile. He was probably the most forthcoming and open 'being' she had ever met. A child with a man's appearance, learning and maturing exponentially fast. And his love for Grace was playing a part in that development . . . or had been. Whatever Grace felt for Bud, it was very strong as well. She had to admit it. She dearly missed him.

She had to push those feelings away and forget them, now. She had obviously driven Bud away. Her vision began to blur with tears and she blinked rapidly, sniffing. She silently told herself to stop feeling sorry for herself. She was a surgeon and she was trained to save lives.

It was time to get to work.

She had a polar bear soldier being cryothawed in the operating room. The soldier needed a new right arm, after having had the limb blown off by an explosion.

Grace changed into clean operating scrubs in the women's locker room and put on her hair covering and surgical mask. After scrubbing her hands with the antiseptic and antiviral soap, she placed her hands in the sterilizer and glover. She could not suppress another deep sigh.

For her, today was the first day back in surgery since the quarantine had begun, and she was on her own, without Dr. Al-Fadi or Bud. She felt an overwhelming urge to race back to her room, bury herself under the covers, and never come out. Grace shook her head. She knew that she was just being ridiculous. She had a responsibility to the patients who needed what little expertise she could offer them. She prayed it would be enough.

What Grace was going through, emotionally, was not important. Injured patients needed help and she would do her best or die trying. That's what Dr. Al-Fadi and Dr. Vanessa Bell would have done, and she would try and live up to their legacy of bravery and devotion to others. She hoped she at least had an experienced SAMM-E to assist her, since Bud was not around. Again, Grace felt some wetness forming in her eyes and she fought the tears back, angrily.

'Stop it!' she scolded herself. 'Stop wallowing in self-pity! You brought this all on yourself, so suck it up!'

She straightened up, pulled her shoulders back, and took a deep breath. She backed up into the door that opened into the operating room, her sterile, gloved hands held up high in the air.

"It's show time," she whispered to herself, recalling when Dr. Al-Fadi had said that to her. She smiled, thinking about how much she was going to miss the small surgeon's antics in the operating room. Through the door she went.

". . . Well! Thank you for *finally* gracing us with your presence, Dr. Grace. To what do we owe this honor? I hope we did not get you up out of your bed, too early? Did you have trouble turning on the shower this morning, may I ask?"

Grace stopped just within the operating room door, frozen to the spot, her mouth hanging open, and her breath catching in her throat. She blinked repeatedly. Was she hallucinating? Was this all a dream?

"Why are you standing there like a lost waif, Dr. Grace? Have I not made it abundantly clear that you are not to be late? Is it not obvious that we are already behind, because of you? There are no flies in this operating room here to catch, so you can close your mouth. I know you are wearing a mask, but I can tell by the position of your jaw, that you have your mouth wide open. Shut it and get over here. Quickly, please. We do not have all day. This patient's thawing injury cannot wait for you to wake up.

"Bud? Please help the stupefied Dr. Grace get into her surgical gown, as I worry that she is not capable of doing it up on her own. Stick her with a cattle prod, if she does not snap out of it or use the cautery. No! Forget I said that! The cautery must stay sterile!"

Grace staggered over, unsteadily, and stopped to stare at the diminutive surgeon in disbelief. She had a desperate urge to poke him with a finger, to see if he was real, but a cattle prod would have been even better. She just had to be gowned first. The adaptation surgeon was sterile and would not have appreciated being contaminated . . . even if he wasn't real and she was hallucinating him.

"How?" she whispered, tears filling her eyes. Her voice was tremulous and her raised hands quivered like ripples on a pond. " . . . How is this possible? Are you for real?"

"If you are going to cry, Dr. Grace, I would kindly ask that you not bend over my patient. Nay, not ask, but demand. I do not want any of your tears falling into my sterile field.

"Bud? Please give the emotional Dr. Grace a gauze to wipe her eyes, and then she will have to go out and re-sterilize herself. Be careful not to contaminate yourself. The last thing I need are *two* surgical assistants unable to assist. Do I have to do everything by myself?"

Bud faced Grace and she could see his eyes gleaming above his surgical mask. Now that he had lungs, he had to wear a mask, just like all the humans. He handed her a clean dry gauze and she blotted her eyes and dropped the sponge onto the floor. A minibot scurried over and picked it up.

Grace did not know whether she wanted to kiss Bud or strangle him. Perhaps it was a bit of both, because she was laughing and crying at the same time as well. If she did either, she would have been yelled at by the small hallucination, for sure. She looked over at Dr. Cech, who was crying too.

"No," Dr. Cech said firmly, shaking his head. "I knew nothing about this, either, Grace. I am as shocked as you! He just walked in a few moments before you did, and started ordering me around, as usual. I have never been so happy to be verbally abused in my entire life. This wonderful miracle is all Bud's doing!"

"Who you see before you, Dr. Grace, is, indeed, the Great—and may I also add younger and more handsome—Dr. Hiro Al-Fadi," Dr. Al-Fadi said. "The Great One is back! Bud cloned my body from the DNA samples taken on the day of the memory printing—how he got access to that information, he is not saying—and then he had my body undergo accelerated growth in the vat tanks.

"Under Bud's constant and careful supervision, my splendid and virile—and did I say 'extremely handsome'?—body grew until it was ready to accept my most impressive and massive memprint data which, oddly enough, Bud also mysteriously happened to have. I shall have to get the truth from my protégé regarding this, after the surgery is completed.

"My unique and magnificent memprint was then uploaded into my unique and magnificent brain yesterday and, as you can see, you have your unique and—may I humbly admit—very modest Dr. Al-Fadi back, younger and therefore more incredible than ever!"

" . . . Whether we really wanted the conceited, pompous, bag-of-wind or not," Dr. Cech quipped. "Of course, his body is a lot younger than the version you knew, Grace. Hiro here still has hair, in the right places instead of coming out his nose and ears. And he doesn't smell as bad as he used to, either, but his memory is only intact right up until the time the memprint was taken. He has no memory whatsoever of the viral epidemic, the quarantine, the attack on himself, or anything else, which is probably for the best.

"Unbeknownst to anyone, other than the station AI, Bud started directing and supervising the accelerated growth of Hiro's body almost the moment after he was discovered dead in his cryopod," Dr. Cech said. "And now, here Hiro is. As you can see, he is his usual irascible, insulting, irritating, immodest, egotistical self. He appears to be normal . . . except for the alleged hair.

"And now, I keep asking myself, 'Why? Why, Dejan? Why were you so upset, when he was gone? You were finally rid of the miserable old madman and yet you mourned and wished he was back. Are you *crazy*?'"

"Why you pretentious impostor!" Hiro Al-Fadi spat. "You had nothing to do with bringing me back. Bud did it all himself. And even if you had, I would not have thanked you," the excitable surgeon exclaimed.

"Why not, you ungrateful wretch?"

"Because you would have put me back in the same old body. You would not have thought of putting me back in a body that looked like Bud's. A true friend would have put my magnificent mind into the body of a god, an Adonis, an Apollo, where it truly belongs. But no, you would have maliciously put me back into this little body that is going to go bald very soon. I have to go through that trauma all over again, you lousy excuse for a friend. Friend? Hah! You are my penance. My albatross!"

Dr. Cech burst out laughing.

Dr. Al-Fadi stopped, mid-tirade, and glared at the anesthetist.

"Oh, welcome back, Hiro! How we have all missed you, even though you did not know it, and probably won't believe it. I know I am going to regret saying this, and I will deny it until I am blue in the face, from this day forth, but I am astonished at how glad I am to have your irritating voice address my ears once more, old friend."

"I am not your old friend, any more, Dr. Cech. I am your younger, more handsome, more energetic and more coifed friend, and don't you forget it!"

Grace started laughing and she laughed until she cried.

Bud stared at Grace with a worried look on his face. Grace went up and hugged the android, not caring about the sterility for once. They could change into new gowns, as far as she was concerned.

"Oh, thank you, Bud," she whispered into his ear. "You are a miracle worker."

Bud looked at Grace with shocked eyes.

"Am I forgiven?" he asked, hesitantly.

"More than forgiven," she said, and gave him a kiss on his cheek. "There was never anything to forgive."

Bud's face looked puzzled, as he tried to work those two statements out.

Dr. Al-Fadi looked around at Bud and Grace.

"WHAT IN SPACE ARE YOU TWO DOING?" shrieked Dr. Al-Fadi. "In *my* OR of all places! Dr. Grace, get your hands off my android! SAMM-E 777 . . . I mean Bud . . . how dare you touch Dr. Grace like that!? HAVE THE TWO OF YOU GONE TOTALLY INSANE? Have you no *decency*? This . . . this OR is a place of *sterility* and . . . and *sanctity* . . . and *integrity*! This patient is thawing . . . and I AM WAITING!

"I refuse to have this form of unprofessional behavior in my OR!"

Dr. Al-Fadi screamed, stomping his little feet and waggling his head around. His eyes looked as if they were about to pop out of his skull.

"What in space went on when my back was turned, anyway?"

Dr. Al-Fadi stared in outrage at all of their smiling eyes above their surgical masks and he listened to their roaring laughter with annoyance. Then he noticed the tears in all of their eyes—Bud had tears?—he would have to investigate this later, too. He began to feel deep satisfaction. They had obviously been helpless without him.

They had truly missed the Great One!

But of course they would have! Why, for one second, should he have doubted that? He frowned and then stamped his foot a second time.

"Well, what are you all staring at? Stop gawking. Stop lolly-gagging. Let's get to work!"

His fury knew no bounds.

That the dim-witted surgical fellow, the meddling station AI, and that insufferable android had all conspired to strip him of his medical license—or at least attempt to do so—was unforgivable. It could not go unpunished. No one could take his medical license away!

Had he not invented the mind-to-mind link that was now used throughout the Union of Solar Systems to treat trauma? Had he not spent years of his life on the Nelson Mandela *Medical Space Station, perfecting the techniques that would revolutionize psychiatric therapy? What had Dr. Grace Lord and her android done?*

Treated a virus! Hardly any reason for acclaim.

No one would believe their accusations. They were nobodies! They lacked his genius, his foresight, his brilliance. No one would miss them, if they were suddenly disposed of! Without their testimony, who would believe the charges? Who would believe the great Dr. Jeffrey Nestor would be capable of such infamy, as they claimed in their accusations.

No one.

All he had to do was get rid of them, that pathetic Grace Lord and her sidekick android, SAMM-E 777. It would be simple. He had the manpower, or should he say, 'woman-power' to achieve his aims. So many of his female patients were primed to carry out his every command, without question, without hesitation.

He had really made only one error.

When he was trying to determine if he could force a patient to kill, he should not have chosen that tiger captain to kill that useless Grace Lord. The captain, although a trained killer out in the field, had not been a patient long enough to be completely under his command. And the captain had been a male sent to attack and kill a female, which may also have made a difference.

If he had used one of his female subjects, he was sure he would have successfully achieved his goal of killing the conceited, haughty Grace Lord, thereby furthering his research into mind control and its boundaries and limitations. Well, even the failure with the tiger captain was a result; an unfortunate failure, but an interesting mistake, never to be repeated.

He would be much more careful next time. There would be no more mistakes or errors in judgement. Dr. Grace Lord had to die and her stupid android had to be destroyed. He would not rest until this was achieved. They had tried to sully his reputation, after all. That was unforgivable!

He had some planning to do, some details to work out, and then he would be coming back to the space station to exact his revenge.

No one made a fool of Dr. Jeffrey Nestor.

No one.

THE END

Acknowledgements

I would like to thank my wonderful husband, David Alan Sherrington, for being a fantastic advance reader, reading everything I write multiple times, and being so supportive through this entire process. I could not have done any of it, without his encouragement, support, enthusiasm, and love. Thank you to my fantastic children, Daniel and Christine, who are such great inspirations to me, every minute, every hour, every day. Their indomitable courage, optimism, and love continually fill me with happiness and pride. Their strength and bravery inspire me to try harder. Their help and understanding with my projects have been invaluable. I love you all more than you can imagine. Thank you for all your help and for being you!

Thank you also to Diane F. Martin and Ian C. Esslemont for comments on the early manuscript.

Thank you to Lauren Sasaki for all things legal. A huge thank you to Bre Boyce of Friesen Press for her invaluable assistance in getting this book to final publication and to Daemon Moore for hooking me up with Ms. Boyce. Could not have done it without you, Bre!

An enormous thank you goes to Edward J. Greenwood, for all of his advice, his comments regarding the completed manuscript, his encouragement, his wealth of information, his wisdom, his friendship, and his generosity with his time. Oh, and for his unique sense of humor that always keeps me laughing!

Last but not least, an enormous 'thank you' goes out to all of the staff of the Guelph General Hospital in Guelph Ontario, Canada, especially the Surgery Department, where I give assistance, wherever I can. A finer group of dedicated and devoted health care workers—including surgeons, gynecologists, anesthetists, surgical assistants, nurses (especially the operating room and recovery room nurses!), porters, secretaries, volunteers, and associate staff—I cannot imagine. I feel very fortunate to have gotten to know you all. It has been an honor and a privilege to be able to work with you and see how you save lives, every single day, in the real world.

This book is a tribute to you.

I salute you all.

S.E. Sasaki is a family physician who works as a surgical assistant in the operating rooms of a local hospital. She lives in a small town in Southern Ontario, Canada, with her chiropractor husband and two mischievous Maine Coon cats.

If you enjoyed reading Welcome to the Madhouse, I hope you might please consider leaving a rating, or even a brief review, about it on your favourite book retailer site. Your assistance would mean a great deal to me, and it helps get the word out about my books. Thank you so much for your help,

S.E. Sasaki

Sign up for your
FREE copy of **GENESIS**:
Prequel to WELCOME TO THE MADHOUSE

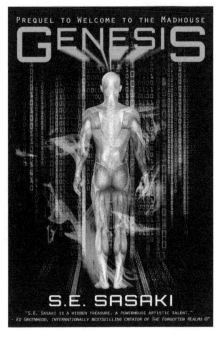

By signing up to my email list about new releases and special deals.
We will never spam you or share your information with anyone else
and you can unsubscribe at any time.'

https://dl.bookfunnel.com/hzm9cwajhe

INTRODUCING

If you enjoyed
WELCOME TO THE MADHOUSE
look out for

BUD BY THE GRACE OF GOD
Book Two of The Grace Lord Series

BY S.E. SASAKI

Medicine. Murder. Mayhem.

Not what one expects to find on the Conglomerate's Premier Medical Space Station, the Nelson Mandela.

When a homicidal ghost, a genocidal general, and a vicious plant alien all land on the station, the bodies start piling up.

Dr. Grace Lord's heart is broken when she sees Bud destroyed before her eyes. Can she rescue the Nelson Mandela from destruction by the conniving Jeffrey Nestor in the few short hours she has left?

'Both a Paean to the science-fi genre and a captivating return to a space station in a complex universe.'
—*Kirkus Reviews Magazine*

Works by S.E. Sasaki

Novels
The Grace Lord Series
Welcome to the Madhouse
Bud by the Grace of God
Amazing Grace
Saving Grace

Novella
Genesis

Short Story Collection
Musings

Praise for the Grace Lord Series

S.E. Sasaki is a hidden treasure, a powerhouse artistic talent who in Madhouse brings us medical science fiction on a personal engaging level that is addictive to read, sometimes scary, and always FUN. Recommended!

— Ed Greenwood
Internationally bestselling creator of The Forgotten Realms©

A layered debut that sings odes to the grandmasters of sci-fi.
Kirkus Review of Welcome To The Madhouse, July 2015

Throughout, Sasaki displays a propulsive inventiveness as she weaves grand ideas with humor and soul.
Kirkus Review of Bud by the Grace of God, July 2016

Lightning Source UK Ltd.
Milton Keynes UK
UKHW010806090223
416681UK00002B/702

9 781988 463018